Saronna's Gift

Other Cracked Mirror Press Books
by Carmen Webster Buxton

The Sixth Discipline

No Safe Haven

Tribes

Shades of Empire

Where Magic Rules

King of Trees

The Nostalgia Gambit

Saronna's Gift

Carmen Webster Buxton

Cracked Mirror Press
ROCKVILLE, MARYLAND

Karen Wester Newton/Cracked Mirror Press
Rockville, MD 20852
http://carmenspage.blogspot.com/

Publisher's Note: This is a work of fiction. Names, characters, places, and incidents are a product of the author's imagination. Locales and public names are sometimes used for atmospheric purposes. Any resemblance to actual people, living or dead, or to businesses, companies, events, institutions, or locales is completely coincidental.

Book Layout ©2013 BookDesignTemplates.com

SARONNA'S GIFT/ Carmen Webster Buxton. -- 1st ed.
ISBN 978-0-9885599-4-3

This book is dedicated to those readers who share their experiences with other readers by posting online reviews of the books they read. Writers write to make connections with their readers. Readers who post reviews let them know they succeeded.

Thank you!

I have been a stranger in a strange land.

– KING JAMES BIBLE

CHAPTER ONE

A warm summer breeze caught Saronna's veil and almost pulled it loose. She stopped to tuck the folds around her face, to ensure nothing showed except her eyes. By the time she had picked up her valise, her father had almost disappeared into the crowd. She hurried to catch up, darting in and out among the throng as fast as she could without attracting notice.

Where were they going? Her father had told her to pack her belongings. That had to mean he planned another attempt to sell her, but he had given her no clue whom he planned to visit today.

Even after their earlier trips to New Jerusalem, the city still disconcerted Saronna. Vendors' cries, chattering voices, ground cars rolling past, and countless footfalls were enough to distract her, let alone the sight of so many strangers. Faces flashed past, some veiled, some bearded, and disappeared into the mass of humanity, never to be seen again.

She caught up to her father just as he turned suddenly, moving through the tall steel supports of the Strangers' Gate, into the off-world quarter. Saronna had never been there. She gripped her valise tighter as a shiver of apprehension ran through her. Would her talent work as well on an off-world man?

After a block, Saronna noticed women in trousers, walking with their faces uncovered. She looked away in confusion, but the men bewildered her just as much. They walked beside the women, sometimes even touched them. Only a few men wore beards, and of them, more were young than old.

The buildings, by contrast, appeared ordinary, even though many were very tall. Ten- and twelve-story structures dwarfed their neighbors, seeming to shut out the sun.

The crowd thinned first, then the buildings, and Saronna realized they had entered a residential area. After a few blocks, her father made another abrupt turn to enter the arched doorway of a large, sprawling house. Saronna stepped back a pace to study the facade as her father waited at the door.

The gray stone house looked very like the ones back in her village, except more spread out. Only the recessed archway that sheltered the entrance broke the line of the featureless walls. A few noticeable oddities caught her attention—two small cylinders mounted on either side of the door, and a flat rectangular screen placed at eye level on the right.

Her father faced the screen and stood tapping his foot impatiently. A moment later, the screen displayed a woman's countenance. She wore a loose-fitting gown and sat behind a desk. In spite of being in plain sight of a man who wasn't a relative, she made no attempt to hide her face, and her expression showed not embarrassment but merely boredom.

"May I help you, citizen?" she said, her tone polite but not overtly respectful.

"I've come to see Sire Trushenko," Saronna's father answered, his voice brusque.

The woman glanced down as if she were looking into her desk. "Name, please?"

"Sire Maynard."

She nodded and moved her hands across the desk. The door hummed, then swung open silently. "Please come in, citizens."

Unused to doors that opened without human assistance, Saronna followed her father into the house with a sense of trepidation. A second later, the woman from the screen appeared before them, and Saronna realized she wasn't wearing a gown, but rather a tunic over loose trousers.

"Come this way, please," the woman said. Her self-assurance amazed Saronna. There was nothing rude in her manner, but there was no deference, either, in spite of the fact that Josiah Maynard stood there—plainly male, plainly a patriarch, and plainly put out at his reception.

Nevertheless, her father followed the woman without looking back. They strode along briskly, passing through a long, dim corridor that ended in a sunny courtyard, much like the one found in the center of Josiah's own house. A fountain tinkled at one end; paving stones provided a level floor; several benches and tables placed in open areas offered comfortable seating; shrubs and flowers growing around the borders, and in a few gracefully-grouped flower beds, supplied bright touches of color. Saronna found the setting pretty, but almost disappointing in its familiarity.

A man sat at one of the tables, in front of a strange machine. Saronna remembered waiting in the women's parlor with her mother and her sisters and her father's wife, and watching through the shutters as her father and the census taker sat in the courtyard. The census taker had moved his hands across a device such as this one while he recorded Josiah Maynard's answers to his questions.

The man at the table seemed to be speaking to the machine, but when he saw them approaching, he stopped his work and rose politely. Saronna judged him to be a little older than her father, but a good deal shorter. His hair and beard had gone white, and years of living had lined his face. Saronna's first impression of him was good; his wrinkles were those made by smiling, and he looked at her frankly—not pretending that she wasn't there, as a hill man would have done.

"Hello," the man said to her father. "You must be Josiah Maynard. Good afternoon, and welcome to my home."

Her father nodded and bowed in reply. "And you are Vladimir Trushenko?"

The man bowed back, exactly the right depth bow. "I'm Vladimir Trushenko, yes. Do you need to see proof of that, or is Abraham Pollard's introduction adequate?"

"I trust his valuation as my own, foreigner," Josiah said, giving the stranger a title that showed he was a peer, but outside the realm of kin or clan.

"Very well, then," Vladimir said. "Shall we sit?"

The two men took seats across from each other. Saronna moved to stand behind her father's chair. She set her valise down beside her on the flagstones, then moved a little so she could at least see her father's profile. She noted that the stranger knew better than to offer refreshments. Accepting food now would have made Josiah a guest, and committed him to accept whatever else was offered. Saronna knew her father wanted at least a minimum price for her.

"Now," Vladimir said, "is there anything you need to ask me before we get down to business?"

Josiah frowned faintly but didn't look entirely displeased. Saronna realized that in spite of having her Uncle Abraham's introduction, her father had qualms about this stranger.

"I would like to ask, foreigner," Josiah said, speaking in a formal tone, "for an assurance that my daughter won't be mistreated in any way, nor subjected to any—indignities."

"Certainly." The off-worlder smiled encouragement. "I can give you such an assurance without reservation. She won't have any arduous duties, nor will she ever be required to, ah, serve in any way she would dislike. In fact, any such, ah, service would be strictly up to her to decide."

Saronna drew in a breath of surprise. She had assumed a man of this age would have only one use for a woman young enough to be his daughter—or possibly

even his granddaughter—and yet Vladimir Trushenko
sounded as if he had no intention of demanding his
rights as her protector, should he come to an agreement with Josiah. Saronna began to worry that the sale
might actually go through.

Josiah looked relieved. "You'll wish to see her, of
course?"

The stranger nodded, but his agreement seemed
more a matter of good manners than good business.
"Certainly."

Josiah lifted a hand in an imperious gesture, and
Saronna stepped out from behind his chair. "Remove
your veil, daughter."

Saronna pulled her veil down around her shoulders.
She kept eyes lowered with maidenly reserve, but she
concentrated her energies on Vladimir Trushenko,
using the techniques that old Brushka had taught her
to heighten her talent and focus it on the right places.
She held her breath. He was just a man, after all. There
was no reason her ability wouldn't work as well on this
off-worlder as it had on the men of the hill clans when
her father had displayed her to them. A moment later
she had a shock, as the stranger nodded approval. Her
father smiled with relief.

"Now the gown," Josiah said, looking determinedly
away from her. It would be most improper for him to
look at her when she wasn't fully dressed.

Saronna reached up and unbuttoned her bodice numbly. Why wasn't it working? She knew she had suppressed all desire in this old man, and yet he still seemed eager to proceed with the transaction. His eyes slid away from her as she pulled her ankle-length dress up over her head, then let it drop to the ground. She stood there in the warm sunlight, wearing nothing but her slippers and a thin shift that barely covered her knees. She darted a glance at the white-haired off-world man and saw that he was nodding again, all the while staring fixedly at a point somewhere over her left shoulder. Panicked, she decided to induce some discomfort. She concentrated on his digestive tract, constricting his stomach to make the acid surge upward, hoping the distress would take the old man's mind off any lustful notions without making him noticeably ill. She had made the last potential buyer itch all over his body, and he had sent them away abruptly, so he could call his physician. Her father would become suspicious if every man they visited became suddenly too uncomfortable to conduct the deal.

"Fine, fine," the off-worlder said, pressing a hand to his mouth. "She certainly looks healthy."

Saronna heard her father's triumphant sigh. She was so shocked, she didn't react to his abrupt gesture, and he had to speak to her to get her attention.

"You may resume your clothing, daughter."

She pulled her clothes on with a haste that made her clumsy. Fear gnawed at her and made it hard for her to concentrate. Her father would sell her to this elderly stranger and leave her here in this house where she knew no one. She would never see her home or her family again.

Vladimir Trushenko leaned back in his chair, pressed one hand against his stomach, and took a deep breath. He made a comment on the weather that Josiah answered politely. Vladimir followed with a joke about the local political situation, an anecdote that would appeal to hill men who saw city dwellers as soft and corrupt. Josiah laughed with genuine amusement. Bitterness filled Saronna; doubtless her father would tell the joke to his cronies when he got home.

"Now," Vladimir said, still smiling, but with a trader's gleam in his eye, "shall we discuss how much a woman is worth these days?"

Josiah settled down to dicker. Among themselves, hill men seldom used money, preferring to barter in the currency of livestock, goods, and services that flourished among their own clans, but they knew what an off-world credit was worth.

Saronna knew, too, and the price her father set stunned her, even considering he would halve it in bargaining. Eight thousand credits would buy a decent-sized house. She was twenty-three and had never married. If he got four thousand for her, he would be doing very well indeed. It was like selling week-old bread at the price of fresh-baked.

Vladimir didn't look troubled by the figure. If anything, he seemed reluctant to drive a hard bargain. He haggled a little, bringing the price down by a fourth, but Saronna could see he was merely going through the motions. His heart wasn't truly in it. A surge of desperation made Saronna consider drastic action. She could make the off-world man pass out. If she was careful, it wouldn't harm him. But she had used that trick on her first such visit, when the prospective buyer had looked at her so appraisingly that she had reacted from sheer terror. To use it again now would be very risky.

Josiah was ready to deal, but apparently a last scruple shook him. "Your son has no wife, and no other woman who might use Saronna harshly?"

Son? Saronna had never considered that the old man could be buying her for someone else. Fathers arranged marriages for their sons; she had never heard of a man buying a woman for his son.

Vladimir Trushenko shook his head vigorously. "Duncan has never married, and he returns today from a long journey to a place where they don't allow men to have women who aren't wives."

Josiah looked repulsed that such a place existed, but he seemed reassured. "Done! Six thousand credits it is."

Vladimir held out his hand to close the deal. "Will you allow me to offer you some refreshment?"

Josiah shook the off-worlder's hand with vigor. It was done. She was sold.

"Certainly," Josiah said, not even trying to hide the triumph in his smile.

Vladimir moved back to the table. He pressed a button on the table top and a voice spoke out of the air.

"Yes, sir?"

"Would you bring us some wine, please, Letitia," Vladimir said, "and perhaps a few wafers."

Saronna wrapped her veil over her face to cover her nervousness, and didn't pay attention as the woman from the front door brought in a tray and set it down on the table. Vladimir thanked the woman, sent her away, and then poured two glasses of wine. He didn't make the mistake of offering a drink to Saronna, even though a third glass stood on the tray. Instead he handed one glass to Josiah, put the plate of wafers down next to him, and then took up his own glass.

It was past time for lunch, but Saronna was too miserable and too numb from shock to feel any hunger pains.

Josiah ate a few wafers, sipped his wine, and then rose to go. "I thank you for your hospitality, but I have a long walk back to my skimmer, and I must be going."

"Of course." Vladimir rose swiftly. "If you'll wait here just a moment, I'll walk you to the door myself."

Saronna knew that the exchange of credits would take place out of her presence, so she assumed that the old man must be leaving to arrange a draft for her father. When he bowed and disappeared into the dimness of the corridor, she realized he was also giving her father a chance to say goodbye to her.

Josiah looked at her gravely, his eyes sad. "Well, daughter, at last I've assured your future. I'm sorry I couldn't find anyone among our own people, but this man has a good reputation, and I'm sure his son will treat you well."

Saronna stood dumbly, unable to think of anything to say. Her father didn't seem to feel a need for speech on her part. He kissed her cheek through her veil and gave her a transitory embrace.

"Will you," Saronna began, but the words stuck in her throat, and she had to start again. This might be her last chance to communicate with her family. "Will you say goodbye to Paul and the others for me, please?"

"Of course," her father said, relaxing the formality with which he had spoken earlier. "Mind your manners, now, Saronna. Don't argue when you're given orders, and make yourself agreeable, as is proper. Remember your upbringing, and behave as a well brought up woman should."

"Yes, Father," Saronna said, more from habit than anything else.

"And don't let their off-world ideas go to your head. This is still Krueger's World. If you're lucky enough to be desired by this man's son, you'll remember that you were once a Maynard, and fulfill your responsibility."

"Yes, Father," Saronna said again, in a whisper this time.

He patted her shoulder and shuffled his feet.

In a moment, Vladimir Trushenko came back into the courtyard. "If you're ready, citizen?"

Josiah answered in the affirmative, then followed his host into the corridor without a backward glance at Saronna.

For several seconds Saronna stood frozen, trying hard not to succumb to a fit of weeping. The strangeness of the house induced a terror that threatened to overwhelm her. She had never been so lonely or so frightened.

Suddenly, she became aware that she wasn't alone. When she turned to look around, a woman stood surveying her from a few meters away, a beautiful woman with red-gold hair and green eyes. Her robe-like gown looked very costly to Saronna's provincial eye. She was several years older than Saronna, but still a great beauty.

She smiled and spoke. "Hello. I'm Naomi. What's your name?"

"Saronna Maynard." She said the last name before she realized that she no longer had any right to it, and then didn't know what to say to correct herself. "Saronna," she repeated.

Naomi's smile grew sympathetic as she moved closer. "It's all right. It takes a while to get used to it. I know."

Saronna looked at her in surprise.

Naomi nodded. "My husband sold me to Vladimir because I had no children. I can't have babies, but fortunately, Vladimir doesn't mind because he already has Duncan."

Saronna took a deep breath and let it out. She loosened her veil and let it fall around her shoulders. She belonged here now—no need for a veil in this house. This was the only home she had.

"Don't worry about Vladimir." Naomi put one arm around her in an awkward hug. "He bought you for Duncan, his son. Duncan's been away for a few years, but I knew him before he left, and he's quite nice."

Saronna didn't answer. No wonder the off-worlder had looked away when she removed her gown. His son's woman would be as forbidden to him as his own daughter. If Saronna had known, it might have worked better to incite his desire rather than to suppress it—

although she had no idea if she could do such a thing. It would be completely against her vows even to try.

"Come inside," Naomi said, holding out her hand. "I'll show you your rooms. They're near mine."

Saronna picked up her bag, took the hand that was offered, and followed the other woman into the corridor.

As they walked, she noticed that Naomi was quite petite. Up close, the faintest of lines marred the flawless perfection of her complexion, but she couldn't be much older than forty, certainly nowhere near the white-haired man's age.

Saronna looked around her. The place seemed familiar, in the sense that the rooms were laid out in a pattern she would have expected. From the courtyard, a network of corridors ran through the house. But when they passed open doorways, Saronna saw men and women sitting at desks and talking together. The mixed setting confused her. "Where is the women's part of the house?"

Naomi laughed. "There isn't one. Off-worlders don't divide living space into men's places and women's places. We can go anywhere in the house we want to go."

It sounded both liberating and frightening to Saronna. More freedom of movement for women also implied there was no sanctuary from men. "Really?"

Naomi nodded. "Yes. Except you have to knock before you go into someone's bedroom because that's their private space." She gave Saronna a sideways glance. "You weren't married, were you?"

Saronna shook her head.

"Well," Naomi said, "if you want to ask me any questions, I'd be happy to answer them. My mother never told me anything, and my wedding night was quite a shock."

Saronna stiffened, unwilling to speak to a stranger about such a personal matter. "My mother talked to me about that. She told me what I needed to know."

"That's good." Naomi squeezed her hand and then let it go. "Besides, they have peculiar ideas off-world. Duncan will most likely wait a while—get to know you first, I mean."

She probably meant it to be reassuring, but Saronna found the prediction chilling instead. No matter how peculiar their thinking was off-world, she knew quite well that she now had even fewer rights than she had when she left home that morning. She now belonged, not to her father, but to a stranger, a man who could make whatever use of her he chose. She couldn't believe that Vladimir Trushenko would have paid her father six thousand credits for a mere companion for his son, or even for a servant.

"Where are you from?" Naomi was asking.

"What? Oh, I was born in Samaria. It's a small town in the hills north of the city."

"I thought so." Naomi's expression held the faintest hint of condescension. "Your dress is made from hand-loomed cloth. No one wears that here in New Jerusalem."

She stepped into the corridor and opened a door.

"Here we are," she said brightly, stepping through the doorway and holding the door open for Saronna. All the interior doors opened on reassuringly ordinary hinges. "These are your rooms, Saronna."

Saronna followed her inside and sucked in her breath. They stood in a tiny square entrance hall, and beyond that she could see a large sitting room, elegantly furnished with sofas and chairs and low tables. Rich textiles of blue and green hung on the walls, and light from a wall of windows shone down on a thick carpet woven in an elaborate pattern of gold and purple. It was nothing like the sparse simplicity of the room she had shared with her sisters.

"The bedroom's through there." Naomi nodded at a doorway. "There's a bathroom, too, of course, and a dressing room for your clothes."

"Clothes?" Saronna glanced down at her valise in puzzlement. "I don't need a whole room for my clothes."

Naomi smiled, her eyes alight with satisfaction "Come and see. Vladimir let me pick them out for you. I hope you like them." She glanced at Saronna's tall frame. "I hope they're long enough. Vladimir said you were tall. He wanted someone tall because Duncan is quite tall. He takes after his mother that way."

Saronna followed her without speaking a word. The smaller woman led the way through the sitting room and opened the bedroom door. An ornate bed occupied one side of the room, and a large oval mirror hung on the opposite wall. Naomi kept going, but Saronna stopped to look at herself. Framed by her dark hair, her face looked bloodless, as pale as it had ever been. Her gray eyes were huge with fear.

Naomi opened the door into the dressing room. Clothes lined the walls—gowns, robes, night dresses, tunics, even trousers, hanging one after the other in exotic splendor.

"There, you see," Naomi said, indicating the open doorway with a sweep of her arm. "You do have clothes."

"Yes."

Naomi shot her a look. "Are you all right? You look a little sick."

Saronna put a hand over her mouth and didn't answer.

Naomi threw her arms around her in a warm embrace. "Oh, my dear, I know it's hard, but you'll get over it. I was terrified when Vladimir bought me, but believe me, no one could have been kinder, really."

Saronna gently disentangled herself from the other woman's grasp. She touched two fingers to her heart in the sign of Mother Eve, but Naomi didn't give the reply, so Saronna knew the other woman wasn't a Believer. She was sequestered in this house with no one to turn to for help. "I think I'd like to be alone for a while."

Naomi gave her an anxious look. "All right, if you're sure?"

"I'm sure," Saronna said, trying to sound firm.

Naomi insisted on showing her how to use a machine she called a com, so that Saronna could ask for anything she wanted, and then she gave Saronna another quick hug and left her alone.

Saronna walked into the bedroom and looked around the room at the elegant furnishings. She had placed all her dependence on her gift. It had kept her unattached and at home for so long that now she was unprepared to find herself in such alien surroundings, luxurious though they might be. It was all so strange and so far from home that she threw herself down on the bed and wept.

CHAPTER TWO

Duncan Trushenko put down his bag and held in a sigh of impatience. Somehow the longer the journey, the more the minor inconveniences of traveling annoyed him. After having come halfway across the galaxy, he now had to wait at the spaceport gate while those needing special assistance were allowed to go ahead of the other passengers. A frail-boned Tryff went first, her species almost indistinguishable within the confines of her bulky gravity suit.

Duncan watched with a tolerant eye as a family of Milorans came next. Milorans were humanoid in shape and about the same height as humans, but wider and bulkier. Each of the well-behaved but massive young-sters probably weighed at least as much as Duncan did.

Finally, there came a last elderly Shuratanian. Two hundred and fifty if she was a day, she still looked spry enough, if a trifle slow in her movements. She was short, even for a Shuratanian. Duncan could easily see the top of her head as he trudged behind her toward the gate. Her long, pointed ears drooped with fatigue but perked up as a younger Shuratanian woman came forward and embraced her.

Duncan moved around them into the spaceport proper, only to find his father standing in front of him.

"Duncan!"

"Hello, Dad." Duncan bent down and returned his father's embrace enthusiastically. "Thanks for meeting me."

"Of course, of course," Vladimir said. "How could I not meet you after almost three years? Welcome home!"

Duncan picked up the small bag he had dropped, and looked around at the open space, crowded with travelers milling about. The absence of anything as formal as Customs or an Immigration Desk told him he was back on Krueger's World, and the time displayed on the wall told him he had arrived in the late after-noon. He had eaten dinner on the ship more than an hour before boarding the landing shuttle, so his internal clock would be off for a few days. "My luggage is being sent later. Do we have transport?"

When they stepped outside, the Kruegerian sun was still high enough in the sky that Duncan felt its warmth on his face. It was good to be back on a planet, even this one.

Vladimir kept up a flow of talk as he led the way to where a ground car waited. Rapid-fire facts about the last few weeks' business developments mixed with personal news about Naomi and the staff at Cameron Trushenko headquarters. Duncan listened with half an ear. Having spent nearly three years visiting the far-flung web of buyers, transporters, and sellers that was the Cameron Trushenko trading company, he was up to date on all but the most recent corporate events.

In the ground car, he leaned back against the seat and let out the sigh he had been holding in. Vladimir put the screen up between them and the driver so they could talk. Duncan looked out curiously at the city of New Jerusalem as they passed through it. He noted that skimmers still weren't allowed in the city; only ground cars navigated the traffic lanes.

"It looks exactly the same," he said. "Rather like a Terran medieval city that's been dug up and then renovated."

Vladimir smiled. "Your mother would appreciate the comparison better than I would. I haven't a clue how Terran medieval cities looked."

Duncan ran one hand through his hair. God, he was tired. "There aren't any left on Terra. Sleeper worlds have closer approximations than anything you'll see on the home world."

"Well, anyway, nothing's changed here in New Jerusalem. Actually, I don't think much has changed on all of Krueger's World. They're not big on change here."

"I remember. The city doesn't just look medieval, it acts medieval."

"Now, Duncan." His father's voice held a scolding note. "Don't be so judgmental."

Duncan shrugged. "Sorry, Dad. But it's hard to believe worlds like this still exist. Families are ruled by patriarchs. Women are virtual slaves of their husbands and fathers. Even sons have limited rights while their fathers live. When you look at the rest of the universe, it's hard not to be judgmental."

Vladimir made a tisking noise. "Well, Krueger's World doesn't look at the rest of the universe. They didn't even want to look at Terra. That's why they came here in the first place."

"I know." Duncan grinned. "That and so old Adolph Krueger could have as many women as he wanted."

"Duncan!" There was fear in Vladimir's voice this time as he cast an anxious glance through the screen at their Kruegerian driver. "Blasphemy is still a crime here in New Jerusalem. And believe me, you don't want to know the penalty."

"All right, Dad," Duncan said, too tired to argue. "I'll keep my mouth shut."

Vladimir pointed out the tall arches of the Stranger's Gate as they drove through it. It seemed to Duncan that his father visibly relaxed once they were through the gateway. Most of the strict rules of Alfred Krueger's followers didn't apply within the off-world quarter.

"So," his father said, "you're sure you're okay with living at home again? We left your room just as it was, but I'd understand if you wanted to move out."

Duncan grinned. "Since home is also the office, I don't think it will seem that strange. And aside from the benefit of not having to commute, having my room and board be part of my salary means I save in taxes as well as living expenses." His father looked so relieved at this answer that Duncan couldn't resist adding a codicil. "Although if you start acting like I'm still a teenager, I might revisit my decision."

Vladimir laughed, but he still looked as if something was worrying him.

A moment later the car pulled up in the interior yard of the house that was both his father's residence and the headquarters of Cameron Trushenko.

"New security?" Duncan asked as he glanced around at the enclosed semicircular driveway at the back of the house. Each end of the far wall had an opening wide enough to admit a ground car, but it was considerably more enclosed than the open space that had been there when he was last on Krueger's World.

His father nodded. "No sense taking chances. One of the MarisCo executives insulted a patriarch without realizing it. The next thing they knew, three young men attacked in broad daylight. They cut up two vice presidents rather badly, and knocked their driver unconscious when he tried to help."

Duncan frowned. "Did this happen in the off-world quarter?"

"Yes, at their headquarters." Vladimir waved a hand and made a tisking noise. "But you don't need to worry. The young men satisfied their honor by drawing blood, and then they left. The Kruegerians benefit from off-worlders being here, and they know it. There hasn't been a death from a blood feud in years. Well," he added, "not in the off-world quarter. They still kill each other off from time to time, but we can't do anything about that."

It didn't sound especially reassuring to Duncan. It was true that off-world presence benefited the local residents, not only directly, through the annual taxes paid to the city, but indirectly by providing jobs and access to improved technology, like skimmers and coms. But it was also true that owning a skimmer didn't seem to make Kruegerian patriarchs any less autocratic or narrow-minded. And his father hadn't specified how many years it had been since the last fatal attack.

His father called out for the driver to take Duncan's bag inside, and then led the way up the steps to another arched doorway. Duncan followed him through a small courtyard into another corridor and then finally into a cozy parlor. He hoped he would remember the layout of the house. It was rather spread out.

"Like a drink?" Vladimir asked, moving to the bar.

"Yes, thanks."

"Still like Shuratanian ale?"

"Yeah," Duncan said, surprised. "I didn't think you could get that here."

"You can now." Vladimir turned to hand him a glass of foaming pale blue liquid. "The Shuratanians have landed in force. You can hardly go for a walk in this quarter without tripping over a dozen of them."

"Are they getting in your way?" Duncan asked as he sipped his ale. A burst of tart, just slightly fruity flavor washed over his taste buds. Apparently Krueger's World had moved into the present, at least as far as beverages. He sank into a chair and stretched out his legs with a faint groan.

"No," Vladimir said, surveying him with satisfaction. "I don't mind. They make me look taller."

Duncan laughed. "I didn't mean literally. I mean, are they cutting into our business?"

"Not yet." Vladimir poured himself a glass of the same ale. "That may change, but for now they seem most interested in the technological aspects of Krueger's World."

"I didn't think there were any."

"There may be," Vladimir said, sitting down opposite him. "If there's any chance this place could produce low cost electronics, the Shuratanians will milk it for all it's worth."

Duncan drank his ale and considered the possibility. He looked up to find his father's benevolent gaze still on him. "What are you looking at?" he asked, without heat.

"You," Vladimir said. "You look well. I swear you look taller."

Duncan snorted with disbelief. "I was twenty-three when I left, and I'm twenty-six now. Believe me, I haven't grown a centimeter in years."

"Maybe not," Vladimir said. "Maybe I just forgot how tall you are?"

"Maybe."

An awkward silence filled the room.

"So," Vladimir said, "are you seeing anyone new?"

Duncan smiled broadly. "No, not since Emily. Why? Are you going to try to fix me up with someone? I thought you'd learned your lesson."

Vladimir's face set in an almost-frown. "I never meant for you to take up with her when I hired her, Duncan. I never thought it was a good idea for you to start a relationship with someone who worked for me, even if she was only a contract employee."

"It didn't hurt anything. We were never serious."

Vladimir snorted. "Maybe you weren't. You can't tell me Emily wasn't trying to make it serious. I knew that the first time I found myself saying good morning to her across my own breakfast table—without any warning at all, thank you very much!"

Duncan remembered the day. He grinned at his father. "I didn't plan it that way. It just happened."

Vladimir didn't smile back. "It scared the *oopla* out of me. When the two of you left Krueger's World a few weeks later, I lived in dread that I'd get an express that you'd married her. I was quite relieved when you told me you had called it quits."

He stopped talking and lifted his brows expectantly.

Duncan smiled to himself but was careful not to let his amusement show. His father had been curious about his breakup with Emily Pulaski since it happened, but Duncan had no intention of satisfying that curiosity, especially as his father had been entirely accurate in his assessment of Emily's intentions. "If you disliked her so much," he said instead, "why did you hire her?"

"I didn't dislike her," Vladimir said. "When it came to navigating the seas of interstellar trade regulations, she had excellent skills. I'm happy you seem to have learned a lot of them from her. I just didn't want you to marry her."

"You can't have it both ways, Dad. Either you want me to get married or you don't."

"Don't be silly," Vladimir said irritably. "Marrying the wrong person is worse than not getting married at all."

Duncan didn't know what to say. His parents had lived apart ever since he was a baby; the few occasions they had been together for any length of time had resulted in epic quarrels. Another awkward silence ensued.

"I'm sorry, Duncan," his father said. "I wasn't trying to cast any aspersions on your mother."

Duncan put his glass down. "I know, Dad. Why all this eagerness to fix me up with someone? I thought that was Mom's job."

"Well," Vladimir said, sounding oddly hesitant, "Your mother and I both want you to find someone— get married, have a family of your own. If nothing else, I'd like to think that someday there'll be someone for you to pass Cameron Trushenko on to. It'll all be yours someday. I won't live forever, you know."

Duncan grinned openly. "You're not giving me the 'I'm getting old' speech, are you? You look pretty hale for that. Naomi must be taking good care of you."

"She is, she is." Vladimir's face lit with affection. "I can't tell you what a change it makes in your outlook to have someone who cares about you in that way. It's meant a world of difference to me to have her with me."

Almost the only good thing about his parents' intense dislike for each other was it took away any guilt he might have felt for being pleased when one of them found consolation elsewhere. "Good. I'm glad you're happy."

"The thing is," Vladimir went on, "poor Naomi had no one to keep her company. I mean, she looks after the house for me, but really, she had no close friends, nothing to occupy her leisure time. And sometimes I get tied up for days on end."

Duncan frowned. What was the old man leading up to? "I know you're busy. Cameron Trushenko is a major concern. Why don't you just hire more help?"

"Well," Vladimir said, a nervous edge creeping into his voice, "the thing is, Naomi wanted more than just to have me free up some time. She needed a friend—a woman friend."

Duncan sat up straighter. "What's going on, Dad? Are you trying to tell me something?"

Vladimir glanced at the window to the courtyard. He seemed almost reluctant to meet Duncan's eyes. "Well, yes, I am, son."

"Son?" Duncan moved to the edge of his chair in alarm. "Son? You never call me 'son' unless something's wrong. The last time you called me 'son,' we had just lost three million credits."

Vladimir looked almost relieved at the accusation. "Oh, it's nothing like that. It's just that, as I said, Naomi needed someone, and the people on this world are so stuffy. There are off-worlders, and there are natives and the two just don't mix. There was no one Naomi was comfortable making friends with, no one who didn't look down her nose at her. And native women almost never leave their homes. They don't need friends, because they all have hordes of relations. And then I found out you were coming home, and I knew you'd broken up with Emily a while ago. It seemed like a perfect solution to both problems."

"What did?" Duncan said, more mystified than ever.

"Well," Vladimir said, still apparently finding it difficult to come to the point, "the thing is, son— Duncan, I sort of—well, I bought a woman for you."

Duncan's mouth dropped open. He must have heard his father wrong. "You did what?"

"I bought a woman for you."

No, he had heard right. But the idea was incredible. "You *bought* a woman for me? You *bought* a sentient being?"

"Now, Duncan—"

The more he thought about it, the angrier it made him. "You thought I'd want some down-trodden, complacent, hapless little female to make use of in my free time? You thought I'd take advantage of a woman like that?"

"Well," Vladimir said, "no, not really. Actually, I just needed someone to keep Naomi company, but there's no way I could get someone on those terms. And besides," he added as an afterthought, "she's not little."

"What?" Duncan jumped to his feet. The old man had gone crazy. There was no other explanation. "I don't give a damn how tall she is! You just send her back where she came from, Dad. I won't have any part of this."

"But, Duncan," Vladimir said, his voice filled with righteous indignation, "when I brought Naomi home, you didn't act like this. You were proud of me for stepping in."

Duncan brushed aside this argument with a wave of his hand. "That was different. Her husband had put her up as his stake in a poker game. You kept her from ending up with some gun-running scum."

"Saronna's father was desperate to sell her." The indignation in his father's voice gave way to a virtuous note. "She's twenty-two in Standard years, and she's never been married. A year ago her mother died, and her father stopped looking for a husband for her and tried to sell her. None of the hill men were interested, so he came into the city. You know very well where she could have ended up if I hadn't made him an offer."

Duncan cringed. Just when he thought Krueger's World couldn't get any worse, he found out he was wrong. "Her own father?"

Vladimir nodded.

"All right," Duncan said, "if he needed the money so badly, let him keep it. Just send her home with no strings attached."

His father shook his head. "I can't do that. If I did, they'd assume she'd been unsatisfactory in some way. If they let her live, it would be as a nameless drudge without any rights."

"God!" Duncan clutched his hair. "Why the hell did you have to move to this miserable, primitive hunk of rock? What kind of place is this, where men sell their daughters to strangers?"

"It's Krueger's World." Vladimir almost snapped the words out, as if he were losing patience. "And you know as well as I do why I moved Cameron Trushenko here. Krueger's World is an ideal location for interstellar trading, and when you add in the tax break from operating outside of ThreeCon, we're in much better shape than we were five years ago. Even your mother approved the move. The combination of New Hong Kong's regulations and ThreeCon taxes was crippling us."

Duncan turned away, unwilling to concede the argument. "We're doing really well now. My two percent of the corporate profits certainly reflects that. Can't we move back into the civilized universe?"

"Not yet," Vladimir said firmly. "I don't know how long it'll be, either."

Duncan shot him a skeptical look. "Are you sure taxes and location are the only reason, Dad? It wouldn't have anything to do with Naomi, would it?"

Again Vladimir wouldn't meet his gaze. "I won't deny that the thought that Naomi might not want to leave this planet worries me. However, it's a moot point for now. We can't afford to move, and that's the truth."

Duncan sighed. "All right, so Cameron Trushenko stays here for a while longer. Is that any reason to go around buying people?"

"Maybe it is," Vladimir said. "So long as we're here, we might as well try to make things better for at least one person when we get the chance. If I hadn't bought Saronna, her father might be walking the streets right now, looking for someone to buy her. As it is, she's safe and comfortable. I presume you don't plan to rape her?"

Repulsed, Duncan put a good deal of heat into his voice. "If that's supposed to be a joke, it's not very funny."

"I wasn't joking at all. I brought her here, and I feel responsible for her."

"Then why didn't you just buy her for yourself?" Duncan demanded. "Why did you have to bring me into it at all?"

For the first time, guilt suffused Vladimir's expression. "Well, I thought about that, but Naomi got very jealous when I mentioned it. She was much happier when I agreed we could find someone for *you*."

Duncan snorted with disgust, but Vladimir continued.

"Anyway, fortunately, I could tell Naomi that this woman stirred no twinges of passion in me. She's not homely or anything, but she's not in Naomi's league."

Somehow his father's reasoning made Duncan even angrier. "And what the hell am I supposed to do with her?"

"You don't have to do anything," Vladimir said, his voice as soothing as it had been sixteen years before, when Duncan had broken his arm and cried all the way to the doctor's. "But it would be nice if you made friends with her. I'm sure she's a little scared. She may have been brought up to think this was all perfectly natural, but still it can't be easy to leave your home so suddenly and move somewhere where you don't know anyone."

Duncan groaned and resumed his chair. "Good God, Dad. When did you buy her?"

"This afternoon."

Less than a day. Just his luck to arrive right as the old man suddenly went crazy. "Damn! Do you mean if I'd gotten here last week, I could have talked you out of this nonsense?"

"No, no. I waited until you were coming home, that's all. Like I said, Naomi was jealous until I told her Saronna was for you."

Duncan groaned again and covered his eyes. It just got worse and worse. "Will you listen to yourself, Dad? You sound as if you were talking about a house pet. You've been here too long, and that's all there is to it."

Vladimir pulled himself upright as if he were offended. "Nonsense. I may have made an effort to blend in, but believe me, I can see the shortcomings of this world easily enough."

Really, for such a sharp businessman, his father could be completely obtuse sometimes. "How can you say that on the same afternoon you bought another human being?"

"I may have done it, but I can still see the innate inequality of it. I know it's a disgrace."

"But you did it anyway!"

"If I hadn't, someone else would have," Vladimir said calmly. "Saronna could have been in much worse shape."

Duncan gave up. He sighed in exasperation and leaned his head back against the chair. "All in all, I would have preferred it if you'd told me we'd lost another three million credits."

Vladimir laughed but shook his finger in a scolding manner. "Stop moping! Anyone would think I'd done something dreadful to you. All I've done is provide you with a companion—someone to tell your troubles to, and maybe rub your neck when you're finished with work."

It had a familiar ring to it. "A geisha."

"A what?"

"It was a tradition back on Terra," Duncan said, sitting up straighter.

"There you go," Vladimir said, sounding pleased. "I knew that year you spent on Terra would pay off."

Duncan snorted. "You were mad as hell at Mom for taking me there. It was too far away from New Hong Kong for real time transmissions."

Vladimir waved a hand dismissively. "Nonsense. Your mother and I always lived up to our agreement. Neither one of us could object to where the other one wanted to live."

Duncan grinned as he remembered his own version of past events. "You both complained bitterly about the fare whenever I had to go a long way. You bitched like crazy when Mom went all the way to Lycandria."

Vladimir frowned at the memory. "Don't mention that, please. When I think how close you came—" he left the sentence unfinished.

"Now, Dad," Duncan said, "we'd been gone more than a month when the Lycandrians attacked."

"Still too damn close," Vladimir said, with a slight shudder. "What if your mother hadn't decided you needed a little time at school before classes star—" He broke off in the middle of a word. "I almost forgot. Your friends are here."

"What friends?"

"Your friends from school," Vladimir said impatiently. "You know, the two who started their own company. What's it called—Kumar and Whisset?"

"Sai and Randy?" Duncan said, in surprise. He had met them at a space station less than two years ago and they hadn't mentioned coming this way. "They're here on Krueger's World?"

Vladimir nodded. "Randy called me a few days ago, looking for you. I told him when you were coming, and he said they'd come to see you soon."

"What are they doing here?"

"He didn't say. But it's not so surprising. The things that made Krueger's World attractive to us also make it attractive to other trading companies."

Duncan frowned, certain that his friends' arrival couldn't be entirely good news. "I can't believe Sai would agree to come here, not with the way they treat women."

"But they won't hassle her so long as she stays in the off-world quarter. She can do what she wants here, same as any ThreeCon world."

Duncan shook his head. "Sai wouldn't buy that. I can't imagine that she'd be willing to live with that kind of restriction."

There was a movement in the doorway. When Vladimir looked up, a warm, contented smile spread across his face. "Naomi, come in, come in. Say hello to Duncan."

Duncan stood up hastily as his father's companion came into the room. He noted first that her lush beauty hadn't faded and second that her clothes looked very fine, as if she were dressing to impress someone. "Hello, Naomi," he said easily. "You're looking well—even more beautiful than I remembered."

"Hello, Duncan," she said with a shy smile.

He bent down and kissed her cheek chastely, treating her to a modest, momentary embrace. Naomi bore it without any signs of unease, and Vladimir beamed at them both.

"I thought it would be a good time for Duncan to meet Saronna," Naomi said.

Duncan frowned, and Naomi looked distressed.

Vladimir patted her arm and oozed reassurance. "Of course, my dear, of course. Why don't you bring her in here?"

Naomi turned back to the doorway and gestured. "It's all right," she said, smiling. "Come in now. He won't bite."

Duncan looked to the doorway, expecting from this encouraging tone to see a small, timid figure, but the woman who stepped into the room was only half a head shorter than he was, and showed no signs of shyness or timidity.

She stood straight, with a great deal of composure and an equal amount of reserve. She kept her eyes downcast, but that seemed to be more from habit than from a reaction to her surroundings. Her dowdy brown skirt came down to her ankles and made her look even taller. She had long black hair and golden skin that reminded Duncan of the Asian women he had seen in his one year on Terra, until she lifted her eyes, and he could see that they were an arresting shade of light gray.

"Hello, Saronna," Vladimir said. "This is my son, Duncan Trushenko."

Saronna nodded gravely, but didn't speak. She looked disconcerted when Duncan held out his hand, but she shook it gingerly.

"Well," Vladimir said, his smile a little too bright. "Shall we sit down?"

They sat awkwardly, with Saronna hesitant until Naomi patted the sofa next to her.

"Would you like some wine, Naomi?" Vladimir asked.

His companion accepted this offer, and Vladimir got up to pour her a glass. "How about you, Saronna?"

The Kruegerian woman looked flustered. Probably she had never seen a man waiting on a woman. She shook her head, murmuring her thanks along with her rejection.

"Naomi tells me that you weave." Vladimir sounded like he was trying for a fatherly tone as he sat down beside Naomi, but it came across more as awkward but well meant.

Saronna nodded. "I did." She glanced around the parlor at the imported off-world furnishings. "It no longer seems a useful skill."

"No, no," Vladimir said. "If you enjoy it, we can get you a loom, certainly."

She gave him a suspicious look from under her brows. "Why? You already paid six thousand credits for me. Why would you spend more?"

Naomi bit her lip at such frankness, and Vladimir looked disconcerted, but Duncan let out a crack of laughter before he could stop himself. Apparently, Saronna wasn't one to disguise the truth.

"Sorry," he said, when his father glared at him.

Saronna was looking at him, too, but it was a more speculative glance.

"Duncan," Naomi said in a determined tone, "how was your journey?"

"It went pretty well," Duncan said. "No problems—not unless my luggage doesn't show up today."

"How long were you traveling?" Naomi asked. The brightness of her tone suggested that she had decided interstellar travel was a safe topic.

"Thirty-four days, in Standard time."

"I forgot about ship time," Vladimir said, suddenly sounding guilty. "What time is it for you?"

"A little after midnight." Duncan noticed that Saronna looked puzzled. "Terran starships always keep Terran Standard time," he said, trying his best not to sound condescending. "And often, when you get where you're going, ship time is nowhere close to local time. A Kruegerian day is longer, I know," he added, addressing his father, "but I forget what the exact conversion rate is."

"One point one three," Vladimir answered. "Just over twenty-seven hours in a Kruegerian day. It'll take you a while to get acclimated again."

Duncan shook his head. "It shouldn't be too bad. Some of the places I visited were much farther from Terran standard time."

Vladimir didn't look convinced, but a gentle nudge from Naomi seemed to make him realize that Saronna might be finding the conversation a little incomprehensible. "Well, anyway," he said, "enough about your trip. If it's past midnight for you, Duncan, then you should get to bed. You must be exhausted."

"I'm all right," Duncan said. He was watching Saronna and he noted that his father's words made her turn pale in an instant. He stood up and looked down at the woman his father had bought for him. "Besides, before I go to bed, Saronna and I need to have a talk."

Her eyes flew up to his and then dropped immediately to the floor.

"So go ahead and talk," Vladimir said.

Duncan shook his head. Things were awkward enough as it was without an audience. "No, we need to be alone."

Naomi rose and tugged on Vladimir's sleeve. "Come along, Vlad. Let's leave them."

Vladimir hesitated, but then nodded. "I'll say good night now, Duncan. You're in your old room. Let me or Naomi know if you need anything."

"Thanks, Dad. I'll see you tomorrow."

His father gave him a brief but energetic embrace and left the parlor with his beautiful companion.

Duncan sat down in Naomi's place next to Saronna. "Well, Saronna, here we are."

Her eyes flew up again, and this time they met his and she stared at him without speaking.

"Don't look at me like that!" Duncan said. "You look like a wild thing caught in a net. I'm not going to hurt you—I'm not going to touch you at all."

Her expression changed from fear to outright disbelief. "Why did your father buy me for you if it's not women you want? Did he hope to change you somehow?"

Duncan had opened his mouth to ask what she meant when it came to him. He leaned back on the sofa and howled with laughter.

Saronna looked bewildered.

"I'm sorry," he said, sitting up straight and composing himself. "I wasn't laughing at *you*. It's just funny that you would put that interpretation on what I said. All I was trying to tell you is that it wasn't my idea to go out and purchase a companion for me. I don't believe that anyone can own someone else. As far as I'm concerned, you're free to go anytime."

Her confusion vanished, replaced by naked fear. "You're sending me back to my father?"

Duncan patted her hand, feeling at a loss. On Krueger's World, even trying to reassure someone was more
difficult than it should be. "You don't have to go back
unless you want to go back. I just want you to know
that you can walk out the door whenever you like. I
have no hold on you."

Saronna's mouth twisted in a bitter smile. "Your
father owns me."

"No he doesn't!"

She looked surprised at the vehemence of his tone.
"He paid my father six thousand credits for me."

"So what? It doesn't matter how much money my
father gave your father. Your father didn't own you, so
he couldn't sell you."

Her eyes grew wide with wonder. "If you said that in
Samaria, they would stone you."

"We are not, thankfully, in Samaria," Duncan said,
with more firmness than was necessary. "We're in the
off-world quarter of New Jerusalem, and here at least I
can tell you the truth. No one owns anyone else."

She pondered this silently, and then studied him
again. "Then why did your father pay my father six
thousand credits?"

Duncan smiled. For someone who had been brought
up to think of herself as chattel, she showed potential
as an independent thinker. Maybe he wouldn't be stuck
with her after all. "If you want to know the truth, Dad
needed someone to keep Naomi company. Off-world

women make her feel put down, and your people are too tightly knit for women to make friends outside the family. He hit upon the idea of finding someone for me—of telling Naomi that he was going to find someone for me—so that there would always be a woman friend here for her."

Saronna nodded. "She said that. She told me that Sire Trushenko was pleased that she would have someone to talk to, and to help her with the house." She lowered her gaze again and added, "But she said, too, that once you felt you knew me, that you would require me to come to your bed."

Apparently, several years as his father's companion hadn't changed Naomi's outlook as much as Duncan had hoped. "Well, she was wrong. I have no such plans at all. And besides, no one can require someone to sleep with them. Even if I were your husband, I couldn't do that."

She gave him a frank glance this time, not hiding her reaction at all. "You wouldn't last long in Samaria."

This made him smile again. "I'm sure you're right. But as I pointed out, we're not in Samaria. I'm not going to demand anything from you, let alone force myself on you. You're welcome to stay in this house so long as you like, or to leave whenever you like. The choice is entirely up to you."

She gave him an appraising glance, as if she suspected him of misleading her. "Then what must I do here?"

Duncan shrugged, conscious of a sudden feeling of helplessness. "I don't know," he said, thinking rapidly. What could she do? He could hardly put her to work for Cameron Trushenko. "Help Naomi with things around the house, I guess. I know she runs things around here—meals, servants, things like that. I'm sure she could find things for you to do."

"Do you have your own courtyard?"

It was Duncan's turn to feel lost. "What?"

Saronna's gesture took in the room around her and beyond. "This is a big house, but the space is assigned in a peculiar fashion. There are several courtyards, but no one seems to live here except Sire Trushenko and Naomi. Will you take one of the courtyards for your own?"

Understanding dawned. "Oh, you mean will I set up my own household within this house?"

She nodded. "You're old enough, even if you don't have a wife."

He shook his head. "We don't do things like that. Actually, grown children usually move out of their parents' house altogether. Dad and I are a little different, because Dad has a controlling interest in Cameron Trushenko—that's our company—and I work for him. He asked me to live here, and I agreed because it's convenient." Although that could change if his father kept going native. He didn't say this thought out loud; there was no need to insult her culture.

Saronna looked just slightly incredulous.

"Is there more than one generation living at your house back in Samaria?" Duncan asked.

She nodded, clearly surprised at his ignorance. "My father's mother is still alive, so she lives in her own small courtyard with a servant to look after her. My eldest brother Gideon has set up his household in the east courtyard; he has a wife and two children. My two unmarried sisters and my other brother still live with my father and his wife in the central courtyard."

To an only child, it sounded like a huge family. "Your father's wife? Did your father remarry already?"

Her brows knit in puzzlement. "Remarry? He's not a widower. He married Leah when he was twenty-five, and she's quite well. He never had another wife."

Duncan blinked. He must be more tired than he thought. "But Dad told me your mother died recently?"

Saronna nodded. "She did. She passed from this world a year ago, from the coughing sickness."

"I'm sorry to hear that," Duncan said automatically. "You must miss her."

She blinked, as if to hold back tears, but went on with her explanation. "My mother was my father's woman, but he couldn't marry her. He couldn't set Leah aside, because she had sons."

"Oh," Duncan said, trying to decide if he had committed a social gaffe by bringing this relationship to light. Apparently not, as Saronna didn't seem at all embarrassed.

"That's why my father sold me," Saronna said in an explanatory tone.

The idea appalled Duncan. "You mean he didn't care what happened to you because he wasn't married to your mother?"

Now she looked offended. "No, of course not. But Leah was always angry at me. She knew my father loved my mother and not her, and so she was cruel to my mother, and then to me. My father thought that if anything happened to him, Leah would most likely push Gideon into selling me. Father wanted to find me the best place he could."

"I see," Duncan said, although he didn't understand at all. He shook his head, hoping that would clear things up, but it didn't help at all. "I'm afraid I'm really too wiped out to comprehend all this. I need to go to bed now—alone, thank you. Maybe we can talk more tomorrow?"

She nodded once. "Of course, if you wish it. How should I address you?"

Duncan yawned, covering his mouth with his hand but not hiding his fatigue. "Call me Duncan. Heck, you can call me anything you like. What should I call you?"

"My name is Saronna."

"Saronna what?"

She looked down at the floor abruptly. "Just Saronna. My family name was Maynard, but once my father sold me, I had no right to use that name."

More sexist crap. Duncan made a noise that started as a yawn but came out as more of a snort. "It doesn't matter to me. You can still call yourself Saronna Maynard if you like."

She shook her head wordlessly.

He got to his feet. "Well, Saronna, I'll say good night. Don't worry too much. I know it must be frightening to find yourself in a house full of strangers, but we're not bad people. No one will hurt you here."

She lifted her eyes to his and nodded slowly. "I believe you."

Duncan thought she sounded almost surprised. "Good!" He patted her arm in what he hoped was a fatherly gesture, and turned to go. "See you in the morning," he said over his shoulder.

BACK in her own rooms, Saronna locked the door to the corridor, then went into the bedroom and opened the cupboard near the bed.

The shrine was very small, meant to hide away in a drawer or behind a dresser. She unfolded it and set it up on the bed, placing the small candle in its holder in front of the statuette. Tomorrow she would have to find a source for candles. They didn't seem to be common in this house.

She knelt in front of the shrine, ducked her head briefly, as a sign of respect, then looked up. The statuette of Eve, the mother goddess, seemed to look back her. The stylized form of a naked woman smiled serenely, her arms crossed over her breasts. Saronna concentrated intently on the wick of the candle. After several seconds, it lit spontaneously. Saronna let out a ragged sigh. Sometimes when she was worried or nervous, it was difficult to make her gift work reliably.

Almost silently she murmured the prayer for women in childbirth, and the prayer for her sisters of the flesh, followed by a prayer for her mother's soul.

"Forgive me, Mother," she said as she began the prayer for forgiveness of sin, "for I love a man. My brother Paul was kind to me, and I failed to keep the proper distance. I ask your forgiveness and promise I'll try not to sin again."

Saronna debated whether she needed to ask for-giveness for not hating Duncan as she ought, but decided that since he had promised not to claim his rights, not hating him wasn't actually a sin. It had disconcerted her when she had thought he was telling her that he was like Paul and cared for men instead of for women. If Duncan had been like Paul, it would have been a relief for her, and yet somehow she was glad that he wasn't.

She felt her face flush. She needed to keep her feelings in control or she would stray from her vows and break her promise to her mother at the same time.

She took a deep breath and began the consecrated woman's prayer. "Oh, Mother Eve, as one who is consecrated to you, I ask that you reward me with the strength of will to keep my vow of purity and to bear my special burden. As I endure the sufferings that men impose upon women, help me to remember the wonderful place you will prepare for me in heaven." After a moment, she added her own plea. "And help me now, alone in this house of strangeness. I have no one but you, Mother."

It occurred to her as she blew out the candle that strangeness might not always be a bad thing.

CHAPTER THREE

When Saronna awoke the next morning, she had been dreaming that her mother was alive. Coming awake brought the pain of her mother's loss back, fresh and new, and tears welled in Saronna's eyes. Morning light filled the room, but no sound broke the stillness. Saronna sat up abruptly, recalled to her new reality by the strangeness of her surroundings. She was not in her father's house; she was not even in Samaria. She brushed the tears from her eyes and got up, determined not to let her grief show in front of these strangers.

She wrapped herself in a robe, then opened the door to the corridor. More silence. There was no bustle of a workday starting, no children running noisily in the corridor, no sound of pots and pans. Only the faintest hum could be heard, the sound of off-world machines.

She shut the door and went to bathe, doing her best to ignore the image of her naked body in the large mirrors that surrounded the enormous bathtub. Afterwards, she tried on one of the dresses that hung in her dressing room. One glance in the dressing room mirror dissuaded her from wearing it. A stranger looked back at her, and strangeness had already overwhelmed Saronna. She opted instead to change into the unflattering familiarity of her second best dress. Dark gray and even more plainly cut than the one she had worn the day before, the dress hung down to her ankles and draped her body in commodious, familiar folds.

Once she was decently clad, Saronna walked through the empty corridors, trying to recall the layout from her brief tour of the house the day before. Unlike her father's home, Vladimir Trushenko's house sprawled over a large piece of land, because it was all on one level. It amazed her that such a large house could be so empty.

But, of course, these off-worlders used their home for their business, something only poorer Krugerians would do. The floor plan at least followed Kruegerian tradition. The large courtyard where her father had sat with Vladimir occupied the center of the huge rectangle that was the entire house. A smaller courtyard marked the center of each of the four quadrants. There was even a tiny dower courtyard on the south side of the house, very like the one her grandmother occupied in her father's house, only here it seemed to be purely a place to sit and enjoy the weather.

Of the many rooms, the majority had been given over to business. The family occupied only the northeast quadrant of the house, while the southeast held storage rooms, pantries, and an enormous kitchen. The remaining rooms had all been turned into offices. The day before, the offices had been filled with people working away at tasks that had left Saronna totally bewildered, but now they were empty.

After wandering the hallways, she headed back to the main courtyard; the sweet scent of the sugar bushes and the familiar drone of morning crickets made the space seem almost home-like. She was surprised to see she was no longer the only occupant of the courtyard. A man stood there with his head back and his arms stretched wide as if he were welcoming the sun.

Saronna waited quietly for Duncan to look down and notice her.

When he did, he bent his arms, stifled a yawn, and grinned. "Good morning. I couldn't sleep any later because I'm on ship time. I didn't expect to see anyone else up, though. You're an early riser."

She considered this comment gravely before she replied. Apparently, everything was different in this house, even the hours of the day. "I'm used to getting up early. In my father's house, I would have had work to do. Here, I don't know what to do with myself."

Duncan looked suddenly struck. "Can you read?"

Saronna debated the question in her mind for a few quick seconds and decided it was safe to tell the truth. It seemed unlikely that her answer would ever get back her father. "Yes. My mother taught me how."

"Good," Duncan said. "Come with me then."

He turned and led the way through a corridor to the northwest quadrant. Saronna followed him, wondering where he was going.

"Here we are," Duncan said, opening the door to a large room near the northwest courtyard. "This is the library. Some of the office staff use it, too, so don't be surprised if someone comes in while you're here. They won't bother you."

Saronna didn't reply. The closest she had ever been to a library was her father's study, which had a shelf with a half dozen books. She looked around the room curiously, wondering what her protector wanted her to do or see here. Comfortable-looking sofas and arm chairs stood against the walls, but the focus of the room was a series of six desks arranged in a circle. A machine such as Vladimir had used the day before sat on each desk, while a totally unfamiliar device sat on the floor in the middle of the circle. Cylindrical in shape, the machine was almost waist high and had a variety of switches down one side. A grid of colored lines etched into the surface covered the concave top.

The room was large and airy. Only one thing was missing. "Where are the books?" Saronna asked.

Duncan looked startled. "Oh! Well, the books are in our system. You can read them anywhere, anytime, but we still like to set aside a room for reading and doing research.

Saronna frowned. "What does that mean, 'in our system'?"

His expression went from blank to almost scowling. "I never realized how bad I am at explaining how things work. Our information system is digital. It doesn't exist in print, only in computers—machines. You can read books on anything that can display text, or you can have a com or a terminal read it aloud to you." He gestured toward the far wall. "We do keep some book readers handy. Some people find them less distracting to use, because like this room, they're dedicated to one purpose."

Saronna felt almost as if the floor were tilting. Did words mean different things in this house? "If I read a book, aren't I a book reader?"

His scowl changed into a reluctant grin. "Yes, of course. But that's also what we call devices that are for reading and only for reading."

Saronna looked where he had pointed and saw that a section of the wall had a shelf of a sort she had never seen before. The shelf contained a row of narrow slots, and each slot held a thin rectangle. "Those don't look anything like books to me."

Duncan crossed the room and pressed one of the rectangles. When it popped out of its slot, Saronna saw it was a little bigger than her hand and less than half as thick as her little finger. It looked as if it were made from plastic; her father owned an antique vase and some dishes made from plastic, but Saronna had only rarely been allowed to handle them.

"Here you go," Duncan said. "This is a book reader."

Could he be teasing her? He hadn't seemed cruel yesterday. She stepped closer. "How can you read a piece of plastic?"

"You have to open it first." Duncan pressed his thumb against one edge. The rectangle opened into two flat halves, almost like a real book, but much thinner and with no pages. All but the edges of the two surfaces lit up. "The reader turns on by itself when you open it. Tell it what you want to read, and then it will track your eye movements and advance the text as you read."

She stroked the smooth surface. "It can tell when I'm ready to go to the next page?"

He nodded, clearly too jaded to see it as a wondrous thing. "Sure." He grinned. "If you find it as annoying as I do, you can tell the reader that you want to turn your own pages, and then just tap the right and left edges of the reader to page forward and backward. You could ask it to read aloud to you, although most people don't bother with a reader if they want that, since a com could read to them just as well."

Saronna took the thing from him and stared at the screen in fascination. The letters had a familiar shape, but words were not all spelled as she would have expected. "The—the something Works of William Sha—Sha—Shakespeare?" she asked.

A blank look crossed his face, and then he laughed. "Sorry. I forgot." He took the reader back and spoke into it. "Attention, reader! Display all text in modern Kruegerian."

When he handed the thing back, the page now said clearly *The Collected Works of William Shakespeare*. Below that line was a date and the name of the person who had compiled the book. As soon as Saronna had read the compiler's name, the display changed to show a page of information about someone named William Shakespeare, along with a crude portrait of a man with long hair and a peculiar flat collar. The next page was a poem.

Saronna blinked, amazed and disconcerted by a device that knew exactly what words she was reading. "Do your people speak a different language, then?" she asked. The idea alarmed her even further.

His smile held reassurance. "It's not that different as a spoken language. We have a lot of words you don't, and your people invented some new words that we don't use. But a few centuries ago we refined our written language to make it easier to learn."

Relieved, Saronna eyed the shelves as she handed the device back to him. "So each of those little squares is a book?"

Duncan shrugged as he took it from her. "It's a reader, a receptacle that can hold as many books as you like. We always keep readers handy for ourselves and for the staff. This one still has poems and plays on it, because that's what whoever used it last asked the catalog for."

More lost than ever, Saronna looked around the empty room. "A catalog is a thing that makes books?"

Duncan faced the wall. "Attention, catalog," he said in firm tone.

A pleasantly neutral voice spoke out of the air. "May I help you?"

Saronna jumped in surprise.

"Yes," Duncan said. "I'd like to add a copy of Crushak's *Analysis of Interplanetary Trade*" to this reader." He moved the reader back and forth, as if he were waving it at the unseen speaker.

"Certainly," the voice intoned.

Duncan opened the reader again. He pressed firmly on the right-side edge and flipped through several pages of text interspersed with strangely solid-looking images of stars and people and what must have been enormous vessels.

For Saronna, looking at the images was like looking into a window.

"See how it works?" he asked.

She shook her head slowly. "I can see what you did to make it work, but I don't understand *how* it works. How did the catalog do that?"

He looked unhappy. "Well, I wish I could explain it to you, but I can't, not without explaining a lot of other concepts first. Maybe once you've caught up on some background, you can look into the how of things a little more."

Saronna looked around the room. It was all fascinating, but alarming at the same time. How would she ever learn her way in this place? In spite of his assurances, she felt rather as if he spoke a foreign language. "What is it you wish me to do?"

"Well," Duncan said, "I suppose what I'd like is for you to work at educating yourself. I'd like you to learn what most people in this galaxy know by the time they're your age."

"Why?"

His expression became severe, as if he were scolding, but he didn't seem angry. "Because I reject the idea that you belong to anyone. You belong to yourself, and that's that. But in order to take care of yourself, you need to know more than you do now. You need skills that will enable you to provide for yourself."

She cast her eyes downward to hide her surprise. She had never heard anyone—male or female—say anything to suggest that a woman could support herself. Mother Eve's rituals concentrated more on heavenly revenge for mistreatment by men rather than what women could do for themselves. "Are you going to make me leave here?"

"No." He said it firmly, as if he were making a promise. "You can stay as long as you like. But I told you the truth when I said you were free to walk out the door anytime. I realize, however, that that's not saying much, when there's no way you could survive on your own. I'd like, ultimately, for you to feel that you could go out the door if you wanted to—that if you stay, it's because you want to, not because you have nowhere else to go."

Saronna looked up at this. It sounded almost too good to be true. Perhaps it was a trick, to test her. "What if Sire Trushenko doesn't want me to leave?"

He smiled, but it was a grim smile that didn't reach his eyes. "If my father tried to stop you, I'd walk out the door myself. I'm not bound here, you know. A child doesn't owe his father squat, legally, not once he's grown."

"But he's your father, and you love him. I can see that easily."

Duncan nodded. "Of course I love him. I'd still love him, even if I left. But if he tried to force you to stay, it would mean he'd swallowed too much of the crap they hand out here on Krueger's World. I'd never stay with him if that happened, not even if leaving meant giving up my stake in Cameron Trushenko."

Saronna was still bewildered. Duncan and his father seemed kind enough, especially for men, but nothing made sense here. "I don't understand you."

Now his eyes lit with rueful good humor. "I can see why it would be difficult. I'll have to look into getting you a tutor or something." He closed the book he had asked for. "But in the meantime let's get you started working on your own. Attention, catalog! Please add a copy of the Ansari history of Krueger's World, translated to modern Kruegerian, to this volume."

Almost immediately the catalog answered, "Done."

Duncan handed the reader to Saronna. "There. You can take this with you anywhere, even add more books to it if you like. Read it whenever you get a chance."

Saronna opened the book reader. The first page now looked completely different. She read the title page out loud, hesitating over the unfamiliar first word. "'*Meg— Megalomania Unchecked: A History of Alfred Krueger's World*, by Deiter Ansari.'"

The idea that information could be stored up like raw material and then made into goods intrigued Saronna. It reminded her of using skeins of yarn to weave different kinds of cloth, only much faster. "So you can make any book you want?"

Duncan chuckled. "Well, someone has to write it first. That one was written about twenty years ago. I think you should read it right away."

She glanced back at the title page. "What does it mean by megalomania?"

He looked inscrutable. "The title refers to Krueger's peculiar view of himself as the center of the universe."

It shocked Saronna to hear how he said the words so openly, without any fear at all. "This book criticizes the Patriarch?"

He nodded but made no comment.

Saronna closed the volume, half afraid it would burst into flame in her hands.

"I realize I've put you in quite a quandary," he said. "Your religion teaches you to revere the Patriarch and to obey me, and here I am, asking you to read a book that's critical of him."

She looked up at this. He knew nothing of her true religion, but on the other hand, his philosophy perplexed her. "Asking? You're not ordering me to read the book?"

"No, I'm not. I don't give orders except to people who work for me, and they can quit any time. It's a good book, well researched, and well written, and I think you should read it, but I'm not about to tell you that you have to read it."

Saronna opened the reader again and tapped the right edge to page forward. The first page of text was displayed. The thrill of discovery suffused Saronna. A whole new book waited for her to explore it. She had read only a few dozen books in her life. And surely one who was consecrated to Mother Eve should know as much about the Patriarch as possible. "I'll read the first part and see what I think."

Duncan looked pleased. "That's all I ask. If you finish it, and you want more books about your planet, I'll be happy to recommend some. You could copy them to this volume."

Saronna didn't answer. She was thinking how pleasant it would be to be able to read out in the open, without hiding what she was doing.

"And," Duncan went on, "at some point, you may want to start an educational program. I'll get you a terminal of your own, one that you can keep in your room, if you like. I hope you won't be intimidated by our machines. You can talk to them if you prefer that to using a keypad. I don't myself, but most people do."

"Like you talked to the catalog?"

He nodded. "Sure. A terminal is a lot smarter than the catalog, and even the reader will understand you if you ask it a question. Book readers always have a dictionary built into them. I'll show you."

He took the book from her and spoke directly into the screen. "Attention, dictionary. What is the meaning of the word 'megalomania'?"

A pleasantly neutral voice answered him. "Megalomania is the delusion of greatness or of wealth experienced by some persons suffering from mental illness."

Saronna was impressed, in spite of herself. She took the reader back from Duncan and wondered how it managed to do all that it did in such a small, featureless package.

"Anyway," Duncan went on, "if you want to use one of these terminals in the meantime," he gestured to the machines on the desks, "feel free. The projector here will give you a better image if you're using a three-dimensional program."

"What's a projector?" Saronna asked, her curiosity inspired by the new marvels he had to show her.

"Just watch," Duncan said, stepping up to the nearest terminal. "Attention, terminal. Display the standard encyclopedia reference on Terra."

In a few seconds, solid-seeming objects appeared in the air over the projector. A sphere—a blue and brown orb streaked with large swirls of white—hung in the midst of a field of blackness that filled half the room. A much smaller, barren sphere circled the larger one, slowly.

"This," a female voice intoned, "is Terra, home world of the Terrans. Its official designation in the register of the Third Confederation of Planets is Sol III."

Saronna jumped from surprise and clutched Duncan's arm. "Oh! What is it?"

Duncan patted her hand reassuringly as the voice rambled on about Terra's size, gravity, and climate. "It's a holographic projection. The projector underneath displays the image generated by the program. This program happens to be about Terra. I thought you might like to see it, since that's where our species originated."

The words were meaningless. "But—is it real?"

"No, no, it's only an image made to look as if it had substance." He stepped away from her and waved a hand through the black field until his fingertips sliced through the blue orb as if it were no more solid than smoke. "You see? You can look at it from any angle, but it'll disappear as soon as the program moves on to the next part."

He moved back to stand beside Saronna, and at that moment, the display of Terra dissolved, and in its place were two human figures, a man and a woman, almost life-sized and completely naked. Saronna gasped again.

"These are Terrans," said the voice. "Terrans are bipedal, bilaterally symmetrical, and come in two genders—male and female. The adults of the species are generally between one hundred fifty and two hundred centimeters in height, with females being, on average, smaller than males."

The figures revolved slowly, clearly displaying all features of their anatomy.

Mortified, Saronna turned her face away. "Please— please turn it off."

"Terminal, terminate program." The display vanished. Duncan crinkled his forehead in a rueful frown. "I'm sorry. I didn't know that part was in there. Besides, I didn't realize it would embarrass you so much."

Suddenly conscious of his closeness, she stepped back a pace. "The man was—was naked."

"Yes," Duncan said. "So was the woman. We all are, underneath our clothes."

Saronna felt her face flame red, half in anger, half in humiliation. "You needn't mock me because I was brought up to be modest."

It was Duncan's turn to look shamed. "I'm sorry, Saronna. I shouldn't have said that."

She caught her breath as she realized that she had criticized him, and he had apologized. Her father would have struck her if he had heard her talk back to any man, let alone one who stood in the position Duncan did. She turned away to compose herself.

"What's wrong now?" Duncan asked.

She shook her head wordlessly.

"Did I do something wrong?" he said insistently.

"You apologized to me," Saronna said, over her shoulder. She made herself turn back to face him. "No man ever did that before, especially not when I spoke to him as I did to you."

Duncan looked as confused by her explanation as she had been by his machines. "Spoke to me how? You didn't say anything wrong. I was the one who was rude."

Clearly, rules of behavior were different here. "A woman isn't supposed to talk back to a man, especially not to her protector."

Duncan made an explosive sound of disgust. "If you ask me, the sooner you read that book, the better."

Saronna looked down at the book reader in her hands. It felt as if she was holding the key to a secret. "Maybe I will read it."

"Good." Duncan glanced at the time display on the wall. "Breakfast should be ready by now. Let's go see if Dad and Naomi are there yet."

Apparently, the family ate in the northeast courtyard when the weather allowed it, as Duncan led the way there.

They found Vladimir Trushenko sitting at a table loaded with dishes of food. He was pouring a cup of coffee when they walked in, and he seemed to Saronna to be inordinately pleased to see them arrive together.

"Good morning, Saronna," he said. "Good morning, Duncan. Did you sleep well?"

"Like a log." Duncan took the chair across from his father. "Sit down, Saronna," he said, waving a hand at the chair next to his.

Saronna sat down a little reluctantly. Until the day before, she had never sat down to eat with men at the table. In her father's house, as in every house in Samaria, women didn't sit down until after the men of the family had eaten and left the room.

Naomi walked out from a door that opened directly onto the courtyard.

"Good morning everyone," she said, bending down to kiss Vladimir on the cheek.

"Good morning, beloved," Vladimir said, patting her hand. "You're looking well."

Naomi beamed and sat down next to him, across from Saronna.

They made conversation on a variety of subjects while they ate. After a while, Vladimir and Duncan's discussions drifted into what products were selling well in specific places. Saronna could determine that the places mentioned were worlds rather than cities, but she had no idea what the goods they described were.

"Vlad!" Naomi said, "can't we please eat breakfast without talking business?"

Having observed Vladimir's doting fondness, and Duncan's extraordinary behavior, Saronna wasn't completely taken aback to hear Vladimir apologize to his woman for his inattention.

"So," Vladimir went on. "What do you have planned for the day, Naomi?"

"I thought I'd show Saronna through the kitchens," Naomi said. "And then perhaps we could do some shopping. There may be things she'd like to buy."

"Fine, fine," Vladimir said. "Where were you planning to go?"

"I thought we'd try the Street of the Drapers," Naomi said. Saronna thought she could detect a touch of apprehension in Naomi's voice, as if she were afraid her protector wouldn't approve of her choice.

Apparently, she was right, because the older man frowned and gave her a displeased look. "That's in the native quarter."

"But, Vladimir," Naomi said, her voice coaxing, "they have the most beautiful fabrics there. You know they do. And it's much cheaper than if I went to one of the off-world shops."

"I don't care if it's cheaper," Vladimir said. "When did I ever criticize you for spending too much? It's dangerous, Naomi. You know it is!"

Naomi lifted her chin. "We'll have a driver with us. We both know how to behave. We'll be fine, Vlad."

Vladimir wavered. "All right," he said finally, "but I'll make sure Frank drives you. He knows the city, and he's up on the local customs. And unlike either of the Kruegerians, he'd do his best to get you out of trouble if you slipped up."

Naomi gave him a sunny smile and agreed to his choice of an escort without protest. She even allowed him to lapse into shop talk with his son without a rebuke from her. Instead, she turned to Saronna, gave her a knowing smile, and began to talk about textiles and shopping in the various parts of the city.

Saronna listened, fascinated to observe the way that the older woman went back and forth between using 'we' to refer to Vladimir's house and company, and 'they' for off-worlders in general.

The kitchen tour would have amazed Saronna if she had seen those rooms first, but having seen the rest of the house, she barely blinked at the sight of pantries that could store fresh fruits and vegetables for months without them spoiling, and machines that could cook food in seconds.

Saronna noted that the three domestic staff were all dressed alike in blue shirts and trousers, with large white aprons covering their clothes. The two women smiled at her, but the man averted his eyes from her as if the sight of her could pollute his gaze. Saronna realized he must be Kruegerian.

After the tour, Saronna followed Naomi to the back door, where a ground car awaited them. The driver, a young man named Frank Chiang, looked rather like Duncan at first. He was older, about thirty, tall and dark-haired, but his eyes were blue instead of brown. He had a twinkle in them now, as he spoke to them both in a polite but bantering tone.

"Ready to go, ladies?" he asked, holding the car door open. His accent confirmed that he was an off-worlder.

Naomi answered in the affirmative, and they entered the back of the car. Naomi put the screen down, so that they could converse directly.

"Could you take a scenic route, please, Frank?" she asked. "Saronna hasn't seen much of the city."

"Sure thing, Naomi," Frank said.

He drove easily through the crowded streets. Only vehicles traveled on the major thoroughfares, but pedestrians and vehicles shared the less traveled byways equally, and not all of the pedestrians were human. The tiny Shuratanians fascinated Saronna, especially once she saw that they had small stubby tails. Milorans were larger; still humanoid, they were so bulky they made Saronna think of crude sculptures assembled from stones.

Naomi complained because Frank insisted on keeping the side windows partly opaqued. "It makes it too dim in here. And we can't see out as well."

"Sorry, ma'am," he said, still cheerful. "But Vladimir was quite firm."

Naomi quit grumbling and instead pointed out all the sights as they passed. After several minutes, they went through the Strangers' Gate, and Saronna knew they were in the main part of the city, what Vladimir called the native quarter. There were no aliens now, only humans, most of them in Kruegerian clothes. Frank guided their vehicle smoothly through the streets, finally stopping in a sheltered spot near a street of shops. He didn't hold the door for them this time. Instead he waited for them to put on their veils and then walked in front of them as soon as they exited the ground car. He walked just as Saronna's father always had, without looking back.

Following a muttered instruction from Naomi, the driver entered a shop that was little more than a market stall, with bolts of cloth stacked high against the walls, and a few choice specimens draped across a rack at the front, to attract the eyes of passersby. The shopkeeper came forward eagerly from the back of the stall and bowed.

"And what can I do for you today, good sire?" he asked, giving Frank a designation to which he wasn't entitled, as shopkeepers were prone to do.

Frank didn't repudiate it. He merely waved a hand at Naomi and Saronna. "My women need some things."

Having been given leave to speak to them, the shopkeeper turned and asked politely, as one speaking to the very young, what they wanted.

Saronna let Naomi do all the talking. She was a little disappointed that their quest had led to a place that was so like home that it could have been on any street in Samaria. Her disappointment vanished when the shopkeeper brought out, for their inspection, bolts of cloth that took her breath away.

There were brocades woven in intricate patterns, shot with gold and silver threads, iridescent satins that took on different hues depending on how the light struck them, silks of every imaginable color, and fabrics so sheer and light they seemed mere shadows.

Naomi selected two bolts of satin, and one of brocade. Happy with her selections, she didn't seem to mind that they had to carry their purchases themselves, since after Frank Chiang paid for them, he made no move to pick them up.

Saronna hadn't expected that he would. She shouldered her burden without complaint as they made their way up the street to where they had left the car.

"Where to, now?" Frank asked, as they resumed their seats.

"Three streets over, please," Naomi said. "And then take us about half a kilometer south."

"Right," Frank said, sliding the car into traffic.

When they stopped again, the shops were smaller and dingier. Saronna glanced at the signs over the doors, and knew immediately that this was a street of herbalists. She said nothing however, as they left the car. Naomi waited until they were almost in front of a shop to speak to Frank.

"Could you wait here, please?" she said, her eyes meeting his.

Their driver looked troubled at this request, but he nodded and took up a post near the door. Saronna followed the older woman into the dim but fragrant interior of the herbalist's shop.

The painfully familiar scent of herbs struck Saronna as soon as she stepped inside. Sharp scents of manglewort, bitter leaf, and myrrh root, spicy odors of comfrey and yew seed, and the sweet aroma of dried sugar blossom petals, all mingled together like colors in a dye pot. Saronna had often accompanied her sisters to such a shop in Samaria, whenever one of her brothers could find time to escort them. Paul would wait outside, just as Frank was now doing, but Gideon had always come in with them as if he didn't trust them not to make foolish purchases.

The old man behind the counter took one look at them and turned without a word. He disappeared into the back of the shop, and a few moments later, an elderly woman came out.

"Yes, my dears?" she said pleasantly. "What did you need today?"

Naomi stepped up to the counter and ducked her head. Without ever quite meeting the old woman's eyes, she explained that she wanted something to ensure that her protector would continue to desire her.

The old woman clucked sympathetically. "Of course, of course. I have just the thing." She pulled out one of many drawers from the wall behind her and then paused. "All is well at the moment? His passion runs hot?"

Naomi nodded.

The old woman selected a bottle of blue powder. She filled a small glass vial, put in the stopper, and handed the vial to Naomi.

"Now," she said, "listen carefully. If his desire for you wanes, you must put half of this powder into a glass of water, or wine if you can get it, and drink it down. After half an hour, make some excuse to be near him, and he won't be able to resist you. If the trouble persists, you may use the remaining powder, but be certain to wait until the same time the next day before you take it. Do you understand?"

Naomi nodded and repeated back the instructions word for word. Saronna glanced at her and realized that Vladimir's woman probably didn't know how to read. Saronna's own sisters had that same ability to repeat any instructions they heard flawlessly, after only one hearing. They had developed it because there was no way they could make a note of instructions; they had to remember them or lose the information. They had often teased Saronna because she seemed to them to have a poor memory.

The old herbalist was counting Naomi's payment when the door of the shop opened and a man came in. The old woman scuttled to the back, clucking in agitation, and Saronna and Naomi also beat a hasty retreat before the frowning man could speak to them. They heard the male proprietor greet his new customer as the door closed behind them.

Frank joined them outside the shop. "Everything okay?" he murmured quietly.

Naomi ducked her head in a quick nod, and Frank started back to the car.

Saronna watched her new friend covertly. It had been a surprise to her to hear that Naomi wasn't certain of Vladimir's affections. It seemed to Saronna that the head of Cameron Trushenko was besotted with his woman, but perhaps Naomi had reason to fear that it was otherwise?

Her thoughts were so thoroughly on Naomi's purchase that she didn't notice when a man passing the other way came too close. Saronna's shoulder made contact with his, and they collided abruptly.

The man turned with words of regret on his lips that died when he saw her. Shorter than Saronna and a good deal older, he wore the full beard of a patriarch, but he wasn't carrying a staff.

Saronna lowered her eyes and murmured a quiet apology.

"Stupid woman," the man said sharply. "You should be at home."

Frank stopped and turned back toward Saronna.

The stranger took one look at Frank's clothes and scowled. "Pho! What are you doing in this quarter, outsider? And how do you come to have two of our women with you?"

Stepping closer, Frank bowed gracefully. "They're not my women, but my sire's. We came to do some shopping for him. I ask pardon if they've bothered you with their clumsiness."

The stranger seemed mollified, so Saronna lifted her eyes, the only part of her face that was visible, to look straight at him. The man spat out an oath and slapped her hard across the face. Saronna's cheek stung from the force of it.

Frank pulled her away from the man. "I'm sorry, sire," he said, his tone deferential, "but I'm afraid I must insist that you don't touch either of them again. My sire allows no one else to strike his women."

The stranger didn't seem overly indignant. This was, after all, a typical reaction where women were concerned. "Your sire should teach her to show respect better than that. He should beat her regularly."

Frank smiled with easy affability, but no warmth in his eyes. "I'm sure he does. She's young, but she'll learn in time."

The man muttered another comment, and stalked off with no more than an angry shrug of his shoulders.

Frank stood watching him, a stiff smile still on his face. "Goddamned son of a bitch," he said under his breath.

He hustled them back to the car, then locked the doors and opaqued the windows thoroughly after they were all inside.

"Sheesh, what a planet," he said, over his shoulder. "Are you okay, Saronna?"

"Yes." In some ways, she was less upset than he was. She was, after all, more used to patriarchs.

Frank shook his head with disgust. "I hope whatever you bought was worth an encounter with the Stone Age."

Naomi gave Saronna a warning look. "Thank you for your help, Frank."

Saronna added her thanks, but Frank brushed them aside.

"Don't mention it. I'd really liked to have punched his lights out, but I can't do that unless I can catch the bastard in the off-world quarter."

He drove them straight home and let them out in the enclosed driveway. A young woman was waiting for them as the car pulled up. Saronna recognized her as Letitia Dubai, the woman who had admitted her to Vladimir Trushenko's house when she first came to it.

"Oh, good, you're back," Letitia said, with no visible enthusiasm. "Vladimir was getting anxious."

Saronna noted that Naomi frowned at this use of her protector's first name by one of his female staff. Her irritation surprised Saronna. It seemed to her that all the employees of Cameron Trushenko were very informal. The day before, she had noticed that his staff called Vladimir sir, rather than sire, when they spoke to him. But she had also noticed that all of them referred to him as Vladimir when he wasn't there.

Letitia left them to inform Vladimir of their return, and Naomi took Saronna by the arm.

"Come with me, please, Saronna," she said, a note of entreaty in her voice.

Saronna followed her, curious to see what the other woman had to say. Naomi led the way to her own apartment, and Saronna was struck again with how luxurious it was. Her sitting room was larger than Saronna's entire suite, and her bathroom had a small pool instead of just an oversized tub. A connecting door from the sitting room led to Vladimir's room. Saronna knew already that Vladimir was often in Naomi's rooms, although she seldom went into his.

"You won't tell Vladimir, will you?" Naomi said as soon as the door shut behind them.

"No," Saronna said. "I won't tell him you bought a love potion. Why do you need it? He seems quite fond of you."

"He is now, but what if it doesn't last? I'll be forty-three on my next birthday. He could decide to get someone else anytime."

"I don't see why he would do that," Saronna said practically. "You're very beautiful, and he loves you."

Naomi flushed as she put away her veil. "I think he does. He paid a lot of money for me—twenty thousand credits."

Saronna opened her eyes wide. It was an unheard of price for a woman. "Your former husband must have bargained very well."

Naomi shrugged. "Vladimir refused to bargain. Twenty thousand was his first and last offer. It was during a poker game that Ephraim sold me. He was angry at me, because he had married me even though I had a very small dowry, and then I never had any children. He finally bought another woman, and once she had sons, I knew that he would put me aside so he could marry her."

Saronna was curious. "How did your former husband know Vladimir?"

Naomi sat down on the sofa. "Ephraim liked to play poker. One night he invited some business associates to the house to play with him."

Saronna sat down on one of the well-padded chairs. "But surely you weren't present if they were only business associates?"

Naomi's face got a faraway look, almost reflective. "Ephraim got very drunk, and when he began to lose, he sent for me. He made me display myself in just my shift for all the men there, and then he offered me as his stake. No one said anything for a moment, and then Vladimir offered twenty thousand credits for me—outright, not as a bet. Ephraim wanted to bargain, but no one else offered a better price. Finally, Vladimir said, 'take it or leave it,' so Ephraim took his money right there."

Saronna watched the older woman's face as she described her humiliation. In spite of the suddenness of the transaction, she seemed proud of having fetched such a large price. "What happened then?"

Naomi shrugged. "They kept playing. Vladimir had me go pack some clothes while he played. He won almost three thousand credits from Ephraim, and then he left and took me home with him."

"You must have been very frightened."

"I was," Naomi said simply. "But Vladimir didn't touch me—not for over a month. I was afraid he didn't really want me, so finally I went to him one night."

Saronna blinked in surprise. Ordinarily a Kruegerian woman would never go to her protector. If he wanted her, he went to her room or sent for her to come to his. It would be a sin for a Believer to initiate sex, and a non-Believer would think it wasn't her place to offer herself. Naomi must have been very afraid.

Naomi lifted her chin as if to suggest she wasn't ashamed of what she had done. "He was very happy to see me, and he was very gentle with me, so I wasn't afraid anymore."

"But you seem afraid now?"

"I'm not really afraid," Naomi said, "but I like to be prepared. Vladimir doesn't like it when I go alone to the native quarter. It seemed best to buy the anodyne now, so I'd have it if I ever needed it."

"I won't tell him about it," Saronna said.

Later, as she hung up her veil, it occurred to Saronna that Vladimir was right to be concerned. Putting on a veil was easy, but it would be difficult to put on the air of humility that was required of women on most of Krueger's World. She would have to be careful if she were ever allowed to visit her home.

IT seemed to Saronna that Duncan and his father were both abstracted when they sat down to supper that night. From their conversation, she concluded that Vladimir had some large deals pending. He and Duncan talked over many of the logistical problems of shipping goods long distances, and assessed the potential problems that could cause delays and eat up their profits. Both of them looked tired.

"I hope I can stay awake at your party next week, Dad," Duncan said after the supper table had been cleared. He stretched his jaw as he spoke, only partly holding back a yawn.

Vladimir grunted. "I hope so, too. The party is in your honor, you know."

Duncan grinned at him. "Using my return as a chance to glad-hand a few prospects, huh, Dad?"

"Okay, so I'm taking advantage of the situation."
Vladimir sighed with fatigue. "But it's good to have you
home all the same."

Naomi tisked her tongue at Vladimir. "You come to
my rooms and soak in a hot tub for a while. You relax a
little, and then I'll rub your back so you can go to
sleep."

Vladimir allowed himself to be led away, his son
watching him with another grin.

Saronna studied Duncan speculatively, wondering if
he would ever expect such an offer from her. He turned
and met her gaze with a suddenness that made her
start.

"No," he said at once, "I don't want to soak in a hot
tub and have you rub my back, thank you."

She was relieved, but she didn't say so. "Very well
then, I won't suggest it."

"Good," Duncan said, sitting up a little straighter.
"Tell me about your day instead. Did you get a chance
to start that book?"

She nodded. She had started reading when she and
Naomi had returned to the house, and she was a
quarter of the way through it. "If you took that book to
Samaria, they wouldn't let you get by with stoning.
They'd tie you to two skimmers and pull you apart
slowly."

Duncan chuckled. "I'll make a point to stay away
from Samaria. It sounds like a hell of a place, anyway."

"I suppose it is, in a way," Saronna said, surprised to find herself agreeing with him. "Is the book true?"

Duncan studied her face before he answered. "Yes, it's true. Alfred Krueger was a lunatic. He had a charismatic ability to convince people he was right, but he was stone cold crazy. He had a large following back on Terra—over twenty thousand people—and he persuaded them all to not only give him their money, but to give him their labor, and in many cases their children. They did it gladly. They believed his line of hogwash about ancient scriptures laying down the proper pattern of life—the father as the master of all his family, women as chattels of men, and himself as the Patriarch over all. They thought he was God come among them, and he could do no wrong. They thought they were earning a place in heaven by serving him, when really they had a place in hell."

Listening to this blistering denunciation of the Patriarch made Saronna's breath catch in her throat. How brave Duncan was to speak so boldly! Even Believers were more circumspect. "How did the Patriarch come here? I haven't come to that part yet, and I want to know."

Duncan pondered. "I suppose I can tell you the bare facts. You'll get the details when you read that part of the book. One of the reasons Krueger was able to sway so many people is that Terra was a pretty crummy

place to live back then. It was very overcrowded,
polluted—worn out, in a way.

"Things were so bad the Terrans had built sleeper
ships. We didn't have spatial fold ships back then, and
interstellar travel took centuries. People who were
desperate to escape from Terra traveled in suspended
animation—a deathless, ageless, frozen sleep. Krueger
organized his own sleeper mission, made his dire
predictions for the rest of Terra, loaded up his people,
and took off."

He stopped and glanced at Saronna, but she said
nothing. Was he wondering if she understood? She
didn't completely, but it sounded very dangerous.
Would she have had the courage to let herself be put
into frozen sleep? She didn't know. But the idea of
leaving a world to escape a miserable life sounded
reasonable to her.

"Anyway," Duncan went on, "they found this world,
built a colony, and things got worse. Women weren't
merely subservient, they were owned. Wives who didn't
fulfill their purpose by having sons could be set aside or
even sold. Scientific knowledge was anathema because
it taught people to distrust Krueger's Book, so
education took a nose dive.

"When ThreeCon found this place, it was a feudal
nightmare. Krueger's World wasn't interested in
changing, so finally ThreeCon left them on their own.

They maintain a consulate for ThreeCon citizens, but that's all."

He had described her world in such negative terms, Saronna wondered why any off-worlders would come to it. "How did New Jerusalem come to have an off-world quarter?"

He looked pleased at her question, as if her curiosity were a good thing. "Well, Krueger's World is an ideal location for trading, so when some Kruegerians expressed a willingness to trade for off-world goods, merchants and other off-worlders signed treaties with the largest cities, to create areas where the rules were relaxed, so they could live as they liked, and do business. They formed their own councils and passed their own laws for the off-world quarters. Each one became a city within a city. And that's the way it is now."

Saronna didn't really understand all of it, especially ThreeCon's role, but she was too curious about something else to ask for an explanation. "What are the other worlds like?"

"What?" Duncan suppressed another yawn. "You mean Terra?"

"No, the other places where the sleeper ships went. What are they like?"

"Well," Duncan considered, "they aren't all alike. Some of them have reasonable levels of technology and some of them are pretty primitive."

"But Krueger's World is worse than most sleeper worlds?"

"I certainly think so," Duncan said flippantly. "But I'm willing to admit that's just my opinion. There's one thing about this planet that's very interesting, though."

"What's that?" Saronna asked.

"Telekinetics," Duncan said. "Comparatively speaking, the place is lousy with them."

Yet another new word. How would she keep them all straight? "What are telekinetics?"

"I guess you could say they're people with an extra ability," Duncan said. "All sleeper worlds have people with psy talent. No one knows whether it was the cryogenic suspension or the amount of time spent in space, but sleeper worlds are the only place you routinely find Terrans—humans—with psy talent. On most worlds, empathy is the most common trait, followed by telepathy, and then precognition. Telekinetics usually run a distant fourth."

"I don't understand you," Saronna said, her frustration rising. If he answered every question with a string of new words, she would never be able to stop asking questions.

"I'm sorry." Duncan sounded tired but truly contrite. "Empathy means being able to perceive feelings.

Just as you and I can perceive the color of someone's hair and skin, an empath can perceive his feelings. Telepathy is a little more dramatic. With varying degrees of success, a telepath can actually tell what someone else is thinking. People with precognition can predict the future—usually only the immediate future. They're not always right, either.

"Telekinesis is the ability to affect matter without touching it. A telekinetic can move objects, provided they're not too heavy or too far away, without ever touching them."

Saronna looked at him with startled eyes. Did he suspect her secret? It didn't seem likely. He hadn't accused her of anything. "And there are people like that on Krueger's World?"

Duncan nodded. "Your people don't like to talk about it, but ThreeCon did some research. They found that about three percent of the population carries at least one gene for telekinetic ability, and some of them have two."

Saronna wasn't sure what he meant by genes, but it was clear that his people had a way to know who bore the mark of Mother Eve. "Then why does no one mention it?" She strove for calm, for the appearance of normality. She had kept her gift hidden for so long that it was terrifying to hear that off-worlders knew so much about it.

Duncan yawned again. "Oh, I don't know. It may be that people here simply refuse to discuss it. They're a pretty superstitious lot, on the whole. Or it may be that they don't know they have these gifts. After all, it's not something people would think to try to do. You could have the makings of a world class wall hockey star, but if you never strapped on a pair of anti-grav skates, you'd never know you had that talent."

Saronna had no idea what his last comment meant. "You're tired," she said suddenly. Best to change the subject before she gave herself away. "You should go to bed."

Duncan stood up. "You may be right." He glanced around at the gathering gloom. It was dusk, and the lights had come on in the courtyard, but there were still dark corners here and there that gave the place a sense of twilight. He looked at Saronna and for just a second, she thought she saw something in his eyes—a warmth that wasn't merely friendship or good feelings. And then it was gone, and he was the same as he had been before.

"I'd better say good night now," he said. "I hope you're feeling a little more at home here?"

His inflection had made it a question, so Saronna answered. "I am."

"Good." Duncan hesitated, and then turned to go without making any move in her direction.

"Good night," Saronna said.

He smiled at her over his shoulder, but didn't turn or speak again. She watched him melt into the shadows, and then looked around her. She was alone, finally, which was good because she had so much to think about.

She had come a long way in a very short time. She had left her father's house an ignorant hill woman, a burden to her family. Now she was a resident in a mansion in the city of New Jerusalem, a pampered toy for an off-world merchant's son—except her protector seemed unwilling to demand his rights with her, something for which she was grateful.

But the more time she spent with Duncan, the less she understood him. Were all off-world men like him? His father didn't seem as strange. It was true that Vladimir allowed Naomi a lot of freedom, but he still controlled her movements, to some extent, and she worried about pleasing him. Saronna could understand that. But Duncan seemed to have no interest in directing Saronna's life. The day before, when she had been surprised into blurting out the suggestion that he was interested in men rather than women, he had not gotten angry, as most men would have. He had laughed as if it would have been of no consequence if he had been that way. Were all off-worlders so tolerant of the predilection that Kruegerians considered an abomination? If she ever saw Paul again, she would have to mention it to him. If his secret were ever discovered, he might find sanctuary in the off-world quarter.

Just as she had. Her secret was even more dangerous than his. Did it not say in the Patriarch's own Book that a witch should never be allowed to live? Saronna shivered. In one way, at least, she felt safer here than she had in her father's house. Duncan had described telekinesis without ever using the word witchcraft.

She glanced around and saw no sign that anyone was near. Vladimir and Naomi were most likely already in bed. Asleep or not, they weren't troubling themselves with her. The regular employees had gone home by now, and it was too early for the security staff to make their rounds. Saronna stretched out her hand toward the last fuzzy apple on the plate. She fixed her mind upon the fruit, and in a moment it rolled across the table to her hand.

Saronna munched it contentedly as she walked to her rooms. It seemed Eve's Mark had another name. All she had to worry about now was keeping it a secret.

CHAPTER FOUR

Saronna stood on the front steps of the house. She hadn't gone out by herself since before her tenth birthday, and it seemed very strange to walk through the door with no man walking in front of her. She waited a moment, to survey the street. She had chosen to wear off-world clothes today, in an effort to blend in, but she felt self-conscious in pale green trousers and a striped tunic.

There weren't many pedestrians to notice her, but a man and a woman turned from the walkway and headed right for the arched doorway where she stood.

Saronna shrank back against the door, tempted to flee inside. The door would open for her. Naomi had pressed Saronna's palm onto a terminal screen and told Saronna she was now part of the household and could open any door she liked.

Before Saronna could decide, the man and woman were only a meter away.

"Hello," the woman said. "My name is Saikirana Whisset, and this is Randal Kumar. We're friends of Duncan's. Did he make it back okay?"

Saronna nodded. The woman was shorter than she was by a good bit, with thick reddish-brown hair that she wore cropped short on the sides, slightly longer in the back. Her features were pleasant without being in any way remarkable, and it was more the steady, measuring gaze of her deep brown eyes that drew attention, rather than their shape or color. She had a wiry build and gave the impression of energy contained.

The man beside her was another story. He was about Saronna's height, but seemed taller because he was so slender. He had high cheekbones, a straight nose, and a warm, generous smile. His eyes, tawny gold circles set deep under black, finely drawn brows, looked warmly at Saronna from under one drooping lock of glossy black hair, as he held out a hand. "Nice to meet you."

Saronna tried to hide her reluctance as she shook his hand.

If the man noticed, he gave no sign. Instead he seemed to expect something.

It occurred to Saronna that she should say her own name. "I'm Saronna," she blurted out. "I'm going now. Goodbye."

She darted past them and hurried onto the walkway. A quick glance over her shoulder showed that they were waiting in front of the door.

She turned her attention to where she was going. Naomi had insisted she take a pocket com with her. Unlike the device in Saronna's room, this com was smaller than her fist. She pulled it out now, flipped it open, and studied the menu. Most of the choices were meaningless to her, but she remembered Duncan talking to the library catalog.

"Com, where am I?" she said.

A view of New Jerusalem popped onto the screen with a red dot blinking in the middle. "You are here," a thin voice said. "For specific directions, please state the location you wish to reach."

Saronna stared at the lines that represented the streets. "Which way should I walk to reach the nearest shops?"

A green arrow blinked on the screen. "Turn east."

It took Saronna a moment to decide the arrow was indeed pointing east. Naomi would have known which way to go. She had offered to come, but Saronna had rejected the offer firmly with the excuse that she needed to learn to manage on her own. She would have been glad of the company, but then Naomi would have wondered why she needed candles.

A man walking on the opposite side of the street gave Saronna a momentary glance and then looked away. Saronna suffered a shock. He could see her face! She hadn't realized how much it would startle her to know that strangers could see what she looked like.

She lifted her chin and started walking, conscious of how different it felt to walk along in trousers, unencumbered by voluminous skirts. She lengthened her stride. It felt wonderful. It felt liberating. For the first time in her life, she could go where she wanted.

She walked for a good ways without seeing anything that resembled a shop. Only houses lined the streets. There were street vendors at some of the corners, but they didn't sell anything but food and drink, and she was neither hungry nor thirsty. The other pedestrians all seemed in more of a hurry than she was. Most of them strode swiftly along without a glance at their surroundings. Certainly they paid no attention to Saronna in her off-world clothes.

Finally, Saronna came to an intersection where a shop occupied each corner. The nearest one looked the most promising. It offered variety, while the other three seemed to have food, clothing, and furniture as their wares.

Saronna stepped across the threshold of the shop and looked around. It seemed ordinary at first glance, but then she realized only the shell of the store was familiar. The shopkeeper had kept the Kruegerian interior more or less intact but stocked his shelves with a multitude of wonders. Gleaming machines, elaborate decorative figurines, house wares, children's toys, and some things that were probably tools all vied for Saronna's attention. She let out a breath as she studied a nearby display and tried to determine if the whirling, lighted objects had a use beyond decoration.

"Can I help you, citizen?"

Saronna jumped, unnerved at being addressed by a young man. He was a little younger than she was, but not by much.

"Yes, thank you. Do you sell candles?"

"Candles?" He looked surprised, but then he smiled warmly. "I guess nothing sets the mood like candle-light, does it? Sure, I think we have some. Wait a second, please."

He disappeared behind a row of shelves and then returned a few moments later carrying a small flat box. "Sorry, I only have them by the dozen."

"That will be fine," Saronna said with relief.

Naomi had assured her that every shop in the off-world quarter would have a terminal, and that Saronna could pay for whatever she wanted just by pressing her right thumb on the screen. Saronna hadn't quite believed it could be so simple until the shopkeeper handed her a small pad, and she pressed her thumb to it. Instantly Duncan's name appeared along with the cost of the candles. Saronna wondered if there was any limit to how much she could spend.

Once she was out in the street, Saronna felt almost uplifted. She had bought something. Admittedly, she had used Duncan's money—or perhaps Vladimir's—but she had managed to find the store by herself and pay for what she wanted. For a woman from Samaria, this was no small accomplishment.

Abruptly, Saronna realized that Naomi would doubtless ask about her shopping excursion. She studied the shop across the street. In addition to clothes, the shop windows held jewelry and scarves. If she could find a reasonably-priced bracelet she would buy it. She had never owned any jewelry, and it was a purchase Naomi wouldn't question.

Saronna stepped off the curb. She would buy a bracelet.

DUNCAN leaned back in his chair and took a moment to scrutinize his friends. Randy didn't look any older, but Sai had a worry line on her forehead that hadn't been there when he had seen her last. Having gotten thorough almost an hour of reminiscing and catching up on mutual acquaintances, he had yet to find out why they were on Krueger's World.

"So," Sai said, "how's what's-her-name?"

Duncan smiled to himself. Sai might look a little older, but she hadn't changed a bit. "Who, Emily? I don't really know. I haven't seen her in over a year."

"Good," Sai said. "She wasn't right for you, anyway, kid. She was too wimpy. You need someone to stand up to you."

Duncan grinned at her. Ever since their brief affair had ended in their sophomore year, Sai had felt qualified to explain to him what he needed in a woman. "She wasn't wimpy, she was devious—too devious to ever be confrontational."

Randy sat up straighter. "Ah! I told you so, Sai. She was out to hook Duncan, and once he figured that out, he cut the line."

Duncan looked at Randy with new respect. It was a remarkably succinct description of the reason for his breakup with Emily Pulaski. "Point to you, Randy. You have no idea how uncomfortable it was working with her, once she realized I was dead serious about it being over between us."

Sai made a tisking noise with her tongue. "We need to find you someone who doesn't see you as a shortcut up the corporate ladder."

Duncan let out an exaggerated groan. "You're not going to start nominating candidates are you, Sai? I get enough of that from my folks—more than enough."

Randy got up from his chair to take another stuffed cracker from the platter of food Duncan had ordered as soon as his friends had walked through the door. They had both eaten a fair amount, even though it was nowhere near dinner time, which made Duncan wonder if they were hard up.

"Has Vonda been pushing babes in your direction?" Randy asked. "I'll be happy to take the overflow if it's too much for you."

Duncan laughed as Randy sat down and put his feet up on the stool in front of his chair. Same old Randy. It was true he was good looking, but that didn't explain his remarkable success with women. "Mom's not the problem at the moment. It's Dad who's gone crazy."

"Why is it crazy?" Sai asked, moving to the edge of her seat. Apparently, sitting quietly still took effort for her. "Most parents try to fix their unmarried kids up with someone sooner or later—especially when he's an only child, like you."

"Yeah, but Dad took fixing up to a new height. He bought a woman for me."

Randy put his feet down abruptly and sat up straight. "What?"

"He bought a woman for me," Duncan said. "From her father."

"Duncan Cameron Trushenko!" Sai's face contorted into a scowl. She looked just as outraged as she had in their midnight political debates, arguing for the rights of Lycandrian refugees. "Have you gone nuts? How could you let him do anything like that? Just because this planet has sunk back into the Paleolithic is no reason for you to revert into some kind of testosterone-induced Cro-Magnon stage!"

"It wasn't my idea," Duncan said. "And I was too late to stop him. Once she was here, I couldn't send her back. Her family might kill her if I did."

The two of them stared at him in consternation.

"Christmas crackers! What a planet!" Sai said. "If Alfred Krueger hadn't been dead for centuries, I'd kill him myself. I hope there is a hell so he can rot in it!"

"Watch out where you say that, Sai." Duncan cast an anxious look around the room from sheer paranoia. "Even in this quarter, there are Kruegerians."

"I know," Sai said. "I had the standard course for off-world women. Don't set foot out of the off-world quarter, or you're dead meat. Don't antagonize any native, even in the off-world quarter, or you could find you've started a blood feud."

"I got that one, too," Randy chimed in. "They do seem excessively touchy here."

"Why are you two here, anyway?" Duncan said, finally getting to the point he wanted to reach. "What's up with Kumar and Whisset?"

They stared at each other for a second, then looked away. Sai grimaced, and Randy let out a profound and weary sigh.

"Not bloody much," Randy said. "We're hoping to do better here."

Duncan looked from one face to the other. Neither looked optimistic. "How bad is it?"

Randy leaned back in his chair and folded his arms. "You tell him, Sai."

She shrugged. "Okay, so we're broke. We thought we had discovered a sure thing, so we sank almost our entire working capital into it. And then it turned out it wasn't actually sure at all. We were lucky to salvage passage here."

Duncan decided it was time to ask the question that troubled him most. "Why Krueger's World? I should think it's the last place you would want to come, Sai?"

"It is," Sai said. "But it's also a wide open port. All we've got left are odds and ends from old deals. We need to sell them for enough profit to get a new stake. This place is crawling with people looking to deal— buying and selling, big deals and small. You don't have to be big time like Cameron Trushenko to find opportunity here."

Duncan nodded. In their situation, it made sense. Whatever the ideology of the planet itself, the cities of Krueger's World provided plenty of mercantile opportunities and little in the way of obstacles. "Can I help? Maybe a loan to tide you over?"

Sai and Randy exchanged glances.

"That's five credits you owe me," Sai said, smiling smugly.

Randy sighed again, and dug into his pockets. "Put it on my tab," he said, coming up empty-handed. "I don't think I've got five credits."

Duncan laughed, wondering who was ahead in their constant game of predicting the future. "What was the bet?"

"Sai said you'd offer on the spot," Randy said. "I thought you'd wait tactfully and mention it to me when she wasn't around."

Duncan tisked with mock despair. "What archaic ideas you have, Ran! Why should I care whether Sai knew about it? I want to help you both."

Sai smiled but shook her head. "No thanks, kid. It's not that bad."

"Oh, no?" Duncan said.

"No," Randy repeated. "We'll make it on our own."

"Oooh," Duncan said. "Was that a slap at those of us who inherit a place in the family business?"

A reddish tinge suffused Randy's golden skin. "Of course not, Dunc. You know I didn't mean it that way."

"Then why won't you let me help you?" Duncan asked. "Is there something wrong with my money?"

"No," Sai said, a note of firmness in her voice "It's just not our money, that's all. We can't take money from a friend—not unless we're desperate, and we're not. Believe me, if we get stuck here and can't get home, we'll accept the loan of two second class tickets soon enough."

"All right," Duncan said, getting to his feet. "If you won't take money, at least accept my hospitality. This house is huge. You two could hide out here for as long as you need a place to stay. At least you'll save on hotel rooms."

"Hotel rooms?" Randy said. "You don't imagine we're wasting our credits on hotel rooms, do you? We're staying at the warehouse where we have our stuff. We slipped the clerk a couple extra credits and he pretends not to notice how much we're using the washroom."

"A warehouse?" Duncan said in alarm. "How can you let Sai sleep in a warehouse?"

"Now who's got archaic ideas?" Sai said tartly. "Randy doesn't *let* me do anything."

"But you don't know this place," Duncan said. "A woman can't take any chances. If there are Kruegerian laborers at your warehouse, and they find you there alone, I hate to tell you what they might think."

"You don't have to tell me," Sai said, unperturbed. "A couple of them did exactly that. Fortunately, I've kept up with my classes since I got my black belt, and I took care of them with no trouble."

"That does it," Duncan said. "You two are staying here."

They protested, but Duncan wouldn't be talked out of it.

"What about your father?" Randy said. "What's he going to say—" he stopped and stared at the window into the main courtyard. "*Stukash haī*!" he said, using a Shuratanian oath that invoked the goddess of beauty. "Who's the babe, Dunc?"

Duncan followed his glance and saw that Randy was staring into the courtyard at Naomi, who was tending the plants in the flower beds. She wore a long moss green gown that set off her hair and showed off her figure at the same time. "That's Naomi, the light of Dad's life. If you want to ever set foot through the front door again, I suggest you think of her as an aunt."

"No way!" Randy said. "Neither of *my* aunts looks anything like that."

"Maybe not," Duncan said, "but Dad will go red in the face and probably have a heart attack if you make a play for her, so I'd appreciate it if you'd just lay off."

Randy's sigh lingered, then trailed off. "Oh, well, if you put it like that."

Saronna came into the courtyard and said something to Naomi. She was wearing trousers today, instead of Kruegerian clothes, and she looked remarkably modern next to Naomi.

"And that," Duncan said, "is Saronna."

The two of them looked confused, and then Sai stepped up to the window beside him. "You mean that's your concubine?"

The word made him flinch. "No. That's Saronna. She's not my concubine or anyone else's. I haven't touched her, and I don't intend to."

"Really?" Randy moved to the window and gave Saronna an appraising glance. "She looks pretty damn touchable to me, Dunc."

For some reason, his friend's lighthearted tone irked Duncan. "What's that got to do with it? The fact that she's attractive doesn't change the situation any."

Randy winced. "Calm down. I didn't mean anything."

"No," Sai said caustically, "don't mind Randy. He was just being his usual sleazy self."

Duncan turned away from the window. It hardly seemed fair to judge Randy when he himself was now in possession of a Kruegerian woman who had had no say in the matter. "I suppose I look pretty sleazy, too. I don't quite know what to do with her. I can't send her back to her father, and she can't survive on her own—not on Krueger's World."

"Is she stupid?" Sai asked.

"No," Duncan said, "she seems pretty sharp to me. She knows how to read, which is an accomplishment for a woman around here."

"So let her learn what she needs to learn to make it on her own," Sai said. "Then she won't need to go back to that slimy father of hers."

"Actually," Duncan said, "her father seems to have been motivated at least partly by a concern for her welfare."

Sai was skeptical, but Duncan explained about the Maynard household.

"I don't know that it makes me feel any better about him," Sai said. "He needed two women to wait on him hand and foot, instead of just one."

"They're big on that hand and foot business here," Randy said, relaxing into his chair. "I've noticed it myself the few times I ventured into the native quarter looking for cheap food."

"Be careful about that," Duncan said. "If you don't watch what you're doing, you could insult a patriarch and the next thing you'd know, his sons and grandsons would be calling on you with very sharp calling cards."

Sai shook her head in disgust. "This place is creepy."

"And weird, too," Randy said. "How can every man have two women? Are they deliberately having more girl babies than boys?"

Duncan smiled at the thought. "No way, not here. Their technology is too primitive. But the young men sometimes kill each other off in feuds and such. And even the ones who make it to their twenties don't get to marry until their fathers arrange it for them. Besides, not every man has two women. A wife comes with a dowry, but an extra woman has to be bought, and most men can't afford to do that."

"So what makes a man a patriarch?" Randy asked. "Is it just having children?"

"Nope," Duncan said. "There's more to it than that. A man has to have sons *and* his father has to be dead before he's addressed as sire. Generally, sons live with their fathers until the father dies. Once that happens, the ones with sons of their own are entitled to grow a beard and call themselves sire, but only the eldest son inherits, as far as land or real property is concerned. Within a year or two, his younger brothers move out of the house and build their own homes. At that point, they can all marry if they're not already married."

"But," Sai said, "I thought I heard one of the servants refer to your father as Sire Trushenko. And you said your grandfather was fine."

"That's true. Dad just lets everyone think his father's dead, because he gets more respect that way. He even grew a beard so he'd look the part."

Randy shook his head in admiration. "Old Vladimir has trading in his blood. He doesn't miss a trick."

"Apparently not," Sai said as she watched Vladimir come into the courtyard and kiss Naomi on the cheek.

"He's my father, Sai," Duncan said gently.

"Sorry," she said, flushing.

"Come and meet everyone," Duncan said, trying for a more congenial note. "You haven't seen Dad in years."

"All right," Randy said, getting to his feet. "You can break the news to him that he has two unexpected house guests."

Duncan grinned. "Dad won't care. It won't make any work for him. It's Naomi who'll get stuck with the bother."

But when he introduced his friends, Naomi didn't seem to mind the addition of two guests to the household. She shook hands with the two strangers as if she had done so all her life, and smiled with pleasure when Duncan told her that they would be staying indefinitely. "Oh, good. You'll be here for the party, then."

"Party?" Sai said. "I don't know if we should go. We're traveling light. I didn't bring any party clothes with me."

"You can borrow something of mine," Naomi said, giving Sai an appraising glance, "or Saronna's if it's a better fit."

Duncan glanced at Saronna to see how she took this offer of the loan of her finery. The woman that Sai had called his concubine was standing as she had when he had first seen her, very straight and very still, with her eyes modestly cast down. She seemed almost to know that he was studying her, because she suddenly raised her eyes to his. Duncan gave her a reassuring smile, and Saronna looked away.

"I'll speak to Margaret about the rooms," Naomi said, and then she stopped suddenly in confusion. "That is," she said delicately, "should it be one room or two?"

Randy laughed and slipped his arm around Sai's waist. "What do you say, sweetheart? It's been a whole week since you cut me off at the knees the last time. Are you ready to come to your senses and make me the happiest man on Krueger's World?"

"No," Sai said, slipping away quite easily. "And don't hold your breath. Two rooms, please, Naomi."

Randy made a show of his disappointment, but his humor didn't seem impaired. He made a joke that had Sai laughing reluctantly.

Duncan laughed with them. It was good to have friends in the house.

WALKING back to Naomi's rooms, Saronna wondered if there were any rules at all for conduct between men and women in this society. Naomi hadn't seemed shocked by Sai and Randy's conversation, so she could only suppose that such behavior was acceptable in the off-world quarter.

In fact, Naomi seemed very curious. "Vladimir told me Duncan had friends who might come to visit," she said, leaning back on the sofa in her sitting room. "He didn't tell me it was a man and a woman, though."

"Does it matter?" Saronna asked.

Naomi gave her a tolerant look. "Of course it matters. I wonder if there was ever anything between Duncan and the woman. They seemed very comfortable together."

Saronna felt a sudden lurch of fear. If Duncan wanted another woman, his father might sell her. "Do you think so?"

"Maybe." Naomi smiled reassuringly. "Don't worry; if there was anything, it's over now. He sees her as a friend or maybe a sister, except he's not so protective as one of our men would be about a sister."

"What about her?"

Naomi shrugged. "I don't know yet. There's something there, but I'm not sure what. She guards her feelings much better than most off-worlders—not like the man."

The remark puzzled Saronna. Randy had seemed pleasant, but not overly emotional. "What about the man?"

Naomi looked almost smug. "He loves her, of course. He hides it behind a light tongue and an easy manner, because he's too afraid to let her see the hurt if he let his feelings show and she still said no."

Saronna stifled a snort of disbelief. "How could you see all this in a few minutes of conversation?"

The older woman made a face. "Pho! Compared to us, these people wear their feelings like a garment, exposed for all to see. They know nothing about the need to share close quarters and pretend that they like one another."

Saronna recalled what Duncan had said about empaths. Was it possible Naomi had that gift? She seemed very sure of her conclusions. "Except for this woman?"

"Yes," Naomi said. "Except for Sai Whisset."

DUNCAN leaned back in his chair. Warhlou hna Nedahna looked almost ridiculous holding a delicate porcelain cup in one massive hand and pursing his wide lips to sip the native tea. His eyes, two dark agates set deep in his craggy, gray-brown face, twinkled at Duncan as if he knew how incongruous he looked.

The Miloran set the cup down gently on the table. "So, have you adjusted to the time yet?"

Duncan shrugged. "Pretty much. I still take a nap in the afternoon. In a way, the four meals a day are harder to get used to than anything else."

Warhlou shrugged. "If you call supper a meal. I don't consider a few pieces of fruit and some bread worthy of the name."

The parlor door opened, and Saronna walked in. She stopped abruptly when she saw them, and cast her eyes downward for a moment.

Duncan watched her eyes travel upward. Even sitting, Warhlou was a lot to take in.

Ever sensitive to Terran manners, Warhlou surged to his feet. Duncan felt the floor shudder as his friend stood up.

Duncan stood up, too. "Saronna, this is my friend Warhlou hna Nedahna."

Saronna cringed. There was no other word for it.

Fortunately, Warhlou didn't seem insulted. He held out his hand. "I'm afraid I'm rather a lot to take in, all at once," he suggested helpfully.

Saronna shook her head and swallowed hard as she allowed her hand to be engulfed by his. "No, it's just that I grew up in the hills, and I'm not used to, ah, strangers."

He chuckled as he sat down, rattling the cups on the table beside him. "Especially not strangers as big as me?"

"Maybe not," Saronna said.

Duncan sat down, curious to see how she would fare in such an alien presence.

She glanced around in confusion. "Oh, there's my book."

She snatched the reader up from a side table, made her excuses, and left them with a hasty farewell.

"So," Warhlou said after she had gone, "that's the woman your father has in mind for you?"

Duncan raised his eyebrows. "I see gossip is as strong an industry as ever in the off-world quarter."

Warhlou gave another crockery-rattling chuckle. "Of course it is. Did you ever think differently?"

"I suppose not," Duncan said. "So what does the grapevine say about Saronna?"

Warhlou looked puzzled by the idiom. "Pardon?"

"What's the gossip?" Duncan said. "What's the rumor mill grinding out in the way of speculation?"

"Ah!" Warhlou said. "What do you think? Your father bought a woman for you. Everyone assumes you're putting the gift to good use."

Duncan frowned. The more he thought it over, the worse it sounded. "It occurs to me that this could really put a crimp in my social life. It's difficult to imagine an off-world woman anywhere in New Jerusalem agreeing to go out to a concert or on a picnic with me if she thinks I'm amusing myself with Saronna right here at home."

This time Warhlou's laugh shook the light fixtures. "I wouldn't bother imagining it. It's not going to happen."

Duncan sighed. "I don't suppose it would help if I strangled my father?"

Warhlou's smile showed a truly alarming amount of teeth. "It seems Terrans also feel a tenseness between the generations."

"From time to time."

"So, is she pretty?"

The question confused Duncan. "Is who pretty?"

"Saronna, of course."

"You just met her?"

Warhlou shrugged. "I can't tell with Terrans. Is she pretty?"

"I really couldn't say," Duncan said. "I think I'd call her attractive rather than pretty. Prettiness connotes a certain delicacy, and I don't think I'd ever call Saronna delicate. She's too—too grounded for that." He studied his caller curiously. "Why did you want to know?"

"Because, that's what every Terran woman of my acquaintance wanted me to tell them, as soon as they heard I was coming here."

Duncan tasted sour discontent, almost as if he had bitten into a piece of fruit gone bad. "Well, they'll all see for themselves tomorrow night. Dad's invited half the off-world population of New Jerusalem."

Warhlou nodded. "I know. I'm sorry I won't make it, but my shuttle leaves tomorrow afternoon. That's one reason I came today, instead of waiting. I wanted to get the date set for our delivery before I left."

"Was there another reason you came today?"

Warhlou gave another fantastic dental display. "Of course. I didn't want to be the only off-worlder in New Jerusalem who hadn't seen Duncan Trushenko's newest acquisition."

"Go to hell!" Duncan said in the Miloran vernacular.

Warhlou's agate-like eyes gleamed. "You need to work on the accent."

VLADIMIR Trushenko watched his beloved preen in front of the mirror in his bedroom. He should host more parties. It always put Naomi in a good mood to be so busy.

"You look more beautiful than ever," he said. "That dress brings out the color of your eyes."

Naomi glanced at him over her shoulder. "You don't know how much the fabric cost."

"Whatever it cost, it was worth it," Vladimir said with conviction.

She smiled, a warm affectionate smile that made his heart glow. Money had a use if it could make her smile like that.

Naomi slipped her arm through his. "Wait until you see Saronna. Her dress came out very well, too."

A nagging sense of guilt assailed Vladimir. He hadn't missed the disapproving glare that Sai had given him when she was introduced to Saronna. She had tried to hide it, but it had come out before she could stop it. He held in a sigh.

"I think Duncan likes her," Naomi whispered as they walked through the corridor. "You picked well."

Vladimir recalled the negotiations with Saronna's father, and his sense of remorse grew. Still, if Naomi was right, it might be that Duncan could find the same happiness with Saronna that Vladimir had found with Naomi. That would make crossing the moral quagmire of buying someone worth the mental anguish of the journey. "There wasn't a whole lot of choice involved." He decided to change the subject. "I appreciate all you've done for the party."

She ducked her head and tried to hide a pleased smile. "It's only my duty." An anxious look suddenly crossed her face. "I just hope nothing goes wrong tonight."

Vladimir squeezed her arm. "It's a party. What could go wrong?"

PARTIES, Duncan reflected, surveying the main courtyard, were a cost of doing business, but at least Naomi knew how to set the scene. The lights had been turned very low, and torches placed around the walls to give illumination without destroying the mystery of the night. A phalanx of hired servants stood ready to serve food and drinks, and a dozen musicians sat in one corner, stringed instruments at the ready.

A noise made Duncan turn. His father came into the courtyard with Naomi on his arm. The Kruegerian woman looked radiant in a blue-green gown.

"Good evening, Naomi," Duncan said, kissing her cheek. "You look like a star come down from the heavens."

Naomi laughed, her eyes shining. "You're as much of a flatterer as your father."

"Nonsense," Duncan said. "Every word is the truth."

Naomi only smiled. She looked past him. "Hello, Saronna. You look very nice."

Duncan turned as Saronna stepped into the torch light from the dim recesses of the hallway. Red satin draped her figure, a deep ruby red that made the black of her hair gleam like polished onyx. Without being too tight, the dress clung to her body, and the fabric reflected the light as she moved. The smooth, silky expanse of the sari-like satin skirt set off the elaborate brocade of the bodice. A faint suggestion of perfume emanated from her as she walked, and her hair had been piled on her head in a way that showed off her slender neck.

"You look lovely, Saronna," Duncan said, much struck by how different she looked.

Saronna seemed pleased at the compliment, but said nothing. Instead, she moved back a little, as if she didn't want to draw attention to herself. She ran the fingers of her right hand over the bracelet on her left wrist as if the plain gold bangle provided some sense of reassurance.

"Well," Vladimir said smugly. "We're ready. Where are your friends, Duncan?"

"They're coming," Duncan assured him.

The butler hired for the evening opened the door to admit the first guests. Naomi nodded at the musicians, and they began to play. The party had started.

The courtyard was full of people by the time Sai and Randy made an appearance. Sai wore an uncharacteristically feminine sheath dress of emerald green Kruegerian silk that made her look as sleek as a Terran cat. She even allowed Randy to lead her into the courtyard on his arm.

"You look great, Sai," Duncan said.

"Thanks," Sai ran one hand down the side of her dress. "I hate to have to give this dress back, but since Naomi is pretending it's one of Saronna's, I guess I'd better."

Duncan shook his head. "I don't think either of them will care if you keep it."

"I notice you didn't mention my appearance," Randy said, slipping one finger into the tight collar of his formal jacket. "And I know this really is one of Vladimir's suits, so I do plan to give it back."

Duncan grinned. "You don't need any more compliments. I'm sure the ladies here will give you plenty."

Sai slipped her hand from Randy's arm. "Just don't forget we're working. We did pretty well from our first deal, and I want to keep it up."

Randy sighed. "It seems a waste of a good party."

Sai pursed her lips in an incipient frown. "There's the Shuratanian woman who bought our glasou carvings. She seemed taken with the Kumar charm. Let's go talk to her again."

Duncan grinned into his drink and looked around for Saronna.

SARONNA took a bite of the Shuratanian delicacy Duncan had suggested she try. A sweet and sour sensation suffused her taste buds. She listened with half her mind to his description of what was in the food, while she eyed the swirling mass of party guests around her. It still felt odd to be unveiled in a room full of complete strangers, let alone wearing a dress that revealed her figure so well. No one seemed to be paying obvious attention to her, but she was aware of covert glances from time to time.

Suddenly, Duncan broke off his description of the menu to stare across the room, a look of total astonishment on his face. When Saronna followed his gaze, all she saw was one of the hired servants talking to a tall woman in a gray traveling suit, who was making her way from the corridor. The servant kept trying to block the tall woman's path, but she simply ignored him and kept walking. The man walked backward, pausing every few steps to plead with her to stop.

"Damn!" Duncan said under his breath.

"What?" Saronna said. "Is something wrong?"

"I don't know. Let's see how they do together."

Saronna looked around the courtyard for some obvious explanation and saw none. "Who?"

"My parents. That's my mother who just walked in."

Saronna looked sharply at the woman in the gray suit. No one had spoken of Duncan's mother except in passing, as when Naomi had mentioned that she was tall. Saronna hadn't realized she was still alive.

Not only alive, but vigorous. Duncan's mother had sailed into the room as if she owned it. Saronna could see where Duncan got his height and his build. His mother had the same tall frame, the same wide shoulders and loose-hipped gait. Younger than Vladimir by a decade or so, her hair was the same dark brown as Duncan's, but the eyes that gazed disdainfully at her son's father were an arresting shade of ice blue.

"Hello, Vladimir," she said calmly. "Have I come at a bad time?"

Vladimir looked her up and down and then threw back his head and laughed. "No worse than usual. Come and join the party, Vonda."

Duncan breathed out a sigh of relief. "Okay, Saronna, come meet my mother."

Saronna went reluctantly, a little apprehensive about the possibility of an emotional scene if they were meeting after a long absence.

"Hello, Duncan," his mother said, when Duncan came up and embraced her. She looked him up and down carefully, but otherwise she might have been saying hello after seeing him at breakfast. "How are you?"

"I'm fine, Mom," Duncan said. "Have interstellar communications gone out completely, or did you want to surprise us?"

"Neither," she said. Was there a tinge of guilt in his mother's voice or was it Saronna's imagination? "I only decided to come when I realized how close to Krueger's World the last leg of my trip would take me. I'd have sent an express, but we were in folded space, and once we came out of it, I knew I might well have arrived before it did."

Saronna didn't understand much of this speech, but she didn't want to reveal her ignorance by asking what it meant.

Vladimir probably understood it, but he looked skeptical as he went off to procure refreshments for the new arrival.

"Mom," Duncan said, "I'd like you to meet a friend of mine. This is Saronna. Saronna, this is my mother, Vonda Cameron."

Vonda's eyes lit up sharply at this introduction. She offered her hand to Saronna, but her gaze was on Duncan.

"Well, Duncan," she said, "do we need to have a talk?"

"If you like," Duncan said. "But not until after the party."

Just as Saronna let go of Vonda Cameron's hand, she noticed Naomi standing transfixed on the other side of the courtyard, her face so drained of color that she looked bloodless. "Oh," Saronna said, tugging on Duncan's sleeve as she nodded toward Naomi.

Duncan's eyes followed her nod. "Damn," he said again.

Saronna waited to see what he would do.

"Well, well, well," Vonda said, smiling derisively. "So that's your father's concubine?"

"Mother," Duncan said, a warning note in his voice, "if you've come to make a fuss, do us all a favor and wait until later."

Vonda raised her eyebrows in mock surprise. "But a fuss would be much more effective in front of company, don't you think?"

"No, I don't," Duncan said. "What it would be is cruel. Naomi's a nice person, Mom. She doesn't deserve to be humiliated just because she and Dad are together. It's not as if you didn't have Pietro keeping you company all those years."

Saronna hid a start of amazement. It sounded as if Duncan's mother had taken a lover—quite openly, as he spoke of it as if it were a matter of course. Could even married women do completely as they pleased, then? Truly, off-world women lived different lives.

Vonda pursed her lips for a second, and then she turned away. "All right. You go and talk to her before she faints dead away. Saronna and I will have a little chat."

She took Saronna by the arm and pulled her away before Duncan could protest. Saronna went, but she looked over her shoulder at Duncan as she walked. Duncan managed to look distressed and disgusted at the same time as he watched them.

"Is there somewhere where we can be alone?" Vonda said. "It's too noisy to talk here."

Saronna turned back to her protector's mother. She owed this woman a level of respect, after all. "The dower courtyard is open. I don't think anyone is there yet."

"The dower courtyard," Vonda murmured. "How quaint."

DUNCAN sighed fatalistically. Somehow he doubted his mother was going to approve of his father's newest addition to the Trushenko household. The sight of Naomi's distressed expression reminded him of the need to deal with the situation at hand. Duncan walked over to his father's companion and pulled her gently by the arm, until they were alone in a corner. "Are you all right, Naomi?"

Naomi nodded, but she seemed dazed. "That's her, isn't it? That's Vladimir's wife?"

"Yes." Duncan put as much reassurance as he could into his voice. "It's okay. Mom has just come for a visit. Nothing bad is going to happen."

Naomi began to tremble. Alarmed, Duncan put his arm around her and maneuvered her through the throng of guests. The rooms that opened onto the courtyard were occupied. Duncan led Naomi through the northwest quadrant of the house and opened the door of the library. A quick glance around the empty room made him sigh with relief. At least he didn't need to chase anyone out.

"Sit down," Duncan ordered, almost pushing Naomi into a chair. "Take a deep breath or something. It's all right, Naomi, really. You don't have to worry at all."

"But what if she's come to take him away from me?" Tears trickled down Naomi's face and fell unchecked into her lap.

Duncan sat down in the chair next to hers. "Don't be ridiculous. Dad loves you. And if you want to know the truth, he and my mother hate each others' guts. They always have. They can't be in the same room for more than an hour and stay polite to each other."

"Really?" Naomi lifted her tear-stained face to look up at him.

"Really." It was no wonder his father had fallen for this woman so quickly, if she could cry like that and not look in the least disfigured by violent emotion. If anything, the tears only made her eyes glisten invitingly.

The door opened. "Naomi," Vladimir said, rushing into the room.

Duncan rose to his feet at once. "I'd better get back to the party now, Dad."

Vladimir nodded absently and sat down in the chair Duncan had occupied.

When Duncan came back into the courtyard, he looked around for his mother, but she was nowhere in sight.

Randy came up beside him, a delighted grin spread across his face. "I saw Vonda. She looks in rare form."

"Where is she?"

Randy assumed an innocent expression. "She took Saronna off in search of somewhere to have a quiet conversation. Saronna mentioned something about the dower courtyard."

Duncan almost ran through the corridors to the south side of the house. He burst into the tiny courtyard, lit only by dim lights around the walls and a single table lamp that threw a pool of light around the two women. His mother sat in a chair with Saronna on a bench beside her.

"Hello, Duncan," Vonda said. "Did you manage to calm her down?"

"Dad's with her."

"Well, that should do it," Vonda said.

"Saronna," Duncan said, "would you mind very much if I talked to my mother alone for a few minutes?"

Saronna rose without speaking, bowed to Vonda, and went quickly back through the corridor.

"What a delightful girl," Vonda said. "I do hope your father didn't pay too much for her, though."

"Now, Mom," Duncan began.

"Don't you 'Now, Mom,' me!" Vonda snapped. "Do you deny that your father bought that woman to be your concubine just like he bought that poor ninny in the other room for himself?"

"Yes, I do."

"Bah!" Vonda said, her eyes glittering. "She told me herself. I asked how she met you, and she explained that your father introduced you on the day that he bought her from her father."

"That's true, certainly, but—"

"But? But what? What kind of excuse can there be for behavior like that, Duncan?"

It was a damn good question. Duncan wished he had a better answer. "Dad didn't really intend Saronna to be my woman. He needed someone to keep Naomi company during the day, and he figured that Saronna's father would sell her to someone with considerably fewer scruples if he didn't buy her himself."

His mother's laugh sounded harsh. "Fewer scruples? How can you have fewer scruples than that? If he wanted company for the bimbo, he could have bought her a dog, couldn't he?"

"Listen, Mom, regardless of what you think, this is Dad's house—"

"This is Cameron Trushenko's house," Vonda said, her chin thrust forward in a clear danger signal, "and I own forty-nine percent of Cameron Trushenko."

It came to Duncan that he had made a major mistake by forgetting that fact. He sat down on the bench next to her. "I know that, Mom, but Dad lives here. This isn't just his place of business, it's his *home* and Naomi's, too. Please don't come into their home and insult them. Naomi is not a bimbo, and if you can't treat her with respect, then maybe you should leave. I'll take you to a hotel."

Vonda looked angry at this assertion, then pursed her lips and took a breath. "Very well. So the little one's not a bimbo. What's the tall one doing here, Duncan?"

"I told you," Duncan said, keeping his voice level. "She's here to help Naomi, and to be her friend. Naomi has a hard time making friends, because the native culture is so restrictive, and she doesn't fit in with the off-worlders."

His mother jumped to her feet as if she couldn't sit still. "I knew it! I knew I should never have let your father bring you to this miserable, backward, misbegotten excuse for a planet. I knew it would suck you in, just like it sucked your father in. This stupid, seductive, macho culture where every man is king of his own little castle."

"I was over twenty-one at the time, Mom," Duncan said, watching her pace back and forth. "It was a little late for a custody battle."

"Maybe. But I could have withheld consent when Vladimir wanted to move Cameron Trushenko here. If he hadn't done that, you'd never have come here and acquired your own little living play toy."

Duncan flinched at the acidity in her tone. "Mom! Stop it!"

Vonda looked at him for a moment, and then turned away. Duncan waited for her to speak again, and when she didn't, he stood up and moved closer.

"Mom?" he said in disbelief. "Mom, are you crying?"

"No," she sobbed. "Don't be silly. I never cry."

It was true—or almost true. "I've never seen you cry before, except for that time when we found that little girl's tomb on Lycandria."

Vonda smiled as she brushed away her tears. "Little girl? She wasn't even human."

"She was still a little girl."

Vonda sniffed. "It was the toys that did it. It was amazing how a top and a doll could tell you right away how old she was, even though she was almost as tall as me."

"It sure got to you. I never saw you break down like that before."

"No," Vonda said absently. "But then you weren't there when I got the news about Pietro."

Duncan said nothing. He had been fond of his mother's companion, but the man's death hadn't devastated him the way it had devastated his mother. It had taken her years to recover—if she truly had recovered. The rigid lines of her face told him she was still holding in the pain of her loss.

Vonda straightened her shoulders, then let them relax. "You seemed to enjoy those last few months on Lycandria, when I let you come out in the field with us. I had hoped, after that, that you'd choose my vocation instead of your father's."

Duncan smiled, recalling his brief foray into archaeology. "It was fun for a few months, but I knew it wasn't what I wanted to do with my life."

"No," Vonda said, pouring volumes of bitterness into the one word. "That became apparent as soon as you left school and started working for your father."

Duncan held in a sigh of frustration. "Don't make me choose between you, Mom. Please don't do that."

"You made your choice already."

Alarmed at the bleakness in her voice, Duncan moved closer. "Just because I decided I wanted to go into business with Dad doesn't mean I don't love you just as much as I love him."

"Doesn't it?"

"No, it doesn't," Duncan repeated firmly.

She held out her arms, and he hugged her tightly.

"Well," Vonda said as she let go of him and straightened up, "that was reassuring. Now there's just the question of what to do about your little hired companion."

Duncan led her back to her chair, pleased that she seemed calmer and sounded less caustic. "You're not going to do anything," he said, sitting down and pulling her with him. "Saronna is preparing for independence already. She reads books and watches educational programs. I'm not trying to keep her in feudal slavery or anything."

Vonda studied his face carefully. "So you see her strictly as someone who needs a helping hand?"

Duncan didn't answer right away. How did he see Saronna? It surprised him to realize he wasn't entirely sure. "How I see her is none of your business, Mom."

She chortled. "Don't you mean it's none of my damn business?"

Duncan smiled with relief at her use of humor. "No. If Sai or Randy asks me that question, it's none of their damn business. With you, it's just none of your business."

She slipped her arm through his. "I suppose I shouldn't be surprised. I was fool enough to marry a man just like my father. It's no wonder your heart beats faster at the thought of trading a bag of pretty rocks for a stack of woven cloth."

It was a remarkably simplistic description of interstellar trading, but on the other hand, he knew next to nothing about archaeology. "We're not that different. Your heart beats faster for a bunch of old bones stuck in a cairn."

Vonda's smile was warm and genuine. She looked more relaxed. "Yes, it does. But I really want you to find a woman to make your heart beat faster—not just things!"

"I'm only twenty-six," Duncan said.

"I know exactly when you were born." She tapped his chest. "You may not remember it, but I was there."

Duncan laughed and grabbed her hand.

"So," Vonda said, "I saw Randy. Is Sai here, too?"

His friends seemed like a good distraction. "Yes. Shall we go and look for her?"

"All right," Vonda said, getting to her feet with a sigh. "I don't suppose you've ever considered trying to rekindle the flame with her?"

"It wasn't much of a flame, and the ashes couldn't get any colder. Give it up, Mom."

Vonda's reply was lost when Saronna came rushing into the courtyard.

"Duncan!" she said, wringing her hands. "I need you!"

"What is it?" Duncan said, alarmed. He had never seen Saronna's composure so disrupted. "What's wrong?"

Saronna looked almost guilty. "I'm afraid my brother has come to call. He's very upset."

Duncan stood rooted to the spot for a second. He had had about all he could take of touchy family situations. Finally, he found relief in a stream of obscenities, many of them in Miloran.

"Duncan!"

"Sorry, Mom," Duncan said perfunctorily. He squared his shoulders. "All right, Saronna. Lead me to your fire-eating brother."

CHAPTER FIVE

Duncan appraised Saronna covertly, as she walked beside him while they hurried back to the front part of the house. She showed no sign of tears, but she still looked anxious. "Where's your brother now?" Duncan asked her.

"The guard put him in a room he called the security office," Saronna said. "Paul was wearing a knife, so they didn't want to let him come in the front door, and he made a fuss about it. Some guests were arriving, and he tried to come in with them, but the security staff stopped him in the entrance hall."

Duncan gave her a sideways glance. "A knife, huh? Is that part of his normal costume or is he out for my blood?"

She seemed surprised by the question, "Paul always carries a knife. He is a little upset with you, but he would never attack you. It's my father he's angry at, for selling me."

Finally, a Kruegerian whose attitude Duncan could identify with. "That sounds reasonable to me. In fact, he sounds more reasonable than your father."

"Paul is very fond of me. We're only two years apart."

"Is he older or younger?"

"Younger. He's twenty-one."

Duncan subtracted one year for every twenty Kruegerian years, to come up with a rough estimate of Paul's age in Standard time. "That's pretty young. How does he get along with your father's wife? Is she mean to him, too?"

"Oh, Paul isn't my mother's child. Leah is his mother, and she's quite fond of him."

The casual comment rocked Duncan. He had assumed that Josiah Maynard wouldn't have had any more children with his wife if he had come to love Saronna's mother. It came to him that he didn't understand Kruegerian society nearly as well as he had thought. "Do you know where my father is?"

She shook her head. Duncan debated about going to the library, but decided he could handle Paul Maynard himself.

The young man waiting impatiently in the security office looked vaguely like Saronna, but he wasn't as dark, and his build was more stocky, with powerful shoulders and a barrel chest. Duncan looked him up and down and hoped Saronna was right about his peaceful intentions.

"Saronna!" Paul Maynard said explosively, as soon as he saw his sister. "Where did you go? I need to talk to you."

"Just a minute," Duncan said. He turned to the security guard on duty in the room. "It's all right. I'll vouch for him."

"He has a weapon, sir," the man said. "He's carrying a knife."

"I know," Duncan said. "But it's okay. It's part of the native dress here."

The man didn't look convinced, but he allowed Duncan to escort their overwrought visitor to an inner office and didn't insist on coming in with them.

"Now," Duncan said when the three of them were alone, "I think some introductions are in order. I'm Duncan Trushenko."

The younger man's face contorted in a mulish frown. "I want to see Sire Trushenko."

"My father's busy at the moment," Duncan said. "You're Saronna's brother?"

The question seemed to remind Paul of his manners. He bowed before answering. "Yes. My name is Paul Maynard."

Duncan returned the bow at the same depth. "Did you come only to see Saronna, or do you need to talk to me?"

Paul's eyes blazed angrily. "I came to buy her back."

"Paul," Saronna said. "Don't be so foolish. You know you can't do that. Father would never allow it."

"I have my own money saved," Paul said.

"Six thousand credits?" Saronna said gently.

Paul opened his eyes wide in surprise, but he set his jaw and answered firmly. "I could earn the rest. Maybe I could get a loan."

"The money doesn't matter," Duncan said. "If Saronna wants to leave now, she can."

Far from reassuring him, this offer sent Paul from red-faced anger to white-faced fear. "You're sending her back?"

"No. But I told Saronna her first day here that she could leave any time she wanted. I don't believe in people owning other people."

Paul's mouth dropped open.

"It doesn't matter what Duncan says," Saronna said. "I can't go back. Father wouldn't allow me to go home, and I have nowhere else to go."

Paul took a deep breath. "I could move out of the house and find a place we could share."

"No," Saronna said.

"Saronna," her brother said, "don't you want to live with me? We talked about it when we were younger."

"We were children." Saronna turned to Duncan. "Could I talk to my brother alone, please?"

Duncan glanced at Paul Maynard's grief-stricken face and nodded. Finally, someone on Krueger's World was reacting as he would have expected. "I'll wait outside."

SARONNA waited until the door closed behind Duncan to speak. Paul had always been hot-tempered—kind and loving, but quick to anger when those he cared about were at risk. It was one reason she hadn't been able to resist loving him back. "How did you find me? Did Father tell you how to find the house?"

"Father told us nothing except that he had sold you," Paul said, sounding bitter. "He refused to say anything more. He punished me when I asked questions."

Saronna put a hand on his arm. "Did he hurt you?"

Paul shrugged negligently. "Not bad."

She smiled, knowing that he would never admit it even if he had been beaten black and blue. "Then how did you find me if Father didn't tell you?"

"I heard him talking to Mother about it. He mentioned thanking Cousin Abraham, so I asked Isaac if he knew anything."

It made sense. Isaac was Cousin Abraham's eldest son; he and Paul were the same age and were close friends.

"Isaac said that his father had done business with an off-worlder named Sire Trushenko and had been impressed with the man," Paul went on. "He said Sire Trushenko kept some of our ways—even to having a woman of our people in his house. When Sire Trushenko asked him if he knew of anyone who had a daughter he couldn't marry off—not too young or too old, and not short, those were his only requirements—Cousin Abraham thought of you right away. He talked to Father and told him about it. Once Isaac told me the name, I found the house by myself."

Saronna moved her arm so that it encircled him. "It was very brave of you, and I thank you for trying to help, but I can't leave here—not yet."

He pushed her away as if he wanted to look her in the face. "Are you pleased to have been sold here?"

She tilted her head as she considered it. She couldn't tell him all her reasons—not what a relief it was to escape his mother and her insistence on enacting the Mother's rituals at every opportunity, and not how much she enjoyed the freedom to read. "In a way, I am. I miss you and my sisters, but I'm treated well. Duncan makes no demands on me except that I try to educate myself. His father is quite pleasant to me, and he has his own woman whom he loves very much, so I don't fear him at all. Naomi, his woman, is kind and she was lonely before I came, so she treats me as a sister. In many ways, I'm better off here than I was at home."

Paul stared at her in shock. Two deep ridges appeared between his brows as he frowned. "Do they know about you?"

"No," she said sharply, with a glance at the door to reassure herself that no one could overhear. "I never even told our family, except for you."

He sighed. "Well, these people won't find out unless you're careless. Be careful, Saronna!"

"I will be," she said. "I don't think they would call me a witch, but I won't take any chances." She let go of him to look into his face. "They're much more tolerant of differences here. You should know that, in case—in case you ever need a place to go."

His face flushed. "No one will find out about me. I won't give anyone cause to suspect my sin."

Saronna recalled the day she had found him sobbing in his room, weeping uncontrollably because a boy he cared about was getting married. He had blurted out his pain to her, and she had kept his secret as well as he had kept hers, well aware if it were known, he would likely be thrown out of their father's house. "Well, keep it in mind. Does Father know you're here?"

He shook his head. "I told him I was going into the city to see a friend from school." He ducked his head. Saronna knew he often went into the city; it had taken her a while to figure out that the friends he saw were more than friends to him.

She laid one hand on his shoulder. "You'd better get back. If you're gone too long, Father will get suspicious."

Paul suddenly threw his arms around her. "Come with me, Saronna. We'll find somewhere we can stay, and I'll take care of you. Please don't stay in this house of strangers."

Saronna didn't try to pull away from him. "No, Paul. Even if I weren't happy here, I couldn't do that. Father would be very angry if I broke with tradition, and his anger would spill out onto you. You have a life ahead of you. How could you ever start your own vineyard or learn a trade if Father disowned you?"

"Pho!" Paul said with disgust as he released her. "I can take care of myself!"

"And I want to take care of myself, too. I think I can learn how here better than I could anywhere else."

He studied her face intently, as if he were looking for any sign of distress or deception.

A quiet knock at the door broke the silence.

"Come in," Saronna said.

Duncan opened the door and stuck his head inside the room. "My father is here if Paul needs to talk to him."

Paul stood a little straighter. "I would like to meet Sire Trushenko."

Duncan held the door open for his father and then stepped into the room behind him.

"I don't think there's any need for you at this interview, Duncan," Vladimir said mildly.

"I disagree," Duncan said, and took a seat in a corner of the room.

Paul looked surprised when Vladimir Trushenko merely sighed and ignored his son.

"How do you do?" Vladimir said to Paul. "I'm Vladimir Trushenko. I understand you're Saronna's brother."

Paul nodded and bowed deeply, in deference to the older man's status. "I'm Paul Maynard."

"How can I help you?" Vladimir asked.

Paul glanced at Saronna, "I came to make certain my sister was well."

Vladimir nodded. "Your solicitude on her behalf is commendable. I trust you're satisfied?"

"Yes," Paul said. "She seems very well."

"Good. Was there anything else?"

Paul hesitated. "I wish to be certain that she'll stay well," he blurted out.

Vladimir didn't look offended. "Your father asked for such an assurance, and I gave it. I wouldn't stay in business long if my word weren't as good as a signed contract."

Paul put one hand on his knife. "In the hill country," he said in a level voice, "breaking your word is cause enough to start a blood feud."

Saronna looked to Vladimir in alarm, worried that he might take offense at the threat.

Vladimir merely nodded. "I know it. You need have no fear that I'll break it."

Paul looked past Vladimir to where Duncan sat carelessly on the arm of a chair. "And him?"

Vladimir smiled. "You need have no fear of Duncan, either."

Paul looked skeptical. "He doesn't obey you. How can you promise on his behalf?"

"Among our people a son doesn't owe his father obedience after his eighteenth year. Nevertheless, I can promise because I know Duncan. He would no more hurt Saronna than he would hurt a child."

If Paul didn't look completely convinced, he at least didn't argue.

Duncan stood up. "Look here. We don't hold with the same customs in this quarter. Saronna is free to have visitors anytime she likes—any visitors. If you're worried, you can come back to see her as often as you like."

Saronna felt a flush of pleasure at the idea that she could have her own visitors. It had never occurred to her to ask.

Paul's eyes opened wide in surprise. "I would appreciate that," he said, gratitude in his voice.

Duncan nodded. "I'll leave orders with the security staff to admit you at any time." His eyes strayed to Paul's belt. "You may want to leave the knife at home, though. Otherwise, they'll want to hold onto it while you're here."

Paul didn't seem concerned by this suggestion. Instead he turned to Saronna. "I'll come back to see you as soon as I can."

She smiled, happy at the thought of seeing him again. She hadn't lost her family completely. She would be able to get news of her sisters, and maybe even send word to them. "All right, but be careful Father doesn't find out where you're going."

"We're having a party at the moment," Vladimir said kindly. "Would you care to stay for a while?"

Paul shook his head emphatically. "I thank you, but no. I must get home soon."

Saronna waited until Vladimir and Duncan had returned to their other guests to say goodbye to her brother. She walked him to the front door and embraced him one last time. When she saw his back going through the doorway, she said a silent prayer to Mother Eve that their father wouldn't find out where he had been.

And then the irony of praying to Mother Eve to help a man made her realize how far she had come from her life in Samaria.

BY the time the last of the guests had gone, the single huge, yellow moon of Krueger's World had risen high overhead. Duncan looked up at it as he stood in the main courtyard. When he looked down, the hired servants had begun to move through the area like a swarm of insects, collecting dirty plates and glasses, cleaning table tops, and otherwise tidying away the detritus of a hundred sentient beings eating and drinking their way through an evening.

Duncan gave a deep, heartfelt sigh. It had been a hell of a night. He had started for his room when he noticed Saronna quietly helping to stack dirty glassware onto a tray.

"Don't do that," Duncan said.

Saronna looked up in surprise. "I don't mind helping. I'm used to it."

"We're paying someone else to do it," Duncan said. "Come and have a nightcap with me instead. I could use one."

"What's a nightcap?"

"It's a drink you have right before bedtime. Let's go into the parlor. I think they've finished clearing away in there."

The parlor was both clean and empty when they entered it. Duncan moved to the bar and took two glasses from the shelf. "What would you like?"

"I don't know," Saronna said. "My father never allowed me to drink anything with alcohol in it."

Duncan glanced over his shoulder at her. "Did you try anything this evening?"

"Randy gave me a glass of wine," she said. "But I didn't like it much. It tasted sharp."

Duncan smiled and selected a smaller glass from the shelf. "Try this instead," he said, putting the glass into the dispenser and typing a code on the old-fashioned bar console. "It's a liqueur. It's considerably sweeter than wine, so you take tiny sips."

When he handed Saronna the glass, she sipped the dark red liquid apprehensively.

"Well?" Duncan asked.

"It's not bad."

Duncan poured himself a glass of Shuratanian ale and sank down on one of the sofas. "Whew! That was quite a night."

Saronna sat down across from him. "I'm sorry my brother intruded on your party."

Duncan grinned. "Don't apologize. He had a right to be concerned. Besides, he didn't make half the stink my mother did."

Saronna hesitated, and then her curiosity seemed to get the better of her manners. "I didn't realize your mother was still alive. Somehow, I had assumed she must have passed from the world."

Duncan's grin grew wider as he thought what his mother would say if she knew Saronna had assumed she was dead. "Nope. Mom is very much still in this world. I don't expect her to go without a fight, either. She may well outlive me."

Saronna's brows creased in a tiny frown of confusion. "I don't understand your customs. Could your father set her aside even though she had a son?"

"No," Duncan said. "Outside of Krueger's World, a man can't set simply set his wife aside. He can divorce her, or she can divorce him, but that's not the case here. My parents are still legally married. They can't get a divorce unless they're willing to lose control of Cameron Trushenko."

Saronna's frown grew as confusion blossomed to bewilderment, "I don't understand."

Duncan leaned back on the sofa, put his feet up on the table in front of him, and took a healthy sip of ale. It would be best to tell Saronna the whole story. She was, after all, now part of the Trushenko household and should know the details of how the company that supported them all came into being. "I hope this doesn't bore you, but the situation started with my grandfather, my mother's father, Alexander Cameron. He inherited a small trading company from his father, and he built it up into a thriving business. He had a family—one son and one daughter—but his wife died when they were both almost grown, and he never remarried."

Far from looking bored, Saronna looked almost relieved, as if family situations were one thing she understood.

"Anyway," Duncan went on, "my mother's brother, my Uncle James, despised business as a profession. He and his father quarreled and haven't spoken in years. My mother had no more regard for trading than Uncle James did, but she was very interested in the revenue that a good-sized company can generate. Mom's one abiding passion through the years has always been archaeology. She digs up old cities, on many different planets. It's what she wants to do, but she has no way to make it pay for itself."

Saronna nodded, as if to let him know she was following the conversation.

Duncan took a sip of ale before resuming. "That's when Dad entered the picture. Grandpa hired him to run one of his branch offices, and he was really impressed with Dad. He liked the way Dad thought, he liked his ethics, and he got along well with him. After a few years, Grandpa promoted Dad to senior vice president of the company, second only to himself. Things rubbed along this way for another couple of years, and then something unexpected happened."

"Your father and mother fell in love?" Saronna asked.

Duncan laughed wryly. "You must have found the romance novels in the library. No, not even close. Mom and Dad had met a couple of times, but with absolutely no sparks. No, old Grandpa Cameron got religion. He became a Neo Buddhist."

Saronna's expression went blank. "A what?"

"A Neo Buddhist." He waved a hand. "It's a strange mutation of an old Terran religion. Neo Buddhists live ascetic, isolated lives as hermits. Grandpa joined a group that had established a colony on a subsistence planet. Right at the moment, he's grubbing out a living in a borderline desert. But before Grandpa renounced the universe, he wanted to dispose of his company— Cameron Intergalactic, it was called then. He wanted very much to keep it in the family, but there was no suitable family to keep it in. So he hit upon the idea of bringing Dad into the family by having him marry Mom."

Saronna's eyebrows lifted in surprise. "But you told me sons and daughters were free to marry as they chose."

Duncan nodded. "Grandpa didn't force either of them into it—he couldn't. He simply offered each of them what they wanted most if they went along with his idea."

"And what was it they wanted?"

"Well, Dad wanted to run the company. To him, the profits are just a way of keeping score. To Mom, they're a sure source of funding for her archaeological projects. What Grandpa proposed was that Mom got forty-nine percent of the new company, to be named Cameron Trushenko. Dad got forty-nine percent, also, along with control of the remaining two percent."

"Control?" Saronna looked actively interested, which surprised him. Her eyes had never left his face. "Is that different from ownership?"

"You bet. Dad votes the stock, but it's owned by a trust."

"What's a trust?"

At least this wasn't a technology question, so he could answer it. "Well, in this case, it's mostly a law firm. Grandpa Cameron's lawyers administer the trust and dispense the income to the beneficiaries."

"And who are the beneficiaries?"

"So far," Duncan said, "there's just me. And since Mom and Dad can barely stand to be in the same room together, it looks as if it'll always be just me."

Saronna stirred restlessly on her chair. "It sounds very complicated. I don't understand why your grandfather did this. Why didn't he just give the company to your father if he wanted him to have it?"

"He did, and he didn't," Duncan said. "Grandpa Cameron believes in family. He split ownership of his company up in such a way so that it would stay in the family. Mom and Dad get equal shares, but Dad gets control only so long as he's married to Mom. If Dad asks her for a divorce, he loses control of that two percent. The trust votes those shares at that point."

Saronna's forehead wrinkled as she pondered the Cameron Trushenko ownership structure. "You mean your father has a reason not to divorce your mother, because he'll lose control of the company if he does?"

So she had understood that much. That was good.

When Duncan nodded, Saronna continued. "What about your mother? What if she wants to end the marriage?"

"She'd have to give Dad a chance to buy her out at a price set by the initial agreement. It's not a whole lot, and Mom is not about to do that. She funds her own archaeological foundation."

"Couldn't she just sell her forty-nine percent to someone else?"

"Nope. Both Mom and Dad actually own only a life interest. The stock is theirs, but when they die it goes to the beneficiaries—again, that's me."

She looked at him speculatively. "So then you will control Cameron Trushenko?"

She had caught on pretty fast, all things considered. "If," Duncan said, "I'm working for the firm when I inherit. Grandpa didn't want his company to go to a third generation that knew nothing about it."

Saronna shook her head. "It sounds peculiar to me. Did your father allow you to see your mother?"

She had assumed his father had full custody. Duncan had to smile at the idea that his mother could be shut out of important decisions without having any say. "Actually, I was raised by both of them in turn, first Mom, then Dad, then Mom, and so on. They usually did a one-year swap, except once or twice when they had to stretch it to two years."

Saronna blinked. "I know you think my people are peculiar, but I must tell you I find yours more than a little strange, too."

Duncan grinned. "That's perfectly understandable. Fortunately, there's an incredible variety of life in the universe. That's what makes it fun to get up every morning. You never know what will happen."

When Saronna made no answer, Duncan drained his glass and stood up. "I'm going to turn in now. It's been a long day. Thanks for helping with the party."

Saronna rose, too. "You're welcome," she said gravely.

Duncan hesitated for a second. She was very close, and he couldn't help but notice how well her new dress showed off her figure, or how the heady scent Naomi had given her still lingered in the air. He took one step toward her, bent his head and kissed her, putting his hands on her shoulders as his lips barely brushed hers.

Saronna didn't move, but her eyes opened wide with fear. She stared at him in total consternation.

Duncan repented. "I'm sorry." She looked even more stricken. Did she think he found her unattractive? "I mean," he added, "I'm sorry if that frightened you. I can't truthfully say I'm sorry I did it."

He left the room leaving her standing as still as if she had taken root to the floor.

SARONNA had dressed for bed in a mental fog. When she bent her head before the shrine to pray, she had to force herself to concentrate on the words to her prayer. What had it meant, that kiss? She couldn't decide. She finally fell asleep worrying about it, about the way it had made her feel, and about why Duncan had done what he had done.

The next morning at breakfast she watched Duncan closely, but he showed no signs of following up on his brief show of affection. It must have been mere friendship or perhaps that strange thing off-worlders called flirting.

A week later, Saronna was spending the morning in the library when she looked up to find Duncan watching her.

"Hello," he said. "What are you reading?"

"It's a history book," Saronna said, "on the building of the sleeper ships. It's very interesting, and the illustrations are wonderful. One of them actually lets you tour a ship."

Duncan nodded. "It was a fascinating period of Terran history."

"Did you want something?" Saronna asked. "Do you have an assignment for me?"

"No," Duncan said, sitting down at the next desk. "I just wanted to ask you if Mom's been giving you a bad time—no, wait. I mean, I know she's been giving you a bad time; I want to know how bad. Do you want me to ask her to leave?"

It was true that Vonda Cameron had been rude, but that seemed to be her normal behavior. Even the Cameron Trushenko staff had received the rough side of her tongue. Nevertheless, such an unfilial attitude shocked Saronna. "No, of course not. This is her house, too. You said so."

"Maybe." Duncan sounded almost grim. "But she's not behaving very hospitably. Mom was never one to take a subtle hint. If she's gone beyond what you can brush off, then I can ask her to move out for the rest of her visit."

Pleased that he was concerned for her, Saronna shook her head. "My feelings aren't hurt. But it's difficult to keep my temper with her."

Duncan grinned. "I don't know of any reason why you have to keep it. If she makes you mad, just give her back as good as you get. Don't feel you should hold back."

"Really?" Saronna had trouble believing such behavior could be acceptable. "Wouldn't Sire Trushenko be angry?"

"Nah! The way Mom has been going for Naomi, Dad would probably buy you a new dress if you got her to lay off."

Saronna recalled how Vonda's comments about illiteracy among Kruegerian women, made over the dinner table, had left Naomi silent and withdrawn. "All right. I'll tell her what I really think."

"Good." Duncan seemed pleased, but instead of leaving, he sat and stared at her.

Saronna felt a twinge of alarm. "Is anything wrong?"

Duncan twisted his mouth into an approximation of a smile. "Nothing's wrong. I'm just feeling like a kid who's been locked in a candy store right after he promised not to eat any candy."

She opened her eyes wide in puzzlement, not understanding his meaning.

Duncan leaned toward her, then jerked away. "Damn!" he said again, and he jumped to his feet.

Saronna watched him pace around the room. What was the problem?

He stopped abruptly. "Do you like me, Saronna?"

She nodded, feeling a twinge of guilt at the admission. Liking a man was only a minor sin, but still it was a sin. "Of course. You've been very kind to me."

"Kind!" The word almost exploded out of him. "I don't think anyone in my family can claim to have been truly kind to you—not from anything but pure selfishness, anyway."

Saronna didn't answer. Was he trying to tell her that he liked her? Would he change his mind and demand his rights as her protector? The thought made her dizzy with fear, but at the same time something stirred in her, a warm feeling deep in her core that alarmed her even more than Duncan's odd behavior.

The door opened, and a young man came into the library. Saronna recognized him as a Cameron Trushenko clerk.

"Oh, hello, Duncan," he said absently. He nodded politely to Saronna and sat down at one of the terminals. "Anyone using the projector?"

Saronna answered no, and Duncan left the room with a muttered goodbye.

She sat for a long time, debating what, if anything, had passed between the two of them. She would have to say a few extra prayers tonight. And she would have to be careful to guard her own feelings as well as the situation.

THAT afternoon, Saronna sat in the family courtyard with Naomi, both of them working their needlework.

The bright sun gave them warmth and plenty of light, and it was easy enough for Saronna to listen to Naomi's chatter with half her mind, while the other half recalled what Duncan had said and how he had looked earlier that day.

All at once Naomi fell silent. Saronna looked up to see Vonda Cameron approaching from the corridor.

"Good afternoon," Vonda said. She looked down at Naomi's embroidery frame where an elaborate version of the Cameron Trushenko logo, interwoven with Kruegerian flowers, took shape. "How lovely."

"Thank you," Naomi said, polite but stiff. "Won't you sit down?"

"In the ancient Terran past," Vonda said, sinking into a chair across from their bench, "young girls sewed what were called samplers. They were usually homilies about the virtues considered suitable for young women, embellished with designs or perhaps flowers, that used many different embroidery stitches. The finished picture would be framed and hung on the wall as a way of illustrating that the girl was both accomplished with a needle and well behaved."

Saronna nodded, willing to assume—or at least pretend to assume—that Vonda meant well. "Our women also show off their skills by making pictures purely for decoration."

"Ah, yes," Vonda nodded, "but of course, there wouldn't be any writing on them, would there?"

"Not usually," Saronna replied for Naomi, who was looking uncomfortable. "How do you come to know about these samplers? Did you dig them up in one of your buried cities?"

"No," Vonda said, her lips curving in a condescending smile. "I've seen them in museums. Textiles rarely survive being buried."

"Oh?" Saronna said. "My people kept very little knowledge of Terra's past. They saw it as sinful, so they made a point to forget about it."

"They forgot quite a lot, didn't they?" Vonda said. "Not only history but science, technology, psychology, even medicine. I understand Kruegerians don't even know enough to use birth control effectively. They breed unchecked, like animals." She glanced at Naomi and smiled again. "At least some of them do."

Saronna could see Naomi almost shrink into herself at this offhand reference to her childless state. How fortunate that Duncan had freed Saronna from any requirement to be respectful! "It's true we've forgotten quite a lot, but at least we haven't forgotten our manners. Even my father's wife at her most spiteful never let her jealousy of my mother make her rude in front of others."

Vonda looked surprised at this counterattack. She gave a light, high laugh and then spoke in a biting tone. "Do you think I care what Vladimir does to amuse himself? I haven't given it a thought in twenty-five years."

"I'm sorry to hear that," Saronna said. "At least jealousy would be an excuse, of sorts, for cruelty. Inflicting pain for no reason beyond your own amusement isn't a pleasant trait."

Vonda's eyes widened; her chin came up. "Why, you ignorant little backwoods rustic! How dare you judge me! Who the hell do you think you are?"

Saronna smiled, serene in the knowledge of her place in the household. "Why, I'm your son's woman. I thought you knew that?"

Vonda paled at this assertion. She opened her mouth as if she planned to refute the statement and then shut it again. Incoherent with rage, she jumped to her feet and stormed from the courtyard.

After she had gone, Naomi sighed. "Thank you for standing up for me. I can't do it for myself, not with her."

"It's all right," Saronna said. "Don't bother thanking me. I rather enjoyed it."

Naomi's eyes lit up as she leaned forward and spoke in a low voice. "Has Duncan—"

"No," Saronna said before Naomi could finish the question. She smiled again. "But his mother doesn't know that."

DUNCAN frowned at the holo image that had formed over his desk. Real-time transmissions tended to suffer both visual fuzziness as well as auditory problems. But the middle-aged woman's image looked clear enough, except around the edges. Had he heard her right? "They had a what?"

She frowned back at him. "A revolution. ThreeCon is imposing an interdiction, and recommending immediate evacuation of all off-worlders. Immediate, as in take what you can carry and get the hell out. They think some of the rebels have dirty weapons."

Duncan's heart sank. He had thought he had found a potential money-maker in exporting the work of the craftsmen of Ishtar, who made amazing artworks from the local volcanic glass. But apparently, the volcanoes weren't the only unstable things on that planet. Months of negotiations would go to waste, not to mention the cost of sending a team. "Okay, get everyone out as fast as you can. Don't worry about the cost. We'll cover it, and we'll replace everyone's lost belongings."

She nodded, relief somehow making the strain on her face more visible. "Will do."

She had just signed off when Duncan's assistant buzzed him.

"What is it, Kaveh?"

"Your mother's here," Kaveh's voice said as the door opened.

"Thanks."

Duncan stood up as his mother stormed into the room, slamming the door shut behind her. "Hello, Mom. Kaveh said you were on your way in. What's up?"

"Duncan Cameron Trushenko," Vonda said, as soon as she stood in front of his desk, "you tell me right now what there is between you and that little Kruegerian witch."

Duncan raised his eyebrows in surprise at this brusque demand. "She's not that little. I'll grant you the Kruegerian part. What makes you call her a witch?"

Vonda gave vent to a sharp exclamation of exasperation. "Duncan! Are you sleeping with her or not?"

He frowned, more than a little exasperated himself. "I've told you before, Mom—whom I sleep with is my business."

Vonda let out a Shuratanian obscenity that made Duncan's frown dissolve into a smile.

"It's no good cursing me with aspersions on my parentage. You're only insulting yourself."

She looked perilously close to stamping her foot on the floor. "Duncan, I want to know just how far this place has dragged you into its sexist, medieval mire. Are you using that woman in the way that men here use women?"

"No. I wouldn't ever do that. What brought this on, Mom?"

Vonda began to pace around the room. "She told me you were."

"Saronna?" Duncan said, astounded. "Saronna told you I was 'making use of her,' as you put it?"

"Not exactly." Vonda stopped pacing and threw herself into one of the chairs placed around the room for visitors. "She merely described herself as your woman."

Relief mixed with confusion in Duncan's mind. What was Saronna up to? Yes, he had told her she should speak her mind, but this seemed more like a deliberate attempt to conceal the truth than plain speaking. "That's hardly the same thing. Around here, as much as anything, that means I'm responsible for her welfare. I don't deny that. Dad put me in that position when he bought her from her father."

Vonda gave him a hard stare. "And that's it?"

"Look, Mom," Duncan said, sitting down next to her, "I won't allow you to pry into my personal life. I never have in the past, and I don't intend to start now. Why are you making such a fuss about this?"

Vonda met his eyes steadily. "Because you're my only child, and I care what happens to you. I don't want you to tie yourself to someone completely unsuitable. How can you meet a normal, educated woman when you have this little witch at home? Will you even look for one if she's laying herself at your feet the way that ninny does for your father?"

Duncan flinched. He hated it when she sounded cruel. "Mom! Will you stop insulting Naomi like that! Are you jealous or something?"

Vonda gave him a scornful look. "Do you think I care how many women your father takes to bed? Bah!"

"No," Duncan said. "I'm not suggesting you're jealous of Naomi because she has Dad; I'm suggesting you're jealous of Dad because he has Naomi."

Vonda looked away, and Duncan took her hand. "Is that it, Mom? You resent Dad because he found someone, and you still miss Pietro?"

She pulled her hand back quickly. "Don't you dare compare what I had with Pietro to your father's relationship with that empty-headed simpleton."

"Oh, come on, Mom," Duncan said gently. "I know you can be tough, but you've always been fair. Naomi was raised in an environment where she was never encouraged to learn anything beyond a prescribed set of skills. Dad may have taken her out of that, but she was already older than I am now when he found her. Is it really fair to call her names because she still shows the effect of her upbringing?"

Vonda made a face, a brief, spasmodic moue of distaste. "And I suppose your father felt nothing but compassion for her?"

Duncan smiled. "No, I doubt it. I'm sure he felt sorry for her, of course, but I'm almost certain he fell for her face as much as anything. She's a beautiful woman, Mom. Dad's neither blind nor feeble. But whatever started them out, they're very fond of each other now. That's as real as Naomi's looks, and it will last a lot longer."

Vonda's eyes studied his face as she spoke. "Saronna's not all that beautiful," she said, making it almost a question.

Happy she wasn't still tossing out insults, Duncan decided it was safer not to argue. "I'd call her attractive rather than beautiful."

Vonda seemed reassured by his assessment. She reached out one hand to stroke his cheek gently. "If I ever thought that Cameron Trushenko was ruining your life, I'd give up my share of it and go back to groveling to academic boards for funding."

Duncan grinned at this suggestion. "I have trouble imagining you groveling, but I know that, certainly."

Vonda sighed. "I wish I got to see you more, Duncan. An express isn't the same thing as being with you—not that you're all that good about sending expresses."

This mild complaint did a better job of making Duncan feel guilty than her angry tirade had. For one thing, this time she was right. "I know that, too. How about if I take tomorrow off and we'll see something of the city—the off-world quarter, anyway?"

"All right," Vonda said, sounding pleased at this offer. "I'll look forward to it."

She left him soon after, and Duncan went back to work. First he updated the project record for the Ishtar team, marking the change as urgent so his father would see it, and then he tried to go back to the sales reports he had been reading before the real-time transmission had interrupted him. After a while, he realized he couldn't concentrate. He had to know why Saronna had said what she said.

IMMERSED in her studies, Saronna jumped when a knock sounded on her door. "Come in," she called, feeling a thrill of accomplishment at the fact that she had control over who entered her room.

She was surprised when the person who came through the door was Duncan. He had never come to her rooms before. A chill of apprehension raced up her spine. Had he come to demand his rights? The fear dissipated as soon as she saw his face. He looked more curious than amorous as he glanced around at the furnishings, and at the terminal in her lap.

"Hello," he said.

"Hello. I thought you were working?"

"I am. I mean, I was. But I took a break because I wanted to talk to you."

Saronna nodded. "Please sit down." She was pleased with herself because she hadn't jumped to her feet when her protector entered the room.

"My mother came to see me a little while ago," Duncan said as he sat down on a chair diagonally placed from her sofa.

Saronna made no comment.

Duncan went on. "She was rather upset at something you said to her."

Saronna shrugged. "You told me I could speak my mind to her."

"I know I did. But you led her to believe that I was taking advantage of you."

Saronna smiled, remembering the moment with pleasure. "She was trying to put me in my place. I merely reminded her what my place is."

Duncan wrinkled his brow in a quick expression of dismay. "Your place?"

"Yes. My place. I told her I was your woman. Shouldn't I have said that?"

Duncan twisted his mouth in an almost grimace. "I suppose it seemed like a reasonable thing to say from your perspective."

"Certainly. I wouldn't have said it if it weren't true."

Duncan stared at her for a moment, and then he leaned over, put his face in his hands, and groaned.

"What's wrong?" Saronna asked, alarmed. Had she somehow broken a rule and not realized it?

Duncan sat up and let out a sigh. "How long have you been here, Saronna? Two weeks?"

"Fifteen days."

"Fifteen days," Duncan repeated.

Saronna made no reply, and Duncan sighed again.

"It seems longer somehow." He glanced at the book reader on the table in front of her that displayed an illustration of a map of Asia. "You've come a long way in fifteen days."

She nodded. "But not long enough if I still don't know the right thing to say."

He laughed ruefully. "Do any of us really know the right thing to say? I say the wrong thing all the time."

"When did you say something wrong?" Saronna asked, curious to hear what he considered a mistake.

"The first day I met you. I said I wasn't going to touch you, and then I did."

Saronna met his eyes but didn't speak. For some reason, her heart seemed to be beating very loudly.

"God help me," Duncan said. "I think I'm going to do it again."

Saronna still said nothing. Duncan moved from the chair to the sofa and slid over next to her. He removed the terminal from her grasp and put it on the table, and then slid one arm around her. Saronna's heart was pounding as he leaned toward her. She closed her eyes from reflex, and Duncan kissed her gently but firmly on the mouth.

Saronna opened her eyes and found him staring at her anxiously from very close range.

"Is it just me," he asked, "or do you feel something, too?"

She wanted to say yes, but she knew she couldn't. She couldn't let herself slip down that path, or she would be lost. What she wanted didn't matter. She had to keep her vow and her promise. Still, it might be possible to defuse the situation. His off-world scruples were strong enough to make him back off if she used them properly. "You asked me before if I liked you, and I said yes."

"Bah!" Duncan said, sounding very like his mother. "You called me kind. I'm not talking about kindness or gratitude. I want to know if you feel anything for me— attraction, affinity, call it whatever you like."

She knew what she had to do. Why was it so hard to make herself do it? Saronna looked at the floor for a moment, and then finally she raised her eyes to his. "Do you mean to enforce your rights," she said in a low voice, "or do I have a choice in this?"

Duncan let go of her as if she had been burning hot. "Of course you have a choice."

She took a deep breath. Why did it hurt to say the words? "Then I choose no."

Duncan stood up swiftly. "I think I get the message. I'll say good afternoon now."

Saronna didn't move until after he had left the room. She got up and locked the door, then went into the bedroom and opened the cupboard where she kept her shrine. She pulled it out and set it on the bed, and then knelt on the floor as she said the prayer for strength, repeating the words over and over in her mind as if somehow the ancient prayer could make her despise him as she should.

CHAPTER SIX

The next day Duncan borrowed a Cameron Trushenko flyter and took his mother on a tour of the plains around New Jerusalem. He swooped low over the ground so she could see a herd of red velvet duacorns racing across the grasslands; they all wheeled together in a turn when the flyter veered off.

Next Duncan took the flyter a little ways into the hills, following the Alfred River so that his mother could see the waterfalls for which it was famous. Beautiful, lacy sprays of silvery water shot out from a cliff face dotted with protruding rocks and crevices.

The water fell in sheets, straight down to a deep blue pool at the bottom.

"It's very pretty," Vonda said.

Duncan banked the flyter for a better view. "They call it Weeping Women Falls. They say the water comes from all the tears Alfred Krueger's women shed when he died."

Vonda snorted contemptuously. "All the tears they shed when he was alive would be more like it."

Duncan agreed, and turned the flyter back toward New Jerusalem. He gave the native quarter a wide berth, approaching the city from the south, the off-world side. Once he had landed the craft, they took a ground car and found a riverside restaurant, where they ate lunch and talked. Duncan found he had trouble keeping his mind on the conversation. His thoughts kept straying to Saronna. What was she doing while he was gone?

"You seem a little absentminded," Vonda said. "Am I keeping you from anything really big?"

Duncan started. "What? No, of course not. I'm sorry if I seem inattentive. I don't mean to be."

She smiled and changed the subject. As they were having dessert, she brought the conversation around to his friends. "So, how much longer will Sai and Randy be staying with you?"

"I don't know," Duncan said, pushing his plate away. "It depends on how well they do in recouping their investment capital. They were always a shoestring operation, but recently the shoestring almost broke clean through."

"She's a nice girl, Duncan. She still seems very fond of you."

"I'm fond of her," Duncan said, smiling a little impishly. "She's the sister I never had."

"Duncan! You're trying to provoke me."

"Of course I am. You're prying again."

Vonda sighed. "It's not fair. I don't get to see you for years on end, and when I do, you won't let me show a normal maternal concern for your welfare."

This made Duncan smile. "Is that what you call it when you try to fix me up with someone? I thought you were just being pushy."

Vonda glared at him, but lost her chance to retort when the servoid waiter rolled up to their table with the bill.

After lunch, they went to the park and watched the hover swans skim across the surface of the pond. A dozen animals spread their black wings out to catch the breeze, and then angled them exactly right so that they hydroplaned across the water, seining for small water insects with their net-like feet while barely getting their feathery fur wet.

Next, Duncan took his mother on a tour of the market where local crafts were for sale, and finally to a coffee shop where he bought her a cup of imported Terran coffee.

Vonda was impressed. "I haven't had real Terran coffee in years," she said with a sigh. "I'm amazed you can get it here in this backwater."

"You can get almost anything on Krueger's World if you pay enough for it."

Vonda gave him a speaking look.

Duncan burst out laughing. "Don't look at me like that! I didn't ask Dad to buy her, you know. And it isn't as if Saronna were some eager, little nymphet. She's damned independent, considering her upbringing, and she's not about to give me the time of day."

Vonda bit back a sound that was suspiciously like a snort.

"What?" Duncan said.

"Nothing," Vonda said hastily. "Nothing at all."

She refused to say anything more, so Duncan gave up and took her home.

"I'LL see you in two years, then," Vonda said three days later, as Duncan waited beside her for her shuttle to be called.

He nodded. "Let me know if you're coming back this way. If not, I can always take a few months and go see you somewhere else."

Her brow creased in a frown that was half annoy-ance and half fear. "I only hope I recognize you after two years in this feudal pit."

Duncan smiled and kissed her cheek. "Sure you will, Mom. I won't change."

She clung to him for a few moments, kissed him soundly when her shuttle was announced, and stifled a sob once he let go of her.

Duncan waited until the shuttle lifted off, and then he rode back to Cameron Trushenko headquarters in a pensive frame of mind.

He was in the parlor having a glass of Shuratanian ale when his father came in.

"There you are," Vladimir said. "I was looking for you. Did your mother's shuttle get off all right?"

Duncan nodded. "No problems."

"Good." Vladimir said, a poorly disguised note of satisfaction creeping into his tone. "I wanted to ask you something. How's Saronna doing with her studies?"

The question surprised Duncan, as his father had never mentioned the subject before. "Fine, I think. I haven't spoken to her about it lately. Which reminds me I still need to find her a tutor. Why do you ask?"

His father grimaced. "Well, the thing is, Vonda gave Naomi a bad time when she was here. I had never realized it, but Naomi's rather sensitive about not being able to read. I did suggest a tutor once, but she was too shy to have a stranger come to teach her. She wondered if Saronna would be willing to try it."

Duncan could see advantages to this plan. It might give Saronna more self confidence to teach someone else. "I think she might. You could ask her, anyway."

"But *you* have no objection to Saronna playing tutor?"

"No," Duncan said, irritated. "I have no reason to object and no right to, either. She's free to do as she pleases."

"I know, I know," Vladimir said soothingly. "Naomi wanted me to ask you first, that's all. I only asked to make her comfortable with it."

Mollified, Duncan went back to his ale, and Vladimir went off to tell Naomi the good news.

"WHEN do I get to read a book?" Naomi demanded.

"As soon as you know enough words," Saronna said firmly. "You've only been studying for a few weeks. Now try it again."

Naomi struggled through the basic vocabulary Saronna had displayed on the screen of a library terminal. She needed help with several words, and finally let out an alien curse in exasperation.

Someone laughed. Saronna turned toward the back of the room and was surprised to see Duncan standing by the door.

"You learned that from Dad," he said to Naomi. "You might want to ask him what it means, some time when the two of you are alone."

Naomi blushed prettily, muttered an excuse about a forgotten chore, and almost ran from the room.

"I'm sorry," Duncan said. "I didn't mean to scare her away."

"It's all right," Saronna said, getting to her feet. "It was time to quit anyway. She gets bored easily."

Duncan moved farther into the room. "There are some educational programs that might help her. They're designed for children, but they're very clever, and they might keep her interested. I could get a few of them if you'd like to try them."

"Thank you," Saronna said, trying not to sound stiff. After what had passed between them before, being alone with him made her uneasy. "That would be very kind."

"Kind!" His expression looked fierce, as if he were angry. "There you go again, calling me kind. I'm not a kind person, Saronna."

"Yes, you are." She said the words with conviction, aware of feeling that somehow even this was a sin.

"No. Believe me, as I stand here looking at you, I'm not having kind thoughts at all."

She looked down at the floor at this, afraid to meet his eyes. She stared at the floor tiles, finding the hexagonal pattern suddenly fascinating.

Duncan took two steps nearer.

"I know I'm almost a stranger to you," he said seriously, "but I feel as if I've known you for years instead of only months. I can't stand it when you look as if you're afraid of me. Do you think you could ever see me in a different light?"

Saronna hesitated, unsure of what to say that would discourage him. She couldn't seem to concentrate; for some reason she could only breathe in short, shallow breaths, almost as if she had been running. Just as she looked up, Duncan closed the distance between them and swooped her up in his arms. Unprepared for him to be so close so soon, Saronna offered no resistance. When his mouth covered hers, she yielded completely, and even put her arms around his neck and clutched him tightly. She felt so safe, and yet so excited, that the contrast made her dizzy.

When Duncan finally let her go, both of them were breathing rapidly.

Duncan's eyes lit with a glad light. "Saronna! You do feel something for me, don't you?"

She shrank back from him in sudden alarm as she realized what she had done.

"What's wrong?" Duncan said anxiously.

"I," Saronna began. "I can't." It was hopeless. She couldn't let herself care for him, and she couldn't tell him why.

"What is it? If I'm moving too fast for you, I can slow down. I just need to know you feel something back."

"Yes," Saronna said, desperate enough to accept the lie. "It's too fast. It's all happening too fast."

Duncan smiled and stepped back a pace. He took her hand and kissed her palm lightly. "All right. I'll go slower. No more surprise attacks."

She nodded wordlessly.

He squeezed her hand before he let it go. "Maybe we can talk a little bit after supper?"

"That would be nice," she heard herself say. Why had she said that? She should have claimed she had a headache or a chore to do.

"Good," he said firmly. "It's a date."

She nodded again. He seemed happy with that response, as he smiled at her before he slipped through the door.

Saronna sat down, transfixed by her dilemma. What could she do? She could try to contact Brushka, to see if the old woman had any kind of potion that would help her fight this feeling.

No, she couldn't do that. If she did, Leah would find out. With a gasp, Saronna realized she could suffer her mother's fate. When she recalled her mother's unhappiness, Saronna put her head on the desk and tried not to cry. After a few moments, she lost the battle.

IT was almost a week later that the security guard buzzed Saronna on the com set to tell her that her brother was at the door.

Saronna rushed to the foyer to meet him. After a brief embrace, she took him into the parlor. She ordered refreshments on the com, feeling almost as if she were Naomi, then asked him to sit down. Paul looked around at the furnishings with interest.

"These off-worlders must be rich," he said, sinking down into a comfortable chair.

"Their business is very profitable," Saronna said, sitting in the adjacent chair. She had already learned that neither Duncan nor his father cared to be called rich, even though to her, it was obvious that they were.

"Are you well?" Paul asked.

"I'm very well. How is everyone at home?"

"They're doing fine. Ruth is going to be married."

"Is she?" Saronna said in surprise. "Who's to be her husband?"

"Eli Pederson."

Saronna had to work to place the name in her memory. "Cousin Abraham's brother-in-law?"

Paul nodded. "Yes. His wife died a few months ago, and he wants to marry again."

"But he's older than Father!"

Her brother's reply was cut off as the door opened and Letitia Dubai brought in a tray. She placed the tray on the table, nodded at Saronna, and left with no more than a casual goodbye.

"That woman seems very forward," said Paul. "And her clothes are indecent. Whose woman is she?"

"She works here," Saronna said. She recalled the few occasions she had met Eli Pederson at their cousin's house. He had not struck her as a kind person. His wife had seemed thoroughly downtrodden, in a way that her mother and Leah never had. "How can Father want Ruth to marry Sire Pederson?"

Paul looked uncomfortable. "It was Mother's idea. He has sons already, so she won't be in danger of being put aside if he has no heir."

Of course. Leah would be concerned for her daughter's status, but not expect or want her to care for her husband. To her, a long widowhood would be an advantage. Saronna bit her lip. Ruth would be married off to another household, and Saronna would have no way to help her if she was unhappy.

Paul took a pastry from the tray. "And since Father made so much money when he sold you, he was able to offer a good dowry. I heard him talking to Mother about it."

Saronna nodded absently, her mind still working on the problem of Ruth's marriage. "He was pleased, I know, to do so well from such an elderly spinster as I was."

Paul frowned as he finished chewing. "He should have tried harder to find a husband for you, instead of selling you like that."

Saronna leaned over and patted his arm. "Don't fret about it. I'm content here."

He seemed more disposed to believe her this time, so she changed the subject to family events. After a discussion of his studies and their youngest sister Rebecca's failings, he rose to go.

"I'll come again when I can," he said, kissing her cheek.

"When are the arrangements to be final for the wedding?" Saronna asked.

"Sire Pederson is coming to dinner tonight," Paul said. "If they can agree on terms, the wedding should take place in a few weeks."

Saronna saw him to the door. He kissed her cheek again and said goodbye. Saronna stood with her hand on the door latch. She had to act fast. She turned and found Duncan standing behind her.

"Oh," she said. Ever since the day he had kissed her in the library, she had avoided being alone with him as much as she could.

Duncan smiled. "Don't worry; I rarely bite anyone."

"Of course not," Saronna said, her mind working on the problem of how she could get to Samaria. She and Naomi often walked together in the off-world quarter, so she had learned her way around that part of New Jerusalem. She knew a place where she could hire a ground car. But once she got to Samaria, she couldn't go anywhere alone or she would be arrested—or worse.

She needed Duncan's help.

"Everything okay at home?"

It was as good an opening as she could hope for. "Not entirely. My father is trying to arrange a marriage for my sister Ruth."

His face went blank. "Isn't that good news?"

She debated the best way to describe the situation in a way that would arouse his sympathy. "He wants her to marry a widower older than himself. I don't think Ruth would be happy with him."

"Hmm." His expression looked not so much sympathetic as guarded, like someone who didn't want to get involved.

"Do you think you could take me to Samaria tonight?" She lifted her eyes to his, trying to assess his reaction.

His expression had gone from guarded to surprised.
"Samaria? Tonight?"

"I'd like to see my sister."

His expression cleared. "Oh, of course."

Just like that. He didn't understand that she wasn't
part of the Maynard family anymore, and thus couldn't
just walk in the door. Well, he would find out very
soon, but she wouldn't explain it now. "Could we leave
right after dinner?"

"No problem. I'll arrange to use one of the flyters."

Now all she had to do was be sure that Naomi didn't
explain to Duncan how much it went against custom to
show up at her father's house uninvited.

But then, Saronna was keeping Naomi's secret about
the love potion. Surely a reminder of that would make
the other woman keep silent. Saronna went off to find
her veil. She hadn't worn it since her second day in the
Trushenko house, but she would need it in Samaria—
her old clothes and her old demeanor.

THEY left the flyter on the open pasture land near
the edge of town and walked through the streets.
Duncan resisted Saronna's direction to walk in front of
her, but she insisted.

"That's how we do things here. Please, Duncan."

He gave in and walked ahead of her, muttering over
his shoulder about primitive customs.

Saronna paid no attention. It wasn't Duncan she needed to worry about. He would do as she asked and knock on her father's door. But would her father let them in? It occurred to her that Duncan and her father had never met. That might work to her advantage. And Paul would support her if it came to pleading for admittance.

The sun was low in the sky as they came near the house. Her father and Sire Pederson would have finished dinner and moved to the courtyard so the women of the household could eat. They would make polite conversation while they waited for Leah to bring them drinks. Only after beer or a similar beverage had been served would they start the marriage negotiations. No one ever rushed these things. Unlike her father's negotiations with Vladimir, marriage linked two families in ways that could never be broken. The dowry had to be negotiated, and a date for the ceremony had to be set, and neither side should feel cheated or slighted in any way.

Hopefully, they wouldn't yet have begun any serious conversation. It was lucky that formal meals were held so much later than the usual dinnertime or she could not have gotten here in time.

They started up her family's street. Saronna glanced at the park across the way, where she had played as a small child, before she was old enough to wear a veil. No one played there now. It was too late in the day.

Her house loomed in front of them. Her father's house, she corrected herself. She didn't live here anymore. She looked up at the tall gray walls covered with gray-green moss-vines, and smelled the sweet scent of the sugar bushes that grew by the front door. She had been born in this house, but it was home no longer.

Duncan turned toward the door. "So this is it?"

"Yes." Better to wait until they were committed to clarify the situation. She waited until they were on the steps, then stepped back behind him. "Would you pull the bell, please?"

He tugged on the rope and Saronna could hear the bell pealing in the courtyard. Would her father come himself, or send Paul or Gideon? "I should explain," she said in a rush. "We haven't been invited. Father will be surprised to see you—to see us. It might be better if he thought this visit was your idea and not mine. In fact, you'll have to introduce me as your woman because Father will pretend he doesn't know me. And he doesn't know Paul comes to visit me," she added, suddenly remembering that revealing this fact could get Paul into trouble. "Please don't mention seeing him."

Duncan swung around to look at her. His eyes hint-
ed at a frown, but before he could speak, the door
opened and light streamed onto the porch.

Duncan swiveled back to face the door. Saronna
peered around him. Her father had come himself. He
wore his best brown suit, so Sire Pederson must indeed
be here.

Josiah Maynard looked up at the tall off-worlder in
front of him. "Yes? Who are you and what do you
want?"

Duncan cleared his throat. "Sire Maynard, please
forgive this intrusion. My name is Duncan Trushenko
and I—uh, that is my father is the man who—um—"

Josiah frowned and tugged his beard, not a good
sign. "I know who you are." His eyes flickered toward
Saronna then back at Duncan's face; the frown
deepened to a scowl. He had seen her.

A sudden chill went through Saronna. He would
think Duncan was bringing her home because she had
been unsatisfactory.

"The thing is," Duncan picked up the narrative, "I
wasn't there when my father, uh, bought Saronna, and,
uh, I thought I should meet you."

Her father's eyes cleared. Saronna saw relief. He
swung the door open wider. "Come in."

"Thank you," Duncan said, stepping over the
threshold. "I hope we haven't come at a bad time."

The slightest of frowns returned to Josiah's face. Duncan shouldn't have used the plural pronoun.

Duncan seemed to realize he had slipped. He bowed and then indicated Saronna with a small wave. "I brought my woman. I hope that's all right."

Josiah nodded and bowed back to Duncan, not quite so deeply, as he was, after all, a patriarch while Duncan wasn't. "She can go to the women's parlor with the others." He looked directly at Saronna for the first time, then jerked his head toward the corridor behind him. "I'm afraid I don't have much time to spare. I have another visitor who has come on family business."

"Of course," Duncan said. "I apologize for disturbing you."

Saronna slipped away. If the women were in their parlor, they must have finished eating. Perhaps Leah had even served the men their drinks. Saronna made her way to the women's parlor and opened the door.

They were all there. Her grandmother sat in the place of honor nearest the fireplace, with the widowed cousin employed to care for the old lady on her other side. Leah sat near her, but Gideon's wife wasn't present. She must be in her own courtyard.

Rebecca and Ruth stood by the window, peering through the slats in the shutters, their two blonde heads together. It seemed very strange to Saronna to see shutters on an inside window again. And how shabby and old-fashioned the room looked!

"Who can it be?" Rebecca was saying. "Mother, come and see. His clothes are very strange."

"His name is Duncan Trushenko," Saronna said.

They all turned to stare at her.

Rebecca gave a tiny shriek and ran across the room toward her. "Saronna! Saronna! It's you!"

Leah stood up. "Why have you come back? Have you disgraced us?"

Rebecca stopped in her tracks, and Ruth gave an anxious cry.

"No," Saronna said. Strange how being away for so long had changed her thinking. She hadn't thought about the disgrace involved in being sent back until she had seen her father's frown. "But Duncan wanted to meet my father, so of course I couldn't refuse to come."

Rebecca smiled with relief and darted forward to throw her arms around Saronna. "I'm so happy to see you. Are you well? Tell me everything!"

Saronna returned Rebecca's embrace and Ruth's more decorous hug, and then went to kiss her grandmother on her cheek.

The old woman smiled up at her, her gray eyes bewildered. "Saronna? I haven't seen you in a while. Did you get married?"

Saronna embraced her widowed cousin briefly, then returned to her grandmother's side. "No, Grandmother, but I have a protector now."

The old woman patted her hand. "Well, well. You're settled at any rate."

"Yes, I'm settled." Saronna looked up.

Leah was still glaring at her. Rebecca and Ruth had gone back to the window.

"I hope your protector's visit doesn't disrupt the negotiations," Leah said.

"What negotiations?" Saronna said, hoping she sounded convincingly curious.

"Her father is arranging a marriage for Ruth," Leah said, her voice laden with maternal satisfaction.

"To whom?" Saronna asked. She moved toward the window to stand beside Ruth.

"Eli Pederson," Leah said.

"Really?" Saronna did her best to sound surprised. "Well, he's older, but then he's already a patriarch. At least he has a nice house." She peered through the slats of the shutters. Eli Pederson sat in a chair across from her father while Duncan sat with his back to the parlor. "And of course, Ruth has met him already, several times."

"Yes," Ruth said.

Saronna couldn't tell if her sister was content with the marriage or not. Leah had brought all her daughters up as Believers, but it had always seemed to Saronna that Rebecca, at least, didn't believe everything her mother taught her. Ruth was more dutiful. Did she truly not care whom she married?

Ruth moved away from the window. "I've seen him before. I don't need to steal a glance through the shutters to see what he looks like."

"He looks a lot like Father," Rebecca said. "Except fatter."

Ruth let out a small sob.

"Ruth!" Leah's voice was as sharp as a vintner's knife and just as barbed. "There will be no more of that nonsense."

Ruth hung her head. "I'm sorry, Mother. I will be good."

"I should hope so." Leah frowned. "Come away from the window, all of you, and sit down."

Ruth and Rebecca moved to obey her at once. Rebecca looked chastened and Ruth resigned. Saronna took one last long look through the shutters at Eli Pederson. He sat with his profile toward her—a long nose, wiry brows, his thick beard more gray than black, his dark hair streaked with gray. He wore a stiff blue suit with buff-colored facings on the lapels. Saronna stared at his chest, where a gold vest was barely visible under his coat.

"Come away!" Leah said.

Saronna took a chair beside Rebecca, but she kept in her mind a picture of Eli Pederson sitting on his chair, sipping a glass of beer with her father.

DUNCAN could feel the hair standing up on the back of his neck. What the hell was Saronna up to with this visit? And why hadn't she warned him he would be so unwelcome? As polite as Josiah Maynard was, it was clear he wished Duncan elsewhere.

Eli Pederson seemed equally annoyed. It was only after several minutes of oblique conversation that it dawned on Duncan that Pederson wasn't merely a crony of Josiah's, he was the potential son-in-law Saronna had mentioned.

Duncan sat there, wondering how long he needed to wait before he brought up the idea of leaving. Clearly, it wouldn't be up to Saronna to initiate their departure. It looked to Duncan like she couldn't even show herself unless she was summoned.

Josiah was asking about the Trushenko business.

Duncan answered, but he was wondering about the Maynard family. "Where are your sons, Sire Maynard? You have two sons, I believe?"

Josiah looked pleased to bring the topic back to family. "Yes. My son Gideon has his own courtyard. Paul has gone out to check on a problem at the vineyard."

Duncan opened his mouth to ask how large the vineyard was when Eli Pederson suddenly gave a small groan.

"What's wrong, Eli?" Josiah asked.

Pederson wiped sweat from his forehead. "Nothing, nothing. Just a touch of heartburn."

Josiah frowned, perhaps seeing this complaint as an aspersion on his hospitality. "Can I bring you anything?"

"Water," Pederson croaked.

"You don't look at all well," Duncan said, noting the older man's pallor. "Maybe you should call a doctor?"

Pederson shook his head. He flexed his left arm as if it pained him. "I'll be fine. We need to talk, Josiah."

Josiah had fetched a glass of water from the table near the window, but now he set it down. "Of course." He looked at Duncan. "Perhaps it would be best—"

Pederson gave a sharp cry and slid out of his chair and onto the floor.

Duncan jumped to his feet and joined Josiah Maynard in bending over the fallen man.

"He has no pulse!" Josiah said after several seconds of holding his hand to Pederson's neck. "I'll send for a doctor."

He dashed from the room.

Duncan rolled Pederson onto his back and made sure his airway wasn't blocked. He debated what to do. Pederson looked paler every second. Duncan pulled out his pocket com, checked the menu, and found the defib setting. He ripped open Pederson's shirt, laid the device on the man's bare chest, and set the timer for a ten second delay. Then he stepped back a pace and waited.

SARONNA sat silently in the flyter and watched the countryside whiz past. The view had no power to entrance her. She hadn't meant to come so close to killing someone.

"You're very quiet," Duncan said. "How was your visit with you sister?"

Saronna stirred in her seat. "She seems well."

Duncan turned his head and gave her a curious glance.

Saronna wasn't used to the idea that he didn't need to steer the vehicle once its flight had begun. His lack of attention to the controls made her even more nervous.

"Well," Duncan said, "I don't think you need to worry about your sister marrying that old guy. Your father seems to have gone off the idea."

"Yes."

He made a face. "I wish you had told me ahead of time that it's not good manners to come calling without an invitation."

Saronna looked at her hands. "I was afraid if I told you, you wouldn't want to go, and I needed to see Ruth."

He said nothing for a few seconds. Then he turned his head back to looking out the front window. "I suppose it's just as well. Your people don't seem to know what to do for a heart attack."

Saronna took a deep breath. A heart attack. She had caused a man to suffer a heart attack. All she had wanted to do was make him look too sickly to make a good husband. "My father was very grateful. It would have embarrassed my family to have a guest die after a meal. My father told Leah that you saved Sire Pederson's life."

Duncan shook his head. "For now. If he doesn't get the problem treated, it'll only happen again. He told the doctor he's been having twinges of pain for days."

Saronna let out a breath. It wasn't all her fault. The man had had a bad heart to begin with.

"Relax," Duncan said. "All's well that ends well. Your father knows now there are disadvantages to having a son-in-law older than he is. Maybe he'll find someone younger next time."

"Yes, maybe he will."

Duncan gave her an oblique glance from the corner of his eye. "And at least we've had this chance to be alone for a bit, without Dad or Naomi walking in on us."

Saronna froze.

Duncan let out a sigh. "I really wish you wouldn't do that."

She caught her breath. "Do what?" she said, as naturally as she could.

"Look terrified."

Saronna lifted her chin. "I'm not afraid of you." She realized it was the truth. Regardless of what Leah had said, regardless of how her parents had lived, Duncan would never hurt her. It wasn't him she had to worry about, it was herself, her own weakness.

He turned his head to look at her full face. "Then why do you get that wild-animal-caught-in-a-trap look every time I say anything at all romantic."

She would have to work on hiding her reactions more. "I'm not afraid of you," she repeated. "I'm just not used to the kind of relationships you're used to."

"I guess not."

A beeping noise sounded from the console. Duncan took the controls. "We're home."

Looking down at the pool of light the roof port made in the darkness, Saronna realized with a shock that setting down on the roof of the Trushenko house did indeed make her feel like she was coming home— much more than she had felt walking through the front door of her father's house in Samaria.

SARONNA heard the laughter before she stepped into the courtyard.

Sai Whisset half reclined on a bench. Randy Kumar leaned against one of the corner pillars. Duncan sat in a chair near Sai's bench, and Naomi did needlework on another bench opposite the off-world woman.

"I remember!" Duncan said, laughing. He pointed toward Randy. "You locked me out on purpose, you bastard!"

Randy grinned. "That's five credits you owe me, Sai."

She shook her head. "No way. I never took that bet."

"Welsher!" Randy jerked himself upright to give Sai a fake glare.

"So who's ahead?" Duncan asked.

"I've lost track," Randy said.

"Randy is," Sai said. "By two hundred and thirty credits."

"Two hundred and forty-five," Randy corrected.

"I thought you weren't keeping track," Duncan said.

"I was just trying to be a gentleman," Randy said.

"What was so funny?" Saronna asked.

"Not that much," Duncan said. "We were just recalling our days at university together. Randy and I used to room together."

"Yes," Sai said. "And Duncan and I were lovers for a while. Randy locked Duncan out during one of our dates."

Saronna met Naomi's eyes. Naomi had been correct in her assessment. Could she also be right that Randy loved Sai? "That seems more cruel than amusing."

"It was cruel then," Duncan said. "But it's funny now." His pocket com beeped. He glanced at it and then stood up. "Good news, guys. You got that membership in the day market. The terminal should be here tomorrow."

Instantly, Sai was on her feet. "Really? I thought it took months."

Duncan tapped the side of his nose with one finger. "Dad knows some people."

"Great!" Randy said. "When do we get it?"

Duncan was still looking at his com. "You're required to install it in a secure location—a room that locks, at the very least. Let's go find an office for you. I know we have some empty rooms."

His friends made no protest, and the three of them left without any more ado.

"What is the day market?" Saronna asked, sitting down across from Naomi.

The older woman shrugged to show her disinterest. "It's a place to sell things, almost like a club. You have to be a member, and everything you offer has to be available for delivery within a day."

"Where is this club?"

Naomi waved a hand. "Oh, it's not a real place. They use machines to post notices and make bids, almost like an auction, but no one is really there physically." She leaned over and whispered. "I was right about those two."

Saronna leaned over and whispered back. "What do you mean?"

Naomi smiled. "He loves her, and she loves him, but neither of them will say anything to the other."

"Are you sure?"

She nodded. "I've studied her carefully. Whenever he's near another woman, she watches him. She does it very discreetly, but I can tell."

It relieved Saronna's mind to know that Sai didn't love Duncan, but still she remembered how casual the off-world woman had been about their past relationship. "She said she and Duncan had been lovers."

Naomi picked up her needlework. "Off-worlders don't always love those they call lovers. Sometimes they just want sex."

The more Saronna thought about this, the less it reassured her. If Duncan wanted sex—and men always wanted sex—and Sai was handy, who was to say he wouldn't go back to her, just as her father had often gone to Leah when her mother had refused him.

All in all, it would be best if Sai were no longer available as a lover.

THAT night after she said her prayers, Saronna sat for quite a while thinking over what she had learned that morning, and debating what she should do about it.

She went over to the terminal Duncan had given her. "I wish to use the encyclopedia," she said firmly, as if the terminal were a servant she was trying to impress.

"Encyclopedia active," a disembodied voice responded. Saronna had become used to it, and no longer jumped when the terminal spoke back to her.

"Tell me about com sets," Saronna said. "I want to see illustrations of the inside of a com set, with an explanation of what the parts do."

CHAPTER SEVEN

"**G**ood afternoon, Saronna."

Saronna looked up from her book. Duncan stood in the library doorway with another man next to him. The stranger had black hair and brown eyes, and a pinched look to his face, as if he worried too much. He was shorter than Duncan, but he had a stockier build, and he carried a portable terminal under one arm.

"This is Kendall Umberto," Duncan said, moving into the room. "He's the tutor I found for you."

She had thought Duncan had forgotten about getting her a tutor, as he hadn't mentioned it recently.

She put the reader down and got to her feet. "Hello," she said, holding her hand out to the stranger.

He fumbled with his terminal, switching it to his other hand so he could shake hers. "Hello, Miss, uh, Saronna."

"I'm so glad you're going to teach me," Saronna said. "I never got to go to school."

Kendall grimaced. "No, well, of course, if you—I mean that is, here on Krueger's World—well, ah—"

Duncan interrupted. "Saronna is mostly self-taught. But she's very bright, and I'm sure you'll be able to teach her quite a lot."

"We'll be fine, Duncan," Saronna said, tranquil in the face of Kendall's obvious embarrassment. She was used to awkwardness from off-worlders. Many of the Cameron Trushenko staff treated her like someone who had escaped from a barbarian regime.

After Duncan left, she invited the tutor to sit, and then took the chair next to his.

Kendall opened the terminal and began asking her a series of rapid-fire questions on a variety of topics.

Saronna answered as best she could. Some questions were easy, but others left her feeling very ignorant.

"Gosh," he said, checking her answers off. "You're all over the map. You have a good knowledge of a few periods of history, a smattering of exposure to natural sciences, only the most basic math skills, and absolutely no awareness of physics."

"My mother taught me how to read, but I had very few books," Saronna said, recalling the hidden volumes her mother had smuggled into her father's house, part of the underground library still treasured by Believers, even the ones who couldn't read. "Until I came here, no one ever encouraged me to learn anything. But lately I've been doing nothing but read."

"Ah, yes," Kendall said, still frowning at his screen. "Well, to get you started, I think we'd better rely on elementary texts for math and the sciences. We can jump up to whatever level is appropriate on the social sciences."

Jumping sounded good. Saronna nodded her approval.

In the next few days, Saronna discovered what the right kind of textbook could do when one knew how to use it. Kendall gave her a child's math book that would count with her in various sequences, prompt her when she made a mistake, give her simple problems to solve, offer help if she needed it, praise her when she got the problems right, and encourage her when she did them wrong.

"You hardly need a teacher at all with a book like this," she said.

He smiled with disdain, almost literally looking down his nose at her as he stood by her desk. "Most people think that, but it's not true. A book is only a tool. Another person is still the best teacher."

Saronna smiled to herself at his pride, but the more time she spent with him, the more she came to appreciate his point of view. She learned a great deal more in the first two weeks he came to the house than she had in the previous two months, when she was merely browsing through the information in the Cameron Trushenko library.

"If you want to learn to read in Standard," Kendall said, the next day, "it would be a good idea." He nodded at the door. "If you ever want to leave here and get a job, it would be easier if you could read Standard instead of needing everything to be translated."

He was assuming she would only work in the off-world quarter. Well, that was probably true, at least until she was too old to sell. Certainly, Saronna saw no joy in living as a servant in a relative's house.

"I'd like to try," Saronna said.

He smiled, obviously pleased. "I'll find a child's text to start, but I'm sure you'll advance beyond that really fast. You're a quick study, Saronna."

Was there warmth in his tone when he said her name? Saronna wished she knew more about men and women's interactions among off-worlders when it wasn't business. Surely a tutor would keep a proper distance from his student. "Thank you."

He opened his mouth like he was going to speak, but it changed to a cough, and he turned his head away.

He seemed friendly but brisk for the rest of the session, so Saronna decided there was nothing in her suspicions.

A little over three weeks later Duncan came into the library one afternoon when Saronna was writing on her terminal.

"How is it going?" he asked.

"Fine," she said, barely looking up.

"You're at it very late. It's almost dinner time."

She nodded. "I have an assignment to finish. I'm working on ecology now. Kendall showed me a program on a variety of worlds, and how the one thing all worlds have in common is that each is a closed ecosystem." She said the phrase with pride, conscious of a sense of accomplishment that she understood it.

"That's a pretty good explanation of ecology for a woman from Samaria," Duncan said.

"Kendall has helped me a good deal already. Thank you for finding him for me."

"Glad you like him," Duncan said, smiling warmly. Suddenly his expression changed to one of concern and he shook his head. "God, I never thought—I hope you don't go getting too fond of him. I'd kick myself if you did."

"Kendall?" Saronna said. She liked the tutor well enough, but the idea that she might develop feelings for him was absurd. She was pretty sure he had tried to flirt with her, but she had politely refused his offers to go on walks through the city, or to attend a concert. "Pho!"

"I hope that means what I think it means," Duncan said, stepping closer.

Saronna hid a smile. "It's not entirely polite."

"Good. I've been very well behaved these last two weeks, don't you think? I stayed away and let you get on with your studies."

"Yes. You did."

"I think I deserve a reward," Duncan said firmly. "I know we're going slow and all that, but I think it would be very nice if *you* kissed *me* for a change."

Saronna's heart thumped in her chest. The fact that he was asking, not demanding, didn't change the requirements of her vow. "Someone might come in."

Duncan smiled and shook his head. "Nope, I thought of that." He held out his hand and Saronna saw that he held the door key. "Well? Do I get a kiss or not?"

Saronna hesitated. He looked so expectant, she hated to hurt his feelings. And after all, he had kissed her before and nothing else had happened between them. Surely merely giving him a kiss couldn't be considered anything but a minor sin, something that could absolved with a few extra prayers.

"All right," she said, rising to her feet.

Duncan waited, and Saronna stepped up to him slowly. She lifted her head, took his face in her hands, pulled him down to her height, and kissed him.

Duncan stood with his hands at his sides until the moment that Saronna pressed her mouth to his. At that point, he suddenly put his arms around her, and Saronna knew that she had underestimated him. He pulled her close and held her tightly.

Saronna let out a little sigh. It felt so wonderful when he held her. How could anything that felt so wonderful be a sin? Surely it wouldn't hurt to let him keep holding her?

And then he pressed his body against hers, and she felt his arousal.

Panic overwhelmed her. He wanted her, and she wanted him—in spite of her vows, in spite of all her mother had taught her, she wanted this man! Fear threatened to swallow her up. How could she stay strong in the face of this temptation? In desperation, she invoked her gift to suppress his desire as firmly as she had once suppressed it in his father.

Duncan let her go and let out a reluctant sigh. "I've been working too hard lately," he said. "But maybe it's just as well?"

"Yes."

"Thank you for the kiss. It was very nice."

"You're welcome."

Duncan tilted her chin to study her face. "You look almost sad. Am I that hard to take?"

"No!" Saronna said, surprised at her own fierceness.

"That sounds better," Duncan said, with a smile. "I'll let you get back to work now. When is Kendall coming to check your assignments?"

"Not until tomorrow afternoon," Saronna said, still a little breathless. "He was here this morning for several hours."

He nodded. "I'll see you at dinner, then?"

Saronna agreed. After he left, she sat down and tried to resume her studies, but she couldn't make herself concentrate on ecology.

DUNCAN returned to his own office to find Kaveh waiting for him with the news that the datawork had gone through on the purchase of a new freighter. A Cameron Trushenko crew would be boarding her in the immediate future.

"Great!" Duncan said. "Just in time for that electronics deal."

"Your father's in the parlor having a glass of wine to celebrate," Kaveh said.

"I think I'll join him," Duncan said.

But when he arrived at the parlor, Duncan found Randy Kumar sitting there by himself, to all appearances lost in thought.

"Hi, Ran," Duncan said. "Is Dad around? Kaveh said he was here."

Randy sat up straighter. "He was. Naomi showed up and took him off to look at some pattern for new drapes, or something."

Duncan poured himself a glass of ale. "Like a drink?"

"No thanks. I already had one with your father. I don't want to get plastered this early in the day."

Sai Whisset strode into the room. "Am I interrupting?"

"Never," Randy said promptly. "Anything up? You look wired."

She did look as if she was holding in some exciting news. "I am wired." She showed her teeth in a feral grin. "I've got us a deal, Ran!"

Randy leaned back in his chair. "Tell me about it."

Impervious to Duncan's presence, Sai dragged a chair closer to where Randy sat, plopped herself down in it, and began to expound on the details of her newfound opportunity.

It did sound to Duncan like it was a good bet for Kumar and Whisset. Sai had met a freighter captain whose biggest customer had gone bankrupt. The customer was unable to pay the shipping fees for the freight he had hired the vessel to carry, and the captain needed to empty his ship in order to take on new cargo and meet his contractual obligation with his next set of customers. The charter for the New Jerusalem off-world quarter gave him the right to dispose of the cargo as he chose, and the captain was willing to let it go very cheaply to anyone who could guarantee his holds would be empty by the following night.

"What's the cargo?" Randy asked.

"Stasis units are the only big ticket items," Sai said. "Eight hundred units. Also, eight gross of recyclers, three of food synthesizers, all low end models. Most of the rest of it is hydroponic lights, two hundred thousand of them."

Randy looked glum. "No way, Sai. It's too big for us. We can't afford that kind of volume."

"But, Randy," Sai insisted, "we'll never get this kind of chance again! The unit price is so low, we'll make a bundle even if we unload it all cheap."

"What the hell does the unit price matter if we don't have the money?" Randy said. "You said the guy wants to move the whole thing as one lot. There's no way we can cover the purchase price, let alone the transport fees."

She shook his shoulder impatiently. "Listen, idiot! We can lay it all out in small lots on the day market tonight, and have the purchase price covered when we take delivery tomorrow. By the time the draft clears, it'll be good."

Randy set his jaw. "*If* this captain is willing to take a post-dated draft, and *if* we can cover the transport and warehouse fees. Then we have to worry that no one stiffs us or backs out at the last minute, or we'll end up in deep trouble. No way, Sai! I may have been the one to go berserk the last time, but this time I'm being smart for the both of us."

"I'll cover it for you," Duncan said.

They both turned startled faces toward him, as if they had forgotten he was there.

"What?" Sai said, frowning.

"I'll cover the purchase price," Duncan said. "You can pay me back after you sell the stuff."

Sai looked hopefully at Randy, but he shook his head.

"No, thanks anyway, Dunc," he said. "We can't borrow from a friend."

"It seems like a low risk loan to me," Duncan said. "Sai is right that you won't beat that price anytime soon. You'd be lucky to do half as well in the regular wholesale market. If you don't have a bad credit transaction hanging over you, you'll have time to bargain well enough to make a sizable profit."

Randy pondered this, and Sai bit her lip waiting for him to speak.

"It's a lot of money, Dunc," Randy said slowly. "We're still not that far from dead broke. I don't want to take a chance on leaving you in the same condition."

Duncan laughed and drained his glass of ale. "Don't sweat it, Ran. I've gotten two percent of Cameron Trushenko's dividends since before I was born. I can afford the risk—such as it is."

Randy's expression hovered between a frown and a grimace. Clearly, he was wavering.

"I have until midnight to close the deal," Sai said. "How about if we check out the day market tonight, and make sure we're covered at least enough to pay Duncan back?"

"All right," Randy said. "But I hope I don't regret it."

Sai lunged forward and threw her arms around him happily. Randy returned the embrace as if she had been made of glass.

"Great!" she said. "Let's get going."

"I'll set up the credit line for you," Duncan called to their retreating backs, as his two friends left the room.

SHORTLY after supper, Saronna knocked on Randy Kumar's door. She waited several seconds, then knocked again. When no one answered, Saronna took a deep breath and put her hand on the door. She was immensely relieved when the door wasn't locked.

Randy's room looked sparsely furnished compared to hers. She took a quick glance around at the tables and in the dresser drawers. No sign of a pocket com. She darted to the bedside table and shuffled through the assorted items—a water pitcher and drinking glass, a few items of jewelry, and a bag of toiletries.

There! Under the bag sat a small almost fist-sized com. Randy had only the one pocket com. Saronna had researched that fact when she came up with this plan.

Now if only Sai was as relaxed about carrying a com, Saronna would be fine.

Her luck ran out. A quick but thorough search of the room next door yielded no sign of a com.

Saronna ducked back into the corridor. She set her jaw. It would be trickier with Sai carrying the device on her person, but Saronna would just have to manage. She had waited weeks for this chance, and she might never get a better one.

A little while later, Saronna carried a tray loaded with covered dishes to the tiny office that Duncan had set aside for his friends' use. She knocked on the door, and Sai's voice told her to enter.

"Oh, hello, Saronna," Randy said, looking up from the terminal screen. He glanced at the tray and smiled. "You didn't have to bring us dinner."

"It was Duncan's idea." It had been his idea to feed his friends, but Saronna had co-opted the task of delivering it. She glanced around the office. There it was! Sai's pocket com sat on the desk next to the single office com.

"What is it?" Sai said absently. "Oh, food. Thanks, Saronna."

Randy laughed. "Try not to overwhelm Saronna with your gratitude, won't you, Sai?"

"What? Oh!" Sai blinked. "Was I rude?"

"Not at all." Saronna slid the tray onto one of the desks. She pushed the desk com a little out of the way and began to set out the plates. "I know you're busy. I hope I'm not interrupting, but Duncan thought you'd be hungry."

"I'm starving," Randy said cheerfully. "Sai will be, too, once the high wears off."

"The high?" Saronna asked.

"Trader's high," Randy said. "No cure for it except to make money or go broke."

"We've done the going broke part," Sai said. "Let's hope this time it goes the other way."

"If it doesn't," Randy said, "we can hang it up."

"It will!" Sai said. She stared at the screen as if she were searching for an important clue to a puzzle. As if drawn to watch, Randy leaned in next to her.

Saronna further rearranged the desk furnishings to make room for the tray. She palmed Sai's pocket com, and then moved to the tiny office-sized sofa to plump the cushions. She kept her back to the desk as she turned the com off then wedged it into the crack between the sofa back and the seat. She would have to make sure the cleaning crew found it later. Once that was done, she took a moment to stare at the desk com.

"Good night," she said, as she headed for the door.

Neither of the partners even looked up. Saronna smiled to herself. They were in for an interesting night.

DUNCAN was surprised, the next morning, when neither of his friends made it to the breakfast table.

"Skipping three meals seems excessive, even for hardened traders like Sai and Randy," he said to the table at large.

"I took them a dinner tray," Saronna said. "They did eat last night."

"I'll check their rooms after breakfast, and see if they overslept," Duncan said. "They have a lot to do today."

No one made any comment on this plan, although Saronna smiled as she sipped her tea.

Duncan was further surprised to find both Sai and Randy's rooms vacant, with no sign that either of them had slept there. He went immediately to the tiny corner office beyond the library and knocked on the door. There was silence for a few seconds, and then Randy's voice spoke.

"Who is it?"

"It's Duncan. Are you guys okay? Did you fall asleep over the terminal or something?"

"Something like that," Randy's voice said. He sounded very light-hearted. "We're locked in, Dunc. Do you think you can find the key?"

Duncan rattled the door latch. After a loud clunk, something fell to the floor.

"Just a second," Duncan said, bending down. "I found the key. It was in the lock on this side."

There was a scuttling noise within the room, a scraping sound like someone moving furniture, and then Sai's voice, sounding almost breathless, said, "Don't come in just yet, will you, Dunc?"

Duncan had already put the key into the lock. He paused now, startled. "Is everyone okay? Should I call for a med team or anything?"

"We're fine," Randy said. "Wait just a sec, will you?"

Duncan turned the key but didn't open the door. What could have happened? If he hadn't heard Sai turn Randy down flat only two days before, he would have thought the famous Kumar charm had finally won her over.

More frantic noises sounded, and then Sai's voice said, "Okay. You can open the door now, Dunc."

Duncan pressed the latch and pushed the door open wondering what he would see. When he stepped inside, the office looked perfectly normal, if a trifle cluttered. A tray of dishes sat on a table in one corner, the com set was on the floor, and both desks seemed rather tidier than usual, but other than that, nothing seemed amiss.

Sai and Randy stood side by side, fully dressed but looking rumpled and remarkably guilty.

"Thanks, Dunc," Randy said. "We've been in here since last night."

"Why didn't you just call Security if you couldn't open the door?" Duncan asked, mystified.

"The com set isn't working," Sai said. "And I can't find my portable. If you'll excuse me, I'll run along."

"Me, too," Randy said, and they started for the door.

"Sure," Duncan said. "Did you close the deal? Are you all set to take delivery?"

They both stopped and stared at each other.

"My God!" Randy said. "We've got to make arrangements to empty that freighter!"

This was too much. Duncan could have believed his friends had stayed up all night working, but not that they had forgotten a deal that had consumed their very being the day before. Something of a momentous nature had to have happened in their office.

"So," Duncan said, "have you got anything interesting to tell me?"

Randy looked at Sai, who lifted her shoulders, as if to indicate a willingness to leave the decision to him.

"Yes," Randy said. "As a matter of fact, we do. We closed the deal on the Empress of China's cargo. We might need some help getting transport for the goods. And we're getting married today—tomorrow."

The correction on the date was made after a nudge from Sai.

Duncan's jaw dropped. "Married? Are you serious? What the hell happened here?"

"We're serious," Sai said. "Dead serious."

Duncan blinked. "But—but you've known each other for years. And you both date other people. And Randy especially—"

"Stop before you get me in trouble," Randy said. "After years of both of us being unwilling to lay it on the line, we both admitted how we feel about each other. We started arguing about who would get the couch and moved on to more serious concerns. The next thing I knew, Sai was proposing to me."

Sai snorted. "Not until after you asked if we could name a kid after your father."

Duncan laughed, still amazed by the development. Who would have guessed they harbored such secret passions? He certainly hadn't. "It sounds as if whoever locked you in here did you both a favor."

"Yes," Sai said, her eyes shining. "Thanks, Duncan."

Duncan shook his head. "It wasn't me. I admit I would have done it in a heartbeat if I had known how you guys felt, but I didn't."

Randy tilted his head to give Duncan a skeptical stare. "Who else could it be?"

Duncan shrugged. "I don't know. Security maybe? But it wasn't me. I'll swear on a copy of Crushak's if you like."

"You didn't rig the com set, either?" Sai asked.

"Nope," Duncan said. "Not guilty."

"Well," Sai said, in a tone that Duncan recognized, "we'll worry about it later. We'd better get moving, Ran. We've got a lot to do today, and I have to pee really bad."

The two of them went off in a hurry, and Duncan stepped into their office to investigate the malfunctioning com set. He might be weak on electronic theory, but he had a certain amount of mechanical aptitude, and he had no difficulty in removing the cover from the base of the communications device. One glance was enough to show him what was wrong. At the point where the power receptor connected to all the leads for the various displays, something had fused the circuits into a corkscrewed lump. It looked as if someone had managed to blast the inside of the com set with a powerful torch, without ever scorching any other component, including the cover.

Duncan frowned as he replaced the cover, mulling over possible reasons to account for such a circumstance. Someone or something had fused the inner workings of the com set at a critical juncture.

But who—or what—could have done it?

CHAPTER EIGHT

Duncan spent the next day helping a frantic Sai and Randy make arrangements. They rented warehouse space, a transport shuttle, and the necessary equipment, but they were unable to hire more than three daily workers.

"It's not enough," Randy said. "We'll never get it all done in time, not even if Sai and I go up and help."

Duncan held up both hands in alarm. "You don't want to try that, Ran. I can tell you from personal experience, you'd just get in the way. A deadline situation is no time to learn how to handle cargo in space."

Sai looked almost relieved, and Duncan remembered that she had gotten ill on the one occasion when she had experienced weightlessness.

"I know someone," Vladimir said. For some reason, he had seemed very pleased with the news that Sai was going to marry Randy. "I had to rely on local talent once, when I needed stuff unloaded in a hurry and the regular hiring hall couldn't oblige me."

"You mean Kruegerians?" Randy asked uneasily.

Vladimir nodded. "They may be natives, but they know their stuff. It's a family business—two brothers and a cousin are the mainstays, with another few cousins added as needed. They hire themselves out as a crew whenever they get a chance. Since there's a prejudice against native workers in skilled jobs, especially topside work, they're often available at short notice."

"Could you call them?" Sai said.

"Sure, I could," Vladimir said. "But if they're available, you'll have to close the deal in person. They work on a cash-only basis, and they'll want to have shaken hands on the agreement before they show up."

"I don't know if we'll have time," Randy said slowly. "Not unless we postpone the meeting to go over the sale of the stasis units?"

"Don't do that," Duncan said. If the biggest part of their deal fell through, they would owe him a lot of money. He hated to think the lengths they would go to in an effort to pay him back. "I'll hire these folks for you. I'm not busy today."

"But you've done so much already," Sai said.

"I don't mind doing one more thing," Duncan said, smiling. It occurred to him their impending marriage provided a good excuse for an extra dose of generosity. "Think of it as a wedding present."

After Vladimir had confirmed the availability of at least the core of the Sopko family, Sai and Randy both agreed, a trifle reluctantly, to let Duncan handle the details of their employment.

"I think I have enough cash," Randy said, handing over a wad of credit notes. "It's everything we made on our last deal." He also provided information on where the Sopkos should report. "If you can't get six men, take what you can get," Randy said earnestly. "I meant what I said about going up there myself if necessary."

Duncan agreed and consulted his father for the address.

"Take the ground car and a driver," Vladimir said. "That neighborhood is a real warren of houses. There's nowhere to leave the car, so he'll have to drop you off."

Duncan nodded. "Thanks for being so helpful about this, Dad."

His father waved away his thanks, and Duncan went to make his transportation arrangements.

The car and a driver were ready quickly; Duncan was pleased with his luck. Frank Chiang knew the city, even parts of the native quarter, and he was better company than either of the Kruegerian drivers, who tended to be overly formal.

"Where to, boss?" Frank asked as he started up the engine.

After Duncan relayed the address his father had given him, Frank keyed it into the map system. He whistled when he saw where they were going. "That's pretty deep into the oldest part of New Jerusalem. The streets are so narrow, I don't know how close I can get."

"Do the best you can," Duncan said. "I can walk a ways if I have to, and I have a com."

"Okay." Frank engaged the throttle and let the ground car slide out of the enclosed drive and into traffic.

Frank's prediction proved accurate. As he maneuvered the ground car through the Sopkos' neighborhood, he had to slow his speed considerably. Fortunately, there wasn't a lot of vehicular traffic, although in many places pedestrians proved a major, if temporary, obstacle.

When Frank pulled onto the correct street, Duncan noted at once that a small utility vehicle parked to one side of the narrow roadway would make advancing impossible. Frank cursed mildly and then studied his map display. "I could try to circle around from the other side?"

"Don't bother," Duncan said, opening the door. "I'll walk the rest of the way. I've got a pocket com with me, and I'll call as soon as I'm ready to head back. Just don't get too far away."

Frank nodded, and as soon as Duncan had shut the door and stepped back, he reversed his vehicle and backed it into an alley to turn around.

Duncan walked down the street curiously. He had been in the native quarter a number of times with his father, but this was only his second time alone. The houses here were clearly older than most of New Jerusalem, dating back to well before ThreeCon's discovery of Krueger's World. The worn, shabby buildings presented a block-like front, with no visible windows and only the edges of their tiled roofs visible. Duncan was pretty certain their roofs slanted inward, to allow for collecting rain water in cisterns. The Sopkos' house, one of the larger ones on the street, stood only half a dozen doors down from where Frank had dropped Duncan, so he didn't have a long walk.

The Sopko who answered the door was one of the brothers. He ushered Duncan into a small courtyard and invited him to sit. Duncan could see the shuttered windows of a women's parlor on one side of the courtyard, and he wondered if they were under observation. The house looked very old-fashioned; there were indeed drain pipes from the roof to a large cistern in the corner of the courtyard, and there was no sign of a central power field. Duncan was impressed that the Sopkos managed to maintain communications with off-worlders in such primitive circumstances.

Sopko offered refreshment, but Duncan declined. His father had taught him enough of the way in which Kruegerians did business to know that this was a test. Sopko nodded his approval and proceeded to lay out his terms. Duncan negotiated vigorously, but in the end, the price was slightly nearer Sopko's original price than Duncan's first offer. They shook hands on the agreement, and Sopko offered refreshment again.

Duncan accepted this time; he was in no real hurry, and there was no sense in leaving bad feelings to save a few minutes. He might easily need the Sopkos again someday. After a cup of tea and a piece of fruit, Duncan asked if he might use his pocket com. Sopko was quick to give his permission, and politely diverted his attention elsewhere while Duncan called Frank Chiang and asked to be picked up where he had been dropped off. Before Duncan could slip the com back into his pocket, Sopko asked if he could inspect the unit.

"Certainly," Duncan said, holding it out.

Sopko turned it over and measured the size of the screen with his fingers, pursed his lips, and nodded. "This is a good machine. We only use portables, because our power is unreliable. Some of them are too tiny to be comfortable."

Duncan could see the innate opportunity of the situation. When Sopko held out the pocket com, Duncan held both hands up as if to block the return. "Allow me to make you a present of it."

Sopko made a show of refusing, but allowed himself to be persuaded to accept. After Duncan had changed the access settings on the com, Sopko walked him to the door and shook hands again.

"We'll meet your crew at the shuttle in an hour," he said. "We'll do a good job for your friends, my word upon it."

Duncan walked through the doorway with a feeling of accomplishment. His good humor evaporated as he looked up the street and saw no sign of the ground car. He felt suddenly exposed, and he realized how much he relied on carrying a pocket com.

The utility vehicle had gone, but the houses hugging the shoulders of the narrow street, with just a strip of walkway available for pedestrians, still made it look inaccessible. Some of the houses had tiny gardens, but most were built right up to the walkway. Duncan felt suddenly claustrophobic. He looked at the narrowness of the pavement, and wondered whether a ground car could drive on it without molesting the pedestrians.

Duncan started walking toward the spot where Frank had dropped him off. He had gone past four houses when he heard a sudden crescendo of noise. First a woman screamed, then several people shouted angrily. After the sound of running footsteps, Duncan heard a child's thin, frightened wail rise above the other sounds.

Duncan hesitated, unsure of what to do. He had almost decided to move on when the door to the house across the street was thrown open and a small knot of people spilled out onto the walkway.

The woman at the front of the knot seemed at first to be the subject of pursuit by the others, but then Duncan realized that it was only the angry man who was harrying her. The others, two women and a little girl of seven or eight, merely trailed in his wake.

Duncan tried to absorb the details quickly. A tall imposing man, about forty or so, and with a full beard, carried a long wooden staff that he used to strike his quarry. His target, a woman bundled up in the all-enveloping embrace of a Kruegerian veil, tried to protect herself with upraised arms. Her long skirt was Kruegerian, but Duncan noticed as she stumbled and fell onto the gravel that she wore distinctly off-world shoes. The two women followers were obscured by knit shawls wound around their heads, as if they had both been in too much haste to fetch proper veils. The little girl wore only a loose smock. All three of them seemed to be pleading with the man to cease abusing the woman on the ground.

The patriarch had raised his staff and brought it down across the woman's shoulders twice before Duncan reached him. Duncan grabbed the staff and held it, forcing the Kruegerian to halt its downward arc.

"How dare you interfere!" the man roared at Duncan. "Get off my property at once!"

"We're on public ground." Duncan pointed to the street.

The patriarch paused and looked around briefly. He seemed surprised to note the walkway under his feet.

He wrenched his staff free of Duncan's grip. "It makes no difference. This is my affair and not yours. Go on about your business, or I'll call you to account."

Duncan glanced down at the woman on the ground. "It is my business. I can't allow you to abuse this woman."

"What is she to you?"

Duncan hesitated, realizing that in Kruegerian eyes only a close relationship could ever justify interfering in such a situation. A lie was clearly in order. "She's my—" Duncan suddenly glimpsed gray hair and a lined face as the woman pulled back her veil slightly— "mother," he ended abruptly.

This revelation gave the patriarch pause as he glowered at Duncan and then at the woman. "You should mind what your mother's about. She was stirring up my household, asking questions—prying where she wasn't wanted. You keep her away from my house, or I'll see to it that she's in no state to pry any further." He reinforced this edict with a swift, sideways kick to the woman's side.

Duncan reacted without even thinking. He lashed out with his fist, smashing it into the man's jaw. It wasn't a very scientific blow, but the patriarch staggered backwards and hit the ground. The other two women and the little girl shrank back against the wall of their house, as if they feared the sky would fall on them.

"Do you dare to strike me on my own doorstep!" the patriarch bellowed, staggering to his feet. He seemed to suddenly take in Duncan's appearance. "An infidel! I'll have your blood for this!"

Duncan had just seen his ground car make the turn into the street. He bent down and grabbed the battered woman's arm and hauled her to her feet.

"You're welcome to try," he said to the patriarch. "My name's Duncan Trushenko, and you can reach me in the off-world quarter."

Frank had brought the ground car to a stop at the end of the street, as a party of young men were crossing the pavement in front of him, taking their time and eying the car curiously. Duncan got a firmer grip on the woman's arm.

"Can you walk?" he said, ducking his head to speak to her quietly.

"Yes," was the one word answer.

"Then let's go." Duncan nodded to the patriarch, who was stammering in incoherent rage as his women clustered around him. "I'll take my mother home now," Duncan said. "My sire will be getting anxious."

The man sputtered an angry demand for Duncan to remain and take his punishment, but Duncan was already walking rapidly toward the car, half dragging the veiled woman with him.

Frank looked very startled as Duncan approached with a total stranger in tow, but he unlocked the doors and let them in immediately.

"Have we got trouble, boss?" he asked, surveying the crowd around the car.

"I have, anyway," Duncan said. "Let's get away from here as fast as we can."

"Right," Frank said, sliding the throttle down carefully, accelerating slowly enough for the pedestrians to move out of his way. He picked up speed as he went, and then slowed again as they went past the house where the two women, the man, and the little girl still stood on the walkway. The patriarch brought his staff down on the front window, but the polymer was built to resist much stronger force than an out-of-shape middle-aged man could deliver with a wooden stick. The staff cracked and broke in two.

"Serves him right," the woman said calmly, pulling down her veil.

Duncan surveyed his passenger and found a pair of bright black eyes studying him back. The woman was either a good twenty years older than his mother, or she had had a very hard life indeed. A network of fine wrinkles lined her face, and her hair had gone completely gray, but the eyes that sized Duncan up so frankly were still full of life and twinkling merrily.

"I'm afraid I'm rather old for a damsel in distress," she said, holding out her hand, "but thank you very much for rescuing me. My name's Zelda Amoy."

"Duncan Trushenko," Duncan said, shaking the hand that was offered. "No problem."

She shook her head sagely. "You're wrong there. You struck Sire Longworth in front of his own house, in full view of his neighbors. If he's hot-headed enough, you could be in real trouble."

"What kind of trouble?"

She cocked her head as she considered the possibilities. "Almost definitely a ritual assault. It's harder to predict if that would end the feud or just get it started. I didn't get a chance to ask about the rest of the household, so I don't know how many sons he has or how old they are. He's young for a patriarch, and sometimes that's the worst kind—too young to have any real wisdom, and no father to check his temper."

"What were you doing there?"

"Research. I'm a sociologist, specializing in sleeper world cultures."

It had never occurred to Duncan that a woman scientist might want to study Krueger's World from so close up. "Wouldn't it be safer to ask your research subjects to visit you in the off-world quarter? The native quarter's not a safe place for off-world women."

"It's not always a safe place for Kruegerian women, either," Zelda said, "but very few of them would be allowed to leave it, certainly not without a male escort. I can't find out much about the female half of this world if I sit at home in my apartment."

She had a point. "So you've been studying Kruegerian women?"

Zelda nodded. "It's a fascinating area for research. Women here are so thoroughly oppressed, they've developed a separate and distinct subculture. They have their own rituals, their own manners, their own social structure. It's amazing, in a way."

Duncan looked at her with new interest. Here was a source of information about a subject on which he could use a tutor. It would be foolish to let such a golden opportunity slip through his fingers. "How badly did that creep hurt you? Shall we take you to a hospital, or can I buy you a drink?"

The sociologist looked him over before she answered. "I'm a little bruised, but I'll live. Are you hot for older women, or are you just being sympathetic?"

Duncan tried not to smile too broadly. He was almost positive she was joking—almost. He decided to be frank. "Actually, I'm hot for a particular Kruegerian woman, and I'm finding it rather heavy going. As you're an expert in the field, I was rather hoping you could help me smooth out some of the bumps."

She sat up at this offer. "Really? You've got a deal. Take me to a bar with nice soft seats, buy me a couple of Miloran whiskeys, and I'll tell you anything you want to know."

Frank reported that they were nearing the Stranger's Gate, so Duncan directed him to drive to the Black Swan, a restaurant known for the intimacy of its tables.

Zelda Amoy seemed to know of it, because she grinned at Duncan when he sat back in his seat. "Are you quite sure you don't have a special fondness for older women?"

"I'm sure," Duncan said, "but if I did, I'd start with you."

She laughed, and patted his arm. "Charm never hurts. It's no substitute for substance, but it never hurts to have it."

When they pulled up to the building that housed the Black Swan, Duncan asked Frank Chiang to call his father and report success on his mission.

"Sure thing, boss," Frank said, giving him a wry grin over his shoulder.

Duncan had a sudden sinking feeling. He should have been more circumspect in front of Frank.

Zelda Amoy shed her veil in the ground car, shook out her gray curls, and stepped onto the walkway with a firm step that belied both her age and her recent suffering. When Duncan offered his hand to help her, she took it, and then slipped her arm though his.

"There," she said. "There's nothing like having an attractive young escort to perk up your spirits."

She clung to his arm all the way up the lift, and didn't let go until they were shown to a table that had a view of the city, but was still sheltered by the high backs of the chairs and a profusion of potted plants.

"This is nice," Zelda said. "Quite cozy."

"Yes," Duncan said. "What would you like?"

They entered their choices into the terminal in the center of the table, and then Duncan pushed it away.

"Are you sure you're all right?" he asked. "That bastard was really laying into you with his staff. I should have broken it over his head."

Zelda's eyes crinkled in a smile, but she shook her head. "No, it wouldn't have helped me any if you had, and in his own view, Sire Longworth was justified in chastising me."

Duncan raised his eyebrows at her wording. "Chastising? It looked like assault and battery to me."

"Oh, it was. But I was in his house without his permission. Legally, he could have done a lot worse to me."

Duncan shook his head, bewildered. "Just for being in his house?"

"Well," Zelda said, looking impish, "I was indeed prying into his household. I had managed to get both his wife and his woman to trust me, and they were getting quite confidential just about the time he showed up. I expect he was considerably annoyed to find an outsider invading the privacy of his domain."

A servoid rolled up with their drink order. "He looked damn mad," Duncan said, lifting the glasses and handing her the one with murky green liquid. "What were you asking them about?"

She took the glass and took a sip before she answered. "Sex. Unfortunately, he heard enough of the conversation to figure it out. That's what set him off."

Duncan almost choked on his drink. "That's your idea of research—to go into a house and ask the people about their sex lives?"

"And other things," Zelda said. "It's just that I had gotten to the questions about sex just as Sire Longworth remembered he had promised to take little Antonia for an iced fruit cup. There's a certain irony," she said thoughtfully, as she rubbed her shoulder, "to the fact that I wouldn't have gotten caught if the man had only been a less involved father."

Duncan was even more amazed. "The little girl was there while you were talking to those women about sex?"

Zelda waved a hand. "No, of course not. They had sent her away, and she was trying to listen through the door. That's what aroused Sire Longworth's suspicions."

"So, what did you find out?"

She sipped her whiskey appreciatively and studied him over the edge of her glass. "A little touch of the voyeur yourself?"

Duncan smiled but shook his head. "I have a reason for wanting to know what Kruegerian women think about sex."

She nodded. "You said that before. I've been trying to think of a situation where you could have met a Kruegerian woman, and there aren't many where you'd really get to know her. I assume we're not talking about love at first sight or blind infatuation?"

Duncan was glad he could answer with no hesitation. "No, we're not. I'm not even sure we're talking about love at all. I only know I've met someone who drives me crazy." He thought about Saronna. What was it about her that made him feel this way? "When I'm not around her, I wonder what she's doing, and when I am around her, I can't leave her alone. She's not the most beautiful woman I was ever attracted to, or the most well built." He shook his head, admitting defeat. "It's just that she got under my skin in a way no one ever did before. She has a way of holding herself in, of looking as if she could speak volumes if she wanted to, but she's not going to say a word. It makes me want to babble the most nonsensical things to her. I don't know what to do."

"How did you meet her?" Zelda asked directly.

Duncan sipped his drink. "It's a long story."

Zelda leaned back in her chair. "Keep the whiskey coming. I've got time."

Duncan debated. He didn't see a down side to telling her the history of the Cameron Trushenko household, and she might have some advice. "All right. Here goes." He took another sip of ale and then leaned his elbows on the table. "A little over five years ago, Standard time, my father decided to move our company here. Dad saw right away that you did better with the Kruegerians if you made an effort not to stand out so much. So he grew a beard, and answered to sire when he was addressed that way, and he struck up a social acquaintance among the Kruegerians.

"Only a few months after we got here, Dad was invited to a poker game by a man he had done some business with. As the poker game progressed, the host got thoroughly snockered and started reviling his luck, claiming nothing had ever gone right for him. He complained about his losing poker hands, his business failures, his barren wife. He said he had married a woman with a pitiful dowry only because she was beautiful, and then she turned out to be barren."

Duncan took another sip of ale and interrupted his tale to ask a question. "Do you know about Kruegerian inheritance laws?"

Zelda nodded. "The eldest son gets virtually everything."

"Right. But it has to be the wife's son, too. A man can't pass his property on to his son unless he is or was married to the boy's mother."

She sipped her drink, her eyes on his face. "Very true. But most men will keep a wife in their household if they put her aside to have sons with someone else. She's not his wife anymore, but she's still his woman."

Duncan recalled how terrified Naomi had been the night he had met her. "Yeah, well, this creep didn't do that. He got drunker and drunker, and then he sent a servant to fetch his wife. When she came in, he made her take off her veil. He was quite right, by the way. She's downright gorgeous."

"Were you there?"

"No. I got this secondhand from Dad."

She nodded. "So what happened next?"

Duncan grimaced. "He sold her to Dad for twenty thousand credits."

Zelda sat back in her seat and opened her eyes wide. "Twenty thousand credits? You could buy a harem for that."

Duncan didn't want a harem, he only wanted Saronna. He went on with his story. "Anyway, Dad stayed long enough to win some of it back just to spite the bastard, and then he took Naomi home."

Zelda smiled. "Ah! And what happened when they got home?"

"Nothing," Duncan said firmly. "Except that Naomi wept for a few days. Dad kept patting her hand and telling her not to worry, and finally she came out of it."

"And then you fell for her?"

Duncan laughed. It hadn't occurred to him she would think that. "No, of course not. For one thing, it was obvious Dad was nuts about her, and for another, timid women who cling pathetically have never been a turn-on for me."

Zelda frowned and shot him a suspicious look. "So, where has all this got us?"

"It's just background. I'm getting there."

She muttered something under her breath, but told him to continue.

"Anyway," Duncan said, "I don't know what happened—it was none of my business, and I never asked—but after a month or two, Naomi and Dad worked things out. He fixed her up with rooms adjoining his, and they started playing house.

"More than a year after that, I left Krueger's World on an extended business trip. While I was gone, Dad and Naomi were very happy, but Naomi was lonely."

Zelda nodded sagely. "Of course. There were no other Kruegerian women in the house. She wanted someone like herself to keep her company."

Amazing how she knew that right away. "It makes sense to you, does it? I confess it struck me as strange. What she did was to urge my father to buy a woman for me."

Zelda froze with her drink in the air. "Did he do it?"

Duncan nodded. "Her name is Saronna."

Her brow lifted; her eyes opened wide. "Saronna? An interesting name. So she's the one?"

"Yes. She's the one."

"So," she said, smiling slightly, "you did get a chance to know her rather well?"

Duncan gave her a stern look. He was tired of everyone assuming the worst about him. "I haven't taken advantage of her, if that's what you mean."

Her smile widened into a grin. "What a nice old-fashioned phrase for it—taken advantage of her. You mean you haven't insisted on your rights under Kruegerian law and taken her to bed."

"That particular Kruegerian law doesn't apply in the off-world quarter. And even if it did, I wouldn't do that."

"Perhaps not," Zelda said evenly. "But that hasn't stopped you from wanting to, apparently?"

Duncan flushed and didn't answer right away. She was, after all, a stranger and she was asking very intimate questions. On the other hand, he wanted answers. "It's not like that. It's not just a physical attraction, although I don't deny that's there, too. I like Saronna, and I enjoy her company. I would never want her to yield herself up to me, like some kind of chattel with no will of her own."

Zelda pursed her lips and tapped them with one finger. "It's an interesting point. Kruegerian women are taught that they have only one role to play in life—serving men. I wonder if a Kruegerian woman could feel otherwise if she were suddenly offered the opportunity?"

"Saronna has. At first all I felt was a sense of responsibility. I didn't know quite what to do since I couldn't send her home—"

"No," she interrupted. "You must never do that."

Duncan nodded. "Dad explained that to me. But I didn't know what to do with her. She had no skills to speak of, unless you count housework and sewing. I asked her to try to get an education as fast as she could. She not only agreed to do it, she seemed to enjoy learning. I hired a tutor for her, and he tells me she's very bright and doing quite well."

"She could already read then?" Zelda asked. She had a curious expression on her face, a mixture of surprise and eagerness.

"Oh, yes. She even started teaching Naomi how to read."

"Really?" Zelda seemed even more intrigued.

"So what do you advise?"

She cocked her head as she looked at him. "About what? The woman's completely in your power. I doubt if she'd object to anything you chose to do."

Duncan gave a short, angry grunt of exasperation. "That's not what I want! And she would object. One reason I like her is that Saronna has a will of her own."

Zelda tisked at him. "I don't think you grasp what you've gotten yourself into with this," she said, her tone sympathetic even while her expression grew stern. "You don't understand the psychology of the oppressed. It would be extremely difficult for a woman who was raised in a Kruegerian household to accept the kind of relationship you're offering her, when she already sees herself as your property."

Duncan frowned, unwilling to accept such a negative prognosis. "Naomi and my father seem to have made a go of it."

"Have they? Or have they simply managed to work out a relationship in which she sees herself as a proper Kruegerian woman, and he thinks of her as his partner in life, without worrying about whether she feels like his equal or not?"

Duncan pondered. It did seem possible. As much as his father doted on Naomi, she still felt a need to ask his permission for almost anything she did. "I don't know. I don't like to pry into Dad's life—I certainly don't let him pry into mine. Naomi did get very upset when my mother came to visit."

Zelda blinked and pulled back in surprise. "Are your parents still married?"

"Legally. There are financial incentives for them to stay married, but they've lived apart—light years apart—since before I was born."

She laughed at this. "My, my! I'd no idea when you intervened to help me that you'd prove to be such a wealth of interesting situations."

Duncan didn't take offense. "I suppose my life looks rather a tangled mess at the moment." He awoke to the time and offered lunch, but his guest declined.

"Thanks anyway, but I'd better get back to my apartment. I need to soak in a hot tub and get some rest."

"Maybe you should see a doctor," Duncan said.

She shook her head. "I'll be all right. But you'd better be careful."

Duncan hoped she was wrong. "Do you really think so? I doubt if I hurt the man. I'm not much of a fighter."

She shook her finger at him. "It wasn't the pain, it was the disrespect. You struck a patriarch on his own doorstep, in front of his wife and daughter and a woman of his household. If he has grown sons, you could find yourself under assault at any time."

"I rarely go into the native quarter."

She slapped his hand as if he were a toddler reaching for a cookie. "Don't let that give you a false sense of security. They could still find you. When they signed the covenants for the off-world quarters, Kruegerians always insisted on the right to conduct ritual assaults and blood feuds anywhere on Krueger's World."

Duncan frowned as he considered this possibility. "What would they do?"

She shrugged. "Knives are the customary weapons, but some of the newer generation are using off-world weapons when they can get them. Don't forget, your whole household is a potential target, not just you."

The thought that everyone in the house might be in danger made Duncan frown even more. "I suppose I'll have to tell my father, then?"

"Definitely. You all need to be careful. Blood feuds aren't always fatal, but they don't call them blood feuds for no reason."

Duncan pressed his thumb to the terminal screen to pay the bill, and then escorted his companion down to the street. He started to reach for his pocket com and then remembered he didn't have one. Before he could ask Zelda if she had a com with her, he saw the ground car edging its way toward them from across the street.

Duncan was extremely surprised to find a uniformed Cameron Trushenko security guard sitting in the front seat next to Frank Chiang.

"What's up?" he asked, as he and Zelda slid into the back seat.

"Mr. Trushenko insisted on sending some help once he heard there'd been trouble," Frank said.

Duncan glanced at Zelda. Frank must see her as an outsider to call Vladimir 'Mr. Trushenko.' Right now she looked impressed.

"Your father knows Kruegerian customs rather well to appreciate the implications of the situation so quickly," she said.

"He's had a lot of practice," Duncan said dryly. "Where can we drop you?"

She gave them her address, and Frank drove there with no trouble. As Duncan stepped out of the car to see Zelda to her door, he was annoyed to find the security guard at his elbow.

"I'll be right back," Duncan said.

"No, sir," the man said. "I stick with you. Those are my orders."

Duncan sighed and didn't argue. He walked Zelda into the lobby, shook her hand gravely, and watched her get onto the lift. His security shadow followed him, jumping in front of him as he went through the door to the street.

Duncan controlled his annoyance and rode in silence all the way home. He was mulling over all that the sociologist had told him, and wondering how much of it applied to Saronna.

When they pulled into the enclosed driveway, Duncan was further aggravated, but not surprised, to see a second security guard waiting by the door of the house.

"Vladimir would like to see you right away, sir," the woman said.

Duncan walked to his father's office in a mood of considerable irritation. He had always valued his privacy, and it looked as if his father was going to make the situation unbearable.

Vladimir looked up and glared at him. "Duncan Trushenko," he said, jumping to his feet, "just what the hell have you been doing?"

CHAPTER NINE

"Hello, Dad," Duncan said.

"Sit down," Vladimir said, "and tell me why a patriarch attacked our ground car with his staff."

Duncan took a seat across from his father's desk. "Well, it started because he was using that staff as a weapon to beat a woman older than Mom. I didn't feel like watching it, so I stopped him."

Vladimir's eyebrows went up. "How did you stop him?"

"I grabbed the staff, and then I told him she was my mother."

Surprise became confusion as Vladimir knit his brows. "But he must have seen that you're an off-worlder?"

Duncan nodded. "Of course, but so is she. Her name is Zelda Amoy, and she's a sociologist who's doing research among Kruegerian women."

His father let out a snort of derision. "In the native quarter? She's nuts."

Duncan couldn't disagree. "Maybe, but she didn't deserve to get beaten for it."

Vladimir twisted his lips into a grimace. "Was that all that happened?"

"No. Even after I told him Zelda was my mother, the patriarch kicked her while she was lying on the ground. So I hit him."

"*Kutra ilas hrogh 'ul!*" Vladimir said vehemently. It was a Miloran curse that meant literally, 'You spawn your offspring,' although usually was it translated more colloquially. If you said it to a Miloran, it would get you thrown through the nearest wall, and Duncan had never heard his father use the phrase. "What do you mean, you hit him?" Vladimir asked.

"Just that," Duncan said. "I punched him in the jaw—not very hard, I'm afraid. I did manage to knock him down, but he wasn't hurt at all."

"Did anyone see it?"

"Yes. His wife and daughter and another woman, and a few of the neighbors."

His father looked even more grim. "Does he have any way to trace you?"

"Well," Duncan said, finally feeling guilty, "I told him my name."

Vladimir groaned and put his head in his hands.

"Is it really all that bad?" Duncan asked. "Don't I get any slack if he believed the part about Zelda being my mother? Was I supposed to watch him kick her and not do anything?"

Vladimir sighed and sat up. "Yes, to the first question. No, to both the others. Believe me, it's bad. I don't think the man has much sense if he couldn't stop himself from kicking a woman after you claimed her as your mother. And I suppose I couldn't expect you not to react."

"Thank you for that," Duncan said dryly. "Maybe it'll all blow over?"

Vladimir snorted. "Quit dreaming. Does this man have grown sons?"

"I don't know. Zelda didn't know, either."

"What's his name?"

"Sire Longworth was the only name I heard. His house is just four doors down from your friends the Sopkos."

"I'll find out," Vladimir said grimly, making a note on his scheduler. "Meanwhile, you be careful. Don't go anywhere without a security escort."

Duncan frowned. "Look, Dad, I know I've caused a problem here, but let's not overreact. I don't need a babysitter. I can take care of myself."

Vladimir threw his stylus down on the desk in disgust. "Take care of yourself? If today is any indication, you're no more fit to take care of yourself on Krueger's World than a baby is."

Duncan clenched his teeth and tried his best to keep his temper. "Now, Dad, I'm twenty-six. I don't need a note from you to leave the house."

"Twenty-six? Then act your age, Duncan. Everyone in this house is now a potential target because of your actions today. Don't give me any crap about being too macho to need a bodyguard."

"Macho? Don't be absurd! Is it macho to want some privacy? I don't want some hulking security guard following me to the bathroom and jumping in front of me when I go through a door."

"Duncan Cameron Trushenko," Vladimir said, his volume rising with each word, "allow me to remind you that you work for me. If you want to remain as—" he stopped abruptly. "What's your title now?"

"Director of Sales Expansion," Duncan said, trying hard not to smile.

Vladimir waved a hand impatiently. "If you want to remain as Director of Sales Expansion, you'll listen up and do as you're told. You don't leave this house without an escort, and that's final."

"See here, Dad," Duncan said, working himself up for an argument. Something in the expectant way his father was looking at him made him pause and change his argument to a question. "So, what happens if I refuse to go along with this edict?"

"You're fired," Vladimir said promptly.

Duncan nodded. "I could live with that. You'd change your mind eventually."

Vladimir smiled triumphantly. "Not here though. Your room and board are figured as part of your salary, remember? You obey orders or you're out the door."

Duncan burst out laughing. "You crafty old bugger! You're trying to get me out of the way."

Vladimir shrugged. "Not necessarily. You can stay if you show some sense."

If his father was worried enough to fire him, then maybe the situation was as bad as he said. "All right," Duncan said. "You win."

"Good," Vladimir said with satisfaction. "You'd better warn your friends to be careful, too."

"You're right." The more Duncan thought about it, the more he could see the sense of being careful. "In fact, it might be time to kick Sai and Randy out—for their own good, of course. They don't know much about Krueger's World."

Vladimir nodded. "True, but don't forget about Saronna. Ritual assaults never target women, but accidents can happen, and there's no sense taking chances."

"Saronna?" She certainly knew Krueger's World, but it would be good to warn her about the specifics. "I suppose I'd better talk to her, too." A thought struck Duncan. "What about Kendall? Would a tutor be a target? He's not a Trushenko or even a regular employee."

Vladimir grimaced. "Since we don't live in big family groups like the Kruegerians, they seem to have defined off-world businesses as households. Anyone who works here or looks as if he works here is a target—although the women are less likely, as I said." He ran his fingers through his hair and sighed. "I'll have a talk with the staff and tell them the situation. You talk to your friends, and to Saronna and her tutor."

Duncan got to his feet. "I'll do that right away." He turned as he was about to go through the door. "I'm sorry I caused such a problem, Dad."

Vladimir smiled grimly. "It wasn't your fault, Duncan. Sometimes you have to do what's right instead of what's expedient." He gave a heartfelt sigh. "Although I do wish you'd said your name was Wong or Jones or anything but Trushenko."

DUNCAN found Saronna in the library, watching a program on the history of the Third Confederation of Planets. As he came into the room, the projector had just displayed an immense swirl of stars, with those that had ThreeCon member planets burning a bright blue. As soon as Saronna saw Duncan, she turned off the projector.

"Duncan!" she said. "Has something happened? You look worried."

She could read him well. Surely that meant something. "Do I? I was trying not to let it show."

She brushed away this attempt at flippancy with a quick flick of her hand. "Tell me what it is."

He sat down at the next desk and related the incident in the native quarter. "Dad seems to think an assault is likely."

She nodded, her face pale and her eyes huge. "You need to be very careful. Don't leave the house unless you must, and don't ever go anywhere alone."

"I won't."

She stood up abruptly and paced the room a few times. "How many sons does he have?"

"I don't know." Her agitation amazed Duncan. He had rarely seen her serenity so ruffled. "Dad's finding out."

Saronna covered her mouth with her hand for a moment, as if she were trying to calm herself. "Was it a big house?"

"Not particularly," Duncan said, getting to his feet. "Certainly nowhere near as big as this one. It's in an old neighborhood, and the houses are quite close together."

Saronna frowned as if she were looking for significance in this.

Duncan captured her hand as she paced near him. "Why are you so upset? Nothing's happened yet. The man was young for a patriarch. His sons may still be in the cradle, for all we know."

She pulled her hand away. "You don't understand. Even if he has no sons, he may have brothers with sons who'll act for him. This is not something to pass off lightly, Duncan."

"But they won't attack you. Dad told me women are never the targets in ritual assaults."

"I know that," she said, sounding scornful.

"Then why are you so afraid?"

She didn't answer.

Duncan recaptured her hand. "Is it for me, Saronna? Are you afraid for me?"

She turned her head away before she spoke. "Yes."

"Then you care about me?"

She said nothing.

Duncan realized she was trembling. "Saronna? Do you care for me?"

Still she didn't answer.

"I'm going to take that for a yes," Duncan said. "You don't seem to have any trouble saying no." He bent his head down to kiss her, but he had no sooner brushed his lips against hers, than Saronna pulled her hands free of his grasp and pushed firmly against his chest.

Duncan opened his eyes, considerably startled. "I don't get it. How can you care so much that you tremble with fear when you think I'm in danger, but you still push me away as if I had the plague?"

She turned away. "I can't explain. Please don't ask me."

Duncan sighed with frustration. "I can't explain it either. I wish I knew what you do to me, to make me so crazy."

She gave him a wild, guilty look. "I don't do any-thing."

He laughed. "Don't look so scared. I'm not accusing you of witchcraft, or anything. It's just that I've never felt this way before."

"Neither have I."

Her voice held a hint of something very like despair.

"What's wrong, Saronna?" He remembered what Zelda Amoy had told him earlier that day. "I'm not constraining you in any way, am I? If you're humoring me—letting me think that you care because you feel a sense of obligation or duty—I wish you'd say so."

"No!" She shook her head vigorously. "You're not constraining me, and I'm not humoring you. I've learned a lot since I came to this house. I can make my own choices."

He frowned as he thought this through. "If you know you have the right to make a choice, and you care enough about me to fear for me, why can't you choose me? What's stopping you?"

She lifted her eyes to his, a mass of conflicting emotions in her face. "I can't tell you now." Slowly, as if she couldn't stop herself, she gently stroked the side of his face with the back of her hand.

The tenderness of the gesture moved Duncan. "Saronna," he said, his voice hoarse with emotion. He pulled her close against him and held her tightly. He couldn't remember a time when physical desire had brought such a feeling of tenderness. "Saronna, I wish you'd tell me what's wrong."

She looked panicked, and shut her eyes for a moment.

Abruptly, Duncan felt his desire ebb.

"I think I'd better go," he said, suddenly remembering the public nature of the room.

She nodded wordlessly.

Duncan stopped with his hand on the latch of the door. "When is Kendall coming? I need to warn him.

Dad's hiring extra security staff, and we can offer him an escort to and from work if he chooses."

She looked numb. "He'll be here this afternoon. I'll tell him about it."

"Good," Duncan said, and he opened the door and left her alone.

"I DON'T like it, Dunc," Randy said heatedly, as they sat in the parlor. "Here you are running all over New Jerusalem doing our errands, and then when you get into trouble—only because you were doing us a favor—we're supposed to duck and run for cover? No way! Not if I have anything to say about it."

"You don't," Duncan said. "Cameron Trushenko needs its office space back, thank you. We may even need your bedrooms for some live-in security staff. Dad's gone totally paranoid."

"We can do without the office," Sai said, "and we'll share a bedroom."

Duncan shook his head. "Nope. Pack your stuff and head on out, guys. There's a travelers' hostel at the ThreeCon consulate if you can't afford a hotel."

Randy waved a hand dismissively. "Don't worry about that. We did pretty well out of the *Empress of China*. In fact we're planning on leaving Krueger's World as soon as we move the last of the stuff."

"If you weren't about to be newlyweds," Duncan said, "I'd ask you to take Saronna with you. I'd like to know she's somewhere safe."

Randy and Sai exchanged glances at this comment.

"So," Randy said, "it's serious with you and Saronna?"

Duncan hesitated. He had firmly resisted his parents' attempts to pry into his love life, but these were his friends, and they had both confided in him in the past. "Yes, it's serious—on my side, anyway. I'm not doing too well at reading Saronna's feelings."

"Oh, I think it's safe to say the woman's got a major case for you, Dunc," Randy said authoritatively. "I can read women pretty well—except for Sai—and I'd say Saronna's gone round the bend where you're concerned."

Duncan grimaced. "Maybe it looks that way to you, but she won't let me get near her. Anything more ardent than holding her hand, and she acts terrified of me."

"Give her some time," Sai said. "After all, I loved Randy for years and never let him do more than kiss my cheek occasionally."

"Besides that," Randy said, "Saronna's father kept her almost locked away in their house until the day he brought her here. Maybe she just needs to get used to the idea of being in love?"

"It would be easier to take your advice," Duncan said, "if I didn't know you two were stupid enough to waste years of your lives keeping your feelings secret from each other."

Sai stood up, an excited gleam in her eye. "You asking for trouble, Dunc?"

"No," Duncan said with a grin. "Are you offering trouble?"

"No, she's not," Randy said, standing up behind Sai and slipping both arms around her waist. "We're still guests here, sweetness—for the moment, anyway. Besides, if you hurt him too badly, he won't make it to the wedding tomorrow."

Duncan frowned. "I don't know if I should go, Ran. I'd hate for your wedding to be spoiled by a ritual assault. Bloodshed does tend to put a damper on that festive feeling."

"Bah!" Sai scoffed. "You're our only real friend here. We'd be sorry to see you miss our wedding, even if it's only at the ThreeCon registry office."

"How about if we have it here, then?" Duncan said. "We could do the service in the courtyard and record the registration remotely."

Sai looked at Randy, who nodded his acceptance. "It's okay with me," he said. "I don't care where I get married, just so Sai doesn't change her mind and leave me waiting there alone."

Sai chuckled and slipped an arm around Randy. "That's not likely now, love—not now that I've finally found out why you're so popular with women."

Randy turned a dull red color.

Duncan let out a crack of laughter. It still seemed a little weird that Sai and Randy were getting married, but at least they hadn't changed.

"I told you I'd make you pay for all those other women," Sai said sweetly.

"Yes, you did," Randy said.

"One down, two thousand, one hundred and seven to go," Sai said, her tone ruthlessly cheerful.

"You're making that number up," Randy said.

"Yes. The real number is probably much higher."

"Two down," Duncan said, grinning.

"Never mind," Randy said, nuzzling Sai's neck. "I can take it. Anything's better than thinking you don't love me."

"I think I'll leave now," Duncan said, hastily jumping to his feet.

"Don't bother," Sai said. "We'd better get moving if we have to pack today."

Duncan shook his head. "What's one more day? Since the wedding will be here, why don't you stay until after the service tomorrow?"

The two of them exchanged glances. When Randy nodded, Sai accepted for both of them.

"I'll go speak to Margaret about the arrangements," Duncan said. "We can have a little party afterwards. Do you want to invite anyone?"

"Just our folks," Randy said, "and I don't think they'll make it in time."

Duncan smiled. "Sorry, but I can't change the laws of physics, much as I'd like to. If there's no one else, how about if I invite Dad and Naomi and Saronna?"

"Sounds good," Randy said, nuzzling Sai's neck again.

Duncan started for the door. In a way he was glad they were leaving. Watching two people who were so happy together was a painful reminder of how little progress he was making with Saronna. "I'm going to find Margaret. Maybe you two should go to your own rooms. Either that, or lock the door again."

Neither of them even looked up.

"STOP it!" Saronna said jumping up from the bench. "Don't you say those things about Duncan. None of it is true."

"Yes, it is." Kendall Umberto stood in the middle of the central courtyard with his chin thrust out and a pugnacious gleam in his eye. "It's all over the off-world quarter that he bought you from your father. How can you defend him after that?"

"He didn't," Saronna said angrily. "It was Vladimir, not Duncan."

"But he kept you here, didn't he? And now you tell me he's put you in danger."

"He was helping a woman. It wasn't his fault."

"How noble!" Kendall sneered. "Or did he want to get in bed with her, too?"

"She's old enough to be his mother," Saronna said scornfully.

"Is that what he told you? A likely story!"

Saronna pointed in the direction of the front door. "Go away! Go away and never come back."

When he didn't move, she started for the nearest corridor, which happened to lead to the dower court, but Kendall caught her arm before she had gone more than a dozen steps.

"Wait, Saronna, wait!" His face crinkled into a concerned scowl. "Don't stay here with him. Come away with me. I'll keep you safe, I promise."

Saronna pulled her arm free and turned to face him. "Don't you touch me, you cretin! I never want to see your face again."

"Don't say that," Kendall said, his face growing red with emotion. "I love you, Saronna. You must know I love you."

He made a determined grab for her shoulders and tried to pull her close, as if he wanted to kiss her. Saronna squirmed out of his grasp and confronted him.

She would need to calm down if she was going to use her gift. "Keep your hands off me! Touch me again, and I'll make you very sorry."

"Saronna," Kendall began, taking one step toward her.

"Is anything wrong?"

Saronna jumped at the sound of Duncan's voice, and Kendall Umberto started violently.

"You!" he said, glaring at Duncan, who had stepped out of the shadows into the sunlight.

"Yes, me," Duncan said. "I live here, remember?"

Kendall drew himself up a little straighter. "I'm going now, Saronna," he said loftily. "I'm leaving this house and never coming back. Will you come with me?"

"Certainly not," Saronna said. "You can't leave soon enough for me."

Kendall turned and stalked from the courtyard with a great deal of dignity.

"We'll deposit your last draft in your account," Duncan called after him.

Kendall kept walking.

Saronna turned to Duncan, almost more irritated with him than she had been with Kendall. "Why aren't you angry at him? He tried to kiss me."

"I know. I saw him do it."

His lack of ire incensed her. A protector should live up to the name. "And you didn't do anything? You could have challenged him."

"What purpose would that serve?" Duncan said. "I don't have any use for a dead tutor. This planet needs all the knowledge it can get."

Saronna tightened her hands into fists. "You didn't mind that he tried to kiss me?"

"Of course I minded. But I also saw you push him away. If you hadn't, then I'd have been upset."

She frowned. "Were you watching to see what I would do?"

"Yes," he said. "And something did bother me, Saronna."

She frowned again. "What?"

Duncan stepped closer. "You weren't afraid of Kendall. You didn't like his touching you, and you made that plain, but you were never afraid of him. I thought maybe you were afraid of me because you're just not used to men, but you weren't in the least fearful with Kendall, not even when he grabbed you. Why are you afraid of me, Saronna?"

She looked up at him for a moment before she answered. "I'm not afraid of you."

Duncan smiled. "If only you could see your face when you say that. You look like a small child trying to convince herself she's not scared of the dark."

"I'm not!"

Duncan walked even closer, and Saronna stepped backward automatically. In a moment, she felt the cool, hard surface of the wall behind her.

"Let's just see, shall we?" Duncan said.

He kept coming until his body held hers against the wall, and then her kissed her gently.

Saronna felt her head swim with confusion as thoughts and feelings warred within her. She felt warm and safe at the same time she was terrified that he would overcome her barriers and she would drop her control. She wanted him so badly, the ache in her heart hurt like a physical pain.

Duncan kept kissing her.

Saronna put her hands on his shoulders, and then moved them to cling to his neck. She knew she should use her gift, but she couldn't make herself concentrate. Instead she almost sobbed out a plea. "Someone could come by at any moment."

Duncan sighed and stepped back from her. "I suppose they could. I always pick the worst places for these scenes. You'd think I'd have more sense."

Saronna tried to pull herself together. "If you had any sense," she said tartly, "you wouldn't have hired such a fool to teach me."

Duncan shook his head. "I can't agree that Kendall's a fool. How can I call him foolish for falling in love with you when I did the same thing myself?"

Saronna gasped. Somehow when she let the air out of her lungs, it didn't seem to come back in.

Duncan flicked her cheek carelessly with one finger. "Sai and Randy are getting married in the courtyard tomorrow. Would you like to come?"

Her mind reeling, she nodded without speaking.

He turned to walk away. "Wear something nice," he said over his shoulder. He stopped and looked at her. "I'll try to find you another tutor," he added with a grin. "A woman might be best, don't you think?"

Saronna nodded again, and Duncan smiled and walked into the corridor. Saronna made herself breathe normally. She waited until he was out of sight, and then she turned and wound her way through the corridors of the house until she had worked her way behind the kitchens and into the family quarters.

As soon as she was in her own bedroom, she threw herself down on the bed and tried not to let her despair overwhelm her happiness that Duncan loved her.

CHAPTER TEN

D uncan picked up the largest glass in the bar and filled it with Shuratanian ale.

"Thanks," Warhlou hna Nedahna said as he took the glass. He drained half the ale and then swirled the remainder with a look of satisfaction. "It's good to be back at something that approaches normal gravity.

Duncan nodded agreement. "I know the feeling. So, was your visit to Krueger's moon worth the aggravation?"

Warhlou shrugged, a violent spasm of Miloran muscles. "Time will tell." He waved a hand. "Enough about my mundane business matters. Tell me about this wild-eyed, stick-wielding patriarch who's stalking you. Does he have grown sons?"

Duncan shook his head in disgust. "I should have known you'd be up on the latest gossip. Dad found out he has three boys. They're nineteen, seventeen, and eleven. From what Dad says, only the eleven year-old can be counted out of their assault plans."

Warhlou shook his head solemnly. "It's almost worse that they're so young. How the *kutra* do you fight off children?"

"I agree," Vladimir's voice said from the doorway. "Hello, Warhlou."

The Miloran offered his hand in imitation of Terran customs. Vladimir looked reluctant as he shook it. Shaking hands with a Miloran was always a chancy proposition. If they were inclined to be absent-minded, they could break bones without ever intending harm.

"Hello, sir," Warhlou said formally. He was a decade older than Duncan, but like many Milorans, he was inclined to extreme civility toward his elders. "It's kind of you to ask me to stay and observe the ceremony, especially after I dropped in without an invitation."

Vladimir waved a hand negligently, as if he were happy to have it back uninjured. "Don't thank me. This is Duncan's shindig. He's throwing this party for his friends."

Warhlou cocked his head. "Shindig?"

"Party, celebration, festivity," Duncan said, "It's an archaic term."

"Is anything ever completely archaic with Terrans?" Warhlou asked. "You all seem quite fond of the past."

Duncan smiled. "My mother would agree with you. She's fond of digging it up, certainly."

Warhlou showed his teeth in a fearsome grin. "Would that be your real mother, or some woman you've adopted for the day?"

Duncan laughed at this sally, but Vladimir didn't look amused.

"You'd better hope Sire Longworth never hears of your deception, Duncan," his father said. "He'll really be out for your blood if he hears you tricked him. That's an insult in itself, let alone knocking him down."

"You knocked him down?" Warhlou said with interest. "I wish I'd seen it. He must be very old, no?"

"No," Duncan said, irked. "He's not all that much older than I am, thank you very much, War. I'm not completely feeble, you know."

"I would have said inept rather than feeble," Warhlou said.

Duncan made a rude comment in Miloran, but Warhlou merely looked inscrutable.

Just then, Vladimir looked through the window to the courtyard where Naomi had entered. "Will you excuse me, please, Warhlou?"

The Miloran made a polite answer, and Vladimir rushed from the room.

Duncan felt a sense of relief when his father left. He was tired of Vladimir walking around with a funereal expression, muttering dire prophecies of doom. With luck, the wedding would take his mind off the possibility of ritual assault.

Warhlou hna Nedahna was also watching Naomi through the window. "Is she really that great looking?" he asked, with a nod in Naomi's direction.

"Yes," Duncan said. "Why do you ask?"

Warhlou gave another convulsive Miloran shrug. "Just curiosity. A lot of Terran men have made comments about her—envying your father, mostly. You Terrans all look so much alike, I just wonder about things like what makes a woman beautiful to you, especially a puny little thing like her."

Saronna had come into the courtyard with a vase of Terran roses that she set down on the table.

Duncan smiled as he watched her sniff the blossoms. "Beauty is in the eye of the beholder."

"What?"

"It's an old Terran saying," Duncan said. "It means that who we are—what we're accustomed to seeing around us, what we see when we look into a mirror, even how we feel about someone—affects how we see them. There's no uniform standard of beauty."

"Ah," Warhlou said sagely, "then maybe there's hope for you yet?"

Duncan laughed. "I certainly hope so."

DUNCAN was pleased when the weather held fine for the ceremony. Sai wore a simple, pale green dress that Naomi had found for her in a shop in the off-world quarter. Randy wore his best suit.

Duncan waited beside Randy as the pastor signaled them to come forward. After Sai approached from the other direction, Randy moved to take his place beside Sai, and the pastor started to speak.

"Welcome, my friends," she said, "and join us now on this joyful occasion."

At her direction, Sai and Randy joined hands and spoke their vows, promising respect, love, and faithfulness. The last vow surprised Duncan, as it had rather gone out of fashion at a wedding service, but Sai and Randy both pronounced it firmly.

The brief service concluded with an exchange of rings. As soon as Sai and Randy had kissed each other and then assorted members of the company, Warhlou took Duncan aside to ask a question.

"Why did they give each other jewelry? Is that required for a Terran marriage?"

"No," Duncan said. "It's a very old custom. It goes in and out of style every century or so. Right now it's considered new and trendy because it's just come back into vogue, but in my great-grandparents' time it was old-fashioned."

"But what's it for?" Warhlou persisted.

"It was a symbol of love," Duncan said. "The idea was to wear the ring on a finger with an artery that ran straight to the heart."

Warhlou looked perplexed. "But I thought all your blood vessels connected to the heart. And why should that organ be a symbol of love?"

"They do all connect eventually. And I don't know why, but the heart does symbolize love for us. It is a critical organ, after all."

"Most of them are," Warhlou said dryly.

Saronna spoke, startling Duncan. He hadn't noticed her standing quietly beside them. "What are Miloran weddings like?"

Warhlou rubbed his face thoughtfully. "They vary. In parts of Milora, people still rely on a go-between to negotiate a marriage. In other places, it's much more relaxed with the ceremony itself almost an after-thought, if they even have one. Some people never bother to get married."

Saronna blinked and looked a little shocked.

After everyone had drunk to the happiness of the newly married couple, a buffet was laid out on one of the tables, and they all helped themselves to local delicacies.

Duncan sat next to Saronna and observed her watching Sai and Randy.

"They look so happy," she said.

"That's customary," Duncan said. "Don't Kruegerian couples look happy when they get married?"

Saronna looked suddenly inscrutable. "They rarely know each other well enough to be truly happy with each other. It's even possible for them to meet for the first time at the ceremony. The bride is veiled, so the man might not even see her until after she's his wife."

Duncan shook his head. "I don't think I'd like that."

Saronna made no comment.

After an hour of socializing, Sai and Randy went off to use the com set to record their marriage with the ThreeCon consulate. When they came back, they exchanged a whispered conversation, and then Randy spoke to the group.

"My wife and I would like to thank you all for being here, and we'll say goodbye for now."

There was a general milling around as the newlyweds gathered their belongings and began to move through the corridor to the back of the house. Vladimir took Duncan aside.

"Is the ground car ready?" he asked.

Duncan nodded cheerfully. "You bet! Frank took care of it for me."

Warhlou looked intrigued, perhaps by the note of subterfuge in Vladimir's voice. "Is there some significance to the readiness of their vehicle?"

"You'll see," Duncan said, pleased with himself.

They installed Sai and Randy into the back of the ground car with some ceremony, and then they all stood in the enclosed drive and waved as it pulled out. The car had gone less than ten meters into the street, and was still plainly visible to the Trushenko household through the open entryway, when a bundle of metal and plastic containers dropped from underneath the vehicle and was dragged along noisily in its wake.

A burst of laughter rose from everyone but Warhlou, who looked surprised, and Saronna, who looked perplexed.

"It's a custom," Naomi explained to Saronna. "Vladimir warned me about it. The groom's friends always try to sabotage whatever transportation the couple take when they leave the wedding—just to make it conspicuous, not to disable it."

Duncan laughed even harder when the ground car pulled out of the traffic, and stopped. Randy got out. He gave a disgusted look back at the house, and walked around behind the car to remove the offending containers, under the curious gaze of a small group of pedestrians who stopped to watch him.

Just as Randy straightened up, two young men darted from the alley between the next two houses up the street and ran toward him.

"Randy!" Duncan shouted. He started forward, oblivious to shouts from his father and the security staff standing by the door. He went through the wide entryway at a dead run, but he was seven or eight meters away when the first young man reached his friend.

Taken by surprise, Randy stood frozen. As the young man drew near, Randy came alert, but he had no weapon, and the Kruegerian held a long, wicked-looking knife. Randy tried to avoid him, but the young man's knife slashed at him in a wide arc that caught the off-worlder across the chest.

Randy staggered back against the ground car just as Duncan reached him. The Kruegerian backed away a few steps, and caught at his brother's arm. The younger boy had a similar knife, and he seemed determined to use it. He took a step toward Duncan with a wild look in his eye, and then suddenly he screamed and dropped the knife, as if it pained him to hold it. Just as Sai jumped out of the car, the older Kruegerian dragged his brother backwards. Three security staff came running up behind Duncan, and the two Kruegerians darted into the street, dodging traffic as they ran.

Duncan was surprised to find that Saronna was beside him. "What are you doing here? Get back to the house!"

Before Saronna could answer, Duncan felt the ground shaking. His immediate thought was that New Jerusalem was having its first earthquake, and then he realized it was only Warhlou running.

Duncan ignored the Miloran, even when he stopped himself by ramming into the car with a noticeable thump. Duncan took Saronna's hand firmly and called to one of the security guards. "Tatiana, see that Saronna goes home now." He pushed Saronna in the other woman's direction, and turned back to Randy before either of them could answer or object.

Sai was examining her husband as he half lay against the ground car. Randy bled profusely from a wide cut across his chest. He seemed to be in pain, but his breathing wasn't distressed, so Duncan hoped the cut wasn't deep.

"I'm all right," Randy said.

Sai's answer was a curt Shuratanian obscenity. Randy grinned weakly. "Okay, so I lied," he said, gasping.

"Let's get you back to the house," Duncan said, putting one arm around his friend to try to help him up.

"Allow me," Warhlou said, and he scooped Randy up in his arms as if the Terran were a small child. He walked rapidly back toward the Trushenko house, with the rest of the party following in his wake, like schoolchildren following their teacher.

Frank Chiang turned the car, in blatant violation of local traffic laws, and drove it back to the house behind them.

"I'm sorry, Ran," Duncan said as he hurried along beside the Miloran.

"Not your fault," Randy said.

Duncan didn't argue, as they were already back in the enclosed drive and hordes of people seemed to be milling about.

There was a confused scramble as Warhlou carried Randy up the steps and into the house. A Trushenko technician trained as a medtech met the group as they came through the door.

"Put him over there," he ordered, waving an arm at a sofa in a small waiting area to one side of the hallway.

Warhlou complied and laid Randy down gently.

The technician glanced at Randy's wound, took a medi-scanner from his kit and ran it over the injured man's body, and then provided the reassurance Duncan was seeking. "I don't think it's life-threatening, but he's still losing blood. He should get treatment right away. Has a med team been called?"

"Yes," Vladimir said from behind Duncan.

The technician had ripped open Randy's shirt, and was applying a pressure bandage as he spoke. "Good. Let's keep him here until they come. They may want to take him to the hospital."

"Shouldn't we take him there now?" Sai said. "It'd be faster than waiting."

He shook his head. "The most important thing is to get the trauma treated promptly. They'll be here sooner than we could get him anywhere useful."

He was proven right a few minutes later as one of the security staff ran inside and announced that a flyter was landing on the roof.

Meanwhile, the head of Cameron Trushenko security pulled Duncan aside to ask him a question.

"Did the second one try to knife you, sir? We couldn't see very well from our position."

"Not really," Duncan said. "He looked like he was going to come at me, but then he seemed to change his mind. He dropped the knife and took off with the other man. Presumably, they were the brothers Longworth."

"Presumably," the chief said. "They must have been waiting for their chance."

"And I gave it to them," Duncan said bitterly.

"It was bad luck," the other man said. "If your friend had gone a little farther before he asked Frank to stop, he'd have been fine."

Before Duncan could reply, Tatiana Devi came up, holding a long-bladed knife. She had wrapped a handkerchief around the blade and was holding it carefully by this makeshift scabbard.

Duncan's first question wasn't about the weapon. "Where's Saronna?"

"I took her back to the family courtyard, sir," Tatiana said. "Naomi was there, so I left them together."

Duncan nodded. "Thanks."

"So this is a Kruegerian ritual knife?" the security chief said, reaching for the haft.

"Careful, sir," Tatiana warned. "It was hot when Izzie picked it up."

"Hot?" He grasped the handle gingerly. "It's still quite warm."

"May I see?" Duncan asked, holding out his hand.

The security chief reversed the knife and handed it to Duncan hilt forward. When Duncan took it, the hilt was indeed warm, almost as if it had been left lying in bright sunlight. Duncan touched the blade experimentally. It seemed cool by comparison.

"Did one of your people manage to hit the hilt of the knife with a stun gun?" Duncan said. "That's pretty fancy shooting."

"It would have been," the chief said, "but a stun gun has no measurable effect on inanimate objects. And anyway, no one could get a clear shot. *Someone,*" he put an emphasis on the pronoun, "ignored our orders and got between us and the attackers."

Duncan was unrepentant. "I had to get to Randy. It was my fault he was in danger."

A moment later, they all had to move out of the way as the med team came down the corridor from the lift, and surrounded Randy Kumar with people and equipment. Their assessment of the wound as not being life-threatening made both Sai and Duncan breathe a sigh of relief. The med team quickly prepared Randy to travel, loaded him onto an anti-grav gurney, and whisked him back down the hallway toward the lift to the roof. Sai went with him, Duncan assuring her that he would have their things delivered wherever she wished.

Events settled down quickly after that. By the time the family sat down to dinner, Sai had sent word from the hospital that Randy had been treated successfully, and would be released on the following day.

"That's a relief," Duncan said. "I'd have gone to see him, except I don't want to take a chance on bringing him more trouble."

"I think it would be best," Vladimir said grimly, "if you stayed in the house for a few days."

Duncan said nothing.

"Duncan Trushenko," Vladimir said, "will you listen to reason for once? There are two homicidal adolescents out there. Let's not give them another target, shall we?"

Duncan frowned, and his father changed his tactics.

"Please, Duncan," he said, a note of entreaty in his voice. "Promise me you'll stay in the house for a few days?"

Duncan found this straightforward plea harder to resist than any order. "All right. I'll stay here unless something really important comes up."

Vladimir seemed willing to settle for this, as he changed the subject to the wedding. "The courtyard looked lovely, my dear," he said to Naomi. "You did a good job with it."

Naomi smiled and chattered happily about her plants and flowers. Duncan listened with half an ear while he studied Saronna.

The younger woman sat with her eyes downcast, eating quietly, and not participating in the conversation except when Naomi asked her a specific question. Had the incident that afternoon upset her enough to make her still so subdued?

Duncan waited until dinner was over and caught up to her as she started back toward her rooms. "Saronna!"

She turned and waited without speaking.

"Is something wrong?" Duncan said. "You were so quiet at dinner. Did something happen to upset you?"

Her eyes flashed at this. "Upset me? But I'm only a woman. Surely I'd be upset by violence."

Duncan wrinkled his brow. "Only a woman?"

She swept her eyes down and didn't speak.

"Let's go to your sitting room," Duncan said. "I'd rather not make a scene here."

She bowed her head slightly. "It is, of course, for you to decide."

Duncan took her hand. "Come along. I want to get to the bottom of this."

She didn't say anything, not even when they were seated side by side on the sofa in her sitting room.

"Now," Duncan said, "what is this about, Saronna? Why are you acting as if you were a mindless child?"

"Mindless?" Saronna said angrily. "Does it strike you that way? But then, no one can compel you to do anything you don't want to do. Even your father has to ask rather than give orders."

Still perplexed, Duncan frowned. "But what has that got to do—" he broke off as he remembered the events of the afternoon. "Oh! You're angry at me for ordering you back to the house."

Her eyes glittered angrily. "Ordering me? You had me taken back like a child who had run away from home."

Duncan recalled his own reactions with a twinge of guilt. She was right. He had run off the rails. "I'm sorry. I had no right to treat you like that. It's just that I was afraid for you. I had to see to Randy, and I couldn't do that if I was worried about you."

She looked down at her hands and didn't answer right away. When she lifted her eyes to his, they reflected hurt rather than anger. "You told me you don't give orders except to the people who work for you."

"I know I did. But when I said that, I wasn't in love with you. I've apologized, Saronna. Can't you accept that my feelings for you made me do something I wouldn't ordinarily do?"

She thought about it for a few seconds, and then she nodded. "Yes."

"Then you forgive me?"

She nodded again, and Duncan leaned forward and kissed her gently.

"We're not in the corridor," he said softly, "we're not in the library or the courtyard. No one's going to come in without knocking. We could lock the door if we wanted to, Saronna."

She didn't answer, but the look of distress in her eyes was enough to give Duncan pause.

"What is it?" he said. "Why do you look so afraid? I could never hurt you. Surely you know that?"

"Yes," she almost whispered the word.

Duncan sighed. "You don't look as if you believe it."

When she didn't answer, he got to his feet.

"Well," he said, "I'm a trader by profession, so I'll make you a deal. Walk me to the door and kiss me goodbye, and I'll leave you alone until supper time."

She stood up beside him. "All right," she said, offering her hand.

Duncan shook it solemnly and then held it as he walked to the door. When they stopped, Saronna waited expectantly. As Duncan leaned toward her, she closed her eyes, lifted her face, and parted her lips slightly. Duncan lost his head for a moment. He caught her up in his arms and kissed her passionately.

Saronna seemed as swept away as he was, softening in his arms. When he ran his hands down her back, and kissed her neck, his arousal grew. Duncan pressed himself against her. For a moment it seemed as if she wanted him as badly as he wanted her, and then she gave a little sob.

It completely killed the mood for Duncan. "Good thing we made that deal," he said.

"Yes."

He bent down and swiftly kissed her forehead, and then opened the door. "See you at supper?"

"Yes," she said again.

He slipped through the doorway with a smile, and the door shut behind him. A moment later he heard a click and knew that she had locked the door. He sighed and went back to his own room.

ONCE she had turned the key, Saronna sat down on the sofa. She knew quite well she should set up the shrine and pray. She knew she had been very close to breaking her vows, but she made no move toward the cupboard. Instead, she sat for a long time remembering how it had felt when Duncan kissed her, how his hands had held her so tightly, how she could feel the warmth of his breath on her neck. She sat for a long time, trying to solidify the memory so that she would have it always.

DUNCAN lay on his back on his bed, staring at the ceiling. He had found he could think more clearly if he stared at a flat, featureless expanse like a ceiling; it was better than closing his eyes for clearing his concentration.

The more he thought over the events of the Trushenko household for the past few weeks, the more they bothered him. There were too many coincidences and unexplained circumstances. How had Sai and Randy come to be locked in their office just when the com set failed, *and* Sai misplaced her pocket com in the sofa? And what could have fused the circuits in the com set? Then today, why had the young Kruegerian suddenly dropped the knife that afternoon, and why was it still warm to the touch, minutes later? Had something made it literally too hot to hold? What could cause such an occurrence?

As Duncan mulled these things over, he remembered the times he had held Saronna close, and then suddenly felt his arousal fade. As Duncan's thoughts slid back to the other unexplained situations, he sat up abruptly.

"No!" he said out loud. "It couldn't be!"

He sat expectantly, half expecting someone or something to dissuade him from this tentative explanation. When no one came forward, he turned toward the desk.

"Attention, terminal. Activate."

"Terminal on," the machine said.

Duncan disliked voice mode in dealing with machines, but it was difficult to work a keypad while lying flat on his back. He lay down again, propping his head up on the pillow and staring at the ceiling overhead. "Activate encyclopedia."

"Encyclopedia active," said the disembodied voice.

"Do a comprehensive search on telekinesis and on telekinetics," Duncan ordered. "Be sure to include absolutely everything about telekinetics on the planet Krueger's World."

"Searching," the voice said. A moment later it continued. "Twenty-seven entries found. Primary entry on telekinetics on Krueger's World is three thousand, two hundred and twenty-seven words long."

"Read it to me," Duncan said. "Tell me if there are any illustrations."

SUPPER was a more relaxed meal. Saronna had forgiven Duncan and enjoyed the light meal more than she had dinner.

Vladimir was tired, too tired even to discuss how his business was doing. He yawned a couple of times toward the end of the meal, causing Naomi to fuss over him.

"You're going straight to bed," she said briskly. "You need a good night's sleep, Vlad."

He didn't argue, and when they were finished eating, the two of them rose together and said good night.

Saronna watched them walk, arm in arm, into the shadows toward the door to Naomi's room. She turned to look at Duncan and found that he was watching her.

"I think I'll say good night, too," he said easily. He came around the table and kissed her forehead chastely. "See you in the morning."

She nodded, a little disappointed at this decorous farewell.

After he had gone, she walked to her rooms and prepared for bed, pondering the unfairness of a life where she was sworn to avoid the thing she wanted most in the world. She had just pulled out the shrine when there was a knock at the sitting room door.

Saronna was surprised. Naomi and Vladimir shared a bed almost every night. Saronna didn't think Naomi would leave Vladimir to see her.

She pushed the shrine back into the cupboard and scrambled to her feet. She hesitated just a second, instead of opening the door, because she was wearing nothing but one of the filmy night dresses that Naomi had thought suitable for Saronna's position.

"Who is it?" she called. Her rooms had Kruegerian doors, and there was no speaker system, so she simply raised her voice to be heard through the door, just as she had always done in her father's house back in Samaria.

"It's me," a muffled voice said. "Duncan."

Saronna was flustered. "I'm not dressed."

"I need to talk to you. I can't stand here shouting. Open the door, please."

Saronna opened the door a crack. "What is it?"

"I need to talk to you," Duncan repeated. "Can I come in?"

"Can't it wait until tomorrow? I'm not dressed."

Duncan moved to peer at her through the small opening between the door and the jamb. "You look dressed enough to me. You could wear that to a party, and no one would know it wasn't a party dress."

Saronna opened the door reluctantly, and Duncan stepped inside. He shut the door behind him and looked around her sitting room curiously, as if he had never been there before.

"What's so important?" Saronna said. "Has anything happened?"

"No. It's just that I was thinking about our conversation earlier today—about how feelings can make you do things you wouldn't ordinarily do."

"What?" Saronna said, mystified.

He took her hand and pulled her toward the bedroom door. "I've never seen your bedroom. Why don't you show it to me now?"

She hung back. "No!" she said, trying desperately to pull her hand free. "I don't want to go into the bedroom."

"Well, I do. Come along."

He dragged her to the door and pulled her through to the other room.

"Why are you doing this?" Saronna said.

"What did you call it? Enforcing my rights?"

She felt her mouth go dry. This couldn't be happening. Duncan would never do this—never! "You said you wouldn't do that."

"I know I did." He grinned, but he didn't look amused. If anything he looked angry. "But that was before I fell in love with you. You seem so shy of me, Saronna. I think it's time you got over that shyness. You'll be fine once you really get to know me."

He pulled her close and kissed her. Saronna could feel that he was very aroused. She tried to pull away, but he wouldn't let her go. Instead, he lifted her in his arms, took three steps toward the bed, and then fell forward, so that they landed on the bed with her underneath him.

"Now," Duncan said, a curious note of anger in his voice, "isn't this cozy?" He ran one hand down her body and then back up to tug at the strap of her gown. He slipped it from her shoulder and then kissed her bare skin. When he did the same thing on her other shoulder, Saronna squirmed under him.

"Let me go!" she demanded. She could feel immediately that it had been a mistake to move, as her writhing seemed to have aroused him even more. She didn't wait any longer, but forced herself to concentrate enough to invoke her gift.

He was still lying right on top of her, so she knew immediately that she had been successful.

Duncan stared down into her face, his expression a curious mix of vindication and animosity. "I didn't really believe it until now."

"What are you talking about? Get off me!"

He obeyed, rolling off her to lie next to her on the bed. "You'll have to tell me how you do that. Considering I took a fool-proof aphrodisiac, that's quite an amazing trick."

Saronna held her breath for a few seconds, debating the implications of this speech. She sat up, and pulled the straps of her gown up over her shoulders. "Get out of my room."

He looked quite stern for someone who had been thoroughly aroused only seconds before. "Not just yet. Although we can go into the sitting room if it makes you feel more comfortable. You and I need to talk."

She stood up and turned to face him, uncertainty making her fear win out over her anger. "You know about me?"

He nodded and sat up. "I figured it out, finally. It took me a while. I felt pretty dumb once I realized what you'd been doing, but then I was too obsessed with other things to notice your psy skills."

Saronna could feel her anger growing as she thought about how he had tricked her. "So," she said hotly, "this scene was set to trap me? You frightened me deliberately, to trick me into revealing my gift!"

"Yes."

She took one step forward and slapped his face with as much force as she could muster.

Duncan made no move to stop her. "I suppose I deserved that." His tone was mild, as if she had merely called him names. "Although, I have to tell you, I don't much appreciate the fact that you felt free to manipulate me—to manipulate my body—without so much as a word of explanation about what you were doing to me and why."

Saronna didn't answer. Shame crowded in to keep fear and anger company. He was right that she had manipulated him. She had done it many times to other men and never felt the least remorse. Why did it feel so bad now? She turned her face away, unable to meet his eyes.

Duncan stood up. "Why did you do it, Saronna? I don't mean tonight; you were scared, and I'm not proud of what I did to make you afraid. But what about the other times? Did you truly believe I was a threat? Did you think I wouldn't stop if you said no to me?"

Saronna shook her head. She couldn't let him think that she was afraid of him.

"Then why?" Duncan said insistently.

"I was afraid I wouldn't say no," she said in a small voice, before she could stop herself.

He took a step nearer. "Then you do care for me?"

She nodded. Duncan stepped close and put his arms around her.

"Can't you say it?" he asked gently.

"No," she said in a whisper. No, she could never say it out loud. She could never sin as her mother had. Someone must atone, and she had promised her mother it would be her.

He sighed and took her by the hand, but gently. "Let's go into the other room."

She followed him and sat down on the sofa beside him.

"Now," Duncan said, "tell me about the telekinesis. How long have you had this ability?"

This, at least, was a lesser sin. She had told Paul about her gift when she had to. "Since I was twelve."

"Your father didn't mention it to my father?"

Saronna shrugged. "Father doesn't know. Mother did, but no one else knows except my brother Paul— and now you." And the other Believers, but she couldn't tell him that.

Duncan looked surprised. "Why not? Why keep it a secret?"

Saronna wouldn't meet his gaze. One lie followed another, just like cattle going off to market. "You said yourself my people are superstitious. My mother was afraid people would call me a witch if they knew, and witchcraft is a crime. Mother told me to keep it a secret, even from my family."

"But you told Paul?"

"He found me practicing, once. I had to tell him then, but he promised not to tell anyone else." Perhaps that was one reason Paul had trusted her with the truth about himself. Both of them had secrets to keep.

"So it was you who fused the com set in Sai and Randy's office? How did you know how to do it?"

"I looked it up in the encyclopedia," she said, unable to keep the pride out of her voice.

"But why did you lock them in? Was it because you wanted them to get together?"

She nodded, happy that she could tell the truth about this part. "I knew they loved each other. It seemed like a good thing to do." She hadn't felt bad about doing it because she had known that, but it wasn't her only reason. She had wanted Sai to go away and not be a temptation for Duncan.

Duncan smiled. "It was a good thing. So you can make objects heat up suddenly. Is that what you did to that boy's knife this afternoon?"

She tilted her head. "Was that what gave me away?"

"Partly." His smile widened to a rueful grin. "But mostly it was when I realized that I could hardly sleep at night because I was so turned on from thinking about you, and yet, whenever I got really close, somehow I didn't stay that way."

Saronna flushed again. She wasn't used to discussing this topic, especially with someone who could be affected by this particular skill.

Duncan expression grew more serious. "Thank you for saving me from that wild-eyed Kruegerian child."

"You're welcome," she said, pleased to be thanked.

"But, you must be able to do more than heat things up. I mean, you heat me up, in the usual way, and then you cool me down quickly. How do you do it?"

"It's," Saronna began shyly, "it's all a matter of knowing how the parts of—of a man work."

Duncan nodded. "I can see where that would help. So you can do other things besides affect temperature?"

A small round bowl full of sweets stood on the table in front of them. Saronna held out her hand, and the bowl slid across the table toward her, stopping just before it came to the edge.

"Wow." Duncan gasped, his eyes wide. "You could put on a magic show."

Saronna shrugged, inordinately pleased but trying not to show it. "I don't care to perform for strangers."

"Can you lift things?"

She shook her head. "Not very far. Lifting requires much more energy than moving something. Gravity is much harder to fight than inertia."

Duncan grinned with delight. "Did you know that before you came here?"

"No," she said. "Not the actual words. Kendall taught them to me. He was speaking of the difference between ground cars and skimmers and flyters, but I applied it to my own gift as well."

Duncan nodded. "I imagine that the more you learn about matter—how it's structured, how it behaves in different circumstances—the more you could affect it with your psy talent."

"Perhaps," Saronna said vaguely, hoping to change the subject away from the ways in which she had changed matter.

Duncan grinned again. "I'll bet you anything Dad tries to figure out a way to make credits from this."

The idea of Vladimir discussing her talent made her flinch. "No! Please don't tell him. Don't tell anyone."

His eyes opened wide in surprise. "But why not? We're not superstitious. No one's going to burn you at the stake for witchcraft, or anything like that."

Fear made her desperate. "Please! The more people who know, the more there's a chance that word could get back to my family. I don't want anyone to know."

"All right," Duncan said reluctantly. "It's your decision."

"Thank you."

He touched her cheek very gently with one fingertip. "Do you forgive me for frightening you tonight?"

Of course. *He* had forgiven her for what *she* had done. "Yes. I'm sorry I didn't tell you what I was doing to you."

"It's all right," Duncan said gravely. "I'll try not to make you feel like you have to do it again." He sighed and looked away. "I think I'd better leave now. The sight of you in that outfit makes it hard to keep that promise."

Saronna looked down at the filmy gown that draped her body. "Do you like it?"

"Yes," Duncan said frankly. "I love it. It's one time when Naomi's taste coincides precisely with my own."

The thought that he found her attractive warmed her. "There are others in the dressing room that are even flimsier. I don't feel comfortable wearing them, though."

He groaned. "Do me a favor and don't tell me about them right now."

She nodded solemnly.

Duncan took her face in both his hands and studied her intently. "What is it, Saronna? Why is it I feel like I've only learned half your secret?"

She stroked his hand gently. More than anything she felt an immense relief that she hadn't been mistaken about him. He wasn't cruel and autocratic; he was the same man who had been so kind to a stranger. She wanted this feeling to last as long as it could, to savor it until the moment came when he realized she could never give him what he wanted. "Give me more time. Please."

Duncan leaned over and brushed her lips with his in the faintest of kisses. "All right, Saronna. We'll do this on Kruegerian time."

And then he rose and went to the door, leaving Saronna sitting all alone.

She made herself say her prayers that night. It took her several minutes to be able to light the candle, and once she had, she stared at it, instead of at the female figure, as she went through the words of her prayers strictly by rote.

ai and Randy stopped to visit on their way to the spaceport, then boarded their ground car in the enclosed driveway where they had departed from their wedding. This time no noisy bundle dropped behind them as the car pulled away. Vladimir hustled everyone inside briskly, and a little while later, Duncan called the spaceport to confirm Sai and Randy's safe departure.

Four days after Sai and Randy had gone, the guard at the front gate called Saronna and told her that her brother was asking to see her.

Saronna took Paul into the family courtyard, as Duncan was in the parlor. She was distressed to see that his face was marked by a bruise on his left cheek, and she could barely wait until he sat down to ask him what had happened.

"Father punished me," Paul said. For one terrible second, Saronna thought their father had discovered Paul's secret. "I told him I'd been to see you," Paul went on, "and he was angry at me."

"Oh, Paul." Saronna laid her hand gently on his shoulder, and he flinched from her touch as if it pained him. "Did he use his staff?"

Paul ducked his head, mortified at her insistence on knowing the details. "It's nothing. I'm fine."

"But," Saronna said, still worried, "how did he know to ask you about visiting me?"

"He didn't," Paul said, with an impatient wave of his hand. "I told him I'd been to see you, because I wanted you to be able to come home for Ruth's wedding."

Alarm flooded Saronna. Had her near-fatal efforts been for nothing? "I thought Father had changed his mind about Ruth marrying Sire Pederson?"

Paul nodded. "He did. One reason was that Caleb Shraeder came to see him. Joshua, his eldest son, wants to marry Ruth. When Joshua found out Father was talking to Eli Pederson, he persuaded his father to let him offer for her. He wants to get married right away so that Eli Pederson can't interfere."

"And Father agreed?"

"Yes. The wedding is tomorrow."

Saronna wondered how this sat with Leah. Whatever claims of oppression she might make in her prayers, Leah had always wielded influence with Saronna's father, and the entire household knew it. "What does your mother think of the match?"

"She's happy because Joshua is the eldest and will inherit one day."

Saronna reviewed what she knew of Caleb Schraeder's household. His wife was a cousin of her father's, so his son had visited the Maynard house occasionally. "But is Ruth happy?"

Paul shrugged his shoulders. "I think so. She smiled when he came to the house."

An eldest son of about the right age who cared enough to persuade his father to offer for her—this was probably the best that Ruth could hope for. No need to interfere again, which was just as well since the wedding was so soon. "But I can't go home for the wedding."

Paul grinned, pleased with himself. "Yes, you can. Father sent me to invite your protector as a guest for the wedding. He can bring his woman with him if he chooses. You know it as well as I do."

Saronna rose to her feet. It might be nice to go home for a happy occasion instead of showing up as an uninvited guest. Leah would be too busy with the wedding to bother her. "Really? Father did that?"

"Yes," Paul said, nodding emphatically. "He was impressed with your protector when he came before. He said we owed him a favor and there was no reason we couldn't invite him to the wedding—his sire, too, if he wishes to come."

"Oh," Saronna said, remembering the Longworths, "if only it were safe!"

"Why wouldn't it be safe?"

Saronna explained about the incident with Sire Longworth, and the assault on Randy.

Paul's scorn was evident. "Do you mean he's hiding here in his house?"

"No," Saronna said, "he's not hiding. This man's sons are little more than children. Duncan doesn't want to hurt them."

"So you think he'd be afraid to come to our house for the wedding?"

"What wedding?" Duncan's voice said from behind them.

Saronna jumped in her chair, and Paul got to his feet.

"Hello," Duncan said, walking around into the sunlight in front of them. "Am I interrupting a private conversation?"

Paul looked nonplused at the idea that Saronna was entitled to keep secrets from her protector. "Of course not. I was just telling Saronna that my father has arranged a new marriage for our sister Ruth. He has invited you and your sire to attend the ceremony tomorrow, at our house in Samaria."

Duncan bowed slightly. "We're honored." He looked at Paul's bruise and he frowned. "Did something happen on your way here? Were you attacked?"

Paul shook his head impatiently. "No, of course not. I was disobedient, and my father punished me for it."

"Really?" Duncan said incredulously.

"It's nothing," Paul said. "Will you come or not?"

Duncan looked at Saronna. "Of course I'll come. I can't answer for my father, but I'd be delighted to attend—with my woman, naturally."

"Duncan!" Saronna said. "You know your father doesn't want you to leave the house just yet. You promised him."

"I promised to stay inside unless something important came up," Duncan said. "I think your sister's wedding qualifies as important, don't you?"

Paul looked gratified at this display of boldness.

Saronna was horrified. Duncan didn't understand the danger. "But, Duncan, I don't want to go."

He smiled at her. "Don't be silly, Saronna. I know quite well you want to go."

"I've changed my mind."

"I don't think so," Duncan said. "And let's not quarrel in front of your brother, shall we? I wouldn't want him to think we don't get along."

Paul was indeed looking uncomfortable. He pulled a folded square of thick paper from his pocket. "I can't stay. I'll leave this with you now, and I'll look for you tomorrow."

"Certainly," Duncan said, taking the paper. "Do you need my father's answer now?"

"It's of no consequence," Paul said, with the indifference of someone who had no part to play in the preparations for the wedding feast. "Another guest or two won't make a difference."

Duncan walked him to the door and bowed one last time as Paul departed. Saronna followed behind him, waiting until they were back into the courtyard to speak.

"Duncan Trushenko," she said in imitation of Vladimir, "you can't go all the way to Samaria tomorrow. It's not safe."

"Why not?" he said. "We can take a flyter. You can't tell me the Longworth family resources include a flyter they could use to follow us. They wouldn't be living on that street if they had that kind of money."

Saronna bit her lip. It sounded convincing, but such an excursion was still a risk she saw no reason for him to take.

"Look at me, Saronna," Duncan said, taking her hand. When she raised her eyes to his, he smiled warmly. "Now, tell me again you don't want to go home to see your family for your sister's wedding?"

She looked away, unwilling to attempt a lie in such a circumstance. "I can see them some other time."

"When? How likely is it that your father would let us drop by uninvited—again?"

She pulled her hand free, knowing he was right in his assessment. "It doesn't matter. They're not my family anymore. I'm your woman now, and that's what counts."

"Don't be silly. You and I both know you're not really my woman. I don't own you, and you don't owe me any loyalty. You don't owe me anything at all, and if you have feelings for me, you can't bring yourself to talk to me about them."

Saronna bit her lip and said nothing. There was nothing she could say.

"Now," Duncan said. "I suggest you decide what to wear tomorrow. I'm going to tell Dad he's been invited to a Kruegerian wedding."

"I won't go," Saronna said flatly, feeling a rush of excitement at her rebellion.

Duncan bowed deeply, as if she had been a patriarch. "Very well. That decision is, of course, up to you. But even if you stay home, I'll just go without you."

He turned and started toward his father's office in the southwest quadrant of the house. Saronna stared after him, and hoped that his father would be able to talk him out of visiting Samaria.

It was a forlorn hope. Vladimir argued and shouted and called Duncan names, but his son wouldn't be persuaded to stay home. There was a brief, almost nasty scene after supper, when Naomi asked Vladimir if she could also attend the wedding with Duncan, and Vladimir lost his temper. He shouted at her, and uttered an ultimatum worthy of any Kruegerian patriarch that she wasn't going anywhere. Naomi looked considerably chastened by this outburst, and not even Vladimir's subsequent apology served to make her less subdued. Saronna went to bed that night enveloped by a feeling of dread she hadn't felt since her arrival.

SARONNA sat silently as the flyter landed. Worry consumed her. Would the Longworths find Duncan so far from the Trushenko home? It seemed less likely here in the hills. She tried to put that worry away, and concentrated on the need to act circumspectly again.

When Duncan opened the door, she wrapped her veil securely around her, trying to walk with the self-effacing modesty that had been automatic for so long. As soon as they were within the town, she tried to drop back behind Duncan, but he kept stopping to wait for her.

"You go first," Saronna corrected him. "I'll follow."

"No. We're together, and we're equals. You walk beside me."

"Duncan!" Saronna said urgently. "This is not the off-world quarter. This is Samaria. Please, do as I ask."

"No."

"You did it when we came before."

"I wasn't in love with you then."

"Please!" She was pleading now. She was as afraid for him as she was for herself. A man wasn't immune to stoning or other dangers. "I'll do whatever you like when we get home—I'll come to your bed if you wish—but please do as I ask now and behave as a Kruegerian man would."

Duncan stopped in his tracks and faced her. "Do you think I want that? Do you think I want you on those terms?"

She couldn't lie to him. "No, I made the offer knowing you'd refuse it, because I need for you to understand how serious this is. Please, Duncan!"

He stared at her for a moment, and then capitulated. "All right." He turned his back on her as he started forward again.

She fell in step behind him, thinking how strange it was to walk behind him just as she had so often walked behind her father. Duncan was taller than Josiah Maynard, and slimmer, and Saronna was quite certain no curious onlooker would mistake him for a resident of Samaria.

Paul met them at the door, greeting Duncan with a formal bow and ignoring Saronna. "Welcome to our home. We're honored that you could join us for this occasion."

"I'm honored to be asked," Duncan said. Saronna had briefed him in the flyter, to give him an idea of what the events of the afternoon would be, and what was expected of him as a guest. "I brought a woman of my household with me," Duncan went on. "I hope you can provide for her as well."

"Certainly," Paul said, finally smiling at Saronna. "My mother will take care of her." He lifted a hand, and a veiled woman who had been waiting in the doorway behind him stepped forward.

"My father's guest has brought his woman, Mother," Paul said. "Will you see to her comfort?"

Leah nodded and took Saronna's hand possessively. "Please tell your father I've taken the woman upstairs."

Saronna looked over her shoulder as she was led upstairs. All at once she felt as if she were leaving Duncan behind her forever. She wanted to pull away from Leah and run back downstairs to Duncan, but she didn't. She knew she couldn't. She was back in Samaria.

PAUL gestured for Duncan to follow as he headed toward the corridor that led to the central courtyard. Duncan went reluctantly. He had an odd feeling that, having brought Saronna to her home, he couldn't be sure of getting her back when it was time to leave.

"I'm sorry my sire is busy with his other guests," Paul was saying, "but there's food and drink waiting, and I'll wait for a chance to present you."

"No problem," Duncan said absently. Saronna hadn't coached him on absolutely everything that could be said, so he was a little uncertain of how to respond.

They came into a large courtyard, and Duncan saw that Paul was quite right about the food. There were tables heaped with all kinds of dishes—cooked meats, fruits, bread, sweets, and some things Duncan couldn't identify.

Over forty men had already gathered for the festivities. All of them looked Kruegerian to Duncan. Several of the older ones wore the full beard of a patriarch. Duncan noticed two bearded men engrossed in conversation. One of them was Josiah Maynard, which suggested the other might be the groom's father.

Paul confirmed it by nodding in that direction and saying, "My sire is conversing with Caleb Schraeder, the father the groom."

"I see," Duncan said. "Discussing the dowry?"

Paul shook his head. "That was all worked out ahead of time. They're probably talking about crops or the weather or some other aspect of farming or wine making. Either that or politics."

Paul offered food, and Duncan tried a few things. Saronna had told him that the sexes would be strictly segregated until the ceremony itself. After that, they would be allowed to mingle. A wedding was one of the few times Kruegerian women were allowed to interact with men who were not their relatives. The women would bring the bride into the courtyard to be married, and would stay to eat and dance and otherwise celebrate the occasion. Since it was assumed that all the men present could claim either kinship or friendship with Sire Maynard, the women wouldn't need to wear their veils.

Duncan chewed a square of bread covered with ground vegetable spread and wondered what Saronna was doing.

SARONNA followed her father's wife up the stairs with a feeling of dread. The aroma of roasting meat wafted from below and mixed with the scent of incense that hung in the air, as she rose upward. That, combined with the muted sunlight filtering down from the high windows under the eaves, exercised a powerful sense of familiarity that overwhelmed her. She was home, but she wasn't entirely sure she should have come.

Leah stopped at the top of the stairs and glanced around. Saronna knew that Ruth was most likely in her room, preparing for the ceremony with the assistance of Rebecca, and a few cousins of a suitable age.

"Come to my room," Leah said quietly, taking Saronna by the arm. "We have a few minutes before the others expect us."

Saronna's heart sank. She could think of only one reason Leah would want to see her apart from the others.

Her fears were realized as soon as Leah pulled her into her own chamber and locked the door. Two of Saronna's maternal cousins sat on the bed along with Brushka, the elderly cousin who had helped her mother to train Saronna in using her gift. They all rose as Leah and Saronna came into the room. Leah pulled off her veil and threw it on the dresser. She was shorter than Saronna, but she had the same black hair and light gray eyes.

"Now," Leah said, "we have just enough time to form the Circle. First, I must ask—Saronna, have you kept your faith?"

"Yes," Saronna said quietly, pulling her veil off as Leah had done. She glanced around her at Leah's room. Nothing had changed. They had always held their rites here, even when her mother was alive to be the center of the Circle. The thick, dark tapestries that lined the walls muffled the sound, and her father allowed Leah to have a lock on her door.

"You say the rite every night?" Leah insisted. "You haven't forgotten?"

"Yes," Saronna said. "I haven't forgotten."

"And you kept your vows?"

"Yes."

Leah took her arm again. "You never gave yourself willingly?"

"I haven't given myself at all. He hasn't forced me."

Leah gave gasp of surprise at this unexpected piece of good fortune. She pushed Saronna toward the bed.

"Quickly now. Remove your clothes. We haven't much time."

Slowly Saronna pulled off her clothing, handing each piece to one of her cousins, who folded it neatly on the bed.

When she was naked, Leah pulled her to the center of the room. Brushka handed everyone but her a candle, and the four of them took their places around her, kneeling on the floor.

Saronna tried to stall. "Why aren't my sisters here?"

Leah glared up at her. "They're busy. And you know your grandmother isn't a Believer. I couldn't make them leave her now without arousing suspicion." She pinched Saronna's arm hard enough to hurt. "Stop wasting time. We must begin now."

Saronna gave up. She closed her eyes and stood, arms folded over her breasts, silent and unmoving as the other women all began to pray out loud, in unison.

"Our Mother, we ask that you give us strength to resist our oppressors. We ask that you keep us firm in our resolve to live as your daughters. We ask that you welcome our souls when we die and join you in heaven."

Saronna opened her eyes. She forced herself to concentrate, to focus on the wick of the candle in Leah's hand. In a second, that candle lit, and a moment later, Saronna succeeded in lighting the other women's candles.

A jubilant note filled Leah's voice as she led the others in their prayer. "Our Mother, we thank you for consecrating this woman to your cause. We pledge her life to you, and ask only that you seat her at your side in heaven when she dies."

Saronna stood mute. She waited desperately for the feeling of rightness, of a connection to her mother that had come to her every other time she had played this role in the Circle. Instead she felt empty. The other women's presence wasn't a comfort, but a chain binding her, confining her to this role. Their heads were bowed reverently. None of them looked up as she surreptitiously wiped the tears from her eyes.

Their prayers changed to a chant as they recited the list of Women's Woes, the cruelties to be suffered by men in hell, and finally the words of the closing prayer. By then, Brushka and the cousins swayed in rapture, their eyes closed, their faces serene in concentration. Leah looked more self-possessed, but she, too, smiled with satisfaction.

Finally, there was a faint sigh, as all four women opened their eyes and blinked at the light. They blew out their candles and got to their feet as if they were waking from a dream. Brushka collected the candles and put them away in a drawer.

Leah nodded sternly at Brushka and the cousins. "You three go first. I'll follow in a moment with Saronna, after she dresses."

When the other women had gone, Leah watched Saronna put on her clothes. Her lips pinched in a sour frown when Saronna pulled on the red dress she had worn to Vladimir's party. "That dress is scarcely decent for one who's consecrated to the Mother."

Saronna shrugged as she slipped into the silk jacket that she wore to cover her arms and shoulders. "I'm as pure as I was when I left. My protector provides my clothes, and this is what off-world women wear."

Leah frowned at this answer. "You're different," she said. "There's something in you now that wasn't there before."

"I've learned a few things."

Leah hissed at her in disapproval. "You said he hadn't bedded you."

Saronna's smile was contemptuous as she slipped her shoes on. She had come so far in a few months, and Leah understood none of her journey. "Do you think that's the only thing a woman can learn?"

Leah suddenly slapped her, hard across the face. "I'll thank you to show some respect to me in my husband's house. Don't you forget your place here, Saronna, and mine."

Saronna put one hand to her cheek and nodded. "I haven't forgotten." She lifted her chin. "I may not be a Maynard any longer, but I'm still a consecrated woman."

Leah gave a harsh laugh. "I'm not the one who's in danger of forgetting that."

Saronna fought a blush. She managed a tight smile. "And do you remember to ask for forgiveness every night? I know very well you love Paul. You've even told him so."

"Pho!" Leah spat on the floor. "My prayers are my business. And if I've sinned, the Mother will forgive me. Paul is a good son, and he would never hurt any woman."

Saronna swallowed a gasp of surprise. Mother Eve's teachings held that a man's attentions were innately harmful to women. Did Leah know Paul's secret?

"Besides," Leah went on, "the Mother understands these things. It's not the same thing."

"Isn't it?"

Leah glared at her. "No. And as we're speaking of your powers, I want to know something."

Saronna had a good idea what the question would be, but to let on would be to answer it. "What is it that you want to know?"

"Did you cause Eli Pederson's heart attack?"

"He had a bad heart," Saronna said. "The doctor said so. He's lucky Duncan was here, or he would have died."

"That's no answer."

Saronna lifted her chin. "That's all the answer you're going to get."

Leah took a step closer. The menace in her eyes was as solid as the blade of a knife. "If you ever interfere in my daughters' lives again, I'll see that you suffer for it."

"If my sisters ever need my help, they will get it."

Leah slipped her right hand into her pocket.

Saronna didn't wait to see what weapon Leah had, if any. She concentrated on the older woman's windpipe. A second later, Leah dropped a small fruit knife and clutched her throat with both hands, gasping but unable to speak. Her face turned pale.

Saronna kicked the knife under the bed, but relented after only a few seconds. She released her concentration, and Leah drew in a sudden sharp breath. She gulped air, breathing deep rasping breaths.

"Don't ever threaten me," Saronna said.

After a few seconds, Leah got her voice back. "And don't you forget that you're a consecrated woman. You may abuse Eve's Mark to taunt me, but if you break your vows, you'll rot in hell, and your mother beside you."

Saronna felt a stab of fear. "I haven't broken my vows."

Leah's face twisted in an ugly parody of a smile. "See that you don't. My sister's soul depends on yours."

Saronna swallowed hard. She remembered her mother's hands, icy cold on Saronna's arm, as she pleaded with almost her last breath for Saronna to atone, to keep her vow of purity and absolve her mother of sin.

Leah bent down to retrieve the knife, reaching under the bed to pull it out and slip it into her pocket. "We must join the others or our guests will wonder where I am." She turned and headed for the door. She didn't look back, but Saronna knew she was expected to follow.

Ruth was almost dressed and ready when they arrived in her room. She wore a white gown covered in gold lace, with a row of buttons up the back and on each sleeve. She was trying to button the sleeves when she looked up and saw them. She gave a glad cry when she saw Saronna, and held out her arms.

"There you are," she said happily. "I'm so glad you could come."

Saronna embraced her sister briefly. "I'm happy to be here. You look beautiful, Ruth."

Ruth looked pleased at the compliment, and admired herself in the tiny mirror that hung on the wall behind her.

Saronna took a moment to greet her grandmother, who sat in a chair in the corner of the room, under the watchful eye of the widowed cousin.

Saronna's grandmother patted her hand, but seemed surprised to see her. "They didn't tell me you were coming, Saronna. Didn't you get married yourself, a while ago?"

"No, Grandmother," Saronna said, bending over to speak softly to the old woman. Her grandmother was getting worse with every year that passed. It was just as well she never left the house, or she would be hopelessly confused. "Father sold me to an off-worlder."

Her grandmother looked distressed. "I hope he treats you well. Be a good girl, Saronna."

"Yes, Grandmother."

Saronna straightened up and glanced around the room. Ruth and Rebecca had removed the third bed, the one Saronna had slept in, but otherwise it looked much the same as it had the last night she had slept here. How long ago it seemed, when her world had been defined by the walls of this house.

After Leah buttoned the last of the buttons on Ruth's sleeve, she draped a veil over her daughter's head and shoulders. Longer than an everyday veil, it masked her completely. The fabric was sheer enough that Ruth could see, but only just.

There were several other women and girls in the room. Saronna knew them all, of course, since all of them were related either by blood or by marriage. She spoke to several of them, and embraced her sister Rebecca.

Leah directed Rebecca to carry the word that they were ready.

Ruth kissed her grandmother goodbye, and then everyone except the old woman and her servant prepared to escort Ruth downstairs. Several other women were waiting in the other upstairs rooms, and they came out to the landing when the bridal party moved noisily from Ruth and Rebecca's bedroom. They all waited at the top of the main stairs until Rebecca came running up with the news that everything was ready.

The whole mass of women swept down the stairs with Ruth at their center. They walked through the front hall and down the corridor into the courtyard, where all the tables had been moved out of the way. The courtyard was already crowded with male guests, and Ruth was pushed forward, passed from hand to hand until she was at the front of the group of women.

Her father stepped up to her and took her by the arm. "Come, daughter. Your husband waits."

The crowd parted as he pulled Ruth along to the small clear space at the other end of the courtyard where a bearded Kruegerian priest waited. A tall, nervous-looking young man stood beside the priest. He was about Duncan's age, and Saronna recognized him as Joshua Schraeder.

The ceremony wasn't lengthy. The priest asked Josiah Maynard if he gave his daughter willingly, and Josiah answered that he did. The priest blessed the bride as a chaste woman, and charged her to be dutiful and obedient in serving her husband, and then turned his attention to Joshua.

He directed the groom to be kind and understanding, but not to shirk his duty as his wife's guardian. He urged Joshua to bring his children up to follow the Book, and to respect their father and the Patriarch.

The priest took Ruth's hand from her father, gave it to Joshua, and then spoke. "Joshua Schraeder, this woman is now your wife. I give both her body and her soul into your keeping. Do you accept this responsibility, with all the rights and obligations that it conveys?"

Joshua answered that he did.

"Then may heaven and the Patriarch bless your union," the priest intoned.

He smiled and closed his Book. Joshua took a deep breath and lifted Ruth's veil. He kissed her delicately on the mouth, and the crowd cheered mightily.

Saronna sighed. At least Ruth was settled.

As soon as the groom had kissed the bride, the ceremony seemed to be over. Everyone milled about in an aimless way, and Duncan noted that the women in the crowd mixed freely with the men.

From his position in the corner of the courtyard, he saw a woman embracing Ruth and weeping. It startled him because for just a second he thought it was Saronna, but this woman was shorter, sturdy where Saronna was willowy, and at least twenty or thirty years older than Saronna. The gown she wore looked suspiciously like the one that Leah Maynard had been wearing when he first arrived.

Duncan realized that she must indeed be Leah, the bride's mother, but her resemblance to Saronna perplexed him. He scanned the crowd looking for his beloved. It wasn't difficult to spot her, because her off-world clothes made her as conspicuous as he was. She was standing next to a very young woman, a girl really, and the two of them were talking in an animated way.

Duncan worked his way through the crowd until he was near them. When Saronna looked up and saw him, she seemed suddenly sad.

"Hello," Duncan said. "This must be Rebecca?"

Saronna nodded, and made introductions. Rebecca looked him over with bright interest.

She was quite short next to Saronna, and her hair was almost blonde. Duncan thought she looked more like Josiah than Paul did. Her face was more square, her eyes dark brown.

"Saronna has been telling me about your house," she said. "It sounds very interesting."

"You're welcome to visit her," Duncan said, "if your father allows it."

The two sisters exchanged glances, and Rebecca sighed. "I don't think that's likely. Not in the off-world quarter."

Duncan didn't say anything. He was finding it diffi-cult to curb his tongue. His disgust with the Kruegerian way of life grew stronger by the minute, and he had promised Saronna he would express none of it to her family, or to any of the other guests.

"Do you really allow Saronna to go out alone when-ever she likes?" Rebecca asked.

"Yes." Duncan would have preferred to have said that it wasn't a matter of what he allowed, but of Saronna being free to make her own decisions, but Saronna's eye was on him, her gaze stern.

"My goodness," Rebecca said vaguely. She glanced around the room and waved at a cluster of young women her own age. "Excuse me, please," she said, and darted off.

"Well," Duncan said, "here we are?"

Saronna's forehead wrinkled in a faint frown. "You're going to behave, aren't you?" she said, keeping her voice quite low.

"Yes," Duncan said. "Although it's difficult."

A tall man came up to them, almost as tall as Duncan, but with some of Josiah's stockiness.

"Welcome to our home," he said, not waiting for either of them to speak. "We appreciate your coming. It meant a lot to my father."

"You must be Gideon Maynard?" Duncan said, fighting the impulse to offer his hand.

The other man bowed slightly in acknowledgement, and Duncan returned the greeting.

"Please make our house your own," Gideon said. He flicked the briefest of glances at his sister, but didn't address his remarks to her at all.

"Thank you," Duncan replied. Gideon bowed again and moved off through the crowd of guests.

"Well," Duncan said, "now I've met them all except the bride."

Saronna shook her head. "My grandmother's not up to company anymore. And my oldest sister is married and living in the next town. She's too pregnant to travel."

Duncan changed the subject. "Why does Leah look so much like you? I would have thought she was your mother rather than Ruth's and Rebecca's."

Saronna looked away. "Leah and my mother were sisters."

This revelation rocked Duncan. "What? You mean your father took his wife's sister—" He broke off, uncertain how to phrase the question.

"Yes. My father bought his wife's sister to be his woman. It's not that unusual."

"It isn't?" Duncan glanced around the room at Saronna's relations. What would it be like to grow up in such a household? He couldn't imagine it. "So your siblings are also your cousins?"

"You could put it that way if you wished," Saronna said stiffly. "We don't."

"Is that why you never say half-brother or half-sister?" Duncan asked. "Because they're doubly related?"

"No. It's because we have the same father. If we had only a mother in common, then we'd be half-siblings."

Duncan stared at her. She seemed different here, stiffer, and less friendly. "Why didn't you mention this before?"

Saronna flushed, but raised her eyes to his. "You never asked me about it."

Duncan would have argued, but he suddenly re-membered where they were. "Come and have something to eat." He took her arm and led her over to one of the tables that had been moved against the wall of the courtyard.

Saronna allowed herself be led, seeming more com-placent than he had ever known her to be, but she shook her head. "No, thank you. I'm not hungry."

Duncan was disturbed by her manner, and by how pale her face looked in the sunlight. "Is something wrong?"

"No. Please don't concern yourself."

"How can I help it? You look as if you'd seen a ghost."

She gave a little sound, like a gasp crossed with a shudder. "I suppose in a way I've been reminded of a ghost. My mother died here."

"I wish we hadn't come. Me and my bright ideas!"

Saronna shook her head. "No, I appreciate your bringing me. I won't get to see my family very often. I would have regretted it if I hadn't come."

Duncan wasn't reassured, but Rebecca came back and, with a brief apology to Duncan, whispered something in Saronna's ear that made her smile. Rebecca darted back into the crowd and Duncan watched her rejoin the group of girls her own age.

"What did she say?" Duncan asked. "Or is it private?"

Saronna paused as if she were debating and then apparently decided to answer him. "She said one of our cousins is very jealous of me because you're so good looking."

Duncan lifted his brows and smiled. "Really?" He glanced over at the gaggle of girls. "Which one?"

"I'm not going to tell you. You look too pleased with yourself already."

Duncan laughed at this, and began to feel more at ease.

Soon after that, the courtyard was cleared for dancing. The tables were moved to the corridors, and guests who didn't want to participate were encouraged to move to other rooms or at least to get out of the way. A cluster of women joined hands to form a circle with Ruth in the middle of it, and then a larger circle of men formed outside the women.

Duncan stood back against the wall and watched with interest. The women began to dance, moving clockwise in a step forward, step back pattern, dipping and bobbing in time to the music of a half dozen stringed instruments and a drum. Duncan saw Saronna laughing and smiling at Ruth as she moved with the others in the steps of the dance. The men danced more slowly, in a counterclockwise direction. As the tempo increased, there were shouts of encouragement, and then Joshua Schraeder was plucked from the outer circle and pushed through the line of women so that he stood with his bride.

The two of them joined hands and began to dance in the same bobbing pattern. There were more cries from the men in the circle, and eventually, Joshua picked Ruth up by her waist and held her up as he continued to dance. As the music reached a crescendo, Joshua spun his wife around and then set her down and kissed her, wrapping her in a passionate embrace. There was a triumphant shout from the company, and the dance ended.

There was some milling around and movement back and forth as new circles formed, with no one in the center. Both the men and women seemed much younger. Duncan noticed Rebecca among the women's circle. After several minutes, the dancing had reached a frenzied pace. A young man broke from the men's circle and crashed through the women's to cheers of encouragement from the onlookers. The boy had broken the circle between Rebecca and another girl. He kissed each of them on the cheek and then stepped back to resume his place. The scene was repeated several times, each time with a different young man.

Duncan felt movement at his side and looked down to see Saronna standing beside him.

"Hello," he said. "You looked as if you enjoyed that."

Saronna nodded. "It was fun."

"Why aren't you dancing now?"

She shook her head at his ignorance. "This dance is for the unattached girls and single men. Superstition says that a man will marry one of the girls who lets him into the circle."

"I see," Duncan said, although it made no sense to him.

Saronna smiled. "You don't really approve of all of this, do you?"

Duncan glanced around. There was no one particularly close. "Not really, but we can talk about it later."

They watched several dances, ate and drank throughout the afternoon, and Duncan began to wonder when they could leave.

"Not until Joshua takes Ruth away," Saronna said when he asked her. "They'll go soon. I heard one of his brothers say the skimmers are ready."

A few minutes later, the bride's brothers and other male relations carried her trunks down the stairs. Saronna explained that these contained not only Ruth's own clothes, but the linens and other household items she was expected to bring to the marriage. The groom's family loaded all the trunks onto two skimmers, and Joshua took his leave of his wife's father.

There was little ceremony to their actual departure. Joshua bowed to Josiah Maynard, glanced around to be sure that Ruth was veiled and waiting for him, and then they started for the door. Joshua went first, with Ruth right behind him. There were cheers as they left, and shouted wishes for many sons. Everyone moved outside to the front of the house to see them off, the women pausing to pull on their veils before they stepped outside.

It wasn't until the bridal party had pulled away, pursued by the children who ran after it for a few seconds, that Duncan noticed the two men waiting across the street.

They were too far away for him to see them well, but there was something familiar in the way they stood together, waiting side by side. They were clearly waiting, because there was no house there—just an open space like a small park, with a bench and some sugarbushes growing beside the walkway.

They had to be the Longworths. Duncan stared at them. So young and so remorseless. It came to him that he could spend months waiting for them to go away. Avoiding them was no solution. He needed to fix the situation.

There was just the problem of how to keep Saronna from interfering again.

Saronna moved away for a moment to speak to Rebecca. Duncan saw Paul Maynard just turning to go inside.

"Paul!" he called, and the young man came over to him.

"Thank you for coming," he said.

"You're welcome," Duncan said. "But before I can leave, there's some business I have to attend to first."

Paul looked puzzled, and Duncan nodded across the street to where the two men stood waiting.

"Longworths?" Paul asked with interest.

"I think so. Will you do me a favor, please?"

"What is it?" Paul sounded suspicious.

"Would you take Saronna back inside and keep her there until I've finished my business? Don't let her come outside no matter what she says."

"Of course," Paul said, looking gratified, as if the request was something he could understand.

"Try not to let her know what's going on. I wouldn't want her to worry."

"All right." Paul glanced at Duncan's belt. "Don't you want to borrow a knife?"

Duncan smiled grimly. "I've never used a knife as a weapon in my life. If I tried to use one now, they'd only see it as justification to slit me in two."

Paul looked mystified. "If you don't intend to fight, then what will you do?"

It was a damn good question. Duncan wished he had as good an answer. "I don't know for sure. I've negotiated enough deals to know the best way to begin is to ask what they want. If their answer is they want my head, I might try threats."

Paul looked unconvinced, and Duncan had to admit he felt far from confident of the outcome himself. Still, he was tired of living a restricted life, and worrying about other people getting hurt. It was time to end this situation, and at least now he knew the Longworths were there, and he could ensure no one else became an accidental victim.

Duncan turned and walked through the steadily thinning crowd in front of the house. Behind him he heard Saronna arguing with Paul. He smiled at her vehemence. She didn't sound like a proper Kruegerian woman.

The two watchers stepped forward as Duncan crossed the road, drawing his attention away from what was happening behind him. In the late afternoon light, Duncan had no trouble recognizing the man and the boy who had attacked Randy. They carried long-bladed knives in scabbards on their belts.

Duncan stepped onto the walkway. It was only a beaten path, lined down the middle with paving stones. The sun had warmed the stones; he could feel the heat rising from them.

"Well," Duncan said, "you must be the Longworth brothers?"

The elder one moved forward a step. "I'm Noah Longworth. And you are Duncan Trushenko."

Duncan nodded. "I am."

The younger brother moved a step closer. Noah Longworth held up a hand as if to tell him to wait.

"What is it you want with me?" Duncan said.

The elder brother answered. "You've insulted our sire. You struck him, and you lied to him, claiming a stranger as blood kin to trick him. We want your blood."

"Your sire was beating an elderly woman," Duncan said. "I stopped him. I'm sorry I had to trick him, but it seemed the best way at the time."

Noah nodded. "We know the circumstances. Nevertheless, our father was within his rights. You acted unjustly."

"Not according to my own rules."

"We are not in your quarter," Noah said angrily. "Nor were you there when you struck my father."

It hadn't occurred to Duncan until that moment that they might feel less constrained by rules here in Samaria than they would in the off-world quarter of New Jerusalem. He struggled to keep his expression stern and unafraid. "I know that. But I tell you plainly that I'd do the same thing if it happened again."

Noah frowned. "That, at least, is an honest statement."

His young sibling tugged at his sleeve. "But, Noah, you said I'd get a chance to fulfill my vow!"

Noah pulled free of his brother's grasp. "Have some patience, Levi. I said he was honest, for once. That changes nothing. A blood debt is still owed."

The boy looked at Duncan with a wild look in his eye. "You have no off-world weapons now," he said, drawing his knife. "You won't make me disgrace myself a second time."

His brother looked at Duncan and frowned. "He has no weapons at all."

"Does it matter?" Duncan said dryly. "My friend wasn't armed when you struck him down."

Noah flushed. "The rules allow for a surprise attack. You knew it. You were being careful."

"Not careful enough. My friend was no relation; he wasn't even an employee of my family's company."

Noah shrugged. "He was living in your house. The teacher told us that."

"What teacher?" Duncan asked in surprise.

"The one who left your house the same day you struck my father," Noah said impatiently. "He said you had hired him to teach your woman." He nodded at Josiah Maynard's house. "That's how we knew where you'd go when we saw the machine head north."

"Kendall Umberto?" Duncan said. "He told you about my household?"

Noah smiled sourly. "Not without some encouragement."

Levi snorted with disgust. "You didn't have to do more than show him the knife. He had no courage at all."

"I see." Duncan folded his arms across his chest and fought the urge to run back to the Maynard house as fast as he could go. "If he told you about our household, I assume he told you my sire is a rich and powerful man."

The elder Longworth came very near to sneering. "We care nothing for that."

"Perhaps not," Duncan said. "But are you so sure that the authorities in New Jerusalem won't object if you murder an unarmed off-worlder?"

"Murder?" the younger boy looked suddenly pale. "We don't have to kill him, do we, Noah?"

"No, we won't kill him," his brother said.

Duncan suppressed a sigh of relief, and held out both hands in a questioning gesture. "Then what do you propose to do?"

Noah drew his knife. "My brother has sworn to wash his hands in your blood. I'm here to see that he gets a chance to do it."

Duncan looked at the boy. Just at the moment, he looked younger than his years. He gripped his weapon with both hands, then shuffled his feet nervously. "How much blood are we talking about here?" Duncan asked.

"Now, Levi!" Noah shouted, and he stepped back as if to allow his brother room to attack.

Levi Longworth took two rapid steps toward Duncan and swung the knife as he moved. The boy's speed surprised Duncan, who flinched from pure reflex. The edge of the blade sliced into his body in an arc, making a deep cut across his ribs and then slashing through the muscles of his upper arm.

Duncan grunted in pain, trying to hold in a scream as his nervous system felt the damage. He swayed as his blood flowed freely, soaking his shirt and jacket, and spattering red drops on the ground around his feet.

Levi dropped the knife and stared at him. At his brother's urging, he stepped up to Duncan and put his hands across the wound as if to staunch the flow of blood. After two seconds, he moved his hands to wring them together in a washing motion.

"Now," Duncan gasped, feeling more light-headed every second, "can I assume the blood debt is paid?"

"Yes," Noah Longworth said. "The debt is paid."

He replaced his own knife in its scabbard, scooped up the weapon his brother had dropped, and motioned the boy to follow him. Duncan stood watching as they retreated through the park to an alley behind a nearby house.

He was still on his feet when Gideon Maynard came up to him with two other wedding guests behind him.

"I'm sorry to make a fuss at such a happy occasion," Duncan said. "I don't seem to have much luck with weddings lately."

Before Gideon could answer, Duncan teetered back and forth, crumpled at the knees, and fell to the ground unconscious.

"BE quiet!" Paul ordered. "You're making a scene."

Saronna was frantic. Why had Paul practically forced her into the house? Something must have happened. "Where is Duncan?"

Paul frowned, his eyes angry. He looked more like their father than he ever had. "He's busy. Leave him alone. It's none of your business."

Gideon came up to them. "What's going on? Saronna, you're attracting attention. It's most unbecoming."

"I don't belong to this house anymore," Saronna said. "You can't tell me what to do."

Gideon glared at her and lifted his hand to strike.

"It's her protector," Paul said suddenly. "He's gone to face the brothers who've been pursuing him."

"Really?" Gideon said. "Where?"

"The park across the street."

Saronna started for the front door, but Gideon caught her arm.

"Saronna!" His voice was low, but his tone held venom. "You will not disgrace this family!" He looked over her shoulder as someone approached. "Mother, please take Saronna upstairs."

"Certainly, Gideon."

Leah's voice was flat and calm, but Saronna heard the menace in it.

She tried to twist out of Gideon's grip, but he held her arm like a vise. And then Leah took Saronna by the shoulders and dragged her toward the stairs.

No one was paying them any attention. The remaining wedding guests were all staring out the front windows. No one saw Leah pull Saronna up the stairs.

Saronna struggled to pull free when they reached the top step. "Let me go!" She twisted and turned, but Leah had her by one wrist. Just as she got herself loose, Leah reached into her pocket.

Saronna stepped back a pace, trying to concentrate so she could use her gift. Leah took a closed fist from her pocket. Saronna assumed Leah would try to strike her, but instead, the other woman opened her hand and tossed something fine and powdery into the air.

Saronna choked on the bitter powder as she breathed it in. Manglewort! Anyone who needed their senses numbed before they had a tooth pulled or a boil lanced got a dose of manglewort. Saronna's head began to reel.

Manglewort clouded the mind as well as numbing the senses. Saronna staggered backwards, away from Leah. Her father's wife waited a few seconds, then raced toward her and grabbed her hand.

"Come along!"

Saronna fought, but Leah was stronger. The older woman dragged Saronna into her room and threw her to the floor.

Saronna tried to push herself up, but she was too dizzy. She heard a thunk as Leah shot the bolt to lock the door.

"Now, Saronna," Leah said, "it's time for a lesson."

She took two steps closer and kicked hard with her foot.

Saronna's head snapped back as Leah's shoe made contact with her chin. She cried out. If only she could concentrate!

Leah grabbed her hair, yanking her head back again. "You little liar—oath-breaker! You promised my sister you'd stay pure."

Saronna sobbed. "I have."

The slap stung, even with her senses dulled by the manglewort.

"Don't lie to me. I can see you want to go to bed with him"

"Stop!" Saronna lifted her hands to protect her face. "I haven't done anything."

"You promised her on her deathbed." Leah slapped her again, then let go of her and moved to the dresser. She opened a drawer, then rooted around in it. When she turned, she held a vintner's knife; the wooden handle had a long curved blade that ended in a barbed hook for catching the stray tendrils of the uva vines. "Do you know the punishment for breaking the oath you made to my sister?"

Desperation made Saronna strong enough to scramble to her feet. She lurched sideways, staring at the knife in Leah's hands. "They'll punish you if you kill me."

Leah smiled. "Then you don't know the punishment? I don't need to kill you. I just need to make sure you can't ever enjoy going to bed with a man. There's an easy way to do that. But you'll wish I had given you more manglewort."

Saronna gasped.

Leah lowered the hand that gripped the knife. She advanced on Saronna. "You'd better hold still, or I might kill you by mistake."

Saronna stared at the barbed hook on the end of the blade.

Leah held the knife level with the floor, pointed straight at Saronna. "Lift up your dress."

Saronna swallowed. "No."

Leah scowled. "Lift up your dress and be still, or I'll have to cut you more to do the job."

"No."

Leah lunged, but Saronna staggered out of her way. The knife caught in her skirt and tore the red satin with a rending sound.

Leah grabbed Saronna's right hand with her left. She yanked hard and dragged Saronna toward the bed.

Saronna screamed and tried to pull away, but Leah's grip was remorseless. And then Leah whirled suddenly, coming straight at Saronna with the knife held out at eye level.

Saronna backed up until she ran into the bed. Leah lunged, knocking Saronna down. In a flash, Leah was on top of her, holding Saronna down on the bed with her body while she yanked up Saronna's skirt.

Saronna twisted and turned, trying to push Leah away. The older woman dug her left elbow into Saronna's chest with all her weight behind it, forcing the air from Saronna's lungs.

Saronna gasped as Leah's knee slid down between her legs and forced them apart. "Help!" Saronna cried weakly, unable to draw breath. "Paul! Help me!"

"Be quiet, oath-breaker!" Leah said, leaning over her. She held Saronna down with her left arm across Saronna's chest while her right hand held the knife. "I'm doing this to save my sister from damnation." She lowered the knife toward Saronna's groin. "Pray that

Mother Eve lets you live long enough to atone for your sin."

Saronna felt the cold metal against her thigh. She was afraid to move her body with the knife so close, so she dug her fingers into Leah's eyes.

The older woman screamed and pulled her head back. The knife point dragged across Saronna's thigh. Saronna felt warm blood flow across her leg as she knocked Leah's arm away and pushed as hard as she could. The other woman rolled off her and onto the floor.

Saronna darted for the door, but Leah's fingers caught the hem of her skirt.

Leah grunted as she rolled on the floor and pulled on Saronna's gown. "Come here!"

Saronna grabbed the fabric and yanked backwards, wrenching herself free. She had so much momentum, she hit the wall hard and grabbed the tapestry for support. She turned and saw Leah on her feet. The door was locked, and Saronna didn't think she could get the bolt slid over before Leah reached her.

Leah's eyes lit with angry resolution. She came at Saronna again, the knife held at the ready. "I'll have to cut quickly, then. Too bad for you."

Saronna yanked as hard as she could on the thick fabric of the tapestry behind her. A series of loud pings sounded as the hooks on which the tapestry hung gave way and sprang from the wall. The tapestry fell on Saronna's head, but she was expecting it, and caught it. She held it in front of her just as Leah lunged at her. The barbed knife caught in the folds.

Leah screamed in rage and frustration as she tried to twist the knife free of the tightly woven threads.

Saronna shoved hard and tossed the heavy tapestry over the other woman's head. Still trying to free the knife, Leah lost her balance and toppled over.

Saronna whirled around, dizzy but still standing, and ran for the door. She got the bolt back and was through before Leah was on her feet.

Saronna made it to the stairs, then gripped the railing to go down as fast as she dared. She stopped on the landing to wipe the blood from her leg, and adjust her clothes and hair so she didn't look totally disheveled. She took a deep breath, and shook her head in an effort to clear the lingering effects of the manglewort.

When she got to the entrance hall, Gideon and another man had just come in the front door, carrying a long bundle between them.

Saronna stared as red blood dripped from the bundle and pooled onto the floor.

"Lay him on the sofa in the parlor," her father said.

Gideon moved to obey, and at last Saronna could see. It was Duncan.

CHAPTER TWELVE

Duncan came to slowly, dimly aware that something bad had happened. He was lying on his back. His field of vision consisted of a small square patch of watery blue sky set in a gray background. It took him a moment to understand that the blue patch was a window in the roof of a flyter. This provoked further confusion, as he had flown himself to Samaria, and he knew quite well Saronna couldn't operate a flyter.

He tried to sit up, but something held him down.

"Duncan!"

His father's face loomed over him. Worry lines made Vladimir look older than his age.

"Dad! How did you get here?" Duncan glanced around and didn't recognize the flyter at all. "Where am I?"

"You're on the way to the hospital," Vladimir said. "Thank God Saronna had enough sense to use your pocket com to call me. I brought a med team."

As if to prove Vladimir's statement, a young woman in an emergency medtech's coverall bent over Duncan and ran a medi-scanner over his body.

"He's okay," she said. "The bleeding's stopped, and we're replacing the blood already."

Duncan noticed a hematological unit strapped to his arm. He couldn't see his wounds because bandages covered his chest and other arm. "How bad is it?"

"Bad enough." Vladimir scowled at him. "It was worse than Randy to start with, and the Kruegerians don't know much about first aid. Saronna followed instructions, but she didn't have much to work with."

Duncan sighed. "Well, I guess the kid didn't have as precise an eye as his older brother."

"Duncan! Stop making jokes. You were an idiot to go to Samaria in the first place, and even more of an idiot to walk up to those two homicidal maniacs of your own free will!"

"They weren't homicidal. If they had wanted to kill me, they would have. I didn't think they wanted to."

Vladimir let loose a string of aspersions, calling Duncan an imbecile in every language he knew.

Duncan paid no attention. "Where's Saronna?"

His father jerked his head as if to point to his left. "In the other flyter. The med team would only let one of us ride with you, and I pulled rank on her."

"But she's coming home with us?"

Vladimir frowned. "Of course."

Duncan settled back against the pallet, his worst fear relieved. "I feel sick."

The medtech fussed over him for a few minutes, and administered a hypospray that settled his stomach. When the anesthetic already in his system wore off, she gave him a second dose that made him drowse off into a half sleep. He barely noticed when they arrived at the hospital.

THE next day, Duncan awoke in the hospital feeling much stronger. Vladimir arrived, looking grim, just as Duncan finished dressing, and announced they would go home together in a ground car.

Duncan didn't argue.

Frank Chiang held the door for them and gave Duncan a cheerful greeting. "Glad to see you looking so well. I heard one of those Kruegerian maniacs sliced you up pretty good."

"It wasn't that bad," Duncan said. "At least now they'll leave us alone."

Vladimir waited until they had pulled into traffic, and then he put up the screen so that Frank couldn't hear their conversation.

"Okay," he said, "you're well now, so I won't hold back. What the hell did you think you were doing, going up to those two? When Saronna told me you'd been attacked, I assumed they'd jumped you, but then her brother filled me in on the details. Were you drunk, or did you just go crazy?"

Duncan grinned, relieved to see his father back to his old self. "Neither. And if you've been holding back, I'd hate to hear you when you're not."

"Well, good," Vladimir said scathingly, "because you're going to hear it now. I'd like to smack you good, Duncan. It was a damn fool thing to do, and I want to know why you did it."

Duncan sighed and leaned back against the seat. "Give it a rest, Dad. It was a calculated risk."

"Calculated?" Vladimir's voice almost hummed with rage. "Calculated? The chance of losing investment capital in a business venture is calculated. Going up to two Kruegerian men bent on vengeance is guaranteed to mean trouble."

"I knew that. But they weren't men. They were boys, really. I figured I'd have a shot at talking them out of attacking me. If it didn't work, at least it'd be me getting hurt instead of someone else. I wanted it to be over."

"Over?" His father made the word sound ominous.

Duncan was beginning to lose his patience. "Look, Dad, I made a decision. Whether it was the right one or not is a moot point at the moment. The fact is, the assault is over. They drew my blood, and they're satisfied. We can go back to a normal life now."

Vladimir's brow creased. "Did they come right out and say that?"

Duncan nodded. "I asked them after the boy cut me, and the older one said the blood debt was paid."

Vladimir let out a popping noise, like air leaving a confined space suddenly. "You asked him? The two of them were performing stand-up surgery on you, and you struck up a conversation?"

"Yes."

"No wonder Saronna's relatives think you're hot stuff." Vladimir shook his head despairingly. "They were very admiring as they showed me where they had you laid out on a sofa. They kept saying it was no bother to have you bleeding all over their parlor."

"How was Saronna taking it?"

Vladimir gave Duncan a patently inquisitive look. At least curiosity had banished his outrage. "I don't know, really. When I arrived with the med team, her father wouldn't let her stay in the room unless she put on her veil. I saw her for a second before she put it on, and she looked like she was about to pass out, but after that she kept in the background. It was only once they had you loaded on the rescue flyter that she spoke up and asked to ride with you."

"Is she all right now?"

Vladimir nodded. "She seemed fine, although her dress was torn up for some reason." He gave Duncan another searching look. "You seem more concerned about Saronna than anything else. How did the wedding go?"

"It was all right," Duncan said absently. "Typical Kruegerian guff. The bride got handed over by her father without so much as anyone asking her what she wanted."

"How did Saronna do back at her family's house? Any trouble?"

"I don't know. Her father's wife—who's also her aunt, it turns out—took her off to join the women for a while before the ceremony. Saronna seemed a little subdued after that, but she wouldn't tell me anything about it."

Vladimir's face reflected the same surprise Duncan had felt. "Her father's wife is her aunt?"

Duncan grimaced, not certain why the idea made him so uncomfortable. "It seems her father took his wife's sister as his woman some years after his marriage. Saronna was her mother's only child, but Josiah had five children with his wife, so Saronna's five half-siblings are also her cousins."

Vladimir grunted. "Interesting."

"Yes." Duncan stared at his feet. "I wish I knew what happened before the service."

"So you're not just looking for a fling? You've actually fallen for Saronna?"

Duncan looked up and found his father staring at him. He hesitated. Should he tell the old man to mind his own business? He remembered his father's anxious face looming over him in the flyter. "I guess I have."

Vladimir waited, but Duncan said nothing more.

"She seems fond of you," Vladimir said.

Duncan shrugged. "Perhaps."

"Is there something wrong?"

Duncan shook his head slowly. "I don't know. I wish I did."

Vladimir glanced out the window. "We're home."

SARONNA opened the door. She knew she was supposed to knock, but after all, Duncan was sleeping, and she didn't want to wake him. She held the edge of the door with one hand to make sure it opened slowly, but in spite of that, Duncan sat up in bed as she came into his room.

"Oh," she said. "They said you were asleep."

"Well, I'm not. Come in, Saronna."

She wasn't ready to talk to him, but she couldn't think of a good excuse. At least he was fully clothed.

She stepped into the room. "I didn't mean to disturb you."

"You're not disturbing me. But why would you come in if you thought I was asleep?"

She flushed and looked down. She couldn't tell him that she had to know he was all right, even though she knew she couldn't see him alone anymore. "You bled so badly yesterday, I was worried."

Duncan smiled. "I'm fine." He pulled his shirt open to show her the scar. "See. It's all healed."

It was amazing. The scar was pink but healed, as if he had been cut weeks ago. The wound Leah had inflicted on Saronna's leg looked much worse, and it had been shallow in comparison. She really shouldn't get too close. Saronna took two steps. Then two more. She put out her hand to touch the scar, but stopped herself just in time. "I see. It's wonderful what off-world machines can do."

Duncan nodded. "It must seem miraculous if you're not used to it."

Saronna glanced around the room with sudden desperation. She had to have something to talk about. Luckily, his living space was alien enough to provide plenty of conversation. "Your room looks very different from the rest of the house."

"I know. I wanted it to look different. Dad kept the rest of the place as much like a Kruegerian house as he could, but I wanted this room to look more modern."

Saronna walked up to a picture on the wall that depicted snowcapped mountains. "This is pretty. It's not a painting, is it?"

"No. It's a projection. If you watch it long enough, you'll see the seasons change. The snow melts, and the trees turn green, and then eventually, it goes back to snow again."

Saronna studied the picture solemnly, afraid to look anywhere else. "Technology allows you to avoid making a choice about which is your favorite season. You can enjoy them all."

"Saronna," Duncan said, sliding out of bed and crossing the room to stand beside her. "What's wrong? Did something happen back at your father's house?"

She looked up at him, startled. "Of course something happened. You were attacked."

Duncan waved a hand in annoyance. "That's not what I'm talking about. Did something happen upstairs, while you were with your aunt, or your stepmother, or whatever you call her?"

She couldn't tell him the truth. Eventually, he would realize there could be nothing between them and find someone else, but in the meantime she couldn't tell him. "I call her my father's wife. And nothing happened."

"Then why did you look so sad? And why do you seem so strange now, as if there were a wall between us?"

It was a good way to put it. "There is a wall. I'm a Kruegerian, and you're an off-worlder. I don't understand you, and you can never understand me."

"Why not? We can both learn what we need to learn."

She shook her head, but said nothing.

"Saronna!" He took her face in his hands and one hand touched the bruise Leah's shoe had made under her chin.

Saronna flinched.

"You're hurt!"

She had a lie all ready, from having had to explain the bruise to Naomi. "When I heard you had been attacked, I tripped running down the stairs."

He frowned. "Dad said your dress was torn."

She swallowed. "It ripped when I fell."

"Are you okay now?"

She nodded.

He bent his head to kiss her. Saronna gave a strangled cry and pulled away.

"Please, don't!" she said. "Don't make it harder for me."

Duncan stared at her in amazement. "What is it? What's wrong? I was only going to kiss you. You don't have to be afraid of me."

Saronna turned her head away, muttered a hasty goodbye, and fled from the room. She shouldn't have come.

DUNCAN stood dumbstruck as he watched the door close behind Saronna. He walked slowly back to his bed and sat on the edge of it. He was still sitting there when the com beeped with one long beep, indicating an outside call. Duncan debated first, and then walked over to answer it.

He was very surprised to see Zelda Amoy's face.

"Hello," Duncan said after he had accepted the call. "How are you?"

"I'm fine," Zelda said. "But I hear you're not doing so great."

"I'm okay. How did you hear about it?"

Zelda grinned. "You must be kidding! Any time an off-worlder is attacked by natives, the news spreads like wildfire. I hear Sire Longworth's boys did a better job on you than they did on your friend."

"I'll live."

She nodded. "I'm certainly happy to hear that. I felt terrible when I heard about your friend, and even worse when I heard about you."

"It wasn't your fault."

"Maybe not intentionally," she said, "but I was certainly the reason you got sucked into the whole mess."

Duncan had a sudden inspiration. She was, after all, almost unique as a source of information. "Zelda, do you think you could do me a favor and come to see me today?"

She gave him a quizzical look.

Duncan smiled. "No, I don't lust after older women. I just need some information. I'd come to see you, but I know very well my father would pitch a major fit if I tried to walk out of the house today. He's old enough that I worry if he has too many fits in one week, and I'm already over the limit."

"Well," Zelda said brightly, "I'm all for people showing consideration for the elderly. I'll see what I can do."

"Thanks. I'd appreciate it."

"It might not be until after dinner time."

"No problem," Duncan said. "Do you know the address?"

She didn't, so he gave it to her.

After he broke the connection, Duncan leaned back against his pillows and pondered the complexity of life on Krueger's World until he drifted off to sleep.

DUNCAN woke early in the evening to find his father standing beside his bed looking down at him. He sat up abruptly. "What is it, Dad? Is something wrong?"

Vladimir shook his head. "Not that I know of; I was going to ask you that question."

Duncan frowned. "What?"

"There's a woman in the parlor named Zelda Amoy." Vladimir sounded almost angry. "*Dr. Zelda Amoy.* Isn't that the woman who was doing research in the Longworth residence?"

"Yes," Duncan said, getting to his feet. "I asked her to come. Would you tell her I'll be there in a minute, please, Dad?"

Vladimir looked resolute. "No, I don't think so. She's not going anywhere. I'll wait and walk you to the parlor."

Duncan hid his annoyance and didn't argue. Instead, he washed his face and rinsed out his mouth to wake himself up. When he came out of the bathroom, his father was still waiting for him.

Duncan let Vladimir accompany him right to the parlor door, but then he paused before he went inside. "All right, Dad. I'm fine. I can walk without passing out, thank you. This interview is private."

Vladimir looked him up and down and nodded. "Don't let her keep you too long. I'll be in my office if you need me."

"Thanks," Duncan said, waiting for his father to be out of sight before he went into the parlor.

Once he was through the door, he found that someone had provided Zelda Amoy with refreshments. She was sipping a glass of murky green liquid that Duncan recognized as Miloran whiskey, and nibbling from a tray of tiny sandwiches—made from chopped vegetables and Kruegerian cheese—that sat on the table in front of her.

"Hello," Duncan said, offering his hand. "Thank you for coming."

"Least I could do," Zelda said amiably, shaking his hand. "Sit down before you fall over."

Duncan sat down across from her. "It's not that bad. I'm fine, really."

"Sure you are. How much blood did you lose?"

"I don't know. What does it matter? They replaced it all."

Zelda snorted. "When you get to be my age, you'll know better than to say stupid things like that. A shock to the system is still a shock."

Duncan gave up the argument. "Maybe."

Apparently Zelda could distinguish between disinterest and surrender. "Enough about that," she said briskly. "You didn't ask me here for medical advice. What is it you need to know?"

Duncan hesitated, and then smiled as he realized he didn't know what to ask. "I wish I knew. I know very well there's something Saronna's not telling me; it's just that I have no clue what it is."

"Saronna is your woman?"

Duncan didn't bother to refute her terminology. "Yes."

Zelda eyed him as if she were debating the best way to proceed. "Are you sleeping with her?"

"No."

"You never have?"

He shook his head.

"Is that because you never asked her?"

"No," Duncan said. "It's because when I've asked her, she said no."

Zelda opened her eyes at this. "You came right out and asked her to come to your bed, and she said a flat no?"

Duncan fidgeted. He had never had this sort of conversation with anyone, and it made him uncomfortable. "You make me sound like some Kruegerian despot issuing a summons. It wasn't like that. Basically, I made a pass—I let her see what I wanted. It seemed to me that she wanted it, too, but she said no."

"And you let that stand?"

"Of course I let it stand," Duncan said, more than slightly offended. "I'm civilized enough to understand the word no."

Zelda smiled. "Don't get your undies in a twist. I wasn't trying to insult you. I just wanted to find out where the problem is. Maybe she just plain isn't interested?"

"It's possible." Could it be that he was seeing interest where he wanted to see it, and really Saronna didn't feel anything for him? "Except that if that's true, I don't understand why she seems to care so much about what happens to me. A couple of times she's either admitted as much, or she's shown it by her actions."

"How do you mean?"

Duncan recalled the incident with the younger Longworth brother and the suddenly-hot knife. He hesitated, unwilling to reveal Saronna's secret to this stranger. "I'd rather not say."

Zelda looked surprised at his reticence. "Why not?"

"Because Saronna told me something in confidence. I don't want to break that confidence."

"I see. Have you asked her what's wrong?"

"Yes. She won't talk to me about it. And then I took her back to Samaria for her sister's wedding, and something happened that made it worse. She said there's a wall between us."

"Really?" Zelda frowned a distracted frown, as if she were considering the possibilities. "By any chance, does this confidence have anything to do with telekinesis?"

Duncan stared at her with his mouth hanging open.

Zelda smiled with triumph. "Don't bother to deny it. Your expression is pretty good confirmation by itself."

"How could you know that?" Duncan demanded. "I haven't told anyone."

"I'm sure you haven't. No one told me. I was simply guessing."

"Based on what?" Duncan said, still confounded.

"Based on several things. Her name, first off. Second, Saronna could already read when your father bought her. And finally, she's held you at arm's length in spite of being in a situation where most Kruegerian women would never even have thought of saying no."

It made no sense to Duncan. "What?"

"There's some background you're missing," Zelda said kindly. "Sit back and listen while I fill you in on some little-known but crucial events in Kruegerian history."

Duncan waited while she took a sip of whiskey and then leaned back in her chair.

"Alfred Krueger's cult started as your basic fundamentalist Christian group," Zelda began, "but he stressed the Old Testament almost to the exclusion of the newer Christian doctrine. When he brought his converts here, there were a larger number of women than of men. Some people think that Krueger created a form of polygamy to deal with this, but actually, he probably would have come up with it anyway, because of his personal preferences."

"I'd heard that," Duncan said.

"Quiet!" Zelda scolded. "I'm talking here."

Duncan was silent, and she went on.

"Anyway, among the first generation that was born on Krueger's World, a small number had unusual gifts. This occurred on most sleeper worlds, but the Kruegerians had no way to know that. Anyway, Alfred Krueger called it witchcraft, and had anyone who demonstrated psy abilities punished in brutal ways, up to and including death by stoning. Not surprisingly, in a very short time no one was willing to admit to having them. An interesting thing is that telekinesis was much more prevalent than was normal for a sleeper world, and in addition, it was more common in women than in men. It was difficult to know this, however, when anyone who had the talent was hiding it, desperately.

"After Krueger died, the fear continued, buoyed up by the text of his almighty Book, which called on the faithful not to suffer a witch to live. At the same time, a small number of younger colonists began to question his edicts.

"Among the dissenters was a group of women who resented their absolute lack of enfranchisement. Back then, most women could still read, and they began to make a point to teach their daughters—in secret when they had to—so that they could pass on knowledge.

When they could, they gave their baby girls names that aren't from the Bible, although that has almost disappeared now, because so often fathers insist on naming even the girls.

"Over time, this movement among women changed. They began to think less of secular power, and instead began to dream of justice in heaven."

"What?" Duncan burst out. "You're talking about a religion."

Zelda Amoy nodded. "Yes, I am. There's a totally separate religion out there—completely at odds with the teachings of Alfred Krueger. Its adherents are all women. They call themselves Believers, but we refer to them as the cult of Mother Eve."

It sounded ominous. "The cult?"

"Oh, yes. It's a cult. It's practiced in secret, but it makes tremendous demands on its members."

"Like what?"

"Well, the primary requirement is to maintain a shrine to Eve. Each Believer is given her own shrine when she reaches physical maturity. She has to pray every night, to maintain solidarity with her sisters."

"That doesn't sound so bad. What's so onerous about saying prayers?"

"She doesn't just have to say them, she has to believe them. The cult of Mother Eve teaches her that men are her enemy. She has to keep herself aloof from men—

not so much physically as emotionally. She's never supposed to form an attachment to any man—not even her own son."

It sounded crazy to Duncan, and much too radical to be hidden. "I don't see how they could keep something like this a secret."

"For all I know, Kruegerian men are aware of it, but if so, they're not talking."

Duncan cast around for anything to refute what she was saying. "It can't be true, not for Saronna. She has a younger brother who came to visit her. She seemed quite fond of him."

Zelda looked interested, but she shook her head. "They moderate the rule somewhat. Complete detachment is what they all aim for, but most of them slip up and become fond of someone—a husband, a brother, a son. The Mother forgives them so long as they continue to pray for her forgiveness."

"So you think this is why Saronna won't let herself show that she cares for me?" Duncan asked, bemused. It sounded bad, very bad. What the hell was he supposed to do now?

"Perhaps." She sipped her drink and then put it down. "But there may be more to it in her case."

This sounded even less promising. "How do you mean?"

"Well, every now and then a girl is born with the gift of telekinesis. It's still there in the gene pool, but

except for the Believers, no one else is looking for it.
Eve's Mark they call it. They test their daughters for it.
A girl whose own mother is a Believer, and who
demonstrates this ability is usually consecrated to the
Mother."

Duncan could feel a strange foreboding when she
said the word. This just got worse and worse. "Consecrated?"

Zelda nodded. "Consecrated—as in dedicated to a
holy purpose. She, more than any other Believer, is to
keep herself pure and free of the taint of men—both
emotionally and physically. Kruegerian life may not
allow her the option to maintain her virginity, but
whatever happens to her, she's never supposed to love a
man romantically or go to bed with him willingly."

"What?" Duncan jumped to his feet. "I don't believe
it. You're making this up!"

Zelda shook her head. "I wouldn't do that, Duncan. I
hope you know that."

He did know it, but he didn't want to believe what
she was telling him.

"Sit down," Zelda said.

Duncan sat slowly.

"Are you all right?" she asked. "You look a little
pale."

He let out a breath. He felt rather like he'd been sliced open all over again. "I'm okay. Is there more or are you finished?"

"That's about it," Zelda said, tossing off her drink. "Except that the reading is a real tip off. Many Believers have lost that ability, but anyone who is consecrated is taught to read." She gave Duncan a glance compounded of sympathy and curiosity. "A consecrated woman has to know how to control a man's physical arousal. Her shrine always has a tablet in the back of it that explains male anatomy and the human endocrine system. They have to be able to read it."

Duncan sat staring as he thought about it. Were there any holes in this theory? He didn't think so. "If it's so secret, how did you find out about this?"

Zelda smiled. "I was tracking the patterns of when men bought a second woman. Mostly it was tied to wealth, but occasionally, a married man would go into debt to buy a second woman, and debt is something Kruegerians frown on. When I researched those families, I found a matrilineal relationship. I persuaded a woman to trust me by pretending to know more than I did, and that's how I found out about the Believers. A man who married a consecrated woman would find that his wife would never give him sex willingly or affection at all, so he would buy a woman who would."

Duncan put one hand over his eyes. It occurred to him that he should have wondered *why* Saronna knew how to do what she had done to him.

"I'm sorry," Zelda said gently. "I hate to be the one to tell you this, especially after what you did for me."

Duncan sat up straight. "It doesn't matter who told me. I needed to know it."

"Yes. I'm afraid that's true."

He rallied from his despondency enough to offer her another drink, but she declined.

"No, thanks, I'd better get going. I'm late for a date as it is."

"Thank you for coming," Duncan said automatically.

"Don't mention it," Zelda said, getting to her feet. "And don't give up hope. I could be wrong about Saronna's situation."

"Yes," Duncan said. But he knew better.

SARONNA was ready for bed when the knock on her door sounded. She inquired through the closed door who it was, and she wasn't surprised when Duncan's voice announced his name. He had seemed to be sunk in gloom at supper, and it had worried her.

"Just a moment," she said. She ran to the dressing room, found a robe, and slipped it on over her night dress before she opened the door. "What is it?"

"I need to talk to you," Duncan said brusquely. He didn't wait for an invitation, but brushed past her into the sitting room.

Saronna followed him apprehensively.

"Well?" she said, once Duncan was seated.

"Saronna," Duncan began abruptly, "do you see me as your enemy?"

She felt herself pale at the question. "You've always been kind to me," she equivocated.

"Don't give me that! Just answer the question."

She pulled back at the vehemence in his voice. "I could never see you as my enemy."

Duncan took a deep breath. "But are you trying to?"

She stared at him with her eyes growing wider every second. "Why are you asking me these questions?"

"Because I have to know the truth," Duncan said, jumping to his feet. "I have to know what you think—what you feel—about me. Is there ever going to be anything between us, Saronna?"

She blinked, feeling a sense of desolation creep over her. She had thought she would have a little longer before he came to this realization. "I told you," she said, keeping her voice level, "I need more time."

"Time!" Duncan began to pace the floor. "Will more time really help?" He looked wildly around the room, and then walked to the wall and began to rip open cupboards and drawers.

"What are you doing?" Saronna cried anxiously.

"Where is it?" Duncan said. "Where do you keep it?"

Saronna stared at him in consternation. He must know about the shrine. But how? She said nothing, but covered her mouth with her hand in horror. She had never imagined he could find out.

"Where is it?" Duncan repeated. He stopped opening drawers and looked around the room. "It wouldn't be in here. It's in the bedroom, isn't it?"

He started for the door, but Saronna got in his way.

"Where are you going? This is my room and you have no right to do this!"

Duncan brushed her aside without speaking and swept into the bedroom.

Terrified, Saronna focused her attention on the cupboard beside the bed. He mustn't find the shrine!

He had pulled open several drawers and rifled their contents before he reached the bedside cupboard. When he tried to open the door, the latch stuck fast. Duncan tugged on it, then turned to Saronna.

"So," he said, "you're back to playing games. What did you do to the latch? Break it? Fuse it?"

She didn't answer, but it made no difference. Duncan glanced around the room and then snatched up a small statuette of a leaping duacorn. He picked it up and rammed the base into the latch of the cupboard. After three blows, the latch fell to the floor, and Duncan wrenched both doors open.

"No!" Saronna shrieked. "No, you mustn't touch it! Please, no!"

Duncan looked into the cupboard at the small brown wooden box. He reached for it, but Saronna tried to get in his way.

"No," she sobbed. "No, please, don't touch it!"

He moved her aside gently, and held her back with one arm while he lifted the box with the other hand. "How do you open it?"

She wrenched herself free and snatched the box from him.

"It doesn't matter," Duncan said. "I know what it is. Is there a tablet in the back, Saronna?"

She stopped sobbing to gasp in astonishment. How could he have found out that detail?

"If you don't tell me," Duncan said, "then I'll take the shrine and open it myself."

"Yes," Saronna said. "There's a tablet."

Duncan nodded. He got to his feet and stared down at her while she sat on the floor clutching the shrine. "How long were you going to string me along before you told me? Or were you ever going to tell me? Would you have just let me think I was crazy and you didn't care about me after all?"

She didn't answer right away. She sat rocking back and forth as she clutched the shrine to her chest. Only when he turned to go did she speak. "I'm sorry. I couldn't tell you. I couldn't."

Duncan said nothing more, but left the room. Saronna heard the sitting room door close a few seconds afterwards.

She sat and sobbed. It was over. Duncan knew the truth. He would hate her now, and perhaps—perhaps he would tell his father to sell her.

THE next day, neither Duncan nor Saronna came to the breakfast table. Vladimir went to his son's room as soon as he saw the empty place at the table.

"Come," Duncan said, in answer to his knock.

Vladimir took one look at his disheveled hair and rumpled clothes and frowned. "All right, Duncan, just what is going on?"

Duncan was lying fully dressed on his bed. He sat up and returned Vladimir's stare. "None of your damn business."

Vladimir's frown deepened into a scowl. "And just what is that supposed to mean?"

"It means I'm twenty-six. It means I'm fed up with having you poke your nose into my private life." He swung his legs over the side of the bed and stood up. "It means as soon as I can, I'm going to find another place to live."

Vladimir drew in his breath sharply. "My God, Duncan. What happened? What's made you crazy like this?"

"I repeat," Duncan said, folding his arms across his chest. "None of your damn business."

Vladimir stared at his son's grim expression and decided to go elsewhere for information.

"I'M sorry, Vlad," Naomi said, coming into the family courtyard. "She's locked her door, and she won't talk to me."

Vladimir took her hand and patted it. "Thank you for trying."

"What's happened?" Naomi sounded anxious.

Feeling helpless, Vladimir pulled away. "I don't know, but don't fret. It's probably just a lovers' spat."

Naomi didn't look reassured, but she went away to talk to the cook.

Vladimir sank onto a bench and contemplated the vines that grew up the opposite wall. The tiny silver flowers on them had just come into bloom, but their beauty failed to move him. "It's all that blasted woman's fault."

His pocket com beeped, and Vladimir slipped it from his pocket to answer it.

"Good morning, sir," said his housekeeper. "I hope I'm not disturbing you, but I wanted to check with you before Duncan leaves the house."

"What?" Vladimir said sharply, staring at the tiny image in his hand.

"He's requested a car and driver. Should I give them to him?"

Vladimir groaned. He had a sudden wild impulse to tell her no, but he realized Duncan had his own resources and would only leave the house on foot. "Yes. Just make sure the driver reports back on where he goes."

"Yes, sir," Margaret said, and the screen went blank.

Vladimir sighed and muttered to himself that it was all Zelda Amoy's fault.

DUNCAN looked at several apartments in different buildings but nothing struck his fancy. He spent the rest of the afternoon roaming through the park and watching the hover swans. He was vaguely aware of Frank Chiang trying to keep him in sight from the Trushenko ground car, but his own problems consumed too much of his attention to spare any time for Frank's.

Late in the afternoon, Duncan gave up his quest in favor of a new one. He tried to send Frank home, but the driver refused to go.

"No way, boss. I'll take you anywhere you want to go, but I can't leave you on your own."

"All right," Duncan said, climbing into the back seat. "Take me to a bar."

"Which bar?" Frank asked, settling into his own seat.

"I don't give a damn which bar." Duncan leaned his head back and closed his eyes.

After that, the evening faded into a blur. Duncan drank slowly but steadily, and soon achieved the desired state of numbness. He sat quietly at a corner table and drank his way through several hours, maintaining mindlessness by never letting his metabolism catch up with the amount of alcohol he imbibed.

After a while, he grew bored with the place and decided to move on. Frank was waiting for him when he stumbled from the bar.

"Ready to go home, boss?" Frank asked hopefully.

"No," Duncan said. "Not yet. Find me another bar, Frank. This one is too damn cheerful."

The driver sighed and held the door open for him.

The next bar was a little darker and a little less crowded. In fact it was almost empty. Duncan decided to make up for the time he had lost in transit, and ordered a Miloran whiskey.

The sharp tang of the off-world drink provided a shock to his nervous system. For just one second, Duncan had a sudden vision of what he was doing to himself, and he resolved to make the drink his last. A few minutes later, the whiskey took effect and he forgot about going home.

A little while later a large, imposing figure slid onto the seat across from him. Duncan had looked up to tell the newcomer that it was a private table when he recognized Warhlou hna Nedahna.

"Hello, War," he said, pleased to run into a friend. "What are you doing here?"

"Nothing much," Warhlou said easily. "What about you?"

"Not a damn thing. Have a drink?"

"Don't mind if I do." Warhlou signaled the bartender, and ordered a Miloran whiskey for himself. When it came, he sipped it silently.

Feeling no need to make conversation, Duncan drank his own whiskey, trying not to spill any of it. Somehow the glass seemed to want to tip every time he lifted it.

"Say, Duncan," Warhlou said after a few minutes, "my ride left without me. Can you give me a lift home?"

"Sure thing. No trouble at all. When do you have to be home?"

"Actually, I'm already late. Could we go now?"

Duncan leaned back in his chair. "You bet, War. No problem, buddy. We'll finish our drinks and hit the road."

Warhlou drained his glass and stood up. "I'm ready."

Duncan tried to do the same, but he spilled most of the whiskey down his shirt, and then he almost fell over when he tried to stand. The Miloran grabbed him and pulled him to his feet as easily as if he had been a rag doll.

"Come on," Warhlou said. "You could use some fresh air."

The cool night air hit Duncan in the face and made him shiver. Frank Chiang pulled the car up just as they stepped outside, and he waited by the door while Warhlou inserted Duncan into the back seat.

"Thanks for coming," Frank said in a low voice.

Warhlou nodded. "No problem. Let's get him home."

Confused, Duncan leaned his head back, closed his eyes, and gave up trying to follow what was going on.

VLADIMIR Trushenko was in bed but not asleep when the com set beeped with the two short, insistent beeps that meant the security desk was calling. The face that appeared on the monitor when he answered was indeed one of his security staff. "Yes?"

"He's home, sir," the woman said. "Frank and that Miloran friend of his just pulled in. They're bringing him into the house right now."

"Is he all right?"

"I think so, sir, but he's pretty well plastered. The Miloran was holding him up."

"Thank you," Vladimir said, and broke the connection.

He waited half an hour, to give Frank Chiang and Warhlou hna Nedahna time to get Duncan settled and leave, and then he went to his son's room.

The door wasn't locked. Vladimir didn't knock, but opened the door and peeked into the room. When he saw the bed was empty, he opened the door and stepped into the room.

"Duncan?"

There was no answer. Vladimir prowled around the room, but saw no sign of his son. He frowned and wondered whether Duncan could have snuck out without security spotting him, and decided that it was unlikely. He noticed that the bathroom door was ajar, and when he looked down, he saw that Duncan's foot was holding it open.

"Duncan!"

His son lay on his back on the bathroom floor, arms flung wide, and a towel clutched in one hand. His face was very pale, almost blue around his lips, and his eyes were closed. For one heart-stopping moment, Vladimir thought he was dead. And then simultaneously, Vladimir noticed a puddle of vomit under the towel, and Duncan's chest rising and falling in shallow, rapid gasps. Vladimir held two fingers to the side of Duncan's throat and felt a pulse so faint and fast it terrified him all over again.

He raced back into the bedroom and hit the emergency switch on the com. "Get a med team here right away," he barked to the security guard who answered. And then he went back into the bathroom to sit beside Duncan and hold his hand until they came.

CHAPTER THIRTEEN

D uncan stirred. His head throbbed with a pounding agony, his mouth felt as if it were stuffed with dry fibers, his stomach churned, and his whole body ached even when he lay still. He clenched his eyes tightly and tried to will himself to go to back sleep, but it didn't work.

He moaned. Something was pressing on his face, and he tried to push it away, but a hand clamped on his and held it.

"Stop that," his father's voice said.

Duncan opened his eyes. He was in his own room, but something strange stood beside the bed, some kind of medical equipment tower.

"What's happened?" The words didn't come out right. It sounded more like "Whuff haffendt?"

"You're on respiratory therapy," his father's voice said. "The med tech should be back soon. I told him to take a break since he'd been up most of the night."

Duncan blinked, and realized there was some kind of breathing mask over his mouth and nose. Daylight streamed in the windows, so it must be morning, but why was he sick all of a sudden? "Whuff haffendt?" he repeated.

"You were so drunk you got sick, and then you aspirated. The stomach acid burned your lungs, and gave you instantaneous pneumonia. If I hadn't checked on you last night, you'd be on your way to intensive care right now—or dead."

Dead? Could he really have been so careless? Perhaps. Dead actually sounded good compared to how he felt now. He moaned again.

His father frowned, but before he could say anything, a middle-aged man in a buff-colored coverall came into the room.

"Is he awake?" the med tech asked.

"Yes," Vladimir said, frowning. "He's awake but not feeling too perky." His face seemed to soften. "Can you give him something to make him feel better?"

"Sure." The med tech glanced at Duncan. "Do you know where you are?"

Duncan nodded. "Homb."At least that sounded close.

"Do know what day it is?"

"The twenty-ninth," Duncan said. He tried to speak distinctly, but it came out, "Da twedydynth."

The med tech nodded, and turned his attention to the controls of the equipment tower. "Okay, you seem clear. I'll add some pain meds to your feed. That should take care of it, and in a few hours you'll be off the machine anyway."

Only then did Duncan noticed the tube connected to his arm. A little while later, the pain began to ebb, and eventually, Duncan fell asleep again.

When he woke this time, he felt much better, but still far from well. He lay still for a while, absorbing the events of the day before.

He had found out the truth about Saronna—about why she was so shy with him, and why she couldn't let herself care about him—and that truth had made him go out and try to drink himself into oblivion. He had come rather closer to oblivion than was really comfortable, and that was bad news. He had been blind drunk a few times, but from jubilation, not from despair. It came to him that he had never before known real despair.

Apparently, he didn't handle it well. He would need to be more careful.

He sat up, and realized first that he wasn't wearing anything but his underclothes and second that he desperately wanted a shower. Before he could head for the bathroom, the door opened and his father walked in.

"Oh," Vladimir said, stopping abruptly. "Sorry, I didn't know you were awake. How are you feeling?"

"Better," Duncan said. The grim lines on his father's face gave him a pang of guilt for what he had put the old man through. "Much better. I'm sorry I put you to so much trouble."

Vladimir lifted his shoulders in a gesture that was half shrug and half question. "It's okay—so long as it doesn't happen again."

Duncan sighed and got to his feet. No point in putting things off. "To promise that, I have to take better care of myself, Dad. And I think I have to leave Krueger's World for a while to do that."

Vladimir looked distressed. "You have a job here."

Duncan shrugged. "I'll take a leave of absence. Kaveh can fill in for me. He's learned a lot while I was away. Or I'll resign if you prefer. I just need to get away."

Vladimir's expression grew inscrutable, rather as if he were negotiating a deal. "Are you going to resign as my son, too?"

Duncan looked at him in surprise. "Of course not, Dad. It's not you I need to get away from."

Vladimir lifted his brows. "Is it Saronna?"

Duncan turned away, unwilling to lie but reluctant to talk. "Yes."

"Why?" Vladimir said. "What's wrong between you two? You both seemed fond of each other—more than fond."

Duncan walked to the closet and pulled out a robe. He slipped it on and tied it while he debated how to answer. How much should he tell his father? Zelda might want to keep her discovery quiet for now, but Saronna hadn't asked for any promise of confidentiality. And after what his father had been though the night before, he deserved to know the truth.

"Basically," Duncan said, "Saronna is a member of a Kruegerian cult—more than just a member. She's sort of like a nun—an old-style nun. The kind that couldn't have men in their lives. I'm a man, so I'm out."

Vladimir's eyes opened wide. "What? You're joking?"

Duncan twisted his mouth in a bitter smile. "Come on, Dad. Did I get blind, stupid drunk for a joke?"

"You mean it?" Vladimir shook his head. "But that's incredible! I've been on Krueger's World for over five years, and I never heard of such a cult."

"I know. They practice in secret because they're the antithesis of patriarchal. Zelda Amoy told me about them. She uncovered the cult during her research. I confronted Saronna with it, and she admitted it. There's nothing I can do, Dad. That's why I need to get away."

"You mean run away, don't you?" Vladimir said.

Duncan didn't see any point in arguing semantics. "Whatever you want to call it, I only know I won't stay on this fricking planet one day longer than I absolutely have to."

"Where will you go?"

"I don't know for sure." Fortunately for him, money wasn't a problem. Wealth made distance feasible, and right now he wanted a lot of distance. "I might go see Mom in the Rim Worlds for a few months. After that, I'll see how I feel."

Vladimir frowned. "You're going to let this ruin your life? You're going to give up everything you've worked for here just so you won't have to sit down and eat dinner with Saronna? I can find her somewhere else to live, Duncan. You don't have to see her."

"No!" The stab of fear these words induced alarmed Duncan. Even knowing what he knew, he couldn't stop himself from worrying about Saronna. "She's not ready to live on her own yet, Dad. Find her another tutor and make sure she keeps up with her education. In a couple of years she should be ready to look after herself. She might even want to go back to the native quarter since she's so religious, but I don't know quite how she'd do that."

"But, Duncan—"

"No, Dad," Duncan said. "It's not just a matter of avoiding her. There's no way I could know she was close and not want to see her."

Vladimir sighed. "I feel responsible. I brought her here. It never occurred to me there was anything more to her than an ordinary Kruegerian woman."

"Well," Duncan said dryly, "that'll teach you to go around buying people. Saronna may be a lot of things, but I would never call her ordinary."

"No, I guess not."

Duncan recalled his promise. "Don't mention the cult thing, will you? Not even to Naomi. Zelda wants to keep it a secret until she's ready to publish her research."

"All right." Vladimir shook himself and sighed. "I feel my age all of a sudden."

Duncan looked at him anxiously. "I'm sorry about last night."

"It's all right. Come and have some dinner. You must be hungry."

Duncan closed his eyes and shuddered. "No, thank you," he said firmly, opening his eyes again. "The thought of food makes me a little sick right now. I'm going to have a hot shower, and then see if I can go the rest of the day without throwing up."

Vladimir gave him a grim smile. "Serves you right," he said, and he went out the door.

THE day after Duncan confronted her, Saronna shut herself up in her rooms. She tried praying, but it no longer provided her any solace. She couldn't even light the candle in her shrine. She read books, but she couldn't concentrate on them either, and she threw the reader down in disgust to pace the floor.

She barely slept that night, and she didn't go to breakfast the next morning. When Naomi knocked on her door, Saronna sent her away.

After Naomi had gone, Saronna sank down onto her sofa and closed her eyes. No matter how much she tried, she couldn't shut out of her mind Duncan's expression as he had looked down at her while she clutched the shrine. She could still recall with perfect clarity the mixture of anger, pain, and disgust in his face when he asked her when she had meant to tell him the truth.

Finally, Saronna slept from sheer exhaustion. She woke the next morning when someone knocked on her door.

Naomi's voice called her. "Saronna? Saronna, you don't have to come out, but could I come in? I brought you a tray of food."

Saronna got up. She would have to face Naomi sooner or later. Besides, she was very hungry. She pulled on a robe and went to open the door.

Naomi stepped inside, carrying a tray with two covered dishes and a tall glass. She set it down on a table and looked at Saronna. "Thank goodness. I was afraid something was wrong with you, too."

"With me, too?"

Naomi nodded. "Yes, we've had a rough time here lately. Duncan was very sick last night. Vladimir had to call the doctor."

Duncan was sick? He hadn't been sick since Saronna had known him. Had his wound somehow opened again? "What's wrong with him? I thought he was healed."

"Oh, it was nothing like that. He got so drunk he got sick, and then he breathed that into his lungs. They had to use a machine that helped him breathe, and gave him medicine at the same time."

Saronna was shocked. "But Duncan never drinks that much. I've never seen him actually drunk."

"Not usually. But he was very upset yesterday. What happened?"

Saronna turned away. "I can't talk about it."

Naomi sighed. "That's all Vladimir will say, too. He won't tell me anything, and he doesn't seem to care about me anymore."

"I'm sure he's as fond of you as ever," Saronna said absently. "They'll both calm down in a few days."

"No." Naomi shook her head sadly. "Vladimir is unhappy because Duncan is leaving."

"Leaving?" Saronna said in alarm. "You mean he's going to live somewhere else in New Jerusalem?"

"No, I mean he's leaving Krueger's World. He told his father he needed to get away for a while."

Saronna fought panic. Duncan was going far away, too far for her to ever see him. "But he works for Vladimir. He has to keep working for him if he wants to keep his place in the company. He told me so."

"That's true, but he's not worried about it anymore. He says he's going, for a few months, at the very least. And even if he comes back, he won't live here."

Saronna swallowed hard, fighting panic. "Won't— won't Vladimir sell me if Duncan's not here?"

Naomi shook her head. "I asked him about you. He said you can stay as long as you like. Duncan wants you to get an education and be able to take care of your-self."

Saronna turned away and busied herself with the dishes. As angry as he was, Duncan still worried about her. She tried to take comfort from that fact. "That's kind of him."

"Is it?" Naomi said tartly. "If he were truly kind, he'd stay with you."

"It's not his fault."

Naomi looked bewildered. "You mean—you mean you said no to him?"

Saronna nodded.

Naomi's eyes went wide in shocked amazement. "Saronna! How could you do that? What would your father say if he knew?"

Saronna set a plate on the table and moved the tray out of the way. "I expect he'd beat me."

"But why did you say no? Duncan's very nice looking and very kind. Besides, he's fond of you. What more could you want in a protector?"

Anger stirred in Saronna. Naomi had a man who loved her and whom she could love back, and yet here she was criticizing Saronna. "Maybe I don't want a protector at all. A woman can live on her own as well as a man can."

Naomi looked as incredulous as Paul had when Saronna had mentioned this possibility to him. "Do you really believe that?"

"Yes. You'd know it, too, if you had studied more."

Naomi cringed. "Do you think I need to worry about Vladimir? He's been very cross with me lately. Do you think he's stopped loving me?"

"Why would you think so?"

Naomi looked down at the floor. "He hasn't come to my bed in days." Tears welled up in her beautiful green eyes and dripped enchantingly down her cheeks. "And he shouted at me twice this last week."

Saronna felt no sense of sympathy. The older woman's situation was so much better than her own that Naomi's fears seemed to her like a child whining about minor hurts. "Don't be silly. Of course he loves you."

Naomi's tears still fell, but she seemed to take heart from this curt assessment. "Do you really think so?"

"Yes." Saronna was tired of talking about Vladimir's feelings for Naomi. Duncan was leaving, and all Naomi could do was prattle on about Vladimir's temper. "Would you mind leaving me alone for a while? I have a headache."

Naomi looked offended at this request, but she left Saronna's rooms without further conversation, merely recommending that she lie down in a dark room with her eyes closed.

Saronna answered absently. After Naomi had gone, Saronna ate the food she had brought. She sat and thought for a long while, staring off into space as she tried to make her mind sort out all the confused thoughts that were milling around in her head. In the end, she took Naomi's advice and lay down with her eyes closed. By then she really did have a headache.

"COME," Duncan's voice called when Saronna knocked on his door. She hadn't wanted to use the speaker in case Duncan was too angry to answer her.

Saronna opened the door.

Duncan turned toward her, a stack of shirts in one hand, and an open trunk on the floor in front of him. He stopped when he saw her and threw the shirts into the trunk. "What are you doing here? Won't you get in trouble for being in a man's room?"

Saronna flinched at the venom in his voice. "No. There's no one to check up on me."

Duncan folded his arms and waited.

"I wanted to see you," Saronna blurted out, before she could change her mind. "Naomi told me you were leaving Krueger's World?"

He nodded. "Day after tomorrow."

Despair gripped her. "So soon?"

Duncan shrugged. "The *Amon Ra* was the first liner that was going anywhere near the Rim Worlds."

"You're going to see your mother?"

"Yes. I thought she deserved to hear me say in person that she was right when she told me you were all wrong for me."

Saronna shut her eyes, trying to block his hostility by not looking at him. "What about your job?" she asked, opening her eyes to watch him covertly. "You told me you had to work for your father to keep your rights to the company."

He lifted his brows and eyed her suspiciously, as if he suspected her of having an ulterior motive for bringing up the subject of his inheritance. "It's nothing you need to worry about. Hopefully, Dad will take me back into Cameron Trushenko in a few years, after I get my head straightened out."

She drew in her breath sharply. "A few years? Naomi said you'd be gone a few months."

He shook his head. "I don't plan on coming back here until you're ready to leave this house. I expect that'll take a couple of years, at best."

"You don't have to go," she said, her desperation rising, blotting out all other fears. "I'll leave here tomorrow—I'll go back to my father's house."

"No! Do you think I don't know any better than that? You can't go back there."

"Yes, I can. My father would let me live there if I told him you didn't want me anymore."

"Don't be stupid," Duncan said cruelly. "If you try to return to Samaria, I'll only have to fetch you back here."

Saronna drew in a breath. She had to stop him. There was only one thing left to do. She let herself get angry. If he got angry back, he might react as so many men did. "Do you think you have the right to stop me?

So much for your off-world ways! I'm surprised you don't enforce your other rights as my protector."

Duncan gave a savage exclamation and took a step toward her. "Just what the hell does that mean?"

She looked up at him with her heart rising in her throat. This wasn't what she wanted, but it was better than nothing. She swallowed once, and looked away as she spoke. "If the reason you can't stay here while I'm here—if you feel a need—" She stopped and started over again. "You don't have to go. I can't say yes, but there's no reason you have to ask, really. You have rights."

Duncan took two steps closer as if he meant to grab her arm, and then he stopped himself. "Is that your solution to this situation? Don't leave just because I love you, and I can't have you! Oh, no, just stick around and be friends. And then when I can't stand it any longer, I can simply rape you, and you won't make a fuss. Doesn't that sound like fun?"

Saronna dropped her eyes and covered her face with her hands. She hadn't thought she could feel worse, but now she did.

"I know men seem abhorrent to you," Duncan said scathingly, "but believe me, I haven't sunk quite that low. I doubt if I even know anyone who has."

Saronna shuddered, feeling suddenly as cold as if she had the chills. "It's what my father did."

"What?" Duncan sounded horrified.

"He loved my mother," Saronna said, "but she was consecrated. She was weak at first. He was patient and kind to her, so she came to love him back. Leah was angry at her, but my mother ignored her. And then, after I was born, Leah brought an old woman to the house—Brushka, my mother's cousin. She was a Believer, too, and she persuaded my mother that she was wrong to break her vows. So my mother began to refuse my father. Sometimes he would accept it, and go to Leah, but other times he would be angry and force himself on her."

"Your father raped your mother?" Duncan said, incredulous.

She shook her head. He didn't understand. There was no way he could understand. "She never called it that. When she told me about it, she said only that my father chose to maintain his right to her body. She said he would weep afterwards, and ask her why she was so cold to him. She never told him why, not even when she was dying."

"Good God!" Duncan's face reflected disgust and horror. "Didn't anyone ever try to stop him?"

"No. There was no one who could stop him. My grandfather was alive back then, but he saw nothing wrong with it. No one else could interfere."

Duncan's expression hardened into disbelief. "But, why didn't she stop him? I mean, if you got your psy talent from her, she must have been able to do to him what you did to me?"

Saronna shrugged. "She did that, sometimes, but she was afraid to use her gift too often. Besides, she still loved him. That made it very difficult for her to want to stop him. The most she could manage was not to let herself respond to him. And then eventually, my father gave up."

"Jesus," Duncan said softly.

Saronna turned away. She shouldn't be telling him this. But he already knew what she was. And maybe if he understood her reasons, he wouldn't hate her. "Mother told me once that she felt she had sinned enough in loving my father. She couldn't compound it by yielding her body as well as her heart. But still, in a way, she was content. She had me, and when she knew I had inherited her gift, she consecrated me to the Mother so that I could expunge her sins."

Instead of understanding, Duncan's voice filled with repulsion. "So that's it? You grew up in that sick household, where people abused each other as a matter of course, and now you think that's normal?"

The scorn in his voice made her unhappiness well up inside of her. Who was he to judge her people? Her grief turned into rage. "Don't you speak in that way about my family! You grew up handed back and forth between your parents because both of them were too greedy to pass up a chance at wealth. You never knew a real home—a place where you could see the seasons change, and know all your neighbors by name, and be sure what color the sky would be when you went outside. Do you call that normal?"

He flushed angrily. "It's a hell of a lot closer to normal than rape is."

"At least he loved her!" Saronna said hotly. "At least he never went off and left her all alone!" She turned and ran from the room before Duncan could do more than call her name.

SARONNA having locked herself up in her rooms again, Vladimir tried to persuade his son to come to supper. Duncan declined.

"I'm not hungry, Dad. I still feel a little queasy."

Vladimir frowned at the glass of ale on the bedside table. "Drinking when you're too sick to eat is not a healthy thing, Duncan."

Duncan's expression stayed impassive. "I won't get drunk again. I promise you."

Vladimir sighed and got to his feet. "All right. I'll accept your word until you break it."

He left Duncan and went to have dinner with Naomi, but he had trouble keeping his mind on the conversation.

"What's wrong, Vlad?"

"I'm worried about Duncan," Vladimir said. "He's taking this awfully hard."

Naomi merely patted his arm. Vladimir continued to eat absently, and didn't make much conversation.

"You'll feel better if you come to my rooms and soak in a nice hot bath for a while," Naomi finally said. "I'll rub your back for you, and take your mind off your troubles."

Vladimir shook his head. "Thank you anyway, Naomi, but I have some work I have to finish. Duncan hasn't been much help lately, and there are some things I have to get done tonight."

She looked away for a moment, but said no more about it. After the meal was over, Vladimir left her to go back to his office.

It was more than an hour later when he looked up from his terminal to find Naomi standing in the doorway.

"What is it?" he asked. "Is anything wrong with Duncan?"

"No," Naomi said, moving across the room to stand quite close to him. "Nothing's wrong. It's late, though, and you really should come to bed."

Vladimir frowned as he noticed she was wearing a diaphanous night dress with an equally filmy robe over it. "What are you doing running around the house in that getup? The security staff might see you."

Naomi drew back as if he had slapped her. "You always liked this gown. Come to bed, Vlad. It's late."

Vladimir waved a hand. "Not for a bit. You go ahead if you're tired. I have to finish this."

Naomi stayed where she was.

"Run along," Vladimir said, not looking up, even when she went through the door.

By the time Vladimir finished his work and switched off his terminal, the house was completely still. He walked back to his room, sticking to the corridors because it was quite cool in the courtyard. When he got to his room, he had a sudden guilty memory of Naomi asking him to come to bed, and he decided that perhaps he should sleep in her bed, so they could at least wake up together. He entered his own room first, to prepare for bed; when he was ready, he walked through the connecting door to Naomi's rooms.

He was very surprised, because the lights were still on. A moment later he was brought up short by the sight of his beloved lying senseless on the floor.

It was close enough to what he had already gone through with Duncan that Vladimir staggered backwards for a moment, wondering if he were in his right mind. He passed a hand over his eyes to make certain that he was awake, and then he rushed to

Naomi's body. She was breathing, but he couldn't rouse her. Vladimir felt dizzy from shock, and found that he had a great deal of difficulty deciding what he should do next. After a moment, he spoke into the com set on the bedside table and asked for Duncan.

A few minutes later, his son's face appeared dimly on the screen, bleary eyed and grouchy. "Yeah?"

"Duncan." Vladimir swallowed convulsively, "I need your help."

"What's wrong?" Duncan blinked once and came awake quickly. "Are you okay, Dad?"

"I'm fine. It's Naomi. I found her unconscious in her room. I don't know what's wrong, and I don't know what to do, Duncan."

"I'll be right there," Duncan said, and the screen went blank.

Duncan's room was on the east side of the family courtyard, directly across from Naomi's room. In a few seconds, Vladimir heard noisy pounding on the courtyard door, and he realized Naomi must have locked it. When he let Duncan in, he could see his son had obviously hurried, as he was clad only in a pair of undershorts.

Duncan crossed the room to crouch by Naomi's inert form. "She's breathing okay," he said, "but she feels clammy."

"I know," Vladimir said. "Do you think she could be sick?"

"I suppose so." Duncan frowned. "But it seems awfully sudden for that. It looks more like she took something."

"You mean drugs?" The suggestion rocked Vladimir so thoroughly he sat down on the bed. He barely noticed another noise at the door from the courtyard. Duncan was here and would deal with it.

DUNCAN looked up to see Saronna's pale face looking in through the window. Just as he stood up to let her in, the door from the corridor burst open. Tatiana Devi and a male security guard stood there, stun guns drawn and ready.

"Are you okay, sir?" she said to Vladimir. "Someone tried to open the door when it was locked."

"Christ," Duncan said feelingly. His father looked too dazed to answer for himself. "There's no security breech. Get out—no wait! Call for a med team, right away. Tell them it looks like a drug overdose."

"Really?" the man said, frowning down at Naomi as he holstered his weapon.

"Come on," Tatiana said, pulling him from the room, with a quick, appraising glance at Duncan's bare legs.

Duncan moved to the courtyard door and opened it. Saronna stepped inside. She had wrapped herself in a Kruegerian veil, and it looked very exotic over her nightgown, but Duncan was in no mood to care about what she was wearing.

"What's wrong?" Saronna said anxiously.

Vladimir was kneeling beside Naomi. "Help me carry her, Duncan."

"I'll get her, Dad," Duncan said, pushing his father gently out of the way as he lifted Naomi's slight body from the floor. He laid her on the bed, and Vladimir began to chafe her hands.

"I'll get some water," Duncan said, moving to the pitcher on the dresser.

"What's wrong?" Saronna said again.

"I don't know," Vladimir answered absently. "I came in and found her like this. She was fine earlier."

Saronna stared at the shallow rise and fall of Naomi's chest. "At least she's alive."

Vladimir didn't answer, and when Duncan handed him a glass of water, he tried sprinkling it on Naomi's face. There was no response from the unconscious woman. She didn't so much as stir.

"What could it be?" Vladimir cried. "What could she have taken?"

"Oh!" Saronna said suddenly.

Both men looked at her.

"You know something!" Vladimir said accusingly.

Saronna scanned the bedside tables. She picked up an empty drinking glass and tilted it. "It's almost empty."

"Let me see that," Duncan said, taking it from her. He sniffed the glass experimentally. "Wine?"

"Is there a vial anywhere?" Saronna asked. "A small glass vial about the size of my finger with a blue powder in it."

They hunted frantically. Duncan found the vial in the trash container.

"Good thing you didn't build a recycler chute in here, Dad," he said, handing his father the vial. "It'd be gone by now."

"Oh, but it's empty," Saronna said when she saw the vial. "It should be half full. The woman said to use half of it at a time." She turned anxious eyes to Vladimir. "Unless she's used it before?"

"Used what?" Vladimir snapped at her. "What was in the damn thing?"

"It was an anodyne," Saronna said. "A potion. It was supposed to make you want her again. She bought it in a shop in the native quarter."

"What?" Vladimir roared. "You let Naomi buy some phony potion that might be poison for all we know!"

"Dad," Duncan said, "Saronna had no right to stop Naomi from doing whatever she wanted to do."

Vladimir stood with his breath coming in rapid, gulping, gasps. His eyes were wet with tears, and he seemed on the brink of losing control of himself.

"I can't take this, Duncan," he said in a ragged voice. "Not after what happened to you in Samaria, and then last night. I can't take this now!"

"Sit down, Dad," Duncan ordered. He pushed his father into a chair, and made him rest his head on his hands for a few minutes. When the old man seemed calmer, Duncan turned his attention to Saronna. "Tell me about this potion. What was in it?"

"I don't know," she said. "I never used such things. I only know the woman told her to use half of it at a time. She told her to wait until the next day if—if Vladimir was resistant and Naomi needed to use the rest of it."

"But why would she even buy it?" Vladimir almost wailed. "Why would she feel a need to use something to attract me? She knows I love her."

"She was worried," Saronna said. "She felt she was getting older. You had been too busy and too concerned about Duncan to pay attention to her—you shouted at her—so she worried that it meant you had stopped caring for her."

Vladimir held back a sob. "I did shout at her. Oh, God, I did."

"That's enough, Dad," Duncan said. "You won't do Naomi any good by falling apart now. The med team will be here in a minute. They'll help her, but you have to stay alert and answer their questions."

Vladimir drew himself up straighter in his chair, as if he were willing himself to stay calm. "You're right."

A moment later, the door opened and two medtechs stood there with a security guard right behind them.

"Come in," Vladimir said, rising to his feet. "She's over here."

He explained what little they knew about what Naomi had taken. One medtech took the vial and the glass of wine and put them in a pouch, while the other one checked Naomi's vital signs and then drew a blood sample. After it was ready, she popped the cube into a portable analyzer.

"Here it is," she said, studying the display on the analyzer. "It's something weird all right. Must be some native Kruegerian stuff."

Her colleague scrutinized the readout and agreed. He began to hook up a monitor to Naomi's arm, as the woman medtech made notes on her terminal.

"Can you do anything about it?" Vladimir asked.

The medtech shook her head. "Not here. We haven't run across this one before. We'll take her to the hospital and filter it out of her blood."

"Is it safe to wait until we get her to the hospital?" Vladimir asked.

The medtech looked noncommittal, neither reassuring nor worried. "She seems stable. We'll monitor her on the way there, and we can put her on total life support if she gets worse. I could try to set up something to treat her here, but it's safer at the hospital."

When they began to prepare Naomi to travel, Vladimir announced that he would go with them.

"Sure thing," the woman said. "Only one of you, though, and we're leaving right now." She cast an interested glance from Vladimir's pajamas to Duncan's undershorts, and Duncan was suddenly conscious of his lack of clothing.

"I'll follow you there, Dad," he said. "I'll bring you some clothes if you don't want to wait to dress. I'll come in one of the flyters. There won't be any traffic restrictions at this hour."

"Can I go with you?" Saronna asked quietly.

Duncan glanced at her briefly. She seemed very subdued by the situation. "Get dressed. I'll leave as soon as you're ready."

Vladimir was on his way out the door behind the medtechs, but he turned at this. "Would you pack some clothes for Naomi, too, please, Saronna?"

"Of course," Saronna said.

Duncan watched as his father shuffled out behind the med team. "I hope he's okay."

"He'll be all right if Naomi gets better," Saronna said. Her eyes flickered to his bare legs for just a moment, and then she stared over his shoulder at the wall behind him

Duncan suddenly felt constrained at being virtually undressed in front of a woman for whom he had strong feelings. "You go get Naomi's things and put some clothes on yourself," he said, aware that he sounded curt. "I'll do the same for Dad, and I'll meet you on the roof."

Saronna nodded and began to look through Naomi's dresser. Duncan left her there without saying another word. It was his turn to be there for his father.

WHEN Saronna exited the lift onto the roof port, she found Duncan waiting by the flyter. The roof port lamps made stark pools of light in the inky blackness, with the hulking shape of the flyter sitting half in the light and half in the shadows. Duncan took the case Saronna had packed, and put it in the flyter next to the one he had brought for his father. She got in and sat down next to him, afraid to break the silence until he did.

All around them, the city slept. When they crossed from the old part of the off-world quarter to the new part that had been built entirely by off-worlders, the streets and buildings below became suddenly much brighter. To Saronna, the new city seemed unnatural, almost hellish in its illumination.

Duncan had punched in their destination and put the controls on automatic. Now he sat with his arms folded across his chest and stared straight out into the night.

"I'm sorry I didn't tell anyone that Naomi had the anodyne," Saronna said, suddenly compelled to speak.

"It's not your fault," Duncan said, still looking ahead, "any more than it was anyone's fault but my own that I got drunk enough to almost kill myself the other night."

She studied his profile. "Why did you do that?"

He turned his head momentarily to look at her full face. "I wanted to make myself too numb too feel anything. I did too good a job, though."

Saronna couldn't think of anything to say so she said nothing.

Duncan watched the night sky again and made no further comment. When they neared the hospital, he took manual control and set the flyter down on the hospital roof port. A sleepy-eyed attendant directed them to the emergency department.

Vladimir was waiting in the small room set aside for that purpose. He was still wearing a robe over his pajamas.

Duncan gave him the case with his clothes.

"Thanks," Vladimir said. "I'm going to change. Will you wait here until I'm back?"

"Of course, Dad."

"Shall I keep Naomi's clothes?" Saronna said.

"I'll take them," Vladimir said. "I'll give them to the medtech."

He took the case, and suddenly Saronna had nothing to do with her hands. She held them behind her.

They waited without speaking until Vladimir returned, fully dressed and looking slightly more alert. Duncan offered to see if there was coffee or tea available.

"No, thanks," Vladimir said. "I'm too tense to drink anything."

A few minutes later, a man in a doctor's coat came through the door of the waiting room and walked up to Vladimir.

"Hello, Vlad," he said kindly. "You do seem to be having your share of late nights, don't you?"

Vladimir stood up abruptly. "How is she?"

"She'll be fine," the doctor said soothingly. "You can take her home in the morning."

Vladimir let out a profound sigh and ran his fingers through his hair. "Thank God!"

The doctor nodded. "It wasn't that close, but it could have been if she had taken more of that stuff. It's harmless in small doses, but it can be pretty noxious if you ingest enough of it."

"Will there be any lasting effects?" Vladimir asked.

"No, no. We've filtered her blood pretty thoroughly. There are no impurities left to cause more trouble." He glanced at Duncan, who was standing a little to his father's left. "You seem to have recovered fully, Duncan."

Saronna watched Duncan's reaction. He met the doctor's eyes but returned an oblique answer. "Thank you for coming so promptly, Dr. Pruitt."

"It wasn't as much bother as it might have been," the doctor said. "I had another call already tonight. How are you feeling?"

"I'm fine, thanks."

"Good," the doctor said. "Don't do anything so stupid again."

Duncan didn't answer, and the doctor turned back to Vladimir. "Anyway, Vlad, Naomi is sleeping now, but you can talk to her first thing in the morning."

"Can I sit in her room?" Vladimir said. "I'd like to be there when she wakes up."

The doctor smiled. "We can do better than that. I'll have someone make up a bed for you."

"I'll wait here," Duncan said.

"Nonsense," Vladimir said gruffly. "You take Saronna home. I'll be fine here. I'm not feeble yet, you know."

Duncan tried to insist, but his father was adamant. Finally, Saronna and Duncan took the lift back to the roof.

Saronna waited, but Duncan didn't speak during their takeoff or the flight. As they were nearing the Cameron Trushenko house, she steeled herself to ask him a question because she wanted to know the answer.

"When the doctor told you not to do anything foolish again, why didn't you answer him?"

Duncan gave her a cold stare. "It's not his business what I do. It's not yours, either, if it comes to that."

Saronna shrank a little, under the weight of his animosity. "Do you hate me, Duncan?"

He looked at her for several seconds before he answered. "No," he finally said. "I wish I did. It would make things easier."

She let out a small sigh before she could stop it, and said nothing else. At least he didn't hate her.

Duncan landed the flyter, and held the door for her when she got out. They rode down the lift together, still in silence, and then Duncan walked beside Saronna as she started to go to her room.

When they reached the turn where the corridor branched to his side of the house, Saronna hesitated. She wouldn't have many chances to see him again, maybe none to be alone with him. "Good night."

"Good morning would be more like it."

She looked at him anxiously. "Are you sure you're quite well? You don't look as if you feel good at all."

"I don't feel good. I feel quite bad, in fact. I feel like I slept all night in a cold, damp, field and then woke up and drank a liter of warm mud."

He had suffered because of her. "I'm sorry."

"You don't have to apologize. It's not your fault."

"Isn't it?"

For the first time that night Duncan stared straight into her face. "No. You tried to tell me something was wrong. I didn't want to listen. I only saw what I wanted to see."

She knew she should let it go, but she wanted to hear him say again that he cared about her. "What did you want to see, Duncan?"

Duncan stared at her as if he would never see her again. All at once he threw his arms around her and hugged her so tightly she could barely breathe. "Saronna! Saronna, don't do this to us!"

She said nothing. She held herself still and limp in his arms and let him kiss her passionately. She wanted more than anything to kiss him back—to wrap her arms around him and hold his body close to hers, to stroke his skin and feel the heat of him under her fingers. But she couldn't. She had promised her mother she would stay pure.

And if she didn't protest, didn't push him away, he might keep going. She would suffer as her mother had suffered, but Duncan might not leave her. She closed her eyes and prayed for the strength not to respond.

After a few seconds, Duncan held her at arm's length. She opened her eyes to find him looking at her with disgust.

"So that's it?" he said. "Do you think I'm going to play your parents' game?" He let go of her abruptly and then turned and stalked off toward his room without saying good night.

Saronna clutched the wall for support. She watched until he was out of sight, and then she went to her own room and tried unsuccessfully to light the candle on her shrine so that she could pray.

CHAPTER FOURTEEN

Vladimir brought Naomi home the next morning. Once he got her into her own suite, he fussed over her—making certain she was warm enough, and not too tired to sit up, and not thirsty. She didn't seem to mind the attention, and Vladimir waited until he was sure she was comfortable to bring up the subject of her lapse.

"Now, my dear," he said, sitting beside her chair and taking her hand. "We need to have a talk."

Naomi cast her eyes downward, much as Saronna had been accustomed to doing when she first came to the Trushenko house. "I'm sorry I caused such a fuss, Vlad."

"I know, I know," Vladimir said reassuringly. "Don't worry about that. I just need to know why you took that drug."

She lifted her eyes to him and Vladimir could see the pain in them. "I was afraid you didn't want me anymore. I needed something to be sure that you'd still find me desirable."

He thought for a second he must have heard her wrongly. "What? My dearest, I love you. I've told you so often enough. Don't you believe me?"

"Yes, of course, Vlad. But men's feelings change over time. I'm getting older, and you might want someone younger one day."

"How could you think that? Do you love me, Naomi?"

She smiled, but her lips trembled. "Yes. Oh, yes."

"But I'm old, dearest. How can you love me when I'm so much older than you?"

"I don't care about that," Naomi said. "I don't care how old you are."

"Why can't it be the same way for me?" Vladimir asked insistently. "Why can't I love you no matter what?"

She gave a little shrug of frustration, as if she found it difficult to explain. "But you're a man. You paid a lot of money for a young, pretty woman you had never seen before. How could you still love me when my looks go?"

Vladimir caught her other hand. "Naomi," he said in consternation, "I didn't pay so much money because you're beautiful! I made that offer because I could see that oaf was humiliating you. I couldn't bear the thought that he would let those other men haggle over a woman as if she were an object up for sale."

She turned her luminous green eyes toward him. "And you didn't fall in love with me for my looks?"

Vladimir smiled warmly. "It made it easier for me to love you, dearest, but that wasn't all of it. The more I was around you, the more I knew I loved you as I had never loved anyone before. I was so happy when you came to my room that first time, and I knew that you loved me, too."

Naomi's eyes filled with tears that spilled down her face rapidly.

"Naomi?" Vladimir said. "What's wrong?"

"Oh, Vlad! Did you love me even then?"

"Of course," Vladimir said simply. He frowned as he considered the meaning of her distress. "Why did you come to my room, Naomi?"

She brushed her tears away with the back of her hand. "Well," she said reasonably, "you never sent for me or came to my bed, and I was afraid you didn't want me for yourself. I thought I'd better see if that were true or not. You were so kind; I wondered if you were afraid that I was too shy."

Vladimir sat back, stunned. "You were afraid?"

She nodded. "If you didn't want me, you might have sold me to someone else."

"Naomi! Naomi, how could you think that?"

She opened her beautiful green eyes wide with surprise. "But it happens all the time, Vlad. It happened to me with Ephraim. He wanted me once, remember?"

"Naomi!" Vladimir said again. He was so perturbed, he rose from his chair and paced back and forth a few times. "This is terrible! Do you mean that all along your feeling for me has been based on fear?"

"Not *all* the time." She made a small gesture to indicate the room around her. "It was just at first, this house was so different, and you and Duncan seemed so strange. I was afraid because I didn't know how to act around you." She gripped the chair cushion as if to reassure herself. "And then when you never touched me, I thought you had some other purpose in mind when you bought me. I thought you didn't want me to be your woman. But then I went to your room, and you were so gentle with me, so considerate of my feelings, and I knew you did want me. I was very happy then, and I came to care for you more than I had ever cared for my husband. And then finally, I loved you, and I knew I wanted to stay with you as long as I could."

Naomi made this declaration simply, but with a great deal of feeling. Vladimir stared at her in confusion.

"Have I said anything to distress you, Vlad?" she asked fearfully.

"What?" He was distressed, but there was no need to let her know that, at least not until he could sort everything out in his head. "No, dear. It's just that I need to mull this over for a while."

"I think I need to lie down for a bit," she said, "unless you need me?"

Vladimir reassured her, kissed her cheek, and left her quarters by way of the family courtyard.

Duncan was sitting at the dining table with a mug in front of him. He rose when Vladimir came outside. "Are you okay, Dad? You look a little wobbly."

"I feel wobbly," Vladimir said, sinking into a chair.

"Have you eaten? Maybe you should have some lunch?"

Vladimir shook his head. "I'm not hungry, thank you, Duncan."

"Then what's wrong? Is Naomi all right?"

"Yes," Vladimir said slowly. "She's well now, thank God."

"Did something happen?" Duncan persisted.

"Not really. It's just that I just found out that the first time Naomi and I—" Vladimir broke off abruptly as he remembered he was talking to his son. "I just realized that Naomi has always lived in fear. Ever since the day I brought her home, she's been living with this terrible fear that I would sell her to someone else."

Duncan said nothing. He looked unsure of what to say.

"How can I reconcile how she feels with how I feel?" Vladimir said. "How can I comprehend her, or she comprehend me? I never realized before how totally different our views of the universe are, Duncan. How can I understand her?"

Duncan nodded. "I know the feeling. You should talk to Zelda."

"What?" Vladimir said sharply. "That blasted woman who almost got you killed?"

"It wasn't her fault. You said yourself that I was an idiot."

A glimmer of humor struck through Vladimir's tribulation. "So you're admitting it now?"

"Maybe. But you should talk to Zelda, Dad. She's studied Krueger's World and Kruegerian women for years. She knows more about the culture than anyone I ever met who wasn't Kruegerian."

Vladimir sat debating and then sighed. "What have I got to lose? Would you call her for me?"

"Sure, Dad. I'll do it right now."

VLADIMIR was in his office when Letitia Dubai told him Zelda Amoy was waiting in the parlor.

Zelda looked him over when he came into the room. She stood up to shake the hand he offered her. "You must be Vladimir Trushenko," she said. "I can see your boy in you. Not in the build, but in the eyes, and the jaw a little—although that's harder to see with a beard."

Vladimir stroked his whiskers with pride. "A beard is a handy thing on this planet."

Zelda shook her head as she sat down. "Yes, but it can be dangerous to look like something you're not."

Vladimir gave her a sharp look and sat down across from her. "So Duncan told you what's wrong?"

"Some of it. He told me about how you came to acquire a Kruegerian woman. Suppose you tell me what's bothering you—in your own words, Citizen Trushenko."

"Call me Vladimir. Everyone does."

She nodded. "All right, Vladimir. What can I do for you?"

Vladimir outlined what he had learned from Naomi earlier that day.

"It shocked me," he said frankly. "I had no idea how much fear was driving her actions."

Zelda looked disdainful. "What did you expect? If you could buy her, then you could sell her."

"I never saw it that way," Vladimir said, thinking back. "And once she—that is once I was fond of her, I certainly thought she was fond of me, too."

"I expect she was. But I expect it was mostly either fear or duty that impelled her to go to your bed."

Her certainty took him aback. "Duncan never told you that. For one thing, he doesn't know it. And for another, he wouldn't tell you if he did."

Zelda nodded. "I agree. He didn't have to tell me. Kruegerian women don't usually think it's their place to offer themselves, but if you make them afraid, they will."

Vladimir frowned. "Except Saronna?"

"Except Saronna," Zelda said. "But that's a whole other story." She leaned back in her chair. "Now," she said with satisfaction. "You want me to help you see things from Naomi's point of view. Let's start with what kinds of things you and Naomi do together."

Vladimir gave her a sour smile. "You sound a lot like a therapist."

She smiled. "That's a good analogy. Think of me as a marriage counselor, and tell me everything."

"Everything?" Vladimir said.

"Everything," Zelda repeated with relish.

IT was late in the day when Vladimir finally stopped talking. He stretched in his chair and groaned. "I feel just a little bit like you put me into spatial fold and then cut the power."

In spite of her age, Zelda still looked fresh. "Do you?" she said brightly. "Then I must have done it right."

"So what do you advise?" Vladimir said. Having spilled his guts, he wanted some payback. "I agree that I've slipped into the patriarchal role Naomi expected me to play, even though I never meant to do it. I can see how she could feel afraid, but I don't quite know what to do about it. How can I get her to see things through *my* frame? How can I make her understand that I truly love her—not merely desire her?"

Zelda shrugged. "I'm not sure how you can do it, but you have to make her feel secure. Fear isn't a positive emotion, and you can't expect her to give up her fear because you pat her hand and tell her she looks lovely."

Vladimir nodded thoughtfully. "I can see that."

"So think of something."

It wasn't much as advice went, but on the other hand, it was a start. And he was certainly old enough to manage his own life. "All right. I will."

"Good!" Zelda glanced around the room, as if she were expecting someone else to be there. "Could I speak to Saronna for a while, do you suppose?"

"Saronna?"

"Yes," Zelda said dryly. "The woman you bought for Duncan."

Vladimir felt himself flush. "I bought her to keep Naomi company."

Zelda smiled. "I suppose Naomi was urging you to do it?"

He nodded. "Yes, she was. Duncan was upset with me, but I didn't want Naomi to be lonely."

"Ah! It was quite an expensive present, surely?"

"Saronna would have been worse off if someone else had bought her," Vladimir said defensively.

"In her case, you might be right. Can I talk to her, please?"

In spite of the help she had provided, suspicion stirred in Vladimir's mind. She was, after all, a scientist with her own agenda. "What do you want to talk to Saronna about?"

"Lots of things. Do you have any reason to object?"

Not one he could articulate. "No. But I understand Saronna even less than I understand Naomi. I know she loves Duncan, and I can't see why she's letting these religious scruples hold her back."

"She loves him?" Zelda said in surprise. "What makes you think that?"

Vladimir snorted. "All you have to do is watch her watching him. It's as plain as the ears on a Shuratanian's head."

"Is it?" Zelda cocked her had. "I had assumed it was a one-sided relationship. What an interesting complication."

Vladimir got to his feet. "I'll go and fetch her—if she wants to come."

Zelda stood up with him. "Perhaps she'd feel more comfortable if we talked in her room?"

"Perhaps," Vladimir said, hoping he wasn't making a mistake. Odd to think that only a few months ago he had had no worries beyond interstellar tariffs and the price of luxury goods. "Shall we go ask her?"

SARONNA sat in the family courtyard with her needlework in her lap, oblivious to the scent of the flowers or the tinkling of the fountain. She was staring off into space when she heard footsteps. She jumped with a guilty start and picked up her needle hastily.

It was Vladimir and a strange woman, an off-worlder with gray hair and dark eyes. He introduced her as Zelda Amoy.

"She'd like to talk to you, Saronna," he added. "If that's all right with you."

Saronna gave the older woman a cold-eyed stare. "Why should I?"

"Why shouldn't you?" Zelda countered. "Are you afraid to talk to me?"

"No." Saronna cast her eyes down modestly from habit.

"Shall we go to your room, then?" Zelda said.

Saronna rose reluctantly, and waited until after Vladimir had said goodbye to Zelda before she led the way to her rooms.

Zelda opened her eyes wide as she took in the opulence of Saronna's suite. "Wow! This is quite a place you have here."

"Yes," Saronna said, offering a seat as she sat down herself. "What is it you want?"

Zelda smiled in a friendly fashion. "I just want to talk to you, Saronna. Is there any harm in talking?"

"Sometimes," Saronna said, her tone cold. "You're the one who told Duncan about me, aren't you!"

Zelda's smile took on a greater intensity. "Did he tell you that?"

"No. But he mentioned you were studying Kruegerian women when he told me about the patriarch beating you. And you came to see him the other day, before he—" She broke off, unwilling to say out loud what had happened.

Zelda finished the sentence for her. "Before he confronted you about it?"

"Yes."

"So finally you admitted the truth?"

"Yes."

"Why? I thought you were pledged to keep it a secret from men—all the way to the grave if necessary?"

Saronna nodded. "He was going to touch the shrine. I couldn't allow that. I had to stop him."

"Yes." Zelda gave her a speculative glance. "But you could have stopped him other ways. A consecrated woman isn't defenseless. A brief spasm of the heart muscle, a constriction of the arteries, and the man is no threat until he wakes up—if he wakes up."

Saronna drew in her breath, remembering Eli Pederson. "I could never do that to Duncan."

"Why not?" Zelda said. "He's a man, isn't he?"

"He's a good man!" Saronna said, seething at her suggestion. "He defended you—risked his life for you."

"I wouldn't go that far. I doubt he knew what he was getting into when he stopped to help me. Although, to do him justice, I don't think he would have acted differently if he had."

Flushed with emotion, Saronna stood up and walked a few paces to regain control of herself.

Zelda leaned back in her chair and crossed one leg over the other. "Do you know why I came here, to Krueger's World?"

Saronna turned to look at her suspiciously. "You study different cultures."

"I study oppression."

Saronna frowned. "And is Krueger's World the only place in the galaxy where there's oppression?"

"By no means, but it's one of the few place where one half of a species oppresses the other half based solely on gender. It's rare, these days, to find a culture in which the oppressed can love their oppressors and vice versa."

Saronna drew a deep breath and let it out. "My mother loved me. My father sold me."

"Your father sold you at least partly because he was worried about you. And your mother may have loved you, but she condemned you to the same unhappiness she suffered."

Saronna stifled a sob. She sank onto a chair and put her head in her hands.

"So," Zelda said brightly. "You do love Duncan?"

Saronna straightened up, her face contorted in a fierce grimace. "No, I don't. I can't love him. I can't love any man. I'm consecrated to the Mother."

Even as she said the words, Saronna knew she didn't believe them. She wasn't even sure she could believe love could be a sin anymore. But it didn't matter. She had made a solemn promise to her mother, and she had to keep it.

Zelda nodded, as if conceding a point. "All right, let's talk about that. I hear your brother came looking for you after your father sold you."

Saronna nodded. "Yes. Paul was worried about me. He's very kind."

"He sounds as if he cares about you?"

"Yes." Saronna said the one word in almost a whisper.

"How about your older brother?"

Saronna shrugged. "Gideon never cared what happened to me. He barely noticed me."

"Why do you suppose that is?"

Saronna sighed. "Gideon is like most men. Paul is unusual."

"Do they have the same mother?"

"Yes. Gideon was Leah's second child. She had a daughter before him, but she died when she was only a few days old, and then Leah had Gideon."

"She must have been happy to have another baby?"

"I don't know. He was older than me, so I don't remember. But I think she resented him for being so healthy when her baby girl had died. I know it was different when she had Paul. He was very sickly as a child, and she nursed him herself. She could never be stern with him after that."

"Ah!"

Saronna waited, but the other woman said nothing else. "What?" she said crossly.

"It doesn't strike you that maybe Leah herself made Gideon into the harsh, uncaring man that he is?"

Saronna had never thought about it in quite those terms.

"And likewise," Zelda went on, "she made Paul able to love by loving him first."

The argument had a certain logic. The more Saronna thought about it, the more likely it seemed. "Maybe. Yes, probably you're right."

Zelda studied her with interest. "How old were you when your mother consecrated you?"

"Twelve."

Zelda looked startled. "You found your gift at a very young age."

"Yes."

"How old are you now?"

"Twenty-three."

"Don't you think," Zelda said, "that eleven years is enough to give Mother Eve?"

The words shocked Saronna. Could it be possible that devotion had limits? Leah would have slapped her for saying such a thing. Even her own mother would have been horrified. "How can you speak that way? We serve Eve all our lives."

"And what does she give you in return?"

Saronna waved her hands in a gesture of frustration. "You don't understand."

"Then tell me. What do you get out of serving the Mother? In what way does it help you to believe in her, to consecrate your life to her?"

"She helps me. When I need strength, I can pray to her."

"Strength for what?"

"Strength to bear what life sends us—what men do to us."

Zelda nodded. "Now we're getting somewhere. What has Duncan done to you?"

"Duncan?" Saronna scoffed at the idea. "Duncan never did anything bad to me."

"Then why do you need strength to deal with Duncan?"

"You don't understand!" Saronna almost wailed. "I need strength to keep myself from loving Duncan. I have no right to love him."

Zelda smiled. "Sweetie pie, people have been falling in love for thousands of years, and not a one of them ever needed permission."

Saronna tried to gather her thoughts. This woman with her calm voice and authoritative manner was trying to tear down everything Saronna had been taught, and it frightened her. "I can't. My mother was weak, and loved my father. I must be consecrated to atone for her sin."

"Ah! So it was wrong of your father to sell you to strangers, but it was perfectly all right for your mother to give away your chance of happiness?"

"No!" Saronna said. "I mean, yes." She threw herself face down on the sofa and wept.

"What's wrong?" Zelda said, laying a hand on her back. "Why are you so unhappy?"

"Because," Saronna said, her pain making her speak the truth, "it's hopeless. I can't love him but I do, and tomorrow he's going away for years and years."

"Now, now," Zelda said cheerfully. "Very few things in life are truly hopeless. Let's talk about it some more, shall we?"

VLADIMIR came into Naomi's room and found her sitting on the sofa doing needlework.

She smiled hesitantly as he sat down next to her. "Hello, Vlad. Have you come to ask me more questions?"

Vladimir took her hand. "Just one, dear heart. Will you marry me?"

Her face froze for a moment in shock. "B-but," she said, almost stammering with surprise, "but, you're already married! You told me you can't divorce Vonda or you'll lose control of the company."

Vladimir shrugged. "Don't worry about the company. I've learned what's most important in my life in the last few days, and it's not Cameron Trushenko. Do you want to marry me, Naomi?"

"But, Vladimir," Naomi said in distress, "the company means so much to you. I can't let you give it up just to marry me."

"I can't make you marry me," Vladimir said gently. "But I'm going to get a divorce no matter what you say, so I only hope the answer is yes."

"Oh, Vladimir," Naomi said, crystalline tears falling like jewels from her eyes, "of course the answer is yes."

A GUILTY conscience prodded Duncan back to work that afternoon. He spent several hours going over the status of his projects with Kaveh, and answering the other man's questions, and then he sat down to clear off his desk and empty out his correspondence queue. He had just concluded that it was hopeless when his father stuck his head in the office door.

"Are you busy, Duncan?"

Duncan threw his stylus down on the desk and lied outright. "Not at all. Come in, Dad. How is Naomi?"

"She's fine," Vladimir said, advancing into the room. "But she's still tuckered out, so she's lying down for a while."

Duncan nodded. "That's a good idea." He waited, and when his father didn't say anything else, he leaned back in his chair. "Was there something you wanted, Dad?"

Vladimir cleared his throat. "Yes, there is, son."

Duncan sat up. "Son? Oh, Christ, what's happened now?"

Vladimir looked almost guilty. "It's nothing bad—or at least, I hope you won't see it that way. The thing is, Duncan, I wanted you to hear the news from me. I've sent a message to my lawyers. I'm asking your mother for a divorce."

It should have surprised him, and yet somehow, as soon as his father said the words, Duncan knew that this day had been inevitable for a long time. "You're going to marry Naomi."

"Yes," Vladimir said in a steady voice. "I realized that losing her—in any sense of the word—would be worse than losing control of Cameron Trushenko."

Duncan tried to make himself look at the future in a positive light. "You've been doing a great job. Maybe the trustees will keep you on?"

"The thing is," Vladimir said, "I don't know what directions your grandfather's charter gives them. They may have instructions that in such a circumstance, anyone but me runs the company." He gave Duncan an appraising glance. "They may want to promote you. Your mother would go along with that."

Duncan shook his head. "I'm not ready yet."

"I agree. But in five or ten years, you will be. If you can just keep the company afloat for that long, you'll be okay."

Duncan snorted. "That's like telling a sailor to dive in and swim for the shore; if he can avoid the sharks for a few kilometers, he can make it. I'm not ready, Dad, and that's that. I wouldn't take it if they offered it."

Vladimir sighed. "Well, I'm sorry, Duncan. I had hoped to turn it over to you myself, but now it looks like it'll be someone else."

"Are you sure you want to do this, Dad?"

His father's face lit in a joyous smile. "Oh, yes, Duncan. I'm quite sure. I've never been more sure of anything since the day the doctor put you in my arms, and I knew that I loved you."

Duncan rose swiftly to his feet and embraced his father. "Congratulations, Dad."

"Thanks," Vladimir said, hugging him back. "I appreciate that. I was afraid you'd be upset."

"Of course not," Duncan said, releasing him. "We should have some champagne to celebrate."

"Maybe tomorrow. I'm not up to it tonight."

Duncan sat down again. "I'm leaving tomorrow afternoon. Unless you can't get along without me? I could wait a few weeks if it's urgent."

Vladimir's shoulders sagged. "I was forgetting. Don't change your plans, Duncan. We'll manage on our own."

Duncan picked up his stylus and tapped it on the desk. It was just as well he was leaving. Watching his father and Naomi be so happy while he was miserable would be hard to bear. "So," he said, with an attempt at joviality, "you didn't need Zelda after all? You figured out what to do all by yourself."

Vladimir looked surprised. "Didn't you know? Dr. Amoy—Zelda came to see me earlier. I spent well over an hour talking to her. She helped a lot, actually."

"It must have been while I was asleep."

Vladimir looked at him critically. "You look a little better, but you're still frayed around the edges. It's almost time for dinner. Why don't you knock off work for a while?"

Duncan shook his head. "I've got too much to finish, Dad. I'll be at it for a while, yet. Don't look for me at meals. Margaret's going to have someone bring me a tray."

His father made one more attempt to persuade him, and then went off to find Naomi.

Duncan looked around his office and wondered who would end up running Cameron Trushenko. It occurred to him that his father and Naomi might have to buy another house. Saronna would have to move with them, as she could hardly support herself.

He sighed and shut his eyes. One more day and then he would be gone from Krueger's World.

SARONNA stared at the door. This was the only door she had seen inside Vladimir's house that had a speaker. She wanted to learn to use technology, but unlike the front door, she didn't see any buttons. "Duncan?" she said at last.

After a pause, his voice came out of the air. "Who is it?"

Saronna glanced around at the dim corridor and tried her best to sound sure of herself. "It's Saronna."

Another pause. "What do you want?"

Saronna drew in a breath. "I want to talk to you. May I come in, please?"

A longer pause, and then the door opened and Duncan stood there, blocking the doorway. He wore a robe similar in style to the one she had on, but while hers brushed her ankles, his showed his bare legs from the knees down.

"What is it?" he asked abruptly. "I was almost ready for bed."

"May I come in, please?" Saronna repeated. She pulled her robe tighter with nervous excitement. She was breaking so many rules, it would be hard to list them all. But she no longer had to worry about those rules. She had to remember that. She let out a little gasp at the thought.

He hesitated and then swung the door open wider for her.

Saronna stepped inside.

Duncan shut the door. "Well?"

Saronna came straight to the point. "I wanted to ask you if you're still leaving tomorrow, now that your father is going to marry Naomi."

His expression hovered near a frown, as if he suspected her of having an ulterior motive. "Yes. I'm still leaving. The divorce will take a few months to work out. I'll probably come back for the wedding."

"I see," Saronna said, stepping farther into the room.

"Was that all?" Duncan folded his arms across his chest, his pose revealing his impatience, or perhaps his anger at her.

"No, it's not all." She turned around and faced him. "If you insist on going, then will you sleep with me first?"

"What?" He almost shouted the word. "I already told you, I won't play your sick games."

"I'm not here to play games. I'm quite serious."

Duncan snorted.

She would have to explain herself. She took a deep breath. How could she explain that she was now someone else, someone new and different? "Zelda Amoy came to see me today. We talked for quite a while."

His eyes locked on her face. "She did? I thought she came to see Dad?"

"She talked to him first," Saronna said. "But she really wanted to talk to me. She had only been able to interview a consecrated woman one other time, and she was very curious about the rite of consecration."

Astonishment replaced suspicion in his expression. "You told her about it?"

Saronna nodded. "I was only twelve, but I can remember it quite well."

His eyes opened wide. "Twelve! You had to make a decision like that when you were twelve?"

"No." That had been the problem. Like so many other decisions in her life, that one had been made for her. "My mother decided to consecrate me when I was twelve."

He frowned and returned to his original question. "So you could tell Zelda about this rite because she's a woman?"

Saronna stroked the soft nap of her robe. Was it going well? He hadn't thrown her out of his room. That was something. "Oh, no. She's not a Believer. I wasn't supposed to tell her anything, any more than I was supposed to tell you about it."

Duncan's frown grew heavier. "Then why did you?"

"Because," Saronna said reasonably, "I don't care about that rule anymore. I'm no longer a Believer, so I don't mind talking about their rituals and things that no longer have any significance for me."

Duncan stared at her face. "What are you saying?"

"I'm saying," Saronna said distinctly, turning from studying the furnishings to look him full in the face, "that my mother had no more right to consecrate me than my father had to sell me. I'm saying I don't consider myself bound by promises based on lies."

There it was out. For the first time in her life, she had made her own significant decision.

Duncan swallowed hard. "You changed your mind just like that?"

She tilted her head. It hadn't been that sudden. She could see that now. Saronna could never have believed what Zelda Amoy told her if she had met her the day she arrived at the Trushenko house. "No, not just like that. I think I always doubted some of what my mother taught me. But since I came here, I haven't been able to believe any of it as thoroughly as I did in the past." She laughed from exuberance. She felt lighter somehow.

"What's so funny?"

"Nothing." She smiled and lifted her arms in an expansive gesture. "Nothing and everything. It's just that I've gotten rid of a terrible burden. Do you know that tonight, for the first time that I can remember, I didn't have to pray for forgiveness for the sin of loving my own brother?"

He stared at her, his expression bemused. Saronna was prepared to give him some time. She had had trouble understanding it herself.

"So you don't consider yourself my woman anymore?"

"I'm my own woman." She said the words with pride and certainty. "I make my own choices. I do what I want, not what other people think I should do."

He nodded slowly, as if he agreed with her. "So what do you want to do?"

She pulled her robe open, slipped it from her bare shoulders, and let it fall to the floor.

Duncan looked surprised, but not displeased, to see she wasn't wearing anything under it.

CHAPTER FIFTEEN

Somewhere morning crickets droned, repeating again and again the pattern of their low humming. Saronna could hear them easily. It must be time to get up, but she was warm and comfortable, so she kept her eyes shut and lay still under the bedclothes.

"Good morning," Duncan's voice said.

Saronna opened her eyes. He was lying next to her, smiling.

"Good morning," Saronna said. A quick glance reassured her. They were in Duncan's room. She hadn't dreamed the night before.

He bent down to kiss her gently.

She twined her arms around his neck and pulled him down to make the kiss more intimate.

He grinned when she let him go. "I must say, you're a quick study."

"Thank you."

He threw off the bedclothes, revealing that he was as naked as she was. He ran one hand down the length of her body in a caress, but stopped when he came to the cut on her thigh. "You should see a doctor about that, right away."

She glanced down at it. "It's not bleeding."

He shook his head. "It could get infected."

It sounded like good advice. "All right, I'll go to-morrow."

He sat up and swung his legs so he sat on the edge of the bed. "Why not today?"

She pulled herself up to sit cross-legged next to him, very aware that she was naked. "We have plans for today."

His smile disappeared into a solemn seriousness. "You're sure you want to go through with that?"

"Yes."

The serious expression hovered at a frown. "Then I think we should plan on living somewhere else— preferably another planet. It seems to me your—uh, your father's wife is going to be pissed as hell at you, as will the old woman who taught you, and any other Believers who know about you."

She couldn't lie to him or try to hide the danger. "I agree they'll be angry." She took his hand and twined her fingers with his. "But I can't change anything unless I'm here. I have sisters, Duncan. I can't abandon them to the life they have now." And a brother who might need her, too. She would have to get Paul's permission to tell Duncan his secret.

His eyes clouded. "So you're sure about that, too?"

She nodded, and almost held her breath. Would he try to urge her not to take the dangerous route?

He twisted his face in a grimace. "Okay, I guess Cameron Trushenko will have to become very profitable if I'm going to fund a revolution with only two percent of the profits."

She laughed, relieved at his willingness to accept her need to take risks. "A revolution? You make it sound like we need to buy weapons."

He got up and grabbed his robe from the floor. "Knowledge can be a weapon more powerful than ignorance. That's what you have to fight. Your ammunition will be the same things you found here— books, teachers, communication."

And courage. He hadn't mentioned it, but Saronna knew she would need it. She thought back to Leah lunging at her with the vintner's knife. It could happen again. She would just have to plan well and try not to get caught alone with a Believer. Or with a Kruegerian man, come to that. She would work against the cult of the Patriarch as much as she worked against the cult of the Mother.

Of course her gift would help. It might be the thing that made Leah angry at her, but it had also helped her to save Duncan. She would need all the help she could get if she was to improve the lives of Kruegerian women, and of men like Paul.

"Time to get moving," Duncan said, tying his robe. "If you're sure?"

Saronna looked at him with exasperation. "How many times must I say that I'm sure?"

He bent over and kissed her again. "Only once more—at the consulate."

She sighed. "And what about you? Are you sure?"

He laughed and grabbed her hands, then pulled her to her feet. "I've never been more sure of anything in my life. Now get dressed so we can get going."

It was only then that Saronna realized she had nothing to wear except her robe.

DUNCAN watched with a smile on his face as Saronna scurried across the family courtyard. She made it without meeting anyone and ducked into her own room.

He turned toward the bathroom, but had a sudden thought. In a surprise attack, it was good to have an ally. Or perhaps accomplice was a better word. He moved to the com and asked for a familiar connection.

In a few seconds, a sleepy Miloran face filled the screen.

"Hello, War," Duncan said cheerfully.

"Duncan," Warhlou hna Nedahna said in a gravelly voice, "why the hell are you calling me at the break of dawn?" He stretched his jaws in the Miloran equivalent of a yawn, a bone cracking exercise that would have dazzled a Terran dentist if one had been watching.

"Sorry, War," Duncan said. "But I need a favor."

The Miloran rubbed his face with one huge hand, as if he weren't happy with the placement of his features and sought to rearrange them. He shook himself slightly, and seemed to come awake. "What favor? I thought you were leaving today."

Duncan smiled. "There's been a slight change of plan."

VLADIMIR was distressed to find Duncan missing from the lunch table after he had already skipped breakfast.

"Where the hell is that boy?" he demanded of his future wife.

"I don't know," Naomi said. "Did you check with security?"

Vladimir nodded glumly. "That animated rock pile called Warhlou hna Nedahna picked him up in a ground car this morning. Duncan didn't say where they were going. I was counting on spending some time with him today."

Naomi patted his hand and made soothing noises. "Saronna wouldn't come out of her room this morning when I knocked, but now she's gone for a walk by herself. Maybe that's a good sign?"

Vladimir made an impatient gesture. "I don't think it matters anymore. Duncan's given up."

Naomi tried to change the subject to more pleasant things, but Vladimir wouldn't be diverted. He fretted all through lunch and went back to his office in something of a funk. His mood didn't get any better as the afternoon passed and the time for Duncan's departure drew nearer.

DUNCAN opened his father's office door. "Hello, Dad. Have you got a minute?"

When Vladimir looked up and saw him, the relief on his face was obvious. "Duncan! Where the hell have you been? You're supposed to be on your way to the spaceport in less than an hour."

"There's been a slight change in my plans," Duncan said, taking a seat across from his father's desk. He wanted a good view to see how his news was received, but also easy access to the door just in case his father didn't take it well. "I canceled my booking on the *Amon Ra*. I'm not leaving for another week or two."

"Oh?" Vladimir said, plainly not displeased. "Did something come up?"

"You could say so," Duncan said, unable to hold back a smile. "Saronna and I got married this morning."

"What?" Vladimir's answer was almost a roar.

"You heard me right," Duncan said calmly. "Saronna and I got married this morning at the ThreeCon consulate. It took a little while, because I wanted to get the datawork straight so that she has some standing with ThreeCon as the spouse of a ThreeCon citizen."

His father was out of his chair now, on his way around the desk. His face reflected a chaotic mixture of emotions—relief, delight, annoyance, and concern.

"What the hell do you mean by running off and getting married without telling me first?" Vladimir demanded, as annoyance won out. "Was there some reason you made me miss my only child's wedding?"

"Well," Duncan said, preparing to jump to his feet if Vladimir's anger grew any worse. "The thing was, I didn't want to wait for Mom to come here for the service, and I knew she'd give me hell if you were present and she wasn't, so I decided the safest course was to ditch the both of you."

His father's eyes brightened as he sat on the edge of his desk. "You didn't want to wait? Is there anything else you need to tell me, Duncan?"

"No," Duncan said, amused. "Saronna's not pregnant. I just didn't want to give her a chance to change her mind."

"Ah! The religious thing?"

Duncan nodded. "She's given it up completely, but it seemed safest to make her position here clear to all concerned. This way it'll be harder for anyone in her family to put pressure on her."

Vladimir gave him a steely stare. "But you didn't invite *them* to the wedding?"

"Nope." Duncan grinned. "Apparently, there are advantages to buying a woman before you marry her. I didn't need to ask their permission, and they're not exactly my in-laws."

His father's expression brightened. "I suppose that will apply to me and Naomi as well." He gave Duncan a confused look. "So what did you mean when you said you're not leaving for a week or two? You're still going? Even though Saronna's changed her mind?"

"Yes. We plan to live here, but we want to take a year-long honeymoon. Kaveh is set to take over for me, and Saronna wants to see more of the universe. We'll stop and visit Mom for a few weeks—give her a chance to get to know Saronna better, and get used to the idea—and then we'll travel. Saronna wants to see Terra, and a sleeper world or two. And I want to get her away from here for a while, so she has a chance to soak up the feel of real civilization."

"And then what?"

"We'll come back here. Saronna wants to work on changing Krueger's World."

Vladimir shook his head. "I can't fault that ambition. I just hope she's careful how she goes about it." He gave Duncan a look from under his brows. "And what do *you* plan to do on Krueger's World?"

Duncan grinned at his father and held out both hands. "That depends on who's running Cameron Trushenko. If the trust balks at your staying in charge, I'll have to suck up to whoever Mom and the lawyers put in your place. Unless you want to start a new venture on your own, Dad? I'd be happy to work for you again."

Vladimir frowned. "No, you need to stay with this firm, Duncan. It'll be yours some day. Besides, I'm too old to do what Sai and Randy have been doing for the last few years."

"No, you're not. I could do the running around part, and you could do the planning. You've got a tidy bundle stashed away; you wouldn't be starting from the same place Sai and Randy did."

"A tidy bundle makes a nice personal fortune," Vladimir said dryly. "But it makes *pouka* feed when it comes to startup capital for intergalactic trading. Think what we spent on that last freighter."

Duncan tried to argue, but Vladimir was resolute. "Don't worry about me, Duncan," he said firmly. "I've got Naomi to keep me occupied. Maybe we'll travel to other worlds, like you and Saronna. I'd like her to meet my parents—in person, not just an exchange of expresses."

Duncan let it go. He could always try again later. "Okay, Dad," he said, finally getting to his feet. "I'm going to see what Saronna is up to, and then I'll take care of a few things I left up in the air when I thought I was leaving today."

Vladimir came toward him and folded him in an affectionate embrace. "Congratulations, Duncan. I'm very happy for you."

"Thanks, Dad. I'm sorry you missed the ceremony."

Vladimir's eyes twinkled. "Not as sorry as you're going to be when Naomi finds out you robbed her of her chance to host the wedding of the season. She may still want to throw a party for you. Any problem with that?"

"Not that I know of," Duncan said, "but I can't answer for Saronna."

"Don't ever try," Vladimir said. "I certainly learned my lesson when it comes to thinking for someone else." He slapped Duncan on the back. "We'll have our own little celebration tonight."

THEY had a cozy dinner in the family courtyard that night, with Vladimir pouring sparkling wine liberally and all of them feeling its effects enough to relax into mellow good humor. Saronna had never had so much wine, and she felt the faintest hint of being out of control. She couldn't recall a time when she had felt such happiness. Even the setting matched her mood. The flowering shrubs scented the air in the courtyard, the night birds called in high, melodic trills, and the moon shone down with golden light.

Vladimir was studying his son with a self-congratulatory air, as if Duncan's marriage had been a personal accomplishment, when his pocket com beeped unobtrusively.

"Dad!" Duncan protested. "Why do you have that thing on? Can't you stop working long enough to eat?"

"Of course I can," Vladimir said, frowning. "It must be something urgent. It was set to take a message for everything else."

"Shall I answer it for you?" Duncan asked.

"No," Vladimir said, getting to his feet. "I'll take it in my office. No sense breaking up the party with business."

He left the courtyard, and Naomi asked Saronna who had been present for the wedding at the consulate. She exclaimed in dismay when Saronna told her that Warhlou and an anonymous clerk had been the only witnesses, but Saronna distracted her with a question about Naomi's plans for her own wedding.

After a few minutes of wedding details, Duncan stood up. "I wonder what that call was about?"

Saronna laughed at him. "Why don't you go and see what it is? You're no good to us once your mind is on business."

Duncan flashed her a smile. "You're a very understanding wife." He kissed her cheek, and headed for his father's office.

Saronna found Naomi watching her. "What's so interesting?"

The older woman shook her head. "Something happened. Not just the wedding. You seem different, but I can't tell what it is that's changed."

Saronna smiled with confidence. "I'm a new woman. Not merely a wife, but a new person altogether. I've learned to think for myself and act for myself."

Naomi looked wistful. "How did you learn that?"

Saronna thought back to the day she had arrived at the Trushenko household, carrying her valise with her shrine carefully packed away beneath her dowdy Kruegerian clothes. "It was a painful journey but worth the trip. You have to know when baggage is no longer worth carrying."

"I don't understand you. Sometimes you don't seem to be from Krueger's World at all."

Saronna smiled but shook her head. "I'll always be from Krueger's World. But maybe someday that won't mean what it means now."

Naomi gave a very unladylike snort. "More riddles!"

Saronna laughed with delight. She felt as if she could conquer a world, even this world. Nothing was too much for her to accomplish. She set her empty wineglass down on the table. "Watch this!"

While Naomi stared, Saronna concentrated. Lifting was indeed more difficult than merely moving, as she had once told Duncan. In a few seconds, the glass rose from the table and hovered a few centimeters into the air.

Naomi gasped and dropped her own glass. It hit the flagstones and shattered into a thousand pieces.

"I'm sorry," Saronna said. Her concentration slipped and her wineglass thudded down on the table top. Saronna wasn't discouraged. "These things take time to learn," she told the astonished Naomi. "And I'm just getting started."

WHEN Duncan arrived at Vladimir's office, he saw that his father had chosen to take his urgent call on the desk set rather than his pocket com. He was staring at the screen with his face frozen in disbelief, and Duncan had a sudden fear that something must have gone terribly wrong with Cameron Trushenko.

"What is it?" Duncan said, without preamble. "Something wrong?"

Vladimir shook his head absently. "No. It's from your mother. She paid for instantaneous delivery, so it came through as urgent."

"What?" Duncan said, even more alarmed. "What is it? Is she all right? What did she say?"

"She called it a wedding present," Vladimir said. He turned the monitor so it faced toward Duncan. "Here, you watch it."

Duncan leaned over the desk as his mother's face appeared on the monitor.

"Hello, Vladimir," Vonda said. "And congratulations." Her face twisted in a smile that held strong hints of amusement but also a certain regret. "I mean that. Congratulations on doing something I wished I had had the resolution to do. I never thought you had it in you. It seems I was wrong."

"She must be thinking about Pietro," Duncan said.

"Hush!" Vladimir held up a hand. "This is the good part."

"So," Vonda said, setting her shoulders. "I think I've come up with a good wedding present. I've attached a proxy statement to this message giving you the right to vote my shares for five years."

"Holy crap!" Duncan blurted out. "You'll have complete control of the company!"

"Shh!" Vladimir said.

"And," Vonda went on, "if you keep the dividends up, I'll renew it for another five years." She smiled more warmly. "Goodbye, Vlad. Tell Duncan I love him. And tell him to send me a damn express every now and then."

The screen went blank.

"Wow," Duncan said. "That was unexpected."

His father let out a happy sigh. "I know. One of the better surprises I've had lately." He gave Duncan a slightly bleary grin. "In ten years, I'll be ready to take it easy, and you'll be ready to take over. It's what I wanted all along, and your mother gave it to me. She gave me you, too. I owe her a lot, Duncan."

How much wine had the old man had? Duncan smiled back at him. "Are you going to invite her to your wedding?"

Vladimir's face reflected conflict as he weighed the chance of Vonda causing a scene against the gift she had given him. "Of course." He shot Duncan a pained look. "It's not like there'll be a lot of family here. You'll be off to God knows where by then."

Duncan looked at him affectionately. "Oh, we'll be here. In fact, we might stick around until after the ceremony. No sense galloping off to the Rim worlds if Mom will be on her way here."

Vladimir looked triumphant. "Vonda might actually come if you'll be here. If nothing else, she'll want to grill you about your marriage."

Duncan laughed but shook his head. "It's not a problem. I'm not afraid of Mom."

His father couldn't hold back a smile. "You're almost the only person I know who can say that."

Duncan smiled back. "She doesn't bite."

"No," Vladimir said, "but she's sure to have an attitude about you marrying Saronna."

"I don't mind," Duncan said serenely. "I was never more sure of anything in my life than I was about getting married."

Vladimir rose to his feet a little wearily. "Well, it's been a long day. I think I'll forget about supper and go to bed now."

"That sounds like a good idea," Duncan said enthusiastically.

His father gave him a sly look. "I suppose you and Saronna can entertain yourselves?"

Duncan assured him it was so without so much as a blush, and the two of them went back to the family courtyard to break the good news about Cameron Trushenko to Naomi and Saronna.

VLADIMIR watched Naomi get ready for bed. She was puttering—putting away her jewelry, fussing with her brushes and other assorted items on her dressing table. Vladimir waited patiently for her to slip off her robe and slide under the covers with him. He reached for her and pulled her close.

"I thought you were tired," Naomi said in surprise.

"I am tired," Vladimir answered. "I just want to hold you. I sleep better when you're close to me."

Naomi sighed and snuggled closer. "How's that?"

"Perfect," Vladimir said. She seemed in a good mood. Now might be an opportune time to ask a touchy question. "Tell me something, dear heart. Would you be upset if I asked Vonda to come to the wedding?"

"Our wedding?" Naomi said in surprise.

"Yes. Our wedding."

"I suppose not," Naomi said slowly. "She was nice about the stock, and I beat her, after all. I've got you now."

Vladimir had to laugh at his intended bride. "Vonda didn't want me, sweetness. She never saw it as a contest for me."

Naomi gave him a skeptical glance. "What about when you were young and newly married?"

"Even then. We never got along."

"What about the honeymoon?"

Vladimir smiled. "It wasn't so much a honeymoon as the opening skirmish in a larger battle. Duncan was conceived a few weeks after we were married. The two of us downed half a bottle of Duncan McDonald single malt scotch whiskey and managed to go to bed together without arguing first. It was the last time I ever made love with Vonda. I'm only grateful Duncan didn't turn out to be a lush."

Naomi laughed with delight. "Is that why you named him Duncan?"

"Yes. Don't ever tell him."

"I won't," Naomi promised. "I suppose I won't mind having Vonda here for the wedding now that I know that."

"After all," Vladimir said, stroking her cheek gently, "she's still family. Old Alexander Cameron was right all along. Family is what counts."

"Yes," Naomi said. "Family is what counts." She kissed his cheek. "Good night, Vladimir."

"Good night, dearest," Vladimir said sleepily. "I never thought I'd say this, but I'm very glad ThreeCon restructured interstellar taxes and drove Cameron Trushenko to Krueger's World."

SARONNA woke suddenly. Her husband stirred beside her.

"What is it?" he said sleepily.

"Nothing." She caressed his jaw. "Go back to sleep."

He opened his eyes. In the faint light from the window she could see his concern as he looked at her. "Anything wrong?"

"No." She kissed his forehead. How wonderful it was to sleep next to someone she cared about. Her mother had missed so much. "Go back to sleep. I had a dream and it woke me up."

"What did you dream?"

"I dreamed of my sisters." She put her hand over his. "I dreamed of their daughters. I dreamed that they were happier than my mother ever was or could be."

He gripped her hand. "I didn't know your sisters had any daughters."

"They don't," she said. "Not yet. I dreamed of the future."

He sighed and shut his eyes. Saronna smiled at him and went back to sleep, to dream again of revolution.

ACKNOWLEDGEMENTS

My writing group helped tremendously in the final draft of this book. I appreciate not only their insights, but the careful balance of honesty and tact with which they presented them.

And as usual, my copy editor provided level-headed assistance in identifying plot inconsistencies and grammatical errors, while my proofreader caught those sneaky typos. Thank you both!

And thank you, the reader, for sticking with the book. Reading has so much competition these days, it's wonderful to know there are still people who read for pleasure.

So, would it kill you to write a review?

Made in the USA
Middletown, DE
13 October 2023

40756054R00263